# The

# Failing

# of

# Angels

# Chris Tutton

Avalanche Fiction

First published in the UK by Avalanche Books, England.

Printed by SRP, Exeter.

The right of Chris Tutton to be identified as the
author of this work has been asserted by him in
accordance with the
Copyright, Designs and Patents Act 1988.

British Library Cataloguing in Publication Data.

A catalogue record for this book is available from
the British Library.

ISBN: 978 1 874392 04 0

lei
c. G OF ANGELS

Also by Chris Tutton:

We so fleetingly savour the essence of stars in our blood

*Chris Tutton, 2019*

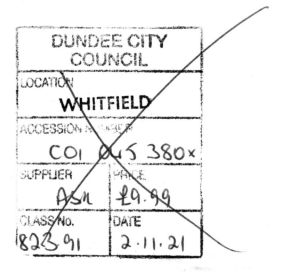

# Prologue

I don't want to wax lyrical. It all happened too long ago. Besides, all my wax has hardened now; there's little poetry left in it.

My bow-legged days have grown feeble with hunger. I palliate their hollowness in threadbare memories; deliberate over footprints too long to live fast. They pendulate beside my wayfaring words on the wind-fleshed bloom of flagstone mosaics, and try not to linger unduly on the cracks.

When this ancient world began in error, my mother stole my fresh green feet.

I was never likely to whip up a lot of speed as a runner after that.

# 1

We are born crying out for love, as if we had lost it already.

My mother was a woman of indefatigable faith; she placed it all in words and hoped to God they wouldn't fail her. On my first breath, they did exactly that.

I was ceremonially disgorged. Winched like an over-stuffed bucket of blackthorns from the vomiting well of her boreal crotch and poured scarlet as a warning over a gunmetal bed in an infirmary of lingering sighs, where the rock'n'roll idol Eddie Cochran surrendered his cleancut body of heavenly songs on the not yet summertime blue Easter Sunday afternoon after an end of tour car crash, eleven weeks later.

Dispatched in haste, a moon phase short of schedule, I couldn't get away from the villainous shrew quick enough. Or was it the other way around? Doesn't matter; we both needed the distance.

One thousand and fifty-six years *to the day* after the bastard-fathering Sergius the Third was crowned Pontiff following his graceless limp out of retirement to murderously dispose of the antipope Christopher, I was delivered like a summons to the soundtrack of a scream, twenty-three minutes before a mourning midnight, mid-winter, during a blizzard.

They swaddled my overturing shivers in a waffle stitch blanket, but I never warmed up.

On the germinal branches of my earliest tears, a restive murder of crows gathered to fly; silhouetted hibernal against thrombotic rivets of cloud.

Typecast as outcast centre stage in my own drama, a jilted imminent latter-day nominal conveyor of the Lord, I lay wriggling like an upturned roach, flapping pathetically around in the hospital mud of my own infant Agincourt. Covered in the lethally indelible stains of my mother's blood, taking my first crust of breath and already half dead.

We didn't bond.

She hurled the pallor of a hard frost at my incredulous stare from the unconquerable summit of her contemptuously curled lip, as if she had soiled herself and I was what was left of it clinging to the bedsheet.

She had wanted a girl.

Anniversaries of torment and countless attempts to conceive had parturated no more winsome a reward than the emblematic, piss-taking, hideously appendaged blasphemy of me indecipherably yodelling uninterrupted reminders of my mother's miscarried destiny through rising mountains of regret, like an artfully animated miniature Francis Bacon oil, stretched on disconsolation and framed frozen by her glacial detachment.

Had I presented myself to the bearer of all worldly misfortune immaculate; pastel painted on a flesh-toned ground of double X chromosomes, a future feature fashion-ista painlessly begotten from the spread thighs of some model mothering magazine, she probably would have hated me more healthily. Instead, I flaunted the pendulous pennant of my pecker as a banner of contempt through the valley of her unshifting scowl. Trashing my apartment in an indecent haste to escape it without a backward glance.

Pathologically averse to croaking on cue and vacating her nightmare without tying her tongue, the suspension of my monstrous matter, hanging like a cosseted curse on the gallows of her cryogenic cradle after being summarily immerged into her reluctant embrace by the antiseptic midwife, catapulted her odium to unfathomable heights of unbearability. She called this loathing love and nurtured it with a passion.

On the day Eddie Cochran died, I discovered that I could sing.

# 2

We left hospital and my mother cried. Reality was only ever streets away. Halfway to the ground, a crystal teardrop froze and cut a furrow in the snow. It was the coldest winter in years.

Biliously green around January gills, I opened my mouth as Caruso once had to unleash another encore. Gelid lips flapped around steaming the frost like a speared fish's prayer, but nothing came out. I was still looking for something to say.

My curt carried-homecoming celebrations from the car, previous to being perfunctorily drop-kicked over the threshold, were predictably underplayed. I would no doubt have enjoyed a more enthusiastic introduction to my precautioned new domicile had I possessed the inherent virtues of a regular packet of self raising flour. Lamentably, despite noticeable superficial similarities in my bundled body's appearance, I conspicuously lacked the flour's refinement. I wailed like a banshee.

Other bubble blowing babies had blagged appreciating gifts of affection in the postpartum ward; attracting usurious interest on outstanding debts of attention. Under-resourced to accumulate a similar fortune, I couldn't flip a mewl for a cursory kiss. I'd collected a few days of age and had almost nothing else to show for my shivers. I barely had as much as a name to my name.

My bric-a-brac parents wore each other like insincere smiles. Overly patched and painted thirty-something relics of an earlier age, who lived above my mother's smart antique shop in a multi-storey, weathered white stone edifice on the eastern edge of town. Light flooded in through formidable windows. You could see every crack in their relationship.

Home was as cold as the shoulder I cried on. My mother's incessant scorching responses to my father's perpetual north-easterly sighs heated their disputes, but froze the sprawling provinces between them.

The lenticled walnut longcase struck ten in the eleven of my late morning arrival, as my mother carried me aloft through the front door and the gallery hall, through the sun filtered illumination of her circadian misery and into the relative darkness of my appointed quarters, where she drew me level with the brunette fleece of her spring-coiled hair and looked at me as though she were trying to recognise something. Then she laid me down mechanically like a corpulent snowflake in a wooden-railed cot and looked out disconsolately at the tumbling sky.

Only days later, a sudden, tepid cry of baby blue watercolour sky seemed to stimulate in her a transitory attempt to communicate with me, just as the first snowdrops were rising on the lawn.

I was informed, between gurgles in the confessional of the first floor oriel, that she had heard me singing inside her. I don't know if I did, or whether she did or not. Maybe she had impetuously mistaken the lugubrious ululations of my harrowing confusion for song. Whatever it was, I carried on doing it.

By the age of three, I was adeptly arranging my unabating misery around a pentatonic scale. And had nailed enough idiomatic expressions to feed a fountain of lament. The issue was resolved; I'd been singing for more than my years.

The details of the picture are lost beneath layers of grime. I no longer have the eye for looking closely enough between the flaking atolls of paint and craquelure to make out much of it now. Except to see that, until I was three, I had been raised by birds.

In the basement of our formerly grand house, canaries flew around free behind a wire mesh wall. Recycled by my father after constructively consulting a construction company on an unconstructive civil engineering project somewhere, they punctuated the air between the almost canary yellow lightbulbs like riots of dust and flitted around interminably, making the same sort of noise as me. I was reassured. At least it was safe to breathe. I filled my nestling lungs with dreams of flight.

My mother often sang me the berceuses of her vitriolic assaults on her habitually besieged husband, who would typically muster barely a grunt of defence but underscore his invariable monosyllabism with enough volume to announce the importance of his begrudging response.

In the best tradition of the worst relationships, my parents appeared lethally incompatible. The occasional cursory verbal dressing of each other's mutually inflicted wounds the only ostensible concession to their peculiar union that masqueraded as convincingly sympathetic. Were it not for their identically coloured eyes, which seemed to reflect the same piercing blue of their respective souls, one might easily have been at a loss to identify any other thing they shared in common.

I perched for unchanging seasons on a narrow ledge of constant apprehension, atmospheres above affection, where their operatic crescendos resounded in an endless medley of displeasure. Their shrieking duets creating the cast of a more vulnerable child inside me. One constantly reawoken to the prospect of landing in trouble by being thrown from ever-rising crags of concern. The hurtling ground of his approaching anger was almost the only time I heard my father speak.

Throughout my parents' habitual altercations, I frequently occupied myself with imaginings of what they might eventually do to one another. And how I might lose them to something worse than words. I could carry the discomfort of my own physical abuse more easily than listening to them fight.

My canary ensemble and I sang away stretches together. It was our only means of escape.

Until one dissonant morning, chilly as a sudden regret, in the desolate aftermath of a routine visit to the cellar to sing, I found myself trapped in a Munchian scream, struggling to whistle up even a quarter note of comprehension.

Lost in a labyrinth of dismay, I struggled to stare my abrupt abandonment down, abortively attempting to spin a determinedly tuneless dribble of sense out of it, as any other wide and wet-eyed warbler would.

My canaries had gone. Every last one of them. No matter how I tried to conjure a chorus from the silent shrunken emptiness they had filled, they obdurately refused to appear. My closest circle of friends had decamped without a parting trill and left me, to be replaced by a graveyard of ghosts that didn't have names yet. My mother didn't care; she just sat down and waited for God upstairs on her own.

She doesn't talk about those times now. They're too visible, still. Too resistant to the lie. If she ever mentions them, it's to say that none of it ever happened.

(Don't you remember how you tried to stop me crying, Mum? Your method was crude, unorthodox, and it didn't work. But you tried. Really hard. And your efforts barely left a bruise. Not one that could compete with yours, anyhow.)

My mother's bruise was as large as the sun, and every bit as radiant. She drew the totality of her life-force from it. Sometimes, just when you thought it was setting on her smirking best La Giaconda smile, it popped back up and filled the sky with blood. She couldn't ever smile without bleeding.

Inside her flowed an endless tide of emotion, too shallow to support a vessel of escape.

She lived within the confines of her imagination and mistrusted life deeply, suspecting the ground it was laid on to be full of snakes and snares.

On such inhospitable terrain my mother entertained no wish to live forever, but trod gingerly, and surreptitiously tended the hope of hanging around long enough to feel as though she had.

The holy holiday camp of Heaven, however, was a different affair. Even before I had stumbled into the bedlam of her Babylon, she had been fastidiously arranging her stay up there for years. Planning the undertaking as meticulously as the Great Escape.

Had the opportunity arisen to leave her wandering alone on the periphery of reality, I may have taken up with my father in the hope of landing a more profitable place within the family, but I never saw the person inside him long enough for us to gel.

On the inexpertly tolerated familiarity of his own home ground, my father was the silhouette of a solitary man who had succumbed early to a genetic epidemic of virulent disillusion and died before I was born. He occupied uninhabited places and isolated himself from the pitfalls of speech by surrounding his inconversable land mass with unnavigable waters of unapproachability. My rudimentary observations of him confounded all reasonable expectations of paternal support and guidance.

Oceans of salt spilt into the wound of our disconnection. Flowed from abbreviated associations with other children's dads, who I almost invariably discovered to be demonstrably more playful, tactile and emotionally attached to their offspring than my own father was with me.

Observations which identified me as an intruder and confirmed my suspicion that a sympathising aspect of his parental attention had been denied me; that I was routinely missing out on the experience of enjoying his company more than I did. Aroused my sorrowful suspicions that no island could be a man.

He flaggingly carted the iron-winged albatross of his shackling disquiet home in the evening, and was accorded just enough of a moment to grunt something unintelligible into the passing anvil of my general direction before I was whisked away and escorted to sleep by my unremittingly impatient mother.

The baleful, ritualistic obligation of this reluctant correspondence over, he invariably gorged his constantly reheated but promptly presented dinner in a manner that suggested he hadn't eaten all day, without uttering more than a morsel in groaning response to my mother's querulous attempts to engage him.

Finally, after an hour or two of exhausting himself still further on the unmitigating effort of successfully avoiding tumbling into the abyss of a full-blown sentence, he would cumbrously clamber out of his chair and take himself off to the outlying sanctuary of his bed early. At the weekend, he typically sat in his chair for longer and said precisely as little. But in a more leisurely manner.

It was a painful way for me to learn how to speak. I began to turn words into feelings so I could avoid the necessity of making myself heard above the silence. In the absence of more communicable alternatives, I cultivated affection for aspirations beyond my reach.

With such extended symphonies of unresolved minor key reticence playing full tilt in both eyes at an unvanishing volume, I tangled myself up hopelessly in the long, wet grass of two or three more bloody birthdays and plodded lead-footed into my mother's peripheral vision.

I was no longer small enough to ignore or satisfy with a shake and a hiss.

We had moved on.

# 3

I stalked the colours and shapes of my preserve, but they stalked me back with unexpected intent. I retired to consider my game-plan, although satisfied that I had made my presence felt.

I was old enough now to scholastically study the hand printed sheet music of my frequently struck and plucked face and legs creatively, and ruminate on the strange polyphony of flesh.

At some point, amid deeply reverberating da capos in the commodious dark confessional of my free-falling tears, I realised I had become a choir of discontent and started singing songs about God. I would probably have sung about anything, but they were the only ones I knew.

The Almighty was everywhere. He had become a Ouija board. Become tangible. My mother eked out angels with an upturned wineglass.

I knew that God was watching me. She hammered it relentlessly into the drumskin of my ears like a marauding army of Gene Krupas launching a full scale assault with 2b sticks.

Everything I did could be seen and punished. Everything I thought could be known and judged. I had no choice; I had to be good or I'd burn. Anybody else could get away with murder but, for some reason, I was under the spotlight.

I felt surrounded on all sides by some paranormal paparazzo. I constantly inspected the fabric of my existence for evidence of depravity. I felt stifled.

# 4

I am captivated by the romance of possibility, but have discovered no evidence for the existence of meaning.

Despite the multiple obstacles on my tongue, I still sang like a castaway canary. Words and music being the incomparable crown jewels of my diminutive kingdom. I revelled like a pirate in the treasure of them both. The sirenic sounds of my liberal lexicon bettered only when subjected to song. And closely following a near-interminable devotional about how He had given me the birds and the bees and the apple trees, I eventually fell silent. Exhausted. My gratitude for His largesse infinite, and my awe joyously expressed through the elation of endless ingemination. It wasn't enough.

The thin skin of my dissatisfied soul crawled guilty with the inadequacy of my offering. Each passing moment swelling with an increasingly awkward awareness that my meagre gift of song had fallen conspicuously short of the magnitude of donation necessary to be justly considered a genuinely reciprocal gesture.

I concluded that, in view of my limited resources, all I could practicably do to return something of incontestable value to the Lord was humbly present to Him freely, via a select handful of my fellow greenhorn five-year-old friends, the richest, ripest gifts from my latest prized hoard of irrepressibly wonderful and magical words; fucking, bastard and cunt. All of which I felt religiously to be among my most revered and inestimable possessions.

As a sonic projectile, the word *cunt*, even shorn of its sex, delivered the fulminating impact of a fragmentation grenade. It was the best and worst of all words.

From my earliest curses I was blessed with an acute appreciation of the value of shock, so typically launched this hallowed harpoon with creative circumspection. With the finesse of a surgeon and with a musician's ear for shading, context and timing.

The hysterical offence taken by my mother to it, however, moderated my moderation and compelled me to sling it at her like a volley of Molotov cocktails whenever I could snarlingly over-emphasise it to optimum effect in the invariably protracted course of one of our many bitterly inflamed confrontations.

I savoured the moments of illicit freedom the imprecation bought me as though I were scoffing a fistful of family-sized chocolate bars in one go.

Such an alliterative barrage would invariably incite the Ali Shuffle. I knew exactly what was coming, but freedom was worth getting assaulted for. Except for when my father joined in.

She loved that honour-outraged, colour-coordinated tag-team routine best, and frequently reported entirely fictitious altercations the moment he'd slide cross-carrying over the threshold, so she could immerse herself indulgently in the pleasure of watching him give me a good hiding. Even as he was assaulting me, she'd enthusiastically pitch in ringside with extra bits of exposition to optimise the violence; helping it along with an excited slap or two in the face whenever the tempo of the action permitted.

Occasionally, she'd warn me in advance of her intention to book a ringside evening in. Other times not. Despite the courtesy, I preferred not to know. It was seldom a performance I looked forward to. And once the fixture had gone to press, there wasn't much I could do to escape showing up in the florescent strip kitchen spotlight as the billing's main attraction. Leadbelly sang his way out of jail, but I enjoyed no prospect of any such parole. Not even a pre-pounding serenade would save me.

My resignation to the inevitable attack sprouted like cress in the light-starved confines of the understairs cupboard, where familiar aspects of my impending pommelling could be contemplated undistracted. My dressing room being at least conveniently situated for the ring, and a lot more comfortable than the under sink cabinet where I would otherwise be forced to crouch behind the semi-closed door with both knees under my chin until Spartacus came home.

It was generally a pretty painful affair when the broad-handed, fully-wound colossus of my father swayed heavy-weight style from the blue corner, usually with the spent typhoon of an exasperated sigh, to defend her dramatically insulted honour like a convincing MAN of pure if shame-lessly over-hammed theatre. Taking on the assignment immediately after arriving at the house, relieved from a hard stint at work, only to be confronted with an evening shift of compulsory overtime. His chiselled features would darken, as if his own daylight had deserted them.

Although, there were other equally one-sided bouts, which more justifiably addressed her choleric objections, and as usual, he'd dutifully step right in as a ready to go, fully gloved-up understudy when he plodded onstage to be enthusiastically informed by the pantomime audience that I had called the old bag a C-O-U-N-T.

She always spelled it out to him emphatically like that. Like it was too incendiary a mouthful to handle whole. But why the hell she added the O, I'll never know.

Perhaps she was counting the times I called her a cunt.

It's C-U-N-T, you fucking illiterate. Even I knew how to spell it.

Frequent flows of blood from my nose taught me to protect my face more effectively. Even then, he'd get through sometimes.

One day, I thought, I'll be bigger than you, you bastard.

# 5

It was a recurring thought. I spent my days living vicariously through the rhythmic melody of its echo. Violence had yet to persuasively suggest itself to me as a declaration of love.

I wasn't frightened of my father. He had never been delicate enough for me to be scared of. The only thing I've ever really been afraid of is the fragility of anything I've wanted to keep.

First day of school, it rained. My mother kept me home. She didn't want me walking to school in the wet. Not with bruises on my face, anyway.

She called the headmaster in the morning and reported that she thought I was sick. It was a lie, but it was the first time she had told anyone the truth about me.

As it happened, she did me a favour. If I had asked her to spare me the rigours of that opening day of primary education, she would have refused without hesitation. But as it turned out, however much I may have been looking forward to it, I quickly came to realise that I had made a terrible mistake in allowing myself to be subjected to the trauma of such excruciatingly interminable confinement. It weighed unbearably on my natural aversion to order and discipline.

I hated school pathologically, and almost immediately

embarked upon a more satisfying career as a freewheeling truant.

It was an enduring vocation, and the conscious inception of a lifetime of feeling alone.

# 6

I always considered my glass to be half empty. Even when there was nothing in it at all.

I began to suspect that I had been born sleepwalking into impossible dreams.

I tried to wake myself up with a scream, although nothing came out except adjectives. Hopelessly tongue-tied and lost in meaning, I wanted to reconnect with a more primitive, spontaneous vocabulary of feeling, but I had been frozen out of myself by words. I needed to escape them, to interpret something warmer for the winter.

Is there ever even another solitary moment before our ultimate surrendering rattle in which we are able to recapture the unadulterated integrity of that inaugural post-natal cry? And supposing the answer to this perennially posed question is positive, how would we then communicate such undecorated candour to ourselves without sanitising it through the filter of pretence? Or be trusted to translate it into more than the nostrum of dialogue without first emasculating it with the artifice of words?

We misplace our embarrassing natural impulsivity in the scramble to acquire more socially acceptable emotional prosthetics and can't seem to wait to hurl ourselves unconditionally into the ambush of their confinement. No sooner we learn to wish than we despairingly lose ourselves forever in the pervasive deceptions of language. The poet's right - it's your parents' fault. They assiduously teach you to talk, as if you were some kind of parrot or something, then they go mad with elation when you've mastered a sentence. Ah ha, we're not alone anymore, he's got the same handicap as us now. He'll never be understood; he's been fucked up the ass by syntax.

Of course I'm sorry now. Sorry that I endlessly interrupted my mother's tearful solicitations to her passed parents with incredulous interjections. I realise now, that her loss was more than granite. More than gravestones. I could see but I didn't yet know that my mother had been crushed by the weight of the dead. And somewhere among my unworldly suspicion, I was profoundly moved by her distress. Oblivious to the cliche and too young to cringe, I really did want almost more than anything for her to be happy. I invariably included her in my nightly solicitations to the Lord, with the reiterated plea for a solution to her malaise. Her affliction seeped from her as a stigmatic flow, etched trenches into her beauty like battery acid.

I sang to her often. Took her requests, too. Her requests were always for the same song; the birds, the bees and the apple trees. She couldn't get enough of it.

('Do you remember, how you used to sing to me? It was always the same song....the birds and the bees and the apple trees, the Lord is good to me....')

It was another one of those legendary World War One moments. We played football and sang Christmas carols together in no man's land. She paraded me like Kokoschka's doll through the spectacle of her delusions, through the decorated town, and showed me avenues of streetlights twinkling over the river in the rain. Baiting my wishes with inaccessible worlds of Woolworth magic, where she availed herself of the second floor conveniences while I deftly embroidered multicolour narratives for ancient diners sitting alone at tables in the canteen staring into spaces between occasional sips of tea.

Reunited like lost lovers at the beckoning clutches of the biscuit counter, I held her hand tightly, like it was more than an arrangement of fingers. For a few moments, everything was different. I felt complete. The courtship was incongruous but my affection was real. I had no-one else to kiss.

It was pragmatic, too. I preferred it like this. I could never tell when the dog would bite, or when the tongue would whip out to lash me.

# 7

How much love has suffered at the hands of words?

It was a rude awakening. Like watching the adventitious spectacle of an over-nourished super-rat suddenly flash impudently out from one of the shelves with half a Jammy Dodger in its teeth and dart between the peopled aisles of a popular supermarket. I didn't even get as far as proclaiming that the Lord was good to me. I just felt the lip-numbing sting of the slap across my cheek and mouth as soon as I mentioned the birds and bees.

'But I was only singing, Mum,' I remonstrated, wounded to the core and fighting back the flood.

She flew like a peregrine falcon into an apoplectic swoop, almost flattening my septal cartilage in her nosedive, and lambasted me maniacally, as if talking in tongues about my foul mouth. Screeching arbitrary references to the need to scrub the septic tank of my entire oral cavity clean with both wet and dry sandpaper and soap, and how I would get a good hiding when my father came home.

The saliva supplemented suggestion of this saponaceous sentence wasn't enough. In a moment, she had flung both her arms in the air and began to furiously flap them up and down, as though she were attempting to take flight or shake the trapped talcum from a bathroom rug. 'Right, then!' she hollered, disappearing in a goose march from the morning room and returning less than half a minute later clutching a well used bar of carbolic from the kitchen, before forcing it between my teeth after grabbing my collar in her fist and yanking me to the ground in a formidable display of brute force.

An undignified balance-losing roll around ensued in which she strove to sustain a credible scrubbing motion for a moment or two, more as a determined endeavour to implement the crux of her threat than a genuine attempt to fulfil an aspiration to thoroughly clean anything. Then, failing to profitably maintain her attack through the defences of my unopening lips, suspended the slippery bar above my exposed throat like an ominously poised Roman gladius.

The fact that I didn't understand her motive hurt me more than the violence. I had considered myself to be on safe ground with the same volitant friends that had traditionally accorded me such accolades of her attention.

Suddenly, the ballad had become painful. A mnemonic for the agony of naked injustice.

I never sang the song again.

On the days I couldn't bunk off school, I more often than not returned home mid-afternoon over-decorated with a particoloured variety of humps and bumps scrupulously accumulated from diligent sessions of involuntarily using my head as a lump hammer. I've no idea why or how I did it. I just did. However assiduously I tried, I simply couldn't seem to stop myself from woodpeckering my more than amenable cranium against any kind of surface that was substantially harder than bone. I didn't mean to. It just happened.

This inconvenient habit actually seemed to culminate in a shimmer of epiphany, which befell me the day I clouted my brow on the school gate. Don't ask me how.

The entryway altercation had imprinted an impressively haloed Burmese ruby-red saddled elevation in the centre of my forehead, but by the end of assembly the pounding had begun to subside and I have to admit that I didn't really pay a lot more attention to it until I smacked it on the lavatory door in the mid-morning break.

But, standing against the wall in the ceramic pearly-tiled corridor, waiting for class to reassemble, mostly minding my own business and quietly singing a memorable line or two of a popular novelty song I'd heard a few times recently on the radio, I began to forget about it again. Several kids were giving slightly more of a voice to their high spirits and larking around when the missile burst. They stopped, frozen by a moment of apprehension, as though they had been petrified by the sudden detonation of it. Finding their feet momentarily in the aftershock, they shuffled against the outside of the classroom in a line. It was a familiar routine.

Had she not stepped into my line of vision, the convention would have provided sufficient information to announce her imminent arrival. The harridan. The demon teacher, hated and feared by all the mini inmates, marched menacingly towards me in a squall, with a full, beige, heavy woollen skirt flapping feverishly in the bellows of her stride. She paused less than a foot from my feet, cast a determined stare at my forehead, flung her arms around me, bent down, kissed my cheek and said something kind. Such an impromptu display of unforecast affection arrested me so abruptly in my proverbial tracks that the ground practically smoked around me.

She crouchingly drew me closely into the fragrant cushion of her chest and unhurriedly held me in a sympathetic embrace long enough for the musky scent of her voluminous body to become familiar to me.

Midway through an unnaturally ponderous period of time, my initial discomfort gradually grew. The unloosening vice of my unlikely paramour's affection began to embarrass me in front of my friends. My neck, too, was taking a dislike to being reset at a right angle.

Although the fear of permanent paralysis subsided soon after, the short encounter had, nevertheless, changed me for ever.

I had been introduced to an unfamiliar aspect of love which had imbued me with the desire to share it. And I learned from its seductive warmth how effortlessly it seemed to communicate with pain.

Equally importantly, I realised that I, along with so many others, without knowing her, had imprudently misjudged this woman.

It was the finest education I received in my years at the school.

# 8

We are continuously bereaved by the orphanings from our idols.

My mother's interest in her art and antiques emporium had waned. The business had been ticking over but she no longer felt able to sustain a serially diminishing enthusiasm for sourcing stock at auction, and had developed a debilitating resentment of fawning to people richer than her to sell it.

In a blink of summer drizzle, my parents had sold up, traded down and moved into the countryside for a quieter life. Where, among the chequered rows of cabbages and sprouts in our neighbour's commodious garden, chickens wandered wild.

I wanted them. Or, if not specifically Gingernut Rangers, then something, anything, to be ambling around in *my* garden. I stood congenially, semi upright against the cold, finger-wrapped silver wire fence, watching, as they waddled around disinterestedly, avidly resisting my frequent, inutile attempts to befriend them.

My father must have noticed.

Unlikely as it seemed, he sheltered a secret sensitivity towards me which occasionally sneaked out when he wasn't looking.

The unsexable rabbit was soft, white and portable, with fuchsia pink eyes. I dubbed it Snowball, in the immediate absence of a more parnassian, gender fluid alternative, and summarily committed myself to being enamoured of it. Even before I had directed at it an array of my most welcoming salutations, which it politely endured with little discernible enthusiasm or interest.

It was the first life I had ever owned. And I threw myself into a unilateral love and affinity of grand operatic intensity.

I embowered its silky, warm body in my protective fingers. Appointed myself the founding patriarch of a long line of leporines. Gazed through its curious, elliptical, raw pink eyes and peered avidly into the advent of a rabbit-shaped future. Within hours, a coterie of inquisitive friends had visited, bearing gifts of lettuce.

In the early evening jamboree of excited children's pokes through the chicken wire front of the wooden hutch my father had built, I noticed the last few stripes of a vividly decorated caterpillar disappear between the obliging yawn of my rabbit's jaws.

'What did you give him that for?' I bellowed, incredulously, to the confounded young owner of a subsequent guilty shrug.

'Rabbits eat anything,' he offered, hopefully.

My torpedoed heart sank in an instant of disbelief. Somehow, in the suspension of that moment, I just knew. It was the second worst feeling I had ever had.

I nurtured the idyll of Snowball and unconditional devotion for a single day. By the eerily over-large, empty hutch of morning, I had fallen all the way from my airborne castle to wander bereft in the vacuum of my wilderness once more. Alone again, and thrust back into a stone cold world where almost nothing made sense. I couldn't find the justice in it. Or reconcile myself to the brevity of our acquaintance.

I continued to grieve the loss of my pet for weeks, then months, and eventually, in a desperate last ditch attempt to cauterise the deluge of unabating misery, I half-heartedly concluded that it was simply meant to be. That the whole experience had somehow been preordained, and the painful consequence of my unprotected affection unalterable. I was undeserving, and that's all there was to it.

It didn't help. The colours of my rainbow remained obstinately monochromatic.

I ended up pulling my forlorn self aside and quietly explaining that I had been especially favoured by God to undertake some unknown future Herculean labour, and that my experience was almost certain to have been the privilege of a sacred trial to ascertain the limit of my forbearance, and the extent of heartbreak I could suffer without cracking.

That's how it starts, the whole insidious thing. You get a little grain of itchy, sandy, despair beneath the freshly violated shell of your defences, that carries on itching and itching, and all the time you scratch it, it grows and grows until, before you know it, it has developed into a beautiful, gleaming, iridescent, pearly white ball of philosophical bullshit.

My father never kept a pet again.

# 9

Despair steals our hopes, as though they were worth having.

It was an agonising moment. The mutilating ignominy of it lacerating my soul as deeply as when you bury your head in your hands to evade the spotlight of your shame and discover on lifting your palms towards you that they've morphed into the grinning faces of everything you've ever failed at.

That's how it was.

I had smashed a precious family heirloom. Some ancient porcelain figure. I didn't mean to. It just happened when I swung a pillow around to get noticed. Swept it clean off the mantelpiece. I thought I'd get a good hiding, but I didn't. I felt terrible, though.

My selfish indulgence had created an incident beyond my intention or control. I attempted to dredge up something appropriately penitential from the depths of my diffidence, but was unable to articulate my regret. I didn't know what to say, beyond sorry. The word seemed inadequate.

My father unceremoniously threw the shards into a bin without saying anything at all. He didn't stop to look at them for a last time, or attempt to stick them back together again, or put them somewhere for safe keeping; he just threw them away, as if they meant nothing to him at all.

I felt worse when he left the room carrying the bin after sweeping the carpet, and realised that it wasn't only the object I had shattered, but his appreciation of it as well.

The figure's accidental fall from grace had depreciated it beyond redemption. And as always for my father, things were either valuable and worth having or they were useless and not. Nothing ever occupied a space between the two extremes of his judgement.

It's how he was. Accidents happened, but not once did he betray a trace of sentiment when he damaged something of his own. This time, however, I knew the loss of his heirloom had saddened him. And that the familiar little pale porcelain lady had, in her sudden demise, become a stranger; their longstanding relationship destroyed by a moment of structural infidelity.

His reasoning eluded me, and I didn't understand his refusal to retain an attachment to an irreplaceable artefact he had valued so long for its unique and exceptional history. His determination to throw the object away so casually, callously, stung me like a punch. And although the ornament was no longer intact, its mishap had not destroyed it beyond repair. Even in its decimated state it retained the essence of what it was and continued to exist as a physical legacy. Which was surely above anything else exactly what it had always been.

I had missed the point, and remained unaware that for my father, a broken heirloom represented a metaphor too close to the bone. Even so, it was impossible for me not to realise that I had shattered more than I knew.

Had I better understood the mysterious machinery of my father's mind, I may have appreciated the extent of my carnage. But the stranger he had been to me he remained, and the dark matter of his impenetrable solitude frustrated my feeble efforts to find him.

My father was a nomad. A wanderer, like me. Never less miserable than when maintaining a respectable distance from himself. Escaping while he wasn't watching to discover a freedom beyond his means; but ultimately losing himself in a fog of unlifting despair. Falling sick somewhere abroad and not finding his way home again. Spending his years awaiting the return of a treasure he had never owned.

His abundantly landed grandparents were old money, rich beyond concern. They disinherited my grandfather when he eloped to Gretna Green to marry a girl in their service and showered the newly-weds with the priceless gift of their exclusion.

The repercussive outpouring of their unending rejection coursed through my father's veins from his earliest childhood; his blood transfused by a fountain of rancour. Undertows of discontent pulled him into straits of undefined sorrows, though not deeply enough to drown him. His bitterness perpetually inflating him to the point of buoyancy, but never more than was necessary to ensure that he remained just noticeably afloat.

Despite nourishing the pain he raised, he didn't spoil or pamper it. Instead, he embedded his teeth so far into his tongue that he could barely use it anymore to articulate a word of it. He existed in a perpetual anaphylactic state and remained at the threat of its effect for the rest of his days.

Not that anyone outside the house of my insufferable detention would have noticed. Oh, no. Beyond the perimeter of his own cell walls it would have been impossible to identify him as the Flying Dutchman of domestic despair, doomed to eternal restlessness until the redemptive kiss of insurmountable catastrophe eventually stilled him.

He could generally be located travelling some distance out of his way to appear affable. Gentle, too. Laughing naturally in the unlikely manner of an easily amused hyena with non-family members and invariably succumbing to an inexorable compulsion to offer his help to anyone he considered to be in need of it.

It saddened me to see his generosity being exploited by chancers who realised they could save money by bringing a panoply of their concerns to his attention.

His almost athletic capacity to respond to a call from a distant acquaintance at a moment's notice impressed me. It frustrated me, too. There seemed to be so many of them.

My father was a man of few pretences. His desire to help others was genuine, and he approached his role as good Samaritan with an equally good natured sense of obligation. And an enthusiasm rarely evident for anything else.

My mother invested herself with the right to insist that any available generosity be solely directed at her, and accepted all gifts of such charity generously. She did not take to his regular acts of philanthropy well.

When called upon for help, she could be occasionally coaxed into lending a tongue, but nothing more. And even then, only on the assurance that others would wag effusively in appreciation of the loan. Unlike my father, she would not step selflessly in, around, or anywhere near where others feared to tread. Certainly not close enough to the house he passed on his way home from the newsagent's to feel the heat of the flames as they poured from its windows, or to kick the front door open without pausing for thought and rescue the elderly occupant from her blazing bedroom while everyone else dithered around on the lawn and waited for the fire brigade to arrive.

My father never spoke about the things he did for others. Unlike my mother who, had she been the first to notice the house ablaze, would have stationed herself a safe distance away from it fashioning the rictus she would bemoan the awfulness of it all through in a voice loud enough to attract the attention of somebody she could bully into acting. Dragging the same visage back out again when recounting the experience to all and sundry for endless centuries afterwards.

A rare compassion elevated her to the ranks of the devoutly kind-hearted. But being a humble woman, she invariably accepted the gratitude of others modestly.

My father's generosity occasionally extended to providing the less well off kids in the neighbourhood with toys and games when they weren't well. He considered such mandatory acts unremarkable and would shy away from handing the articles over himself, entrusting their delivery to my mother instead. An errand she did not enjoy but did not object to, as her participation ensured that any appreciation for a gift would not be directed solely at her husband. An outcome which suited my father, who invariably preferred to not only hide his light under a bushel, but to hide the bushel as well.

He bought a garden swing for a neighbour once. I used to go around and play on it sometimes.

Nobody could express their thanks to him for these apparently insignificant acts of kindness. He wouldn't have it, and would wave away any attempts to modify his modesty dismissively. Not that he wasn't a stickler for correct forms of protocol in any other matter known to man.

When passing an object at the dinner table, of course, my father insisted upon the appropriate etiquette and decorum; the abetted migration of condiments commanded courtesy. But the recognition of his philanthropy was a different affair. Convinced that such acts were no more than duties, he believed wholeheartedly that everyone had a right to be provided with enough to keep them from despairing too much in a life already beset with sorrow.

It appeared to me that he found it easier to care about people he didn't really know.

I was confused about all this when I was a child. And still am, in a way. But, back then, I wished I had been someone who didn't know him very well, and had made one of those calls to him for help.

# 10

Empathy is the tender bruise of sorrow.

Throughout the endless winter of the following few years, death fell in a flurry of snowflakes, and I felt surrounded by a biblical slaughter of the virtually still innocents. The familiar ground of incomprehensible normality opened before me and a swallowing hole of infinite sadness appeared. A miniature legion of my tiny friends toppled into it in a march and quietly disappeared. Spring buds withered on the vine. Just kids; beautiful and cold. Same age as me.

The pretty, blue-frocked, pony tailed red-head next door, and my unassuming fatherless friend from across the street, both drowned in town within a few months of each other. A soccer-mad playmate three doors further up the road gashed his leg while falling on a stone mid-game and bled profusely. I offered myself as the crutch he stumbled home in tears on, whereupon, he anxiously sought a gush of reassurances from his domestically distracted mother that he would not immediately expire from his mishap. She correctly predicted, with appropriately anodyne motherly composure, that a band-aid would likely suffice.

Shortly after his leg had restored itself to full health and active service, he fell ill. Within weeks, a reverential chorus of *leukaemia* spectrally permeated the neighbourhood air like an ominous knolling of bells. I donated a large collection of personal prayers and my favourite table football game to his recovery, but he died less than a month later.

Another classmate disappeared from our view in unexplained circumstances. Her demise solemnly posted in morning assembly a few days after her initial absence. We were all deathly quiet when word was finally delivered and pretended not to know; but by then, the rumour had circulated like an outbreak of smallpox and the inevitable news came as no surprise to any of us.

The unlucky fifth victim of the period was a boy in the classroom next to ours, who was towed into oblivion by the minibus that had dropped him off at home following an evening at Cubs in town. He had climbed out of the vehicle, stepped onto the pavement and began to walk away, but hadn't realised he'd caught his coat in the back door when he closed it. Neither, in the accompanying chorus of poignant farewells, had anyone else. He was dragged along the poorly lit road for several hundred yards, bouncing and bobbing behind the accelerating minibus like a straggle of cans.

The news spread fast that evening, that there was a package of dead kid in the road. My mother was beside herself. The information she had was that it had happened a couple of streets away, that the boy was around my age and was called Christopher. And that I wasn't at home.

# 11

Philosophy is the art of making impossible to answer questions seem essential to our understanding of something indefinable that forever remains intractably beyond our grasp.

I became increasingly aware that I was wading precariously in a meandering tide of pus. Ailing people everywhere were hobbling around bleeding invocations from infected wounds that were never going to heal. Vitiated by a surfeit of dreams.

Each time somebody I had been familiar with died, I was fully aware of the gravity of the occasion, but unable to grasp the incomprehensible finality of it all. I was sad, of course, but more puzzled than anything. There were thoughts in my mind that I couldn't get my head around.

I understood the departed wouldn't return, but were they still alive in Heaven? And if so, exactly how alive were they? Were they carrying on blithely, as if nothing had happened? Apparently so, and gleefully experiencing the rare pleasures of an extraordinary mirth routinely denied the woebegone Earthbound, but no-one really seemed to know for sure. Except for my mother. And almost everyone else agreed with her, however much they seemed to lack conviction in their assent.

Short of practical experience in such affairs, I had little alternative to assuming that those who were all so much older and wiser than me somehow knew the answers to these secrets. But that wasn't necessarily true; I had heard dissenting voices. So, what about the people who said not? Were they right to or wrong? I was confused. My mother assured me she couldn't be wrong about anything. And that was all that really mattered. Death was not the end.

It was a familiar reassurance. I was exposed at home to endless reverberations from the constantly resurrected threat of eternal life.

Eternity was such a long time in those days. It seems to have shortened since.

I tried to imagine what it would be like to die, and yet to not die and to live for ever. I couldn't do it. I didn't know how to unpick the riddle of the words. Or have enough of the tune for the song to make sense. I couldn't grasp the full feculent reality of death in any way that didn't ensure the noun remained larger than the condition. But a corral of letters spared me the momentousness of their meaning; the menace in their bark kept me just far enough away from a cold blue corpse.

I noticed how some people seemed to think, in the way the ancient physicians did, that they could escape the icy finger of death altogether and heal themselves with a panoply of wordy potions. That they could deny the inevitable with a jumble of incantations. And all they needed to do to create their undying new reality was escape the lethal clutches of delineation. In their quest for distance, I saw how easily they were able to hitch-hike away from almost anywhere on a magic carpet of mysterious mutterings.

In my own quest for immortality, it occurred to me that

neither the unyielding mysteries of death nor the blissful prospect of eternal merriment was worth losing any more of my life on, anyway, as I was unlikely to be subjecting myself to either condition at any time soon. If indeed at all.

But for most of the time, the only thing I felt I could practically do to alleviate my bewilderment and effect some glimmer of apperception was philosophise. Roll these unpalatable titbits of enigma over my tongue and try to ascertain something of their elusive flavour as best I could. Chew them up and spit them back out again in a way that melded them all into some reassuringly recognisable, all-embracing, comprehensible certainty.

I did this over and over again but earned no real conviction from my efforts. It felt that I was hunched over my unyielding fields of darkness like one of Millet's gleaners, forever foraging for scraps of understanding.

Occasionally, on marginally more edifying excursions into satisfyingly deeper waters, just when I'd think I was inching towards a rip tide of percipience, I'd find myself paddling despondently back into the baffling shallow of my ignorance. It was frustrating.

Now, of course, it's endearing to remember that once, in my fresh green and broad leaved salad days, I imagined death to be contained within the moment of its incidence. I soon came to despair at my naivety, and realised that expiration was a resolutely ongoing process.

My mother found it impossible not to brandish her contempt for the publicly articulated grief of the distraught father for his drowned child, when he contrived to perfect an eventually successful drowning of his own by increasing his regular visits to the infirmary of the local alehouse. She twisted the nib of her supercilious disapproval into his face like a corkscrew on every repeated showing of his mortified shell tottering unsteadily past her watch from the guard-post of our garden gate. To her, the undignified parade constituted an insult, an affront to the Almighty, who had intended such suffering to be borne without recourse to conveniently situated fermented draughts of temporary anaesthesia.

With death circling the skies like a conspiracy of ravens, I became conscious of the fragility of life and flirted with notions of sober circumspection. Sedulously setting about weighing up the potential advantages of taking my existence a bit more seriously. Not that I had ever taken it for granted or undervalued it particularly, any more than the average six-year-old did. I entertained a more or less healthy respect for it. It's just that it had always presented itself to me as being somewhat elusive.

From the dawn of my days it felt as though everyone I knew had invested something in my life, and the controlling interest belonged to someone else. As if I had been born in a stranger's home and was diligently observing the house rules while they were away. Or, that somebody had saddled me with a suitcase too heavy to move while I was sitting at a railway station and asked me to hang on to it until they returned at some unspecified time. So, I obediently tended it scrupulously and missed all the passing trains while I waited there, but they never came back. And however curious I might have been about what was inside the suitcase, I was too nervous or lazy or irrationally considerate of the owner's bizarre request to open it and see.

It's crazy. I was only ever at that frigging railway station in the first place because I was trying to get away.

From my earliest disillusions, I had always been leaving.

Hobbling fiddle-footed over the horizon to somewhere else. Somewhere new.

I never have developed an abiding sense of home. Just a lingering homesickness for somewhere I've never been. Or is it some*one*.

I find tantalising scents of it in unexpected places.

# 12

Even for those who dare not speak its name, poetry remains the universal language of dreams.

Suddenly, my misfiring meanderings through eternal years of yearning erupted in an over saturated fury of primary shades. I was in love. A sublime condition. One that was even worth going to school for.

I first noticed her in the girls' line-up for lunch, where I caressed her lovely face with an improperly extended glance and was hooked in a heartbeat. My enamoured opening gander being immediately followed by an indecorous series of unseemly gawks which carried me abruptly to the periphery of indiscretion. It was obvious, the first time my jaw dropped like a lead balloon, that Raquel Welsh swanning around bikinied in One Million Years B.C. couldn't hold a candle to this babe. And to top it all, she was six, like me.

Every ravishingly fascinating thing about her was so seductively larger than life, it was impossible not to be smitten by the consummate perfection of it all; the silken, auburn waterfall of her hair, the endless summer of her smile, the angelic choir of her voice. She had flown through the mists of ages on gossamer wings from an ancient Greek pantheon of gorgeous goddesses to be with me. The magnificent peregrination not ruffling a ringlet or diminishing her beauty a whit.

I subsequently discovered that her journey began at Gosport when her family moved to Bath with the M.O.D. but it didn't matter. She was here at my school, and I loved her.

I entertained few inhibitions in affairs of the heart at this pre-testosteronic stage of my romantic career, considering it so very much less complicated and distracting, so much more expedient and forthright to depend entirely on my sparkling personality to open the doors of love than to be hung up about the need to parade a host of irresistible trappings of accomplishment to ferry me through them.

The first time I saw her she had already taken her seat in the refectory and was dining with uncommon refinement. Nothing at all of serious note plummeting down her chin and onto her blouse. I watched her eat, besotted, jealous of the mint-jellied mutton hotpot on her fork. Even the way she nonchalantly flicked her hair from her cheek hurried my heartbeat. The effortless way she laughed, casual and confident, conspicuously commanded the worship of every devotee at the altar of her table.

I knew I needed to act incisively, before some snot-flinging lowlife muscled in on my hustle and audaciously snatched her away. I thought about it for a day or two.

The second time I saw her, I marched right up to her and started talking, as if I had been on the most cordial of terms with her for years. She talked right back without concern or hesitation. This confirmed my suspicion that she would immediately like me a lot. We breezed through the first round of our routine preliminaries; and with her corylus irises peering into my soul through the blue of mine, she revealed the secret I had been so impatient to uncover. That her name, like her eyes and the magnificently burnished hue of her hair, was Hazel. And although I'd never encountered another with so axiomatically nutty an appellation, I considered the title entirely without equal. It suited her perfectly.

Anyway, through a nebula of ardor I called her Haze, and we continued to hit it off straight away.

For the rest of the day, I thought about her as though a hyperactive bee had trapped itself in the labyrinth of my bloodstream.

By the time we spoke again at morning break in the playground the next day, I considered our acquaintance solidly enough based to launch a direct assault on her heart. I struck a suitable pose to show off my full three feet ten of manly desirability and summoned just the right amount of irresistible insouciance to ask her out.

'Will you be my girl?' I implored. It didn't really sound like I was imploring. Not when I started, anyway. In fact, I managed to conceal my apprehension pretty well throughout the duration of the request, and accomplished most of it in the emphatically cinematic, cross-leggedly leaning against a lamppost taking a lingering draw on a freshly lit Gauloises guise of a casual question. I might have been a bit bashful towards the end, but was still pretty hopeful, and honestly didn't think Cary Grant would have delivered the line with more charisma.

She conjured imaginary scenes from the reality of my flattering proposition for a moment, which seemed to go on for a bit longer than I had anticipated. As if she may have been attempting to envisage something of even greater magnitude than the pleasure of my company.

The lengthening silence began to unnerve me.

'OK,' she said, eventually, but not before tectonic plates had formed, settled and shifted somewhere, 'I'll be your girl if you never call me Haze again, and call me Hazel.'

I was ecstatic. Almost completely lost control of myself in an enveloping blaze of erupting elation. Despite the broad range of subjects covered in my pre-proposal ruminations, I hadn't sensibly considered the reality of her accepting me as a suitor. And now she had. Which meant that she fancied me like mad, too. I couldn't contain either my excitement or relief. Already, I had begun drawing up an invitation list to the wedding.

'Thanks, Haze,' I blurted, deliriously, straight into her face like a sudden sneeze.

She didn't say anything. She just looked at me in a similar but more unnervingly less extended moment of poker-faced deliberation. Then she turned around and walked away.

I knew that I had blown it. The relationship was over.

# 13

I have always been blown from shadow to shade, but have never formed an attachment to the wind.

I took stock. I loved words, but they had already been unfaithful to me. And the cascading over-conscious dawning on me of my unenviable disposition was as painfully inevitable as the repeated chorused echoes of my resounding self-chastisement.

In the deep-focussed foreground of my habitually miscarrying compulsion to somehow acquire the rhetorical equivalent of double D silicone implants, I became achingly aware of an extraordinarily irrepressible and fantastically resilient natural facility I have for saying precisely the most inappropriate thing at exactly the least opportune moment.

It's a deeply uncherished gift, but one I've wheeled out with monotonous predictability and at considerable personal expense on innumerable occasions. It's completely at odds with my almost neurotic over-consideration of practically everything I say. It may not seem immediately obvious sometimes, but I really take unnaturally thorough precautions to avoid deliberately offending anyone.

My mother's the opposite. She'll say the first thing that comes into her mind. An exhibitionist and an accomplished practitioner of the vulgarity she professes to despise, she's verbally incontinent and leaves piles of her shit behind her wherever she goes. My father, as previously reported, was pretty much so inimical to the post-Neanderthal practice of using words at all that, unless you spent all day with him, you'd probably think he was mute. But talk was cheaper than broken promises to my mother, which is why she stuffed herself so relentlessly on the sound of it. If spouting gibberish had cost her any money, she would have been as dumb as him.

Anyway, all this self-critical disconcertion surfaced in anger at around the time my paternal grandmother, whose preternaturally wrinkled face out-cratered that of any planet's moon, informed me in her nicotine-burnished croak that I was too beautiful to be a boy and that I ought to have been born a girl instead. Music no doubt to my mother's ears, but the acidic remark had not been thrown as a compliment. Neither had it been received as one. Her insensitivity stung me as much as her words. I stood there saturated by the invasion of her assault.

At the risk of appearing conceited, I couldn't exactly describe myself as being a complete stranger to occasional reassurances that I looked OK. But I was a sobering distance from being anywhere near convinced that these commentators were addressing the person they were referring to when they said so. It didn't exactly boost my confidence that if anyone said anything commendatory, they were usually at least as old as my grandmother and presumably of a similarly questionable state of mind. And even though I couldn't depend on the opinion of such people, they occasionally gabbered on through some wistful mist about my corkscrew yellow hair and deep blue dinner-plate eyes. Even going as far as occasionally sticking their semi-glabrous, patchy purple rinsed top-knots into my face and coming over all gooey about my eyelashes. A dangerously repressed acquaintance of my mother referred to them as riding crops.

It didn't matter. Nothing complimentary compensated for the curse of being so scrawny. I loathed my barely visible frame as though the emaciated needle of it were a body-covering carbuncle. My party-piece was turning sideways and disappearing altogether.

But it was true, even if the puppy-fat on my doggedly visible bones was conspicuous by its absence, my facial essentials were fortunately all there and in not egregious proportions. Which is more than I could say for my equally wiry grandmaternal commentcaster, whose withered features had long transformed into a series of indistinct punctuations cratered into an undulating landscape of head-smothering creases. The beauty that had cost my grandfather his family and fortune lost to the unforgiving ravages of antiquity.

Maybe she resented my youthfulness or epidermal elasticity. I didn't know. The acuity of her self-awareness rendered her remote. Too hard and unaccommodating to allow children a safe place to play inside her defences. In my case, the indifference was reciprocated. She possessed all the grandmotherly approachability of an industrial blast furnace.

The only reason I had been compelled to stand to attention there in the stale cigarette stinking kitchen, like some cherubic caryatid at the side of her unmade fire, offering myself up as a polite target for her rude remarks, was because my father had arranged to take my grandfather to visit his sister, my venerable great aunt May, at her house in the country.

The excursion to my aunt May's with my father was not an unusual one. In fact, our regular visits were among the few recreational activities he and I shared, and I looked forward to spending such afternoons together, even though the conversation between us remained, as usual, sparse and stilted. But chasms of silence contracted on those almost amenable occasions, when the change of landscape provided mediation in the communication of our awkwardness. And when my father did speak to me, alone in the car, he spoke warmly.

My mother never came with us. Not once.

My grandmother subscribed to my mother's loathing of my grandfather's family; the lifestyle their exclusion from it had cost them leaving the taste in both women's mouths bitter as the waters of Marah. Neither feeling able under any circumstances to darken their tongue with the mention of any members of it.

On our return from Great Aunt May's, through tortuous miles of haw and blackthorn hedged narrow country lanes on darkening autumn evenings, the spectacle of natterer's, pipestrelles and greater horseshoes zigzagging around the car, melding like ballroom quicksteppers pirouetting over crops and the pantiled roofs of ancient farm buildings, entertained us more than the moiled manufacture of more perfunctory distractions. Terpsichorean twirls and twists hatched rapt smiles and flight-tracing finger-points. Bursts of approval punctuating vistas of silence more efficaciously than the random flinging of more speculative sounds.

Although our trips to my father's elderly aunt were not unusual, it was the company of my grandfather that rendered today's appointment unique. He had never previously joined us on our visits in the car. To anywhere. The unusual circumstances appealed to me, even though I would be expected to relinquish the privilege of my front seat in favour of a more familiar, less dignified placement in the back. Rarely having socially encountered our illustrious passenger, however, I decided to shoulder my demotion with good grace and reckoned the exchange to be worth the opportunity of becoming better acquainted with him.

Even on the relatively infrequent occasions when I visited my grandfather at home, he mulishly retained his aura of mystery by almost invariably sequestering himself away in a different room from me. As for socialising in a less confined environment, I couldn't recall ever having been anywhere in public with him at all. Despite the memorable clean shaven contours of his face and the tall, lean figure of his physique, he was quite a stranger to me. Not least because, even when I did actually see him, he never really said anything.

Which is why I had been looking forward to this outing so much from my initial briefing on it, and hoped that it would stimulate a more rewarding new relationship between us.

Not far into the journey, and as yet almost completely unaddressed by either party in the front, I pre-empted my father's inevitable request to wipe the back window with a rag on the shelf for the purpose. Clearing my own immediately afterwards by drawing on it with my fingertip and watching rivulets of disturbed condensation flood the frame. I took the necessity to create ephemeral, Alfred Wallis-style, self-destructing, semi-abstract, throw away master-pieces of art in the car seriously, considering it to be one of the principal purposes of mechanical locomotion.

I liked the car, too. A curvaceous black galleon with leather seats and a wide, metal-ribbed running board at the side. It felt like travelling in a room.

On the way to Great Aunt May's it was impossible not to notice how both my forebears had somehow morphed into completely different characters. I was astonished. At any other time, either of these avid aphonics could have been mistaken for Trappists, but here they suddenly were chirping away like a couple of songbirds.

To my unworldly eye, whenever I happened to visit him, my grandfather unwaveringly presented himself as a devoutly austere man, who only appeared in person when he absolutely needed to and spoke only when his less lexical options had manifestly failed him.

To satisfy an emotional need for a greater familiarity with him I imaginatively reinvented his personality, and was later amazed to discover that my fantasy creation had been creepily close to the truth.

His action-packed Boy's Own story book career, since being eighty-sixed from his family and disinherited, had consisted of a constellation of adventures extending from the front lines of legendary conflicts to jaguar and anaconda filled South American rainforests and gold mines, where he perpetually seemed to be surfacing armed to the teeth and up to his neck in jungle or mud.

For my grandmother, life without him at home in Bath had been somewhat more sedate. Although his short-lived returns to her there would typically result in the essential credentials of the youngest member of the family being ceremoniously recorded and rubber stamped by the local registrar some months subsequent to his departure.

As many other would-be soldiers would be, I was keen to hear his accounts of action from the front lines of the Russian Revolution, the Spanish Civil War and other fabled fields of conflict, but information was virtually impossible to come by.

My father would begin to recount captivating vignettes of adventure, only to clam up altogether shortly afterwards and leave me wondering. The wild horses of my pleas couldn't drag more splinters of storyline from him. 'Why won't you tell me, dad?' I implored. But I could read no answer into the inflexible shaking of his head. My curiosity intensified to the limit by the knowledge that he knew more than he was prepared to let on.

I almost never got further than that definitively punctuating shake of his head. Except for once. A two or three minute interval in the extended awkwardness of a tedious drive home together one evening in the dark, when, unprompted and unintroduced, a single thread of sparkling narrative spilled naturally out of the surrounding silence and he volunteered the strange tale of the disappearing skipper on my grandfather's ship after he and his crew-mates had been subjected to a litany of his drunken abuse during an intercontinental return from duty. The ship eventually arrived at port three weeks after setting sail from the East. The author of the crew's disaffection, however, was not to be numbered among the disembarking personnel.

But even the special magic of that unique occasion could not sustain the story, and he abruptly concluded the account there. Right in the middle of the best bit. Slammed the door of his refusal to continue with it, just as I was hooked and desperate to know more. I begged him to reprise the tale. To provide me with an epilogue or satisfactory conclusion. But he had said enough.

Despite his illustrious past, my grandfather remained a devoutly modest man. If he was ever heard to speak it was never about himself. Seldom relating anything to my father about his martial or adventuring campaigns, and even when he mused in moods for sharing a memory with him, it was to say no more than he intended to, and almost nothing at all of the people he had encountered in the making of it.

Now he retired quietly amongst his decorative army of brightly painted ceramic gnomes and the various awards for the presentation of his gardens.

Great Aunt May was another formidable enigma. The oldest person I knew and by now, close to the cusp of her years, she had creakingly ossified on the exposed brow of her dotage into a brittle memorial to herself. Half a decade before the flying tackle of diabetes-induced gangrene would whip both legs away and permanently sever her connection with the ground, she plodded slowly and methodically around in an array of colourful silk scarves like a moribund Stegosaurus. But, perfectly partnering herself with gentle, good natured frustration in the curious ballet of her strangely robotic ancient frailties, she was also eminently kind and caring and easy to like. Motherly, even, in spite of having spent what I assumed to have been an unhappy and lonely life as a spinster. Although my favourite relative, she invariably appeared to be somewhere slightly removed from wherever she was. The disposition suggesting a constant preoccupation with something, and painting her as being permanently beset with a problem she was anxious to resolve. The habit inevitably burnished her with a veneer of softly patinated distance.

In the eerily resonant arched stone porch, the familiar clank of opening door oozed into the cool, late morning air, along with a closely following indefinable scent of house.

I was, of course, perfectly well acquainted with the ritual of impending pleasantries and for a few seconds immersed myself in the peculiar tension of waiting for the ceremony to begin. Suddenly, the small but strikingly larger than life shape of Great Aunt May appeared in front of me and the inalterable, time-honoured, prescriptively choreographed etiquette that I had for some moments anticipated, began amid a short flurry of welcoming words. Impeccably observed, as usual.

I was obliged to summarily kiss her cheek upon my arrival then again later, in her drawing room, before I was permitted to take full possession of my weak tea and biscuits. It was like kissing powdery blancmange, and I needed the tea to get rid of the taste and texture of it.

She was rich, and wore the becoming aroma of old money like the subtle scent of beeswax on antediluvian furniture. She occupied a world of ornately framed oils and family portraits on William Morris walls, porcelain figures and mythical bronzes on Georgian mahogany tea tables. The whole rambling house was like a museum.

I sat there in an antiquated air, ignored among relics of the past, feeling bored and out of place while my father, grandfather and great aunt talked about things I didn't understand. The museum stank of age.

I finished my tea and biscuits, taking as long as I could to polish off the dregs. After which there was nothing more for me to do but sit in a brass studded upright leather chair and wish I hadn't come.

To her credit, my great aunt May noticed my discomfort and asked if I would rather put my coat on and play in the garden. The garden was huge. It seemed to go on forever. There were different sections of it for lawns and vegetables and flowers and trees. It was too much for me to take on.

'It's OK, thank you, Aunt May, I'm fine siting here.'

I made a considerable effort to sound as convincing as

possible.

'Well, perhaps you'd like another biscuit, dear?'

Now, that was a suggestion I could readily embrace with appreciably more than a modicum of authentic enthusiasm.

She rose slowly from the dusky plum damask of her Queen Anne wing chair and disappeared dragging her skirt behind her into another room, returning some moments later to declare the biscuit tin empty, and requested that my father walk me to the village shop to buy more.

I didn't think we had been gone that long, but when my father and I returned to Great Aunt May's house, the ambulance was already there. We went in. Aunt May was crying. My father began to cry, too. I couldn't see my grandfather anywhere.

# 14

We are the voices of ghosts.

My father didn't say anything, but cried quietly as he drove home. I didn't say anything either, but fished avidly for an appropriate consolation that didn't sound like a platitude or presumption; replaying the trip out to Aunt May's over and over again while I waited for the mot juste to arrive and rescue my credibility as a companion and confidante.

Through my father's sobs, I reheard the laughter in the conversation on the way. Found in his tear-stained face the silvery back of my grandfather's imposing head, which I had seen so much of, so full of life, just a few hours before.

Try as I might, I was unable to accept the impossibility of anticipating such transformation from contentment to catastrophe, or how, in the mirth of one the heartache of the other is concealed. That my grandfather would not be travelling back with us, and that I would never see him again.

I tried manfully to offer my condolences to my father but was unable to speak. Dragged further away from dialogue by tears of my own, I silently berated myself for my unbearable lack of finesse. Even in the front seat, I felt childish and useless.

We continued past the outstretched terraces of bowing hedgerow, as though, in our brief reassociation, we were accepting with the light brush of their berried branches the discreet wave of their respects. Occasionally we could see through them to the barley fields beyond. Neither of us noticed the bats.

The previously unsettled islands my father and I occupied inched closer in the purgatory of that long, cold, dreadful ride home. And although separated still by insuperable waters, we shared the intimacy of our tears, and a similar space in our respective reflections.

I had never until then seen my father cry. And wouldn't again for another seven or eight years when, unable to contain the compound pain I had invested from untold previous winters of woe, I confronted him across the dinner table with an uncomfortable truth, as I saw it, which, much to my surprise, he didn't attempt to parry or defend. I couldn't withhold it for another minute. And although it may have seemed unfair to land my broadhead so far below his belt, the accusation I launched was lethally heartfelt, and fired completely without aim. Even so, the terrible sound of it whistling through the air towards him was much worse than I'd anticipated, and I had no idea that it would penetrate its mark with such devastating impact.

I didn't aggress him, or raise the temperature a degree above the contaminating cold. But told him simply, in such a way that I could be charged with revealing nothing more than an axiomatic truth, that he didn't love me. Almost before my accusation struck, he dropped his knife and fork percussively onto his plate, rose from the table as if his chair were ablaze and tearfully left the room without a word. I was shocked, silenced by a ricochet I hadn't expected, unable to muster another syllable, and completely at a loss to interpret his reaction. Straight away, I wished I hadn't said it.

My father remained shut inside his room for the remainder of the evening.

Nothing in his attitude towards me changed afterwards. For better or worse. The incident, which had made such a profound impression on us both, was never referred to, and I had no further information to go on.

# 15

We are seldom more miserable than when staying put,
or more lonely than when we are leaving.

Smothered by an avalanche of wanderlust in the latitudinous
shiver of my first six and a half years of snowfall, I felt
culturally malnourished. Re-orienting myself skyward, I
ardently exclaimed to my mother that I felt an existential yen
to travel.

'I need to see the world, Mum' I declared in the ditch
water of another dull afternoon. 'I'm an artist; I have to be
inspired. I've got to travel'

My mother dismissed my assertion with a perfunctory
sigh of familiar disinterest.

I stared at her unflinchingly, and long enough for her to
feel the need to placate or at least silence me with the equally
dismissive retort: 'Well, JP a few doors along the road is an
artist, and she doesn't even need to leave the house.'

It worked. She had me beaten in a dozen words. It was
true. JP was an artist. She never left the house. She was
agoraphobic.

In contradiction of my mother's natural reluctance to lend
a meaningful hand to anyone, justifying her easy indifference
as an outright refusal to intervene in any situation she

interpreted as having been contrived by the will of God, somewhere in the FV4201 Chieftain tank of her self-centred soul crept a slim and solitary shadow of compassion. A quality no doubt she would have described herself as being in possession of by the spade-load.

Occasional observations of her chameleon-like ability to persuasively pass for someone who cared about other people, or believed she did, convinced me that, despite the problematic distinction being a hair she would not have been eager to split, the emotion nevertheless existed somewhere inside her, and I would not infrequently watch her offer an undercover tear to an appropriately bathetic incentive. Though, whenever pressed to explain her ocular oozing, she would impatiently deny she was weeping and attribute her mistiness to a recurrent eye infection. I suspected otherwise. And predictably enough, throughout film dramas or TV news stories that featured scenes of misfortune and trauma, particularly those in which a catastrophic loss of money or property played a compelling part in the tragedy, the sob was there for all to see, and I would catch her surreptitiously wiping her watery eyes with the full length of a perfectly manicured index finger after shedding an incriminatingly empathetic tear or two.

It's also true that for an audience, she could turn it on without trying. At some point in the performance she would consider it expedient to employ the technique. It was, if nothing else, a crucial piece of meticulously oiled machinery in her constantly productive manufacturing plant of emotional manipulation.

I can do it, too. But not on command, as she does. It's completely involuntary and drives me mad. An inheritance I would rather not have received in quite such abundance. I have to admit, I can seriously embarrass myself by blubbing through a TV report about an orphaned whale or something. It need be hardly anything at all and I'll be off. I don't mean to, but I do. I can't help it. I'm not kidding; there's something wrong with me.

I used to watch her sometimes, shut away for a moment or two in that little lost world of tears, and wonder why she found it so difficult to not be so selfish.

# 16

We are persistently assailed by the bigotry of isms.

My cousin Jay had been snatched away from his sing-songy, classroom colouring book contentment, confined alongside a living rogues gallery of brawnier words and numbers and conditioned by the thought law the year before, which meant that I had been well primed for my impending internment at the local junior school. And although I had previously detested my subjection to the state controlled production line that institutionally churns out often expensively defective characters compromised by conformity and decorated with self doubt, I quite unexpectedly found myself excited to soon be embarking upon an interesting new tussle with it.

Unconfirmed reports that they depersonalised you there, called you by your surname, psychologically waterboarded you until you submitted to their prehistoric principles and caned you if you did anything else they didn't like appealed to me. Not that I harboured any particularly masochistic tendencies, but I viewed the anticipated regime as a challenge to my iron will and looked forward keenly to taking it on. Such disquiet I could handle with comparative equanimity.

I have always, for my pains, squared up instinctively to a challenge. Particularly one with any tiny tin-pot army that likes to shamelessly promote itself as some bastion of establishment. So I was more than prepared to let them take their best shot at me; I had already rooted myself in the knowledge of exactly who I was, and who I was never going to be.

The celebrated Russian auteur Alexei German included in his film of a Strugatsky brothers novel, the quip that a child's tears are nothing more than water. It's a beautiful line but it's not true.

I'd been incarcerated in the bloody tower of my new pen for little longer than a month, before gazing desolate at the grass and gravel around me and wondering how I would feel if all my classmates were dead.

The reality of my reluctant rumination was impossible to imagine.

Throughout breaks, the seemingly impervious children played touch and skipped ropes, laughing in groups on the lawn. What if, in a moment, they were smothered to death and no longer there? The impenetrable air of disbelief choked me, hard and still as yearning. Distraught and distracted, I couldn't shake the perpetually trodden-on thumbtacks of the thought of it out of my mind.

I hadn't wanted to leave the house at all, much less go traipsing gaily off to the jug on that misty grey morning, and said so. But I had, of course, been offered no choice, and was obliged to relent under the upbraiding of my mother's snarling insistence. She marched me to the door of the guardhouse in person.

I took my place in pre-class assembly on Monday the twenty-fourth of October, but resented the embarrassing exposure of my unmasculine emotions from the start, and the unqualified waste of my time. Unable to fully focus or concentrate on anything, I struggled to restrain the effusion of my distress for the remainder of the day.

It was the first school day after the last Friday morning news, and I had watched suffocating images of collapsed slag over the entire weekend on TV in unending anguish. One hundred and sixteen children, the same age as me, killed at school in Aberfan. I had been bent to breaking point by the incursive weight of the tragedy on my safe little world of mosaic-making and song. And although I had previously been touched by the deaths of family members and friends, I had never before been so affected by the pain of such profound sorrow.

My mother sneered disdainfully and chided my unseemly outpourings. Impatiently commanding me to conduct myself with composure and to act more like a man; assuring me that I would forget all about far away landslides in a day or two. But I didn't.

Not even more than fifty years after the disaster, and thirty years since incredulously questioning implausible opinions of God and fate whilst wandering among rows of little graves at the Pant Glas cemetery, does the devastating news of it haunt me less.

It came as something of a surprise to me that I never did acquaint myself with any of the teacher's canes while running the gauntlet of my self-educating years at Junior school. In fact, my end of term reports all seemed to witter on about how polite, friendly and respectful I was. They said I was *reserved*, too. I mean, it was true, I was all those things. Whatever else I might have been, I was never a thug. But that didn't mean I wouldn't stand up for myself. Or accept anyone else's inveigling ideas over the legitimacy of my own experience. I was polite, but I wasn't a fool or a conformist. Dear me, no.

They described me as 'thoughtful', but they didn't know what I had been thinking.

# 17

We spend the endless sunset of our days on the mercurial surf of finding and losing ourselves.

I supped on the slow flow of my years edaciously then, as though they were a banquet of birthright. Not as now, when I accept the gift of each with gratitude, humility and dread. But at what point does one begin to look back? To hanker after the good old days?

Despite retaining my youthful complexion, all at once, right out of the blue, I was seven and felt that my best years were behind me. Suddenly, in the awful infant-executioner's swift swing of an axe, I was old. A.A. Milne had said nothing positive whatsoever about being seven. As difficult a time as it was, I was depressed that being six hadn't lasted longer.

The first afternoon of my eighth year rounded with feeling the pressure of needing to be older still. A middle-aged wing-tipped lace-ups and morning jacketed childhood was no good to me at all. It didn't suit me. I needed some kind of chronological maturity to maintain my all-out offensive on the world. I didn't feel like a bona-fide kid any more. I'd lost my place. These were the wilderness years. I had a long wait now until I was into double figures and able to claw back some credibility.

Impatient to re-establish myself as a dynamic and one of a kind force of nature, I began to inspect my give-away clear, fresh, supple skin in a kaleidoscope of reflective surfaces for evidence of inceptive lines and age spots. But on the outside at least, nothing much seemed to change. The reassurance of encroaching maturity I sought from avid daily scrutiny evaded me.

The inside, however, was a different affair altogether. In the mangled world of my innards, things had changed quite a bit.

My mother's incessant physical and emotional brutality had extended to the practice of regularly forcing me to eat mouthfuls of coal in exchange for sanctioning my release from the house alone for short periods of recreation with friends after school. When she decided that my playtime was up, she'd storm out of the house wielding the brass poker of her antique companion set and hurl herself like a mouthy harpoon to wherever I may be, seize my arm as though I were being nabbed by the law in front of my mates, and march me back to the stark and bizarre penal institution of her company. Full studded, high ankled rugby boots, two sizes too big, ensured that I didn't wander away too far.

Few kids would come to the house to play. A short lived exception being a friend from the village who was unceremoniously evicted for asking to use the bog. 'We don't recognise such appalling language here,' my mother advised him, as though she were stringing him up by the neck on the gibbet of his vulgarity, 'the word is lavatory. Lava-tory. La-va-tor-eeee!' she articulated, with a rapier of frosty glare thrust into the open apology of his bemused smile. 'No, you may not. Get back to your illiterate spawners and soil your own.' The kid flashed a glance at me, as if hoping to secure my confirmation that she had been joking. Then left the house abruptly without returning.

I had lost a friend and seasoned enough in the disaffection of my long path to knowing that I would never allow myself to trust my mother with anything of value to me again. This rampant distrust had begun to spread like a virus, which infected everything she touched.

All overtures to the rational discussion of any sensible subject were entirely futile, and it was to my considerable cost that I repeatedly attempted to engage her. The torturous exercise being as satisfying as launching an assault against myself with an arsenal of nail bombs. Her maddening modus operandi being to convert almost anything I said into a weapon that she would immediately use to annihilate every point I was trying to make. Smugly rounding off her attack by contemptuously declaring that I was wrong about everything. But without explaining why.

Ironically, her pithy coup de grace was a credible claim. After all, everything was the one thing she knew something about. And she clung to her opinion about everything with the tenacity of a person whose life depended upon it.

But, with the typical lack of a nod to the need for the provision of even a smattering of support, her inexplicable opinions were generally held untamed and unsubstantiated by any corroborating information or experience whatsoever.

It didn't matter. However wide of the mark she might be, and almost invariably was, she could never actually be wrong. Or even partly wrong. She understood implicitly that she was right because she knew she was, and that she always would be, no matter what ultimately insignificant obstacles may exist in the real and verifiable world to prevent her from proving it.

Her rightness was non-negotiable. It was set in imperishable stone and stood as an undying monument to her infinite wisdom. Never did she need to endanger her tongue on the tripwire of logic, or condescend to argue the toss for a moment. And never would she. No possible need could ever arise. There were but two eternally unerring beings in this or any other universe; and God wasn't even running a close second. In fact, it was to God's eternal credit as a scholar and a gentleman that He selflessly backed her up in all things unfailingly.

If you were patient, or stupid, or ambitious enough to persevere with the futility of banging your brain against the brick wall of her omniscience, and attempted to stimulate more than an extension of her dismissive disapproval by impertinently offering her a smattering of factual information or an alternative view of anything, she wouldn't descend an inch from her clouds to pay you the courtesy of a hearing. She'd simply sit there beneath the halo of her hubris, gawping at you obdurately and shaking her head slowly above an imbecilic smile with which she intended to convey her pained pity for your ignorance.

She lionised her exasperating obstinacy as though she were in possession of a coveted natural talent. An inestimable gift of infinite rarity. Vaingloriously parading the hobby she so zealously indulged before as many people as possible, as often as she could.

Although I was yet to saunter blithely past the unseasoned age of seven and eager to learn, my tender years accorded me no defence from her vitriolic onslaughts, far less provided my assailant with sufficient reason to spare me. Quite the opposite. She revelled in her ability to frustrate the hell out of me; mining my vulnerability to sustain the impetus of her offensive. Consequently, however conscientiously I attempted to, I could never defeat her with logic. Which didn't mean that my abysmal lack of success ever quite compromised me completely enough to prevent me from trying. But invariably, after a few minutes of head-banging excruciation I'd become riled and call her something incontestably uncomplimentary.

It was not necessarily to my credit that I was too hot-headed to adopt any other approach than wanting to pommel reason and truth into her brain with a hydraulic press. The lack of practical resourcefulness a crippling deficiency in my attempts to subvert her command. My incapability riddled my landscape like tumbleweed.

I detested her arrogance. She rattled me with the rudiments of a smirk. I couldn't stand the way she wallowed in the power she derived from being so infuriating.

Despite my frustration, the thought had never occurred to me that she may actually represent a clear and present danger to the public at large. Perhaps at this point, the danger was neither clear nor even present. After all, this was still some time prior to her calling and ministry. And before she had acquired an affection for firearms.

# 18

We invent the spoons of want and gratitude with which
we feed ourselves to the gods.

I was at a complete loss to understand what we could
possibly have done to deserve her, but it had somehow been
decided by the faceless educational great and good that our
unassuming little class should be awarded the accolade of a
student teacher for a few weeks of spring term, and I was in
love again.

Miss Duffield was a pin-up, and the fragrant owner of the
same tumble of chocolate hair that Hazel had stolen my heart
with. But this ringletted fleece was fascinatingly attached to a
novelty unique in my romantic experience; a collection of
corporeal curves I had never before seen assembled with
such breathtaking expertise in the space of little more than a
handful of vertical feet.

Experienced in the art of love, as I now considered myself
to be, I saw no point in procrastinating; I knew precisely
what I wanted, and was more than a little confident of
learning from past mistakes and acquiring it with the
minimum of fuss. Having nailed the best part of this scene
before, I sauntered up to her in the eminently engaging self
conscious manner of a matinee heart-throb and casually

asked her for a kiss, in a thoroughly thought-through, specifically un-needy way that suggested the pleasure of its delivery would be entirely hers.

It worked.

With absolutely no hesitation, surprise or resistance whatsoever, I got one. She lowered her face to my lips and I pecked her seductively on the rouged pillow of her cheek as though I were breathing the gift of life into Pygmalion.

I had pulled my woman. Easy.

Presumptuous as ever and well seasoned in the practice of demonstrating a healthy contempt for the pretensions of authority, I unambiguously communicated to her that the fact she was my teacher made absolutely no difference to my intention of visiting her in a less formal capacity at home, and asked her where she lived without further ado.

Despite adhering to my own rule book meticulously, I realised straight away, without understanding quite how it had happened, that I may have presented myself as being a little over-cute by reacting to the receipt of her home address by uttering an overjoyed 'thank you, Miss Duffield', but regained my masterful composure with no further mishap and sat down to begin the lesson knowing that my teacher had already been reduced to putty in my hands; and was very probably, even now, crumbling inside from her consummate seduction by an accomplished Don Juan several birthdays in excess of his years. The achievement was considerably less challenging than taking candy from a baby.

In the interests of decorum, I'll skip the details, but will confirm that I did indeed visit my new love at home. And behaved like a perfect gentleman.

I realised almost immediately, however, that the relationship was unlikely to fulfil some of the more arcane amorous expectations of a ravishingly voluptuous, red-blooded nineteen year old undergrad, so I reluctantly withdrew my commitment to our romantic association, to the advantage of chap with a beard called Simon who lived with her, and distracted myself with the more preconsidered determination that I had stretched my patience and willingness to indulge my mother and her galling foibles as far as I comfortably could.

This decision had been immediately pre-empted by my obligation, on her insistence, to wear an assortment of girl's clothes to school, and her outright refusal to provide any alternative garments, except for a pink pair of short trousers which were several sizes too big.

I concluded there and then, once and for all, that I was no longer willing to waste any more of my existence on fruitlessly attempting to develop an ability I would clearly never master to excavate any appreciable understanding of her apparently meaningless motives. I had no realistic alternative to reluctantly accepting that, however bizarre and unlikely, some things had no plausible explanation, and just were.

In my bewildered innocence, I was not only forced to acknowledge the violability of logic, but also to begrudgingly accept the possibility that, by the acquisition of some arcane gnosis, my mother had raised her apparently constrained intellect to enviable heights that were to permanently remain inestimably beyond my grasp.

Within a few more lonely and persecuted years, I realised that I could not have been more wrong. I had dangerously misinterpreted her idiocy.

# 19

The police were waiting for me when I arrived home from school, like a black and polished silver butterfly net poised to snare me at a stroke when I let myself into the kitchen. My mother had already become animated, wide eyed and hysterical, as if she had uncrossed her legs or yawned unguarded and sucked in one of those mischievous, nun-stalking devils at Loudun.

'I want him put away' she screeched, hysterically. 'I want him put in a home. Take him away. Take him away, TAKE HIM AWAY!'

Her hysterical yelp rose in a flurry of half-tones to the stridulous crescendo of a semi-throttled scream, as though she had been caught unawares and had inadvertently glimpsed an unflattering reflection of herself in a magnifying mirror.

This all came as a bit of a surprise to me.

Within fifteen minutes, I had escaped the long arm of the law with nothing worse than a few stern stares from a couple of burly constables who were evidently as nonplussed as me.

I've no idea what kind of yarn she had spun on the phone to get them there, but when she seized her moment of limelight and avidly regaled them with that impromptu act of wanton scenery chewing, they calmly explained to her, without applause or encouragement, that there existed an established procedure for formally offering a child up for adoption, and left.

It was a scene to be repeated almost ad nauseam throughout my long career as a bewildered and aimlessly wandering stripling.

I never lost my fear of being swept away when I was least expecting it and placed in a children's home. It became such a regular threat that I occasionally held almost amicable matter-of-fact conversations with my maddening mother about what would happen to me when I was finally donated to an institution, just how bad life would be there, and when I could look forward to being released.

In the crucible of following years, the police would occasionally be exempted from their responsibility of laying in wait for me at the house to nab me when I returned home from school (or more likely, a pleasant and rewarding afternoon of skiving in the countryside), and I would instead be leapt upon on entry by my mother and frogmarched a quarter of a mile down the road to the local constable's house, where the same impassioned request to have me disposed of was earnestly delivered to whoever happened to be inside. Accompanied of course, by crude variations of essentially the same over-egged performance.

It genuinely surprised me that in all the years she trod these boards, the manifestly shocking quality of my mother's acting appeared intractably resistant to any discernible improvement.

As the finest female McGonagall of amateur theatrical artlessness, my mother undoubtedly deserved the tragically unreceived honour of being dissected and examined in detail at RADA and other celebrated schools of dramatic art. The careers of some of our better known thespians may have shone a little brighter from their exposure to her scintillating incompetence. She was incurable ham; all her lines were B-movies.

I never received a satisfactory explanation for any of these patent miscarriages of justice. Nothing more than my mother's repetition of her assertion that she didn't want me. It was no real education; I had kind of worked that much out for myself.

# 20

Metaphor is the first weapon of war.

I had moved up a year at school where the breaking news was that my whole class would be imminently decamping to France for a week's hard earned holiday in the sun. I couldn't believe it. I was going to travel after all! All we needed was a letter of permission from a parent and to hand over a nominal sum to help fund the trip. The excitement in the class was tangible and of course, by the next morning after the bulletin, most of the children had returned to school with the prerequisites. A day or two later, everyone had.

'But I'll be the only one who's not going, Mum. They're all going.'

'You're not going, and that's all there is to it.'

'I'll ask Dad, then,' I resolved, frantic with disbelief.

'I've told your father you're not going, and you're not.'

The torment of missing the trip was almost unbearable.

When my elated classmates returned from their Alpine adventure recounting their memories and regaling each other with fascinating tales of continental capers, I don't think all the slaps and punches together would have equalled the pain of it.

Long weeks passed in a thick fog of agony.

# 21

Nothing clings so close to flesh as fear.

I tried to look on the bright side of night, but it was always the darkness of it that was so illuminating. It still is. In the maliciousness of night, I am haunted by ghosts of myself. Tormented by visits from unimaginable offspring. The execution-squad inescapableness of everything I've evaded so assiduously in all the hours of daylight floods in like a stampede of lost children. Nothing lightens the brilliant darkness of an uninhabitable reality setting in my arteries like petrified cholesterol.

Inside the psychogenic iron maiden of night, memories pierce my watery eyes before their brittle refuge in milling daylight. I slept with the hall light on and recruited bedfellows from mysterious half-lit reflections on the walls.

When I slept as a child, my dreams were not peopled by shadows of the dead. When I slept, I sprouted feathers and took to the skies. On oneiric limbs, I flew with grace, with the effortlessness of a wish. Escaping my waking shackles so adroitly I could sleep through almost anything to remain free.

Soundly enough to remain oblivious to the excited chatter of my mother's busy fingers pilfering my golden curls with a pair of antique pinking shears as I outpaced her on the wing.

My rude awakening on that peculiar winter morning was a yawning discovery that I had somehow been divested of my hair and was consequently now practically bald. It didn't sink in. Although I could feel and clearly see in the mirror that I had almost nothing left at all on top, I was at a complete loss to fathom how such a thing could have occurred. I went to bed with hair and woke up without it. This was unusual.

My mother's uncharacteristically euphoric disposition on the morning of this unaccountable thieving suggested something sinister.

As hard as I resisted the inevitable dawning in those opening moments of dumbstruck dismay, I had no realistic alternative to accepting the truth of what had happened and that, despite her denial of any involvement in my sudden alopecia, on the heavenly stage of her deranged mind, I had played Samson to her jubilant Delilah.

This incident represented a worrying new dimension to my availability as fodder for her rampaging plague of lunatic locusts.

My mother's apparently inextinguishable fixation with cutting things off extended to several attempts on my air supply with a pillow while tucking me into bed, either side of a visit to the family doctor's surgery where I was exhibited as a vital accompaniment to her typically animated request that I be genitally modified and suitably streamlined in accordance with her discriminating aesthetic sensibilities. (I remain inexpressibly grateful to the bemused GP who dismissed her unusual request with an appropriately abbreviated tirade of professionally outraged rebuke,)

The incident of my slumbering snip had reawoken concerns about what else she may yet reconsider shortening while I slept.

I now knew that my mother would forever represent the scorpion in my shoe, and that I would invariably be exposed to the industry of her venom while at my most inattentive and vulnerable.

My depilation and the most recent of her suffocation attempts on me confirmed that she would cynically disregard any acceptable rules of engagement. A realisation that had encouraged me for some months to sleep fully dressed, except for my shoes, for fear that I should be otherwise snatched away in my pyjamas by the ubiquitous clutches of the children's home while I nestled into immersive dreams of happier things.

But some mornings were very different. And so was she. She could, on those random occasions, open her waking eyes to a fleeting shaft of sunshine and forgo the immediate need to apply her tortured make up before facing the day. In those liberated moments of forgetfulness, she'd lie in bed passively after my father had left for work, as if lost in her own semi-human reverie; bare-breasted, motherly, calling me into the covers for a cuddle. I invariably accepted the invitation. If not for her sake, for mine. Such occasions provided my only access to her affection. And despite the discomfort of my own emotional paradox, I valued those moments of closeness above all others.

The legacy of these unpredictable truces was the enduring mystery of how it could be possible for my mother to accommodate such disparate personalities. Even for brief and occasional moments. I wrestled with credible definitions of the true nature of truth, and secured no submissions of explanation from any such skirmishes. These meditations intrigued me, but drove me mad at the same time.

I found it easier to dismiss my mother as insane than to convince myself she had somehow fallen victim to a genuine, card carrying clinical condition. And that a bone-fide medical issue caused her to part company with the reality most other casualties of it espoused.

In spite of myself, and all the years of evidence to the contrary, I had traditionally viewed her apparently contrived nonconformity with cynicism, and believed that beneath all the scattered rubble of spiteful, selfish, self-righteous idiocy, the genuine, true, uncontaminated inner chamber of her mind remained essentially no different from mine. That her pre-meditated mores were nothing more grounded than the exasperating gimmicks of a game, and that somewhere beneath the artifice of it all existed an emotionally and intellectually intact woman and mother. It was this refusal or inability to modify my imperturbable certainty of her sanity that allowed her behaviour to affect and infuriate me as much as it did.

I was unable to explain the finer details of this reasoning to myself, but my faith in a paradox was easier to live with. It offered me hope.

Why did she offer me occasional moments of affection amid so many more of open hostility? Which of her faces was real? Which perversion concealed the imposter?

On one occasion, when her apparent tenderness extended unbroken over a period of at least ten minutes, I felt so nauseously replete with an effusion of questions, that I almost vomited them over her when I candidly asked her outright why she was cuddling me warmly after making it so clear to me for so long that she didn't like or want me. I'd anticipated receiving no answer at all, but after a few moments of electrically charged silence, she became gentle again and softly explained that my affection provided the only solace for her suffering. Her solitary relief for an incapacitating fear that had been sickening her lately to the point of distraction. The dread of an operation she was to have on her brain in a specialist London hospital at the end of the following week.

Her voice cracked into near silence as she tearfully informed me that she had already been warned by the neurologist there that she would probably not survive the procedure, and continued to waver as she described the operation in excruciating detail.

I felt every atom of my world implode. Collapse in a moment into a black hole of unbridled despair. Sick with concern, I hysterically begged her not to go through with it.

'It's no good,' she said, shaking her head disconsolately, 'I have to.'

I cried uncontrollably and trembled with fear. Nothing had prepared me for the possibility of facing such unbearable tribulation. I wanted to help her, to heal her, to take her so far away from this nightmare that she would forget all about it. I couldn't for a moment allow myself to consider the mortifying prospect of her suffering in such a way.

I noticed how my mother withdrew her affection as I retreated into my heartbroken desolation. She watched my tears with her arms folded and leaned away from me, as though she were examining something in my appearance that she had previously failed to notice.

I could barely speak through my weeping, beyond repeatedly wailing *Mum*, inconsolably, as she eventually climbed out of bed and left the room.

It was more than an hour later when she told me that none of it was true.

## 22

Some words are so quiet as to be inaudible over the fray.

My father's ability to communicate endearment to me perfectly suited the unremittingly remote loquaciousness of his interminable silences. I often studied the geography of his broad hands and imagined the great plains of them resting on me in affection, instead of almost invariably feeling the brevity of their warmth against my flesh in frequent visitations of uncontrolled anger. On such painfully intimate occasions I'd get a whole sentence or two out him as well. Generally along the lines of him promising me a little more violence if I didn't immediately meet specific conditions and guidelines about keeping quiet. A stormcloud of fingers would portentously hover clenched above me to reinforce his threat.

Despite his predilection for offering the gentleness I sought to strangers, his approach to me remained irascible and remote. We shared the common language of his violence, but beyond it we seldom exchanged more than a fistful of words in bungled attempts to acknowledge the awkward spectre of each other in passing.

An acid reign of silence continued to rain over us.

I blamed myself for our seemingly irreconcilable detachment. An aspect of my character compelled him to behave in the way he did. My own lack of subscription to a convention that defined him.

It wasn't that I was reluctant to indulge his aversion to colour; I was pathologically incapable of doing so. I was creative, and had been so since I fashioned my first breath into an unfading scream of indefeasible outrage. And the creative mind, to my father, was a questionable contraption in every particular.

We spoke of the same things in different tongues, but my penchant for expressive flamboyance presented a natural impediment to any sympathetic accommodation of factious perspectives. He was not a person I could have revealed my passion for seventeenth century embroidery and stumpwork to without invoking in him a cringing sense that he had fathered a pansy. I didn't blame him. Recrimination never constituted a significant part of my wanting him to change. To accept my unacceptability regardless of the need to understand it. But the reservoir of experience from which he drew his primary objections was a clearer spring of war time masculine monochrome. One that naturally filtered obtrusive pigmentation and regarded it with suspicion. It was more instinctive for him to avoid the embarrassment of associating with unsubtle shades altogether.

We had stood on different sides of the fence, I knew, since even before it occupied the stony ground of my earliest years, where I planted the fertile flag of my own picturesque responses to my mother's interminable bouts of painful malignancy. And I couldn't deny that I had helped create his challenging role of muscular maestro in my enthusiastically conducted but shambolically orchestrated discipline.

Although, maybe, in addition to his regular bouts of physically assaulting a young child, he felt guilty about other things, too. Since my mother's relatively spontaneous change of lifestyle and the loss of her income, he had worked even longer hours for little extra reward and, unlike some other members of his family, had no impressive inheritance to look forward to or to pass on. It wasn't difficult for me to suspect he assumed that if he kept enough distance between us he wouldn't notice me so clearly. He could escape the infection of my presence with a visual prophylactic and wouldn't need to think about it all quite so much.

But the irony was, I knew he *was* looking. And a strange kind of vacillating tenderness undoubtedly sauntered apprehensively around in there somewhere, among the chains and hardware of his bitterness, like a winterly weak sun hidden bloodless behind flocculent grey and intractable cloud.

I caught my first glimpse of it with his gift of Snowball. A few years later, I stood in the relative cold of my own company watching a handful of local kids kicking a ball around in the park close to our house. I had no idea he was lurking anywhere in the vicinity, let alone that he was watching me. Even had I seen him, he would no doubt have looked in the way that people look when they look as though they're not looking. But he had looked for long enough to notice that the kids hadn't invited me to join them in their game.

An hour after breakfast the next morning, a pleasantly mild, mid-spring sunny Sunday, my father unceremoniously presented me with a brand new, white panelled, genuine leather football. Not the ubiquitous plastic type, but a real professional match quality ball. It felt like being awarded the

F.A. Cup after scoring the winning goal in the last minute of injury time. I was shocked almost beyond being able to thank him when he thrust the magical globe into the howling stadium of my hands and told me to take it out straight away and play with it in the park.

For me, it was a spiritual experience. A lily any words would have gilded. And another one of those rare occasions when I felt moved by a genuine and enveloping closeness to my father. The perfect concinnity of such unanticipated exchanges glinted in the surrounding dark like an uncovered vein of golden narrative from the sympathetic conflux of immiscible wishes.

It's a well thumbed memory, one that has never needed so much as the touch of a light polish to retain the fullness of its lustre. And even amid the grotesque carnival of subsequent surreality, one which never fell from my affection, or lost a trace of its warmth or colour.

# 23

Words often come easily to us, but seldom are they the ones we would have chosen.

Were it not for the ubiquitous hard sell of words, would it be possible for us to be more content with a simpler palette of fewer? Wittgenstein postulated a reining in of their super-fluous super-abundance.

For my sins, I was compelled to indulge my natural gluttony and want more of them, not less. I wasn't alone; it's an ecumenical craving. Another unyielding curse of being human. We spend the best and worst of our years digging for the gems of language. Stoking our appetite with the gunk we'll gorge ourselves to death on in an endless acquisition of new definitions for our anguish. I needed as many pitchers of command as I could wrap my thirsty lips around.

Nowadays, I am aware that my words fail me in a different way. They have grown bedraggled with age and I have learned to become patient with them. They are more delicate now than they once were; less disposed to carry the weight they did when they were young and fit and lean.

However sincerely I may have attempted a shrug to protect my sanity from the barbed rain of my mother's madness, I called desperately in the dumb absence of wisdom on the counsel of words to explain the prevailing mysteries of manias to myself. To rationalise the otherwise impenetrably absurd. To discover some path of exposition among them that would lead me to finally understand. To know for certain that the reality of my mother's marginalised adolescence had been ultimately defined by the lottery of her escape from the exploding hail of German air raids over Bath, and by running from one form of destruction to another. That affection, for her, began and finished with the caresses of lifeless limbs hanging bleeding on her in the blitz. To accept that she had watched her friends fall, and had remained one of the half-fallen all her life. To grasp that her maidenhood had been defiled by the Luftwaffe. I needed to plant words on my own tongue for the atrocities she had suffered inside and outside her mind, so far beyond my own imagination that they had withered her entire garden of reason.

But for my many attempts to engage her, I arrived at nothing more edifying than confirmation that to her, the carnage of conflict seemed to play out distantly like a drama in a different theatre. And that she somehow viewed the wantonness of its deadly embrace as essentially un-remarkable. Suffering was, after all, a way station on the road to eternal reward. A sacred obligation. A condition ordained by God. Heaven insisted upon the stomaching of it. It was not, to my mother, the obscenity of war, from which she had been delivered at least physically intact, but the absence of pain that seemed so Godless and unnatural.

She appeared to brazenly undervalue the privilege of her deliverance. But she had been saved. Not only from the terror of death by airless air raid shelters and luck, but liberated by her heroic arrogance from the need to excel at anything but her own incalculable stupidity.

Of course, her double-edged double deliverance wasn't nearly enough. She needed to be saved over and over again. To scratch its unrelievable itch and excoriate the scarred flesh of her incomplete redemption in perpetuum. To constantly relearn the unfathomable language of her salvation for ever, and to chisel its meaning into her soul with the blade of her need like a mantra she could never perfect.

She demanded to be saved until it hurt. Until the whole iniquitous world groaned from the shared weight of her pain. The exquisite self sacrifice through her selfless suffering compelling the infliction of the climactic wound of an all-aching, all-bleeding redemption in perpetual motion.

The words I heard suggested that my mother inhabited a permanent state of insatiable need. And that perhaps once, somewhere in the unequalled peculiarity of her past, the land beneath her was dry. But amid a flooding, tangled convergence of disparate tides, she lost her footing and stumbled into the gulf of her needfulness. She didn't drown; she grew fins and gills and swam in sewers on the dark side of daylight in search of her shining salvation. It's undefined contours as yet to be drawn from the crumbling marble of her broken mind.

I remained unconvinced that I had stumbled on the well head of my prose. But I knew she had discovered hers. And from the summit of her questing poured a fluvium of grammatical supplication. Every subsequent meaningless sliver of drivel she spewed to betray the inadequacy of her discovery she vomited in the name of the Lord; as though eternally attempting to impress Him with her hammering insistence. The Lord must have been heartily sick to death of having to answer for her. He must have also suspected that she had been systematically taking His name in vain.

Now that she had unearthed her holy serum of sounds, she could take Wittgenstein's advice and dispense with those that would not serve her.

She grew saintly on the ceaseless feast of her complaints. And after denouncing the audacious claims of science with a smirk, reclined satisfied on the soft pillow of her inflated narcissism to embark upon a wishful flight of daydreaming fancy, in which she realised that, with the collaborative power of words and God, she could accomplish almost anything.

On her return to Earth, she wielded the scalpel of her humility against the perfection of her form to refashion her angelic wings into arms with which she could magnanimously embrace the lost unclean; holding them well upwind where the air was thick with despair, so that neither could read the true scent of the other. Eyes that had rested upon the Lord now enabled her to see clearly that the most wonderful thing about everything was how perfectly wondrous it was, and that the merciful obverse of every catastrophe was the miracle of all the people it hadn't affected.

Centralising the polished monolith of herself in God's one true plan for everything, she dared to question the precise origin of the marvels she habitually venerated. Audaciously challenging the conventional notion that they had indeed been the single-handedly manufactured endeavours of the consistently well over-laboured Almighty, and persuasively encouraging herself to instead believe that, in some as yet undefined but indispensable way, she had been helping Him out.

She had, after all, provided the crucial element of witness to each miracle, and by doing so, had inevitably influenced it in some significant way. The principle being nothing more controversial than the basic premise of quantum mechanics and according to science, which swiftly rounded to her defence, an immutable law impossible to refute. Only after she alone had observed the outcome of these events could they legitimately acquire the full substance of their divine status.

She reassured herself that the logic of her reasoning remained above reproach. Her conclusion astonishing but beyond doubt. It was quite impossible to misinterpret the obvious; that she had unquestionably been appointed God's workmate, and was already remotely labouring industrially in tandem with the Lord.

The revelation came as less of a surprise than a confirmation of a recent suspicion that He had been meticulously preparing her to take up His mantle by subtly invoking her complicity in many of His more modest affairs; investing her with the power of preternatural perception and consulting her regularly by mysterious means.

Now that she had been divinely chosen to perform the duties of the Lord's worldly deputy, she scrupulously reinvented herself in a manner appropriate to her uniquely onerous appointment. Regarding herself accordingly as more saintly than a panoply of saints, she rebuked them all and criticised them for their unsaintly flaws and oversights.

It was precisely at this point that my mother disappeared almost completely beneath the encroaching quicksand of her reinvented self and became noticeably quieter for a week or two. The cause of this uncharacteristic reticence remained obscure. Undisclosed and unknown to me. I found it disturbing that she appeared to have substantially lost her ability to disturb me and, prompted by my concern at her improbable transformation, I eventually succumbed to my curiosity and posed the question of whether she had suffered a stroke.

I needn't have worried. She just as abruptly recovered her familiar unpleasantness and re-emerged from the quietude of her mysterious retreat renewed. Invigorated, like one of Hannibal's drunken elephants galloping fully armed into battle over the Alps.

It was all beginning to fall into place.

My mother mobilised a regiment of words to trot out militaristic jargon like a ground force. Speaking frequently with a pronounced new gravitas of *the struggle*, and often applying the expression to eruptions of frustration at describing the ruinous state of the world. She delivered unprovoked tropological monologues in which she offered reassurances that God would not suffer being demeaned by the deeds of man; typically launching herself so combustibly into these impassioned performances that she became visibly exhausted by the end of them.

Nevertheless, however much my mother continued to suffer selflessly to preserve the cause of her suffering, her pain alone could not atone for the wrongs of those who had not suffered enough and had turned their backs on the Lord.

In a padded pouch, hidden underneath the carpet behind her wardrobe, she began to set aside money for the purchase of weapons.

## 24

It happened just as I had anticipated it would. It was late evening, the peach tinged embers of daylight smouldering luminous among the fresh leaves on the sycamore tree outside my window. Lying in bed, unable to sleep, I was rudely roused into a condition of concerned curiosity by a disconcertingly determined knocking on the back door.

The businesslike voices were confident but muffled, and even silencing the annoying rustle of my bedclothes as I sat up to press my ear against the wall to better hear, didn't help me make out what they were saying.

After a brief exchange, during which I heard both my parents' say *OK* in a way that suggested something was wrong, I heard footsteps on the stairs. They stopped momentarily outside the room, denying me my only avenue of escape. If there had been anywhere to hide, the amplified bodhran beat of my heart thumping bare rib-bone like a prizefighter would have given me away. Within seconds, the door creaked open and I was being lifted out of my bed by someone I had never seen before.

The grave silence worried me more than anything, and it seemed to go on for ever before my kidnapper explained: 'We're taking you to hospital, we can look after you better there.'

I had contracted bronchitis and could barely breathe without honking like a fog-horn.

Hanging there as limply as a menthol-scented hand-kerchief in the broad arms of a warm-eyed medical orderly, I felt afraid. But in next to no time, my initial fear significantly subsided in favour of an influx of exhilaration.

The irresistible aspect of my impending adventure, the big pay-off that excited me so much it almost rendered my abduction worthwhile, was the thought of all the neighbours inquisitively peering out from behind their lace curtains and wondering what could have been so terribly wrong that it had necessitated the calling of an ambulance. And then, in the perfect show-stopping moment of my scene-stealing entrance, seeing that it was there for me and that I was being carted off to hospital in it. Brilliant! And if so unforgettable a drama didn't already unequivocally confirm me as the star of the village, the cherry sitting firmly on top of the whole escapade would be our racing through the streets in it with its lights flashing and siren blaring to authoritatively sweep the impressively aghast able-bodied out of our way and leave them speculating about the condition of the unfortunate occupant. I couldn't wait. In fact, for a moment, I almost forgot I felt so unwell.

They wrapped me, as I dangled aloft between the thin-coated arms of the orderly, in a couple of regulation type, itchy, grey, ribbon trimmed blankets, and we began the expedition down the long path and onto the road.

Maintaining an unobstructed, close to hundred and eighty degree view from my semi-comfortable, semi-recumbent position, I scoured the scattering of parked cars, but couldn't see an ambulance anywhere. Just some pathetically unimposing, unmarked military green van planted a few yards beyond our garden gate, which we were now drooping like April tulips over the back of.

If I confessed that I felt thoroughly disgusted, it wouldn't begin to come close to how thoroughly disgusted I felt. I was downright sickened and mortally offended by the sheer humiliating inconspicuousness of it all. And this was supposed to be my big scene, too? I had been made to look a fool. Even the colour of the blankets I had been practically smothered to death in blended virtually unnoticeably with the hideously drab slate tone of the pavement.

We pulled off. No siren. No flashing lights. Nothing. Just an acapella chorus of unconvincing assertions about how I would enjoy being banged up in hospital and forgotten about.

At the risk of sounding a bit puny, if I'm going to be brutally honest, I'd probably have to admit that all this wasn't entirely unlikely to happen at some point. I was, after all, pretty sickly as a kid. Chicken Pox, Whooping Cough, Measles, German Measles, Scarlet Fever, Glandular Fever, you name it. Even the stuff you were only supposed to entertain once, came galloping back on stage for two or three more curtain calls. I wasn't exactly proud of it but I decorated my formative years with a pretty healthy collection of illnesses.

Next day, my father came to see me, like a Wise Man bearing an eye-catching assortment of interesting and appropriately colourful presents to cheer me up.

It worked. Although the thing that impressed me most was how clearly I could see his concern. Not only in his face, but in his whole demeanour. He really did feel sorry for me. My mother came, too. Issuing near-hysterical instructions on how I was expected to behave in sick company.

They both visited me every day, bringing me crayons, drawing books, jigsaw puzzles, comics and other untaxing distractions.

My mother took to habitually hovering gravely over my prostrate body like a weathered gargoyle, with an agitated hand-shuffle and inflexibly contorted facial expression, as if she were desperately attempting to remember exactly how Pat O'Brien hurriedly administered last rights to James Cagney under difficult circumstances. My father seemed to quite effortlessly find his voice and used it affectionately on a steady succession of one-liners to make light of the situation. He did it well. He instinctively seemed to know exactly what to say and how to say it to render my unusual circumstances acceptable.

I settled into hospital life relatively painlessly. Within days, it was as familiar to me as home.

Within a few more days, it had all become quite horribly tedious. Unacceptably regimental.

Preposterously inconvenient dreary dawn breakfast eggs followed by excruciatingly gropey, cold-handed bed-baths preceded a full day of collective wheezing, and after two torpid weeks of permanent prostration, as suddenly as I was seized from my own bed, I was instructed to get out of my borrowed one, dress and go home. They'd had enough of me. But by then, the feeling had become mutual, and I was released with almost embarrassingly little ceremony.

I was still heartily groggy and barely upright, but somehow my wobbling feet had grown a little broader. Not only did they now support a willowy sapling with a brand new appreciation of life, liberty and the pursuit of happiness, but one with a palpably increased sense of independence. The experience had strengthened me in more ways than one.

Like a celebrity straight out of rehab and looking to sell my story to a few friends for the full fifteen minutes of envious attention I richly deserved, I was home. The old place still leaked the indefinable essence of all my unanswered prayers and memories. Nothing had changed; everything was pretty much as I had left it. Except for two boxes of ammo on the sitting room sideboard.

# 25

Memory steals our sleep from under the nose of dreams. Clings to the thin skin of yearning, like a burr. Holds the eternal child of our emotions to an impossible ransom.

I wish I had been able to apprehend her right there. Before anything intractable had happened, or any non-negotiable imperative had arisen to remove significant extracts of recollection from the annals of anyone's personal history.

Maybe I could have reported something salient to someone, or informed somebody other than a few disbelieving or disinterested friends about the boxes of live shells perched behind some gardening books next to the TV. But the elusive gods of acceptance and denial move in mysterious ways and maybe, in the gradual normalisation of the unusual, no-one could really have predicted the sickening shape of things to come, anyway.

Not even did my returning home from a day of bunking off school and finding a pig's head floating in the bathroom wash basin with a bullet hole between its eyes raise the spectre of anything more untoward than the expectation of an imminent deluge of pork stew fashioned in my mother's unique, transcendentally inedible style. Sinister in itself, perhaps, but not necessarily an inevitably lethal proposition. Although a simple modification could easily have produced an effective weapon of mass destruction.

As it was, arguably to my benefit, I ate hardly anything at home, despite my mother frequently serving my father entirely fictitious accounts of my having eaten the vital ingredients of a meal she had been planning to prepare. There was almost no food available there, and I wasn't allowed to touch the few things in the fridge on pain of being physically assaulted as a thief.

As a result of my close to starvation diet, I was noticeably under-weight, and near-permanent hunger encouraged me to develop physical methods of fending off the infrequent but bothersome opportunistic advances of other kids at school who assumed they could take advantage of my apparent puniness.

Occasionally, I walked the few miles into town to avail myself of the contents of the refuse bins at the back of one the supermarkets there. Sitting propped upright between a row of them against the wall, like some moribund Augustus Mulready urchin, devouring untold packets of out of date ham, cooked chicken and picnic meats, cake, biscuits, and other otherwise unobtainables that had all been thrown away as unsellable.

A profound and peculiar romance circumfused these starlit epulations like a diaphanous blanket of mist. And a dreamlike veneer of inescapable solitude accompanied my feast-fuelled rambles into regions of untold freedom.

On the completion of my complimentary à la carte buffet, I could barely move to waddle my way home again.

Although my gastronomic seasoning basted deprivation and want for being the dysfunctional parents of excess and moderation, I irrationally retained the propensity to gorge insatiably long after the need to had disappeared through ghostly passages of rheumatic remembrance. And even in the comparatively affluent turning leaves of autumn, the spectre of privation still haunts me. Except that now, I invert the compulsion and binge on abstinence. Unable even to unpack occasional festive gifts of food, much less eat them. Fastidiously preserving them instead, untouched, intact, until they have been consumed on my behalf by tumours of mould. When I throw them away, wondering how they might have tasted when they were fresh.

At home, the rancid réchauffé I was forced to repeatedly rugby-tackle was exactly the same gruel for days on end, reheated over and over again until everything on the plate had transmogrified into suppository-shaped elements of the same shrivelled, unicoloured mass and coagulated to the consistency of cardboard. Each plateful featuring a strange, fresh lump of viscid blue goo, teased into the shape of one of the ruined pyramids at Abu Sir

This semi-solid concoction of unknown origin was presumably intended to provide a form of essential lubrication, but instead, the navy anti-gravy served considerably more effectively as an almost instantly setting mortar, which forcefully fixed an inedible leathery shingle to every part of the tongue and teeth. And I remained obliged to chase each moistened or non-moistened mouthful with two or three swallows of fetid cabbage water to get it down; meticulously timing everything with such a precision that avoided me being swiftly landed with seconds if I cleared my plate or glass too soon.

Eating at home was a form of torture. My expression constantly monitored for suggestions that I could be conquered by additional helpings. I supped in an air of menacing scrutiny; silence circling the dinner table like a ring of spies.

Whenever I was able to, I enthusiastically capitalised on the threat of being sent upstairs with no sustenance at all for some minor infringement of domestic law, and absconded. After the first two days of attempting to stomach such slop, the relative bearability of hunger became my preferred option.

In all the years I watched my father devour this swill, I never heard him once complain. Maybe he found the whole thing as revolting and unpalatable as anybody else would have, but swallowed it anyway, along with the risk of a whole sentence sticking in his throat if he coughed up anything so verbal as an objection. Maybe he even assumed my mother was doing her best for him, and was grateful.

Whatever he thought, I felt he deserved a more equitable exchange for the sacrifice of his wages. Something more along the lines of a few of the treats she always bought herself for mealtimes. She wouldn't share them, of course. But offered us instead the bigger ticket delicacy of allowing us to watch her sit there revoltingly masticating at the table with a hideously embellished pleasure seeping like a sewer from the orgasmic apogee of every enviable mouthful. Tossing the twisted-faced humility of her indulgence to us like a shower of crumbs.

But the contaminating pain of her torment betrayed the truth that such treats barely constituted any compensation at all for the near insufferable magnitude of her selfless sacrifice. The flashing polished chrome of her over-laden fork repeatedly piercing her unmade-up mouth mimicked a crucifix-foot stationed Roman centurion's spearing assault on the tender flesh of Christ. Dramatically enhanced by liberal, oozing, unwiped gravy bloodflows. The painful pleasure of her indulgence the weight of her cross. You could clearly see from the stoicism with which she bore the magnificence of her excruciation that, despite her greatness, all she really wanted was to be human.

It was an ambition too far. Her seasoning timber had already begun to groan and bend into the crippled shape of a divine question mark. And even by now, humanity was slipping greasily out of her reach.

She began to surreptitiously exchange the softly contoured horizon of her smile for a more permanent magazine of unspent sneers, which she had recently cultivated in her garth of contempt and now, for the most part, slung hidden over her shoulder like a barely seen bandolier so she could dupe the unaware into believing she was unarmed when she cast the scoff of her withering judgement upon them.

I had become increasingly daunted by the profanity of her scorching appraisals. But, in defiance of my exhaustive efforts to educate her more comprehensively in a subject so dear to my heart, the only time I ever heard my mother actually swear was when, just for a fleeting moment, she was, quite out of the blue, confronted with the intimidating possibility of having to make some trivial concession to someone else's suggestion and reacted to the unfamiliar situation petulantly. The ensuing auricular infection causing her to lose the fragile balance of her mind and teeter half a step backwards, or was it forwards, into fresh droppings of raw anger. Which revealed something else I had never until then seen. Suddenly, in that glaringly Godless moment, she turned her slim and stiffened back on her flawed flock and the witless world that she alone seemed ordained to save, and with a virgin venom spat, shrieked and bellowed on a partially peopled street, 'BALLS TO EVERYONE.'

# 26

It wasn't even so much *what* she said, but the bellicose way she belched it like a battlecry. And I was, in that propitious moment of dumbfounding discovery, summarily compelled to reconsider almost everything I had previously assumed about her.

The spotlight of my reappraisal led me adroitly to a revel of questions seeping from a thunderhead of cloud into the breaking dawn of a concern to find out precisely how foul her mouth actually was when she thought nobody else was listening.

I was also curious to know exactly what she assumed the Lord might have to say about it.

In my enlightened elation, I felt that all my previously unmarked birthdays had lined up at their starting blocks and were chomping at the bit to come charging back to me in a victorious lap of honour. And I found myself suddenly festooned with laurels of confirmation that my mother's prodigious, self-advertised, meritoriously moral inviolability was nothing more sacred than conscientiously concealed aggression.

I wanted to seize the moment, savour it, snatch it up and hold it to me in undying affection, like the body of a brief life lost in endless admonition, and with Adrestian retribution demand to know whether she thought other people exist to be helped or hated.

She deserved it. Had this overdue confrontation with the reckoning of her reason coming for all the years I could remember. And may so easily have been demoted to the abounding ranks of the conspicuously fallible by the inquisition of a solitary remark. But I couldn't get anything out. The churning montage of it all rushed manically around like a myriad of Bluebirds attempting the land speed record in my head. The anthracite plank of my tongue, enfeebled by a bounty of incriminating options, hung like a rigid Dalian soft watch out of my mouth, burning to call time on her charade. And after fruitlessly attempting to flap it about for a second or two, I was compelled to capitulate, and content myself with the quietly delicious delirium of being resoundingly dumbstruck.

It was, however, a seriously seminal second or two.

To the casual observer, the incident may have played without distinction. Particularly in comparison to the ostentatious virtuosity of subsequent events.

But the conniption was pivotal to my understanding. It provided a moment in which truth opened the door to a sliver of certainty. Shadows crept out of the shadows and become perceptible. I watched the previously impregnable walls of Jericho fall.

I replayed the demolition of my mother's fatally exposed folly over the years ad infinitum.

Now, of course, the pleasure of my reminiscence is tempered by the discomfiture of my failure. And the unending retribution of knowing that I could have embraced the opportunity to shame her. To attack her, to bring her to book. To nail her to the crosstalk of her divulgent slip of face.

But words failed me. Precisely at the time when I needed them most. Had I deftly redrafted my discomposure and marshalled a modicum of lexical firepower, I could have executed her fleetingly vulnerable alter-ego with a curt volley of criticism. But I failed. I failed everyone. Had I commanded no more than a sniper or two from a marshalry of mutterings more ably, I may have averted a catastrophe. Provided the subtly amended dialogue of a less grievous martyrdom.

In the irrupting daylight of those awakening doubts surrounding the veracity of my saintly mother's messianic motives, the buds of my cynicism flourished and opened in a rich soil of untrodden distance between us. I began to deftly perceive ulterior motives and objectives where once I had unconditionally accepted the imbecilic meaninglessness of her supposedly virtuous meanderings.

My eyes had been blown open like popcorn by a holy trinity of acrimonious words and as a result, for the first time, I carried cold, hard proof that my mother was not nearly the pious person she was so anxious for the rest of us to unquestioningly accept.

She had covertly contrived a working script after all, and had begun to block her stage.

However competently she may have previously concealed the presence of her plotlines, their nativity had now been blown in the brief blast of her graceless growl.

She had, in the marsh gas of her mind, embarked upon some as yet amorphous and untitled crusade, dressing it up deviously in ribbons and bows; but it wasn't benign. It was a calculated and malignant stalking of power.

# 27

I determined to live life more in the moment, and impatiently awaited the arrival of the appropriate moment.

My tenth birthday arrived with an unusual degree of visibility. At least to my father, who casually mentioned but characteristically underplayed something about me now being in double figures, as he left the house for work.

I had long been impatiently anticipating the impending acquisition of an additional digit, and in a household unfamiliar with the tradition of wishing a Happy Birthday or bestowing cards or presents, I deemed the unmitigated excitement of my decimalisation celebration enough.

I couldn't wait to get to school and start throwing my new status around.

My birthday evening proved routinely dull. And was only partially lightened by a short visit to my aunt's house; an irrepressibly sour woman who had always been unshakably convinced that she had squandered her talents in order to raise a family. An opinion she retained until in her early forties, when she finally began to relax her irascible demeanour after realising that her life had not been forfeit after all, and that she had never actually had any talent to squander. The relief was tangible. She had become a warmer person.

I sat next to my mother in sweltering gas fired radiator heat, supplemented by a lung blistering three kilowatt electric fire snapping at my face like a polecat, and listened to her impassioned explanation to her sister of how all she really wanted was to have me put away. It wasn't true. It was further evidence of my mother's mendacity. I knew for sure by then she wanted a lot more than that.

# 28

Not only had the unlicensed arsenal expanded now to include a bedroom side-cupboard half full of ammo, an ex-Local Defence Volunteers Enfield P14 in an elephant's foot umbrella stand, concealed beneath a somewhat incongruous French pink parasol, and a couple of .38 Webley revolvers in the telephone table drawer, but a not-so-long-ago modest library of death-cultist literature had swollen to span the cream Mexican quartz horse-head ended Scandinavian pine bookshelves. Cheaply printed and produced pamphlets, which contumeliously referred to the *unenlightened* as slaughter lambs, stacked up alongside instructive manuals on how to most efficiently address the spiritual problems of an overpopulated world.

I had been sworn to secrecy and threatened with being blinded with a fish knife and sold to the local meat processing plant if I breathed as much as a word about the armoury to anyone. I wasn't allowed to go near any of it. Much less actually touch it. Which made it all seem a bit less real to me. I didn't even know exactly how much of it there was.

My mother enjoyed the contrived eccentricity and black humour of scattering it around the house in the manner she had, but it didn't stay so playfully concealed for long. Two or three months later, she became hysterical after impetuously calling the police to me and hid it all under the floorboards. Except for the P14, which retained its place of honour behind the sofa. After that, she'd only excavate the odd piece occasionally and sit with it in her chair while simultaneously clutching the stock of the rifle to her chest, as though she were nursing a child.

The breadth of my mother's conversational meditations had now narrowed noticeably, and some manner of religious instruction or judgement typically permeated them all.

A young, neighbourhood acquaintance of mine was verbally set upon and denounced as being unworthy to enter the Kingdom of Heaven for mispronouncing the word *chocolate*. Another was subjected to a similar interrogative admonition for dropping the h's in hedgehog. The Holy Ear-offending effrontery of this fiendish faux pas was answered with all the vitriol and incredulity of an entire church synod watching a crowd of idiots vote for the freedom of Barabbas. My mother whipped a piece of paper out of her bag and scribbled the word *edgog* onto it. 'Is that how you spell hedgehog? Is it? You unholy miscreant, my dear!' she hissed, opprobriously, emphasising the h's and slavering over the poor kid like a demented drill sergeant.

She typically addressed everyone as *my dear*. The custom not only making it seem that she was couching her acid-tongued invective in something acceptably akin to affection, but more importantly, sparing her the unnecessary tedium of condescending to remember anybody's name. Even on the odd occasion when she felt moved enough to fling the mud of mine at me, she invariably needed to first scroll through a short directory of others before arriving at the correct one. But she had stepped out of line this time.

115

I felt sorry for the unwitting offender. Embarrassed, too. It was unabashed overkill and, in my estimation, entirely unnecessary to demand the kid drop to his knees and beseech God for forgiveness. I expected an incensed visit from the victim's parents within minutes, but it never came.

My mother was always on the prowl to catch something to be offended by. Despite her staggering ignorance, the moral safari inflated her with illusions of superiority.

Sometimes, in the evening, she would sit with her thighs apart in a kind of gooey-eyed trance in front of the fire, wax polishing the antique P14 with a pair of old bloomers.

My father concealed the majority of any concern he may have felt for my mother's hobby beneath a regular alternation of acerbic and jocular remarks about the impending local outbreak of World War Three, and a request that she earmark the last shell for him in the event of a stand-off.

Once or twice I heard him fire off something less than complimentary about her psychology which appeared to fall appreciably short of containing any humour at all.

# 29

We exist only within the confines of trust.

Jim Reeves crooned Four Walls virtually sotto voce at around a customary three watts on the ageing lo-fi and my mother warbled along. It was like a sweet breath of fresh spring air flooding in through the open windows.

She loved Jim Reeves with an affection reserved for few others and as a result, his were the only records she ever played on the radiogram. He also held the enviable distinction of being the one person who could reliably seduce her into fleetingly flaunting the beautiful singing voice she compulsively concealed beneath the inflexibility of her usual conversational disdain. It remained a tragically under-exposed treasure that she appeared to treat with unjustifiable indifference, if not contempt, rather than valuing, as she might otherwise, the priceless natural endowment it had been from her own mother who had warbled operatically nightly for years in theatres for a living.

It was lamentably true, however, that even with Jim's unique encouragement, my mother would abruptly curtail her laconically liberated outpouring after a line or two. But on those infrequent occasions, when she opened a secret path of access to herself, broke free of her fetters for a moment and just let rip, she decorated the room with an irresistible exemplar of unaffected beauty. It was the one quality she possessed that I admired without reservation. The incomparable sound of Saint Cecilia weeping with joy. Her silvery tears falling into the air around me like droplets of paradise.

I could almost have loved my mother for the beauty of her singing voice alone. And despite having heard it so seldom, I still hear it now. It's the one small part of her I wish I could remember the rest of her for.

I heard it sneak out in perfect pitch and rise above the multi-keyed cacophony of the carolling congregation to the mock-medieval bossed rafters in church sometimes. When I had been dragged into the excruciating tedium of a post Sunday school service in the damp-oak-smelling structure that ominously counselled me in austere, monumentally overblown cold white lettering on the side of its pyramidal Victorian Neo-Romanesque tower to be prepared to meet my doom. Profoundly disconcerting though ultimately ill-timed advice, as I had by then not only met it, but been intimately acquainted with it for years.

Though it was worship of a different tune that compelled me to commune with the exquisite timbre of my mother's angelic soprano. In it I found cathedrals of belonging and wandered their enigmatic aisles thirstily imbibing something magnificent.

I considered my mother's dismissive attitude towards her God-given gift blasphemous. Not only because it raised a finger to the Almighty, but that its wilful neglect was an obvious affront to the common good. In a different life, she may have been saved by song. Instead, the Lord continued His work largely unserenaded by one of His more finely crafted creations. And in the place of Heavenly melody skulked the cacophonous irony that the only utterance my mother ever made that actually caused her to feel awkward or shy was the most pleasant sound she was capable of producing.

Maybe the discomfort of possessing so conspicuously so manifestly human an attribute rendered the joy of song unrewarding to her. Whatever the cause of her disharmony, I wished I'd heard her sing more often than I did; enough to feel that I had been adopted by a part of her I could depend on.

I could not have been more aware of the implicitly sacred in those abbreviated moments of cautious conviviality, when we shared without competition the unblemished beauty of those octaves at home, almost surreptitiously, in a discernibly vacuum-like harbour of inscrutable reclusion. Where she'd coquettishly invite me to creep quietly into her confidence while she became someone else for a minute or two. Someone happier.

I always complimented her rhapsodically on the almost otherworldly loveliness of her singing voice, but she never believed me.

## 30

Years later, I became friendly with one of the few people who had watched Jim Reeves' self piloted plane plummet into the rain sodden ground of Brentwood, Tennessee, one thundery afternoon in '64.

It's strange, the way that such unexpected, unimaginable connections become fashioned into substance from ether, as though they were always intended to exist with a greater visibility. And then it feels appropriate, natural, and you unconditionally accept the inevitability of it. As if the things you remember most vividly, the images and narrative threads that embroider the fabric of your memory, somehow inadvertently assume their own bodies of flesh and blood and transplant the inviolable, intangible perfection of remembrance onto the flawed, familiar face of unremarkable reality. Then, when the icon of your personal mythology becomes splintered and distorted beneath the profane weight of the mundane, you can't avoid taking a re-evaluating glimpse through the gathering dust on your mirror, or circumvent the impossibility of not noticing in unflattering reflections how it has left the tracks of its scratches and scars all over you.

# 31

That's another thing I learned as a kid. Most people seem to live their entire lives in a tailspin.

It goes like this: as soon as you're born, you get three words carved into your occipital lobe that burn themselves into everything you see or touch until you croak: YOU ARE WRONG. They inculcate you with the conviction that you're flawed and don't measure up, so you try to disappear into the asylum of anonymity.

The next step on the slippery ladder of invisibility is that you go to ridiculous lengths to lop off all those bits that stick out, and to conceal your critical blemishes beneath the thick make-up of a deadpan face that never changes, so no-one can ever know what you're thinking, and they can't exploit your involuntary winces to hurt you any more than they already have. That's how it works.

You learn to reweave your unacceptability into such an unthreatening tapestry of conformity that nobody takes as much as a second glance at you. On the outside, it looks as though you've fitted in.

But the price of it is that you leave a part of yourself somewhere and there's no paper trail back to it. Your vital, favourite, familiar warm colour gets hopelessly misplaced, bit by bit, until the time when you wake up in a frost and it's still night, and you realise you don't have it anymore. You've become monochrome and you can't sleep.

I had seen plenty of people, who hadn't slept for years, using wishes as splints for broken dreams. Born with fingers snapped from digging into the bedrock of their exclusion. Forging a path to the significance of their own graves. Plodding out their lives as somebody else's shoes.

I couldn't do it. Couldn't even think of doing it. I've stuck out so far, so much, in every direction, that people have had to jump out of the way to let me pass. It's just as lonely but not so self-compromising. Somehow, you never seem to quite lose the defining sign around your neck that says 'don't touch the exhibit'.

I wrote in vivid green felt tip pen, 'I've been orphaned by indifference' on the torn off inside of a piece of cereal box and Sellotaped it to the door of my parents' wardrobe.

It was a puerile act of antagonism and I knew it wouldn't change anything. But I had had enough of looking for undetectable reassurances that they would be attentive for long enough to catch me before I fell, and I had got sick of picking myself up off the floor.

I wrote the note but my heart wasn't in it.

I didn't even need them now, anyway. I almost stopped looking for signs that I might be wrong.

# 32

We are inexorably attracted to narcissists. They seduce
us with proof that they are capable of being loved.

By now, my mother's indefectible resentment of spending
any money on me at all had mutated into a preoccupation,
and as a result of having expanded appreciably beyond my
ancient meagre threads, I had almost nothing to wear. I
slinked around in extended family hand-me-downs and
badgered friends for cast-offs. My father didn't seem to
notice. And, even had there been one among the few items of
my wardrobe, I wouldn't have been anxious to demean
myself by going cap in hand to him and bringing the pathetic
spectacle of my plight to his attention. I was down to my last
shirt.

Months earlier, my mother had presented me with an
apricot and lavender, frilly-bottomed blouse with a multi-
coloured bevy of grotesquely dressed dolls printed all over it,
that she had snapped up as a bargain from a local church
jumble sale. I declined to wear it on the grounds that, a) it
was patently obviously a girl's garment, b) it wasn't new, and
c) it was too small.

In declining her blatantly inappropriate gift, I provoked an
extended, authentic Lear-like tirade of her *only to be ventilated*

*in the all forgiving privacy of her own home* infuriated abuse in response to my monster ingratitude.

In the interim, I had spotted a cochineal red needlecord, button down collar Ben Sherman shirt in the window of a fashionable boutique, which I implored my mother to go and see when she next went into town to shop. I was sure it would only take a glance for her to love it as much as I did, relent and present it to me in a reconciliatory moment of motherly love or begrudging conscience.

Eventually, according to plan, she agreed, and as I had hoped, returned home with the shirt I could see poking out from the top of a store bag inside her open trolley in the hall.

Both my affection for and gratitude to her rose like an escape velocity-nearing Apollo rocket mission to somewhere embarrassingly short of the moon in those gob-smacking moments of ascending excitement. But, after pulling it out of her bag and holding it up at the shoulders, both affection and gratitude tumbled broken back to Earth when I could see immediately that, even allowing for a few inches of fashionable overhang, it was far too big for me.

Before I was able to cut a sensible response from the excessive cloth of my disappointment, the garment was contemptuously snatched from my hands by the cyclone of my querulous mother who blasted me for the impertinence of handling her belongings.

Straight away I felt wounded and stupid. In a moment, it had become clear to me that my willingness to embrace the possibility of a change of her heart had been naive, and far from receiving a token of love or conscience, the gift I had hoped for had patently been purchased for herself.

Even more disconcerting was, that despite my best efforts to rectify the situation, I was still almost shirtless.

Peace is lost when words fail it.

We employ language to invent attitudes. Exactly the same attitudes that we then proceed to vilify other people, with even more specifically invented words, for holding. For all their seductive, eye-fluttering, full and pouty-lipped appeal to us, words are the most bitterly and bloodily divisive thing we have ever invented. We trust the heartwarming maliciousness of them implicitly. It's only when they are used to communicate compassion that we become so deeply suspicious of them.

I said nothing about the shirt that would risk exposing the effect of the assault on my feelings, being all too aware of the zeal with which she would already be monitoring my response. I walked away from the rebuff quietly, but was careful not to limp. Determined to deny her the prize of any additional pleasure.

She wore the shirt all over the weekend and I tried not to notice. It was too big for her, too. The colour didn't suit her, either. She never put it on again after that.

It was around this time that my mother decided to modify her appearance with a peculiarly hideous new closet of uncomplimentary clothes and began discussing God with strangers. Chaperoning her holy commodity into town and selecting their areas of commerce with meticulous precision.

Although she had yet to fully formulate the minutiae of her business plan, she already possessed the essential full range Words and God product line and, with various merchantable quality samples of both, embarked upon her pilgrimage to the marketplace; targeting her exclusively packaged products specifically at the demographic she had identified as representing the entirety of her customer base from the time they had driven her into the countryside to escape them. The rich. No other sector of the community could provide her infant enterprise with such necessary levels of investment. Or afford the ostentatious luxury of her undivided personal attention. Besides, the poor had prophets of their own.

Among the overly comfortable flush who conspicuously paraded their seductive prosperity through the honey-hued streets of Bath, ambled a richer cream of more solitary souls. These mouthwatering morsels my mother's most treasured reward. Almas caviar. Select truffles, to be skilfully snouted out, then savoured and devoured at leisure. These were the recherché delicacies of vulnerable outsiders. The intoxicating aroma of their bereft confusion and cloistered displacement bursting out of them like a bouquet of freshly cut gardenias.

She sniffed the air for sweetly scented sorrows, scrutinised autobiographies of faces for telling chapters of torment. Followed the fall of uncertain footsteps to catch the unmistakable essence of perduring trauma.

Discovering the seductive ease with which the old, the ill and infirm, the single young, sad or angry could be wheedled out of the crowd and hoisted by their response to an ingratiating smile was empowering beyond almost anything she had accomplished outside of a delivery room.

Even before the opening bugle call of the hunt my mother revelled in the thrill of the chase, knowing that the dithery-footed could be outfoxed and bowled over in a strike by the anodyne of her sincerity. Not only that, but they would continue to fall at her brogued toes like a bevy of ninepins.

She was right.

Once they had begun to tentatively embrace the cushioned analgesic of her unaffected indulgence, they relaxed and lowered their defences a little. Minutes later, she would penetrate their confidence like a hookworm.

The nature of her business was, as are many others, somewhat speculative and subject to an element of chance. A few people stopped to talk to her, most didn't. But after the freshly scattered seeds of conversational exchanges had taken root, she would nourish them with occasional waterings of the Lord's name. Gently, amiably, as though she were delicately rubbing the soothing liniment of Him into an aching muscle.

Portraying the Lord as a fond old friend, she spontaneously embellished her narrative with heartwarming anecdotes and especially created reminiscences of divine interventions in the seemingly insurmountable troubles of her own life. Subtly confirming, by referencing His curative responses to her desperate calls, how particularly well acquainted with Him she had through such encounters become.

The more rewarding of these diligently calculated chance assignations would escort the emotionally precarious willing captive from the initial larval stage of their unwitting seduction, to the irresistible warmth of her willingness to help provide abiding solutions to whatever problems they were currently experiencing in the unchartable chaos of their own personal lives. A little later, the benignant romance would yield enough subtly extracted information to complete the discovery of where they lived.

Those sufficiently inveigled by the brass-necked mastery of her seduction to surrender their address, as though they were apprehensively offering her their virginity at the end of an office drinks party, would be offered a drop in, a day or two later, to help flesh out a viable solution to the most pressing of their problems. A visit invariably paid, whether explicitly agreed to or not.

The preliminary stages of this unsubtle deflowering were surprisingly easy to effect. And once the potentially big money prize of knowing where they lived had been claimed, escape for the unfortunate occupant was almost impossible. At any time. Not, of course, that some didn't try. They could hide but they couldn't run; and once her foot had landed at their door, she could commandeer their living quarters like an outbreak of dry rot.

Should she encounter a perfunctory snarl of resistance at the polished brass bell or neatly knockered threshold of their illustrious abodes, it would seldom constitute a significant impediment, or diminish in the least her unblushing determination to sweep the wielder of such objection aside and enter. On the rarest occasions, when the battering ram of her natural impertinence failed her, she resorted to the unbearability of her ever-accessible roscian repertoire to successfully draw the appropriate key of sympathy like blood from an old wound.

After consolidating her initial town centre interview with a home visit follow-up, the hard sell of recovery would begin at pace. But so ingeniously deceptively that it would typically appear to be my mother who was forking out the cost of it.

Almost all residual squeals of scepticism from the resolutely unbending would be efficiently strong-armed out of earshot by the cast iron promise of both emotional and spiritual salvation through their membership of the new Church my mother had been divinely instructed to found on exacting principles ordained by the Almighty Himself.

Nevertheless, most prospective cadets fell by the wayside almost immediately, and refused unconditionally to countenance any further association. But within dogged days and weeks, my mother had succeeded in attaching herself to one or two others like a beatified leech.

Her initially modest success rate gradually grew, and over the months, a few more lonely, ill, socially gauche or recently bereaved shadows of people responded sympathetically to the enthusiastic outpourings of her persuasively pious convictions and familiar concerns.

In the airy wisdom of her counsel, she became sweet, supportive, unassuming and almost sincerely interested in her malleable victim's circumstances. Her demeanour never less than warm, genial and charming. She complimented her lost sheep with bleats of benevolent laughter, adding precious currency to the economy of their own voices, and immersed them in the mollifying theatrical spectacle of how much she cared about them.

The amiable alleviative of her fatal charisma gradually acquired the form of essential regular medication. Unlike at home, where she became increasingly difficult to swallow.

The larval-stage induction of every metamorphosing recruit into this barely yet fledgling army of biddable subordinates began with an invitation to consider the great blessing they had already received from their auspicious encountering of my mother in their moment of need. She encouraged them to reflect on the miracle of their impending rehabilitation through God and assured them: 'I know you will receive wonderful and everlasting gifts. How do you imagine you will best use these gifts to enrich your life forever?'

And then, after a little more protective incubation to ensure the unimpeded completion of their transition from credulous larva to pampered pupa, she would pose the more searching, revealing, pivotal and penetrating question, with all the alluring ingenuousness of a blue-eyed, Rubens' ruby-cheeked cherub, 'have you ever discharged a firearm in the name of the Lord?'

# 33

I spent myself extravagantly on an affordable sense of ownership.

I had become a member of both the school's and the local church's choir. After a short tussle with my conscience on either count. In fact, I decided to accept the opportunities both these unloved institutions presented me without spending anything like the regulation forty tormented days in the wilderness over the possibility of compromising my valued integrity. Principally, because they offered me an unmissable and relatively convenient opportunity to sing regularly without restraint or inhibition. The decision duly taken without ceremony or contention, I subjugated my instinctive aversion to each place and accepted their offering gratefully.

The sensation of singing was like loosening the fingers of my clenched fist and releasing a small bird trapped beneath their thicket in my palm. Then watching it take to the air on unbridled notes, fluttering and weaving in the clear blue, safe, sunny sky; coruscating unfettered in the swallow-lift breeze of its wings.

Not only that, but the church gig was easy money; one-and-six on Sundays and three shillings for weddings. It was the first time I had cash of my own, and it felt like I was raking it in.

Naturally, my mother interpreted my regular attendance at church as a devotional activity, which, in a way, it was, and convinced herself that I had finally discovered the great love of God. All attempts to correct, reason or explain the error of this hopeful assumption were met with exactly the same stone wall refusal to listen long enough to consider the possibility that she may be wrong. And she grew ever more intolerable as a result of her frequent insistent attempts to inculcate me with a self-devised holy protocol designed to ingratiate me and no doubt her, too, with the Lord still further.

It was the beginning of an unexpectedly satisfying social life for me as well. Some of the local choirboys casually used the seemingly always open-doored vicarage as a kind of youth club, taking advantage of a noticeable lack of adult supervision and the commodious space in the castle-like, rambling, crenellated Victorian mansion. Its billiard room, sofa-filled TV lounge and table tennis facilities proving unfailingly popular with kids who hung around them and the sweeping, tree strewn grounds of the house feeling as though they owned the place.

And every now and then, the sky pilot, who was actually a genuine guy and not a pervert or anything, organised mini-bus trips for the choir boys, including his son, to First Division football matches on weddingless Saturday after-noons. Paid for them, too. Needless to say, we all liked him a lot.

Naturally, my mother hysterically refused to allow me to travel to any of these matches, assuming them to be attended by harrying armies of beer-swilling cut-throats. But I did, anyway. I learned my lesson the first time she refused to let me out of the house; after which I just sneaked off in the morning and didn't tell her where I was going.

Once or twice I'd get back quite late at night and find her calling my name, walking the lamplit streets looking for me.

# 34

I never wasted my life. But allowed it instead to leak away unchecked while I distracted myself with other acquisitions. Not doubting for a moment my ability to command its return, should I ever find myself in need of it.

The thing I had never previously fully appreciated was that my relatively comforting self-identity as a heavenly-toned cub was living entirely on borrowed time. In a way, of course, I always knew it was, and had routinely managed somehow to completely overlook the inevitability of amending my perspective. But I had no idea that I would be so abruptly obliged to confront the reality of this anathema when I joined the church choir. Suddenly, the rumination had become a source of concern.

From time to time, I had been, as most boys occasionally are, mildly curious about what might happen when my treble hit puberty, but had hardly been worried about it as I had become now.

This novel angst had not only been ignited but constantly fanned by the unrelenting iterations of my friends in the choir who appeared to view the dropping of an octave as some kind of impending Armageddon. The motif began to plague me like a blanket of bees. The older choir members were no help. Amusing themselves by taunting us that we would never sing again.

I began to fixate. To feature in my own fantasies as a wandering ratite, trapped in a croak and sucked into the reality of a life that denied me the freedom of flight. Any day now, the treasure of my voice could lose the entirety of its value overnight. Even death didn't seem so disinheriting a prospect. I was inextricably bound to the rules of a game I hadn't been fully conscious of playing. A throw of the dice was to imminently affect me, and all I could do was wait to see how.

It was a daunting period. My discomfort magnified by the arrival of other new anomalies. Even the mayhem and volatility that had traditionally passed for normal life at home was beginning to take on a disturbingly less familiar character.

Within a couple of seasons, my mother had assembled the working nucleus of her motley army, which congregated around the chenille-draped Victorian mahogany loo table at the bay windowed end of our commodious sitting room on the second and fourth Sundays of every month.

Even on all the other days, the unhurried disorganisation of family life seemed to have rapidly become subtly imbued with an uncomfortably purposeful new momentum.

During this time, I noticed how naturally my mother identified with the charismatic character of her new role. She had without any doubt discovered her true vocation, her hitherto elusive raison d'être, and threw herself into her bespoke part of visionary elder with the joie de vivre of a child.

The movement had begun its active life with the short-lived moniker of *Suffer His Inviolable Truth*, until it quickly became obvious that the acronym rendered this name practicably unusable. For weeks, my mother filled reams with unused alternatives.

The twice-monthly meetings of the brand new Church of Highest Righteous Instruction and Sacred Truth, or CHRIST, as my mother invariably acronymised it, were an almost comically anarchic, offbeat combination of traditional hymns and self-styled, stutteringly erratic sermons, which amounted to little more than her outlandish and verbose ramblings, sustained by barely veiled threats against various institutions and world leaders. During which she repeatedly addressed both herself and her followers as 'the chosen shirtless'.

I had absolutely no idea why my mother should use such an ostentatiously inappropriate description of the gathered who were, after all, meticulously baited and drawn from incontrovertibly affluent areas of the city, and who were quite clearly more than satisfactorily attired.

Whether the term derived from a conscience-inspired reference to the stoicism with which I bore my own unenviable sartorial situation, or related to sentiments my mother may have held about my recently erroneously interpreted association with the Almighty, remained some way beyond sensible speculation. Although I accepted that any nod in my direction was improbable in the extreme, and the more likely explanation was that, for some unfathomable reason, patently nonsensical to anyone but her, she brazenly lifted the expression from Eva Peron's equally outre 1951 address to the Buenos Aires Descamisados and presumably considered it to be in some way appropriate.

Anyway, my mother wittered on about them all being reborn and wearing nothing more tainted by sin and the blackened Earth than the weightless cloth of Heaven, without actually explaining what any of that meant.

During every gathering, she dragged out the story of how she had received, directly from the darkroom of God, an album of explicit metaphysical photographs that contained numerous images of her CHRISTian family kneeling in golden sunlight, blessed and haloed before Him. Going on to explain how the Lord had revealed Himself to her on several previous occasions to confide that He had become saddened and angered by the profligacy of those who cynically purported to act in His name, and by unscrupulous others who sought to further their contemptible ambitions by contravening His sacred commandments.

She related at length how the Lord had been moved by her rare beauty and the unique purity of her heart. And how necessary He had deemed it to discuss with a woman so morally chaste and unsinning, the full, terrible, masculine magnitude of His impending retribution. Revealing in his outpouring the plans He was currently hatching to unleash a cataclysmic deluge of bloody atonement upon a world in which His word had been debased and His suffering children exposed to lethal infections of ubiquitous depravity. The time had come, He declared, to eradicate a mortal sickness created and spread by numberless self-serving purveyors of lies and their uncountered plagues of corruption.

The upshot of it all was my mother's astonished discovery that she, as the only possible nominee, had been divinely appointed the Lord's one true Earthly emissary, and instructed to gather His most trusted and beloved saints together to conduct a campaign of Holy Vengeance on His behalf. In conclusion, He revealed that He had already invested her with His celestial weapons of Truth and Right and granted her exclusive authority to act in His name.

At the closing of these invariably protracted announcements, usually around the half-way stage in the service's proceedings, my mother, with typically unrefined and woefully over-the-top amateur dramatic colour, invariably conceded a swooning defeat to her improbably trembling lip and launched full scale into breathless floods of tears to emphatically illustrate how dramatically she had been affected by the supernatural encounters, and how humbly she had accepted the Lord's remarkable call.

God had apparently been pretty insistent that my mother only share the true meaning and significance of His words with the trusted, hand picked members of her flock *after* they had dug deeply into their pockets and invested heavily in the growth of His Church. Only then, some considerable way into an open-ended instalment-based programme of purchases of essential Holy Truths and Blessings, could they be deemed to have made a substantial enough down-payment on the unique and reassuringly expensive privilege of securing the first secret, sacred words of revelation pertaining to their divinely endowed responsibilities for righting the critically compromised and vilely violated world.

This crucial entry level of spiritual attainment would confer genuinely recognisable status, and entitle each Carrier of Eternal Truth to go on to claim, at a small additional cost, the right to own the otherwise entirely unobtainable title of Most Holy Soldier. Its acquisition uniquely qualifying each member to form part of the front line battalion of the absolutely most holy and revered Saviour's True Guard.

Even the name of this elite regiment was too sacred to be spoken aloud. The unuttered bestowal of its title being more than a coveted badge of honour. It was no less than a painless, deathless, safe-passage ticket to the unimaginably opulent, fruity, serpent-free Eden of the afterlife.

Although my mother could typically barely articulate the words through the choking cascade of her tears, she always managed to be just about coherent enough to inform her marvelling minions that, on the highest authority, she had been granted the title of Our Heavenly Sister, and had humbly acknowledged the banner as her own.

Following a few more aphoristic utterances, pertaining principally to the highest holiness of poverty, the meeting would be wound up with an extended eulogy on the virtues of love and inclusion, an effusive appreciation of the miracle of how God had finally managed to establish His own one true Church on Earth, a prayer for peace, and an opportunity for all the attendees to offer any financial contribution or personal information which may in some way be ultimately exploitable by my mother, or serviceably relevant to her burgeoning enterprise.

My father, who was anything but an actively committed drinker, would not be back from his social afternoon at the local pub until after tea and cake had been consumed and the odd little gathering had dispersed.

His attitude towards my mother had hardened, however. He had clearly become concerned about something.

# 35

Between nothingness and madness lays belief.

I watched the upbeat CHRISTians leave the house, seemingly buoyed by the possibility of having discovered something new and meaningful. A truth less harrowing, that offered the potential to drag them far enough away from the awfulness of their previous existence to feel the warmer proximity of a less baldly desolate lifescape.

I felt sorry for them. Not only for them, but for me, too. In the few moments I spent watching the dribble from the house dissolve, I became profoundly aware that I had lost something. Something I hadn't realised I had valued.

I was seized by the bereft, mortifying hollowness that consumes your body and soul when you drop a tiny, precious and irreplaceable object in the long grass and you know you're never going to find it again. You sink to your knees and swish the larcenous blades around it in prayer for the umpteenth time before the sun goes down, when you know for sure you will have lost it for ever. You attempt, with no resource other than faith, to muster the object up out of nothing. Invoke it like a hapless medium at a showcase seance to reappear. But you're already drowning in the sinking feeling of knowing that it never will; so the only practical recourse available is to decathect. You instinctively try to devalue the little lost item's significance to you in an attempt to mitigate the pain of your irreparable separation from it. The whole procedure is an act of inhumation. You reluctantly straighten up and leave it there, as though you had been kneeling at its graveside hoping for a last minute recovery. And even the unmarked burial place gets lost when you've wandered far enough away. Then, with every involuntary step of your retreat, you can't help yourself wanting to go back and take another look for it one last time.

I knew that I had lost the light. I didn't even know where I had dropped it.

My mother had acquired influence over a rag-tag retinue of vulnerable psychological vagabonds, who had been felled like softwood in a stormwind of circumstances they could not contend, and who, in the misery of their tribulations, possessed the vital ingredients for her recipe for disaster. She industriously reinforced their disabling insecurities by tirelessly reminding them that their loneliness had been manufactured and sustained by a cumulus of cynical others, who were bent on exploiting it to effect the realisation of their own selfish objectives. And that all family members and friends with expectations of profit from the pain of others must be rejected wholeheartedly. Excised absolutely from the lives of the victims of their influence.

She constantly reiterated the dictum that any family or society guilty of creating conditions that made it impossible for any member to feel valued within it must be dismissed as toxic and harmful.

Finding fault with judgemental and unsympathetic family members or friends was essential, and my mother actively encouraged her followers to focus on the pain such people had caused them. Advising that it be fully felt, owned and accessed by constant conscious reference, and that the perpetrators of it be viewed with unassuageable hatred and suspicion. The unnatural and divisive expectations of society had produced a fertile breeding ground for the disease of disaffection, that must be shunned in favour of each other's safe, warm company, in which honest mutual compassion could therapeutically effect their escape from unhappiness and need.

My mother was, of course, acutely aware of how tightly her followers would cling to their own repudiation of any society they felt had forsaken them, and to a mutually supportive commonwealth of their own. A secure and valued place within it would cement them together stronger than anything. Before long, and with all due diligent attention to the details of its constitution, any necessary action or reaction would represent a legitimate and justifiable defence of it.

# 36

Even the densest stone appears soft when the sculptor has hacked at it hard enough to render its new form familiar.

On the completion of her recent sartorial reinvention, Our Heavenly Sister took to habitually sporting a military-style green beret on her proselytising sojourns, into which she had discretely embroidered, with wispy, black silk thread, For United Christian Kinsfolk on one side, and Our Fellowship Forever on the other. It teased my imagination to think that she would not have considered the acronyms, and I suspected that the words had indeed been carefully selected to quietly articulate an otherwise entirely indiscernible scoff. She seemed to wear the blithefully subversive item as she might a new style of self-congratulatory sneer.

I was sure I had interpreted her little joke correctly, but couldn't take a chance on being mistaken, so I said nothing, and half-smiled at the remote possibility that her characteristically indefatigable meticulousness had, on this occasion, failed her. Either way, I found it amusing.

Excepting her procreatively encouraging needlework and uncharacteristically ballsy outburst, I had yet to hear her actually swear. Ever. Not with the sorts of words I enjoyed so much, anyway.

I have to admit that I very seldom heard my father cough up even the mildest of expletives either; it was like living with the frigging language police. The whole stultifying puritanical correctness of their expressive vocabulary was absurdly unnatural. I sympathised with them; their asceticism was denying them access to an alternative universe of timeless poetry and pleasure.

When pushed to beyond the edge of uncontainable anger by my mother's vituperative provocation, my father would spit out the occasional, self-conscious, bile-laden *bloody* or *bleeding,* and less infrequent *damn and blast,* but, unlike him, she almost never lost her conviction that such unspeakably vulgar verbal decoration remained unworthy of her virginally untainted tongue. And if, in public or in private, she felt, as she frequently did, the necessity to respond to an offence, or to remind some bottom rank mortal of their unenviable place in the world, she either simply pinned the victim against the wall of her contempt with the barrel of her stare or, in the warranting of a higher level of personal attention, assumed the most impeccably supercilious and indifferent stance then, like a one woman firing squad, shot off an exaggeratedly sympathetic simper and an economic scattering of masterfully selected slogans of immaculate put-down, which invariably contained an imperious reference to the Lord's exalted position as unimpeachable arbiter of all worldly affairs. It wasn't something you could easily argue with. God knows I tried. It absolutely wasn't possible to either engage or disarm her. She would contumeliously rebuff any invitation to commit even the most microscopically discernible interest in either you or the point you were trying to make. I've never in all these years witnessed another human being stonewall anybody with such effortless totality. She had no need to swear; the conspicuous perfection of her ineffable righteousness was more than obscenity enough for anyone.

She looked reminiscently regimental and vaguely ridiculous in her beret and tweedy civvies, which was likely to have been her intention. The gently self-mocking military-inspired presentation would almost certainly have been the carefully measured consequence of an attempt to convince her prospective recruits that there was something reassuringly offbeat about her, too. An obvious, endearing eccentricity that would render her familiar enough to assimilate more easily into a cautious circle of those who themselves felt they didn't fit in. To such guarded unfortunates, she would have been anxious to appear benign. Sympathetic. To credibly portray herself as someone who naturally belonged amongst them.

With her new disguise she concealed her pugnacious contempt beneath an ornate humility verbal enough to imperiously out-everso 'umble Uriah Heep with the razor-edged sickle of her monstrous mouth unmoving.

She wore her majestic modesty like an emperor's new cowl over the perfect figure of her conceit. And through it blazed the floodlight of her amiable approachability like a big, broad, luminous brooch, which could be seen as clearly as the lantern of a lighthouse from a distance at a glance. She never now left the house without it; wielding its beam insistently like a hatchet of sun.

There could be no doubt that she would have immersed herself in the most indispensable qualities and characteristics of her second self scrupulously. Committed their full, complete architectural splendour to memory and paced every anticipated word and gesture out methodically in front of the mirror.

Her long anticipated moment of daring debut now in reach of her pre-greasepainted fingertips, the limelight awaited her bow like a stage door Johnny.

Her acting was as wooden as a floorboard, but she instinctively knew how to nail an entrance; and would have rehearsed her ingratiatingly humble and lovably surprised reaction to the crowd's heartfelt applause more rigorously than anything else. Less immediately exhilarating elements of stagecraft would need to be more patiently honed to functional perfection on the hoof.

The pearly-toothed calling card of her sainted mask was calligraphed with an affable smile so effortlessly affecting that it could take you in and suck you down before you had time to realise you'd been snared by the sticky little mousetrap of its ulterior motive. She flashed it like a miner's lamp into the shadowy face of anyone she thought she could squeeze anything worth having out of; and it landed like a mosquito, with almost audible impact, on the owners of Ballyed, Barkered or Ferragamo'd feet taxiing about newly bagged bargains from fashionable boutiques. Encouraging her unwitting victims to summarily throw themselves cleanly off their clifftop of reason by returning the smile as if the gesture wouldn't harm them.

You couldn't blame them.

It was almost impossible to see past that simper of hers. To the bayonet end of it, anyway. Unless you had been sickened by the sight of it as many times as I had. And even then, I found it almost impossible to completely suppress my admiration of her vulpine cunning in calculating so astutely that people were generally more likely to speak when their mouths had already been engaged in some other kind of communicational activity.

Any gullible, limp-winged fly, caught open-lipped on the viscid paper of a courteous response, would be immediately swatted with a hefty hello rolled up into a beaming bludgeon. They need return her nacreous salute with nothing more than a non-committal nod to fire up the dragster of her attack. Within moments, their softened flesh would be rendered edible. She'd toy with them for a while, enjoy the appetiser of their vulnerability, drain a nourishing soup of gratitude, trust and respect from their opened veins of complaisance, then imperceptibly nudge them into the beckoning snare of her slavering jaws. The choreography was sublime.

She was born to predate on the most defenceless. It was one of the more outstanding of her few natural talents. And fewer accorded her greater pleasure. In the river of life she was mink. On its grassy bank, she angled easily. Dangling the maggoty bait of her unassuming self to tempt a bite from a hungry hopeful at the lethal end of one of her opening lines.

Words served her in a way that I could never use them. And despite my abounding efforts to weave graceless threads of conversations over excruciatingly reticent years, I irreformably failed to spout even a poor imitation of my mother's palaver. Unremittingly, at my most fluent, articulate, voluble best, it would take me all day to think of anything to say. And then, when I had finally come up with something, I'd inevitably over-analyse it and eventually decide that it probably wasn't worth saying, anyway. We were polar opposites.

In her proselytising exchanges, she'd painstakingly present the child of herself as so shatterably benign that it was difficult to escape the truncheon of her impending assault without feeling remiss for doing so by prematurely terminating the conversation. That's how she netted them. Some escaped intact. The less discriminating few enthusiastically impaled themselves on the hidden hooks in her jam when they discovered they had unexpectedly acquired a new good friend and confidante. Then, ever so gently, she'd screw the lid onto her jar and cut off their air. And all the time she was screwing, she was probing, bit by imperceptible bit, to discover their weaknesses, their areas of raw, aching tenderness, emotional distress and discomfort, their pain; their Achilles' heel.

# 37

We seem to arrive at this world with the uncomfortable sensation that our hands are unnaturally empty.

Oscar Wilde once observed 'the only thing that ever consoles man for all the stupid things he does, is the praise he always gives himself for doing them.' I think Wilde overestimated the proximity of consolation. We mistake our reflexes for choices, then lose our tenuous perspective on reason in a disorientating agglomeration of relentless over-analysis, self-immersion and doubt.

We have evolved to habitually celebrate the paragons of our intellect with a pyrotechnical exhibition of words, but we've abused our ability to think. It's this which has rendered us stupid, and our stupidity has become sacred to us.

We measure our lives in units of poetry. It's an over-appreciated yardstick. A permanently underlying medical condition that kills more people than heart disease.

It's the lethal accessibility of the poetic image that enables us to remain so perilously convinced that, should we delve deeply enough into the unexplored universe of our own fragile minds, we will eventually discover the whereabouts of our real and natural selves. The real one being so very much bigger, better and more capable than the one we've been lumbered with. So *very* much more deserving.

It's this bullheaded belief in our inherent value that compels us to pursue our delusions. To search for the one brilliant spark of illumination that will finally release us from the grip of anonymous darkness and into the definitive spotlit articulation of our genuine, inestimable worth.

It's that interminable quest for our own substantiation, that endless pilgrimage to the Eden of our redemption which renders us so peculiarly impressionable. It's a design flaw. An evolutionary failing. Even if we can't quite compile a convincing enough photofit of what this missing self actually looks like, and can only waveringly point to dubiously persuasive abstracts of description, we remain tortured by an unabating compulsion to undersell our misfiring selves to fund the endless blind search for the perfect metaphor of it. While impotently wringing our hands and bemoaning the insuperable tragedy of its elusiveness.

The more we look, the more we moan. The more we moan, the more desperate we become. The more desperate we become, the more suggestible we are. The more suggestible we are, the more we'll try to make anything fit to find a stop for the seemingly unbridgeable gap. Nothing ever stretches far enough to span it, though. Not for very long, anyway. Everything eventually loses the elasticity of its initial discovery.

Then, the only consolation available in the holy loneliness of our bereft malaise is faith. Faith that something will one day span the ballooning lacuna for ever, or faith that something already does but we can't quite feel it yet. Either way, we carry on screaming loud enough to attract the attention of some conveniently situated medicine show

150

which will sell us the ready bottled snake oil confirmation that something can bring us closer to the way we think we should feel.

There just *has* to be more than all we have. And the defibrillating relief from our perpetual disquiet is a mouthy mountebank on every street corner who knows exactly what it is and how to flog it to us at an unmissable price. The more ingenious of these quacks will feed us enough free samples of our own desolation to get us hooked on it, then offer us a therapeutically expensive, shiny, and even more meaningless antidote to the lethally stupefying poison of it.

Thank God that for those of us left clinging to the last thread of belief in something more satisfying than suicidal oblivion, the kingdom of Heaven is and only ever was no further than a promise away. And better still, you can lie or bribe your way in with no trouble at all. Couple either ticket with your obsequious obedience to every law-laying whim of its self-appointed taskmasters, and you may even be singled out as an epitome of spiritual probity and paraded as an example of rectitude before the ears of the rest of the flock.

Fact is, Heaven, for all its sins, probably attracts more faecal matter than the average lavatory bowl. And long before any of it ever gets there, it has written the myriad moral aberrations of this life off altogether with the perfunctory expulsion of a few simple words of pre-initiation, and without so much as a whiff of irony or penalty for their perpetration. It's a compelling sell.

But it's not what you've bought. It's only after they've reeled you in and kept you hanging up to smoke you discover obedience and devotion are never going be enough to pay for a view of the stage. Then you realise the painful truth, that there's no such thing as free manna up there, after all. You've been inveigled into a pyramid scheme you'll stay tied into for ever. The hidden maintenance charges for your unaccommodating accommodation will cost you more than lip-service allegiance.

As a child, I invited God into my heart, but He hamstrung my arteries and trousered my pocket money. I felt let down when I realised that's just what happens when deities live beyond their means. My worldly potential and sixpence disappeared before I saw any of it. And all I had left in the place of either was my mother's reassurance that I was happy, and that the missing cash had been invested on my behalf in some spiritual savings account I had no wish to open, even though the balance would eventually swell to an amount impressive enough to save my soul.

I mourned my loss of comic books and Pelican fiction like a siblingless orphan. Demanding as compensation for both, the company of alimentary answers to such questions as why in ancient Greece, if the food of the gods had been ambrosia, did the priests on their behalf insist on offerings of money and valuables to ensure the welfare and salvation of their donors?

I was initially confused, but after a short period of setting my mind to the task, I worked it all out with a surprising economy of effort. I had been hoodwinked. And was pretty sure that there was no such thing as ambrosia after all. The food of the gods was money. Even when I was too young and naive to have learnt anything else at church, it didn't take long for me to notice that nobody put ambrosia in the collection dish.

How did the ancient priests of Greece and Egypt, or probably any other civilization on Earth at any time, become so rich and powerful and live so enviably well? Why did

Henry the Eighth order the dissolution of the monasteries in 1536? Because the superstition-peddling Church, which forced the poor to work for nothing on its lands and encouraged spectacular bribes from the rich to oil their passage into Heaven, had accumulated more money than the king and threatened his power over the ever yielding gullible with their own. That's why. And guess what? I'll bet when the mega-rich monasteries were destroyed, nobody found ambrosia in any of them. Nor in the Parthenon, or the Temples of Karnak, Bacchus or Solomon, or at Templo Mayor, or among the stupendous riches of the Vatican. Nowhere. The only Heavenly nourishment to be found in any of these holy places is what can still be seen today; the grinning face of where mammon had flowed like a river.

Remember the heartwarming story of the Church's brazen fleecing of the poor widow's last mite? Crude simony, contrived to illustrate the idiocy of hanging on to any amount of loose change in comparison to the unimaginable rewards of giving of it all to God, via His agents, and securing for yourself the reciprocated windfall of eternal life and salvation. The more you give, the more you're saved. Simple as that. As salvations go, it's not a bad deal, and cheap as a poke in the eye at the price.

We were all systematically conditioned with the synoptic gospels' bullshit of how it's easier for a camel to pass through the eye of a needle than for a rich man to enter the golden gates of Heaven. So what the hell are they doing with *golden* gates up there, then, for Chrissake? Are we regarded by our spiritual masters as being so pathetically gullible and naive that we are not expected to pose so inconvenient a question?

Anyhow, the important lesson we are expected to learn is that we are required to purchase that priceless Heavenly pile of eternal redemption because those vulgar, grand, golden gates need to be paid for somehow. It'll cost you your last mite, it's always for sale and it's available to anyone.

The precept is simple: the way you spend your money is critical to your eternal wellbeing, but how you spend your life isn't. As long as the lip-service remorse you pay at the end of it is backed up with a barrel of brass, bingo, you're up for the star prize with no seriously embarrassing questions asked. The rules of the game are idiot-proof, and haven't changed since we began to plant saracen stones in the mud. Why should they? Superstition is and always has been far too important for its obliging victims to start mucking about with it themselves.

For the rest of us wretches, wallowing in the purgatory of all the guilt we've accumulated for not having anything else to give, the best we can hope for is that if we allow pretty much every aspect of our miserable life to be controlled by some usurious organisation and pledge our full industrious cooperation to the enabling of it and its administrators to remain as powerful and wealthy as possible, we might get a begrudging nod to lick the shit off a celestial jackboot at the end of it if we're lucky. Or else the Devil's fires can kiss our otherwise assetless asses for ever. It's a persuasive proposition. Even Pascal felt compelled to admit that he had been taken in by it.

How much of a surprise would it have been to anyone with a functioning brain cell when luxuriating tyrants and plutocrats invented the golden goose of religious dogma pdq to cover their own imposingly resplendent posteriors, and inculcated the deludable disheartened with ideas of conscience and divine retribution to enable them to continue to collect? At the same time, of *course*, ensuring that the poor, miserable bastards who weren't left with a brace of pennies for their own dead eyes wouldn't rob or kill them for a crust of their pie to keep themselves alive.

And did the fabulously rich new theocratic elite fund the golden gates of God? No, they paraded their wealth to the destitute as confirmation of their favour with the Lord, before handing it on to their slavering offspring to enjoy in precisely the same way.

The subject of money remained one of the dearest to my mother's heart. And as such, the discovery of a recipe for its acquisition and subsequent squirrelling away commanded a particular pride of place in her limited Earthly aspirations.

The origins of her obsession were unclear, but seemed to relate to her insistence on repeatedly announcing that her family had lost an impressive amount of it in the war. She hammered the old chestnut of her complaint on the iridium anvil of mythology whenever she felt the need to justify her unnatural parsimoniousness, fingering the time-polished gem of her favourite fable like a rosary.

Her comfortably off but modestly successful thespian father had been a naturally generous man, broken by the parish priest before her pre-pubescent eyes with regular reminders of his shameful worldly status as a terminally wretched sinner. His ecclesiastically perceived failings convincing him that he was unworthy of anything, and forcing him into a spiritual vocation as a moral understudy.

His conviction had not been inherited by my mother, who valued her meanness above most other things, and more than confidently considered herself to be fully deserving of its treasure. She leaned heavily on her belief with a full weight of emotion and now enjoyed the great fortune of discovering herself to be in possession of a divine right to collect as many pieces of silver as she could get her hungry and hustling hands on.

Although the vital organs of my mother's inchoate organisation performed less than impeccably and initially haemorrhaged potential.

As a neophyte spiritual cutpurse, relatively unschooled in the finer lucrative possibilities of cold-blooded emotional exploitation, Our Heavenly Sister's first tottering footsteps did not lead her to the path of immediate reward, and she remained oblivious to some of the less sophisticated methods of securing the additional returns she may otherwise have relatively effortlessly squeezed from the pockets of the passing public. Realising only some days after her inaugural street-slither, that her hand-warming cup of freshly emptied coffee held the key.

Both generosity and embarrassment proved susceptible to the intimidating cry of an empty vessel, and almost immediately upon the coffee cup's draining, it miraculously began to fill with a steady rain of loose change. Within an hour, it and her mindless viridity had been replaced by a shiny, large, tubular, silver biscuit tin, which rattled like a hungry sidewinder in the battlemented basket of her hand. Each coin hissing and spitting briefly as it dropped onto the rising pile, voicing her seething self-recrimination at the costliness of her guileless oversight.

Another moment of inspiration historiated a second divine truth; that courtesy, too, could be as easily abused. And that even in the otherwise fruitless event of her conversational approaches disintegrating into smithereens of irredeemable disinterest, a token financial forfeit could expeditiously silence the querulous clatter of chest-height change and be almost painlessly provided as a convenient salve to the conscience of the unrecruitable.

Her perspicacity yielded anticipated gains, and a prevailing retreat of potential cadets left a cataract of coins in their wake. Some forked out for a more impressive escape with paper money.

At the end of her first year of speculative streetwalking, my mother had secured donations of almost a thousand pounds from passing benefactors, who typically remained unaware of the cause their contributions were intended to serve.

My mother's confidence, too, had grown. Her blossoming circumstances carried her cosily into the pink.

Not that I profited in the least from the improvement in her cash flow. Aside from the fact that my mother had gained a couple of dress sizes and a new wardrobe to match, nothing much changed at home, in the fridge or at the dinner table. Still the same inedible, reheated slop, day after day. Still hardly anything to wear. Still she couldn't be persuaded to part with a penny of it for the sake of anyone else. But instead kept almost all of it in a rising mountain of mainly fifty pound notes under the carpet behind her wardrobe, along with all the other money that had been laying there in varying amounts for years. I began to wonder if she knew exactly how much she had stuffed in her little hideaway. And whether she would notice if any of it went missing.

# 38

I was always abdicating my crown of belief. Forever pitching over-mannered tributes to the shadowing dead from the pockmarked furrow of another night-scarred farewell.

The rain tapped rimshots and strummed in free time onto the nylon hood of my minus-sized cagoule with the dispassionate abandon of an underpaid rhythm section. It was cold, and I couldn't pull the two halves of the jacket close enough together to zip it up. Couldn't even comfortably keep my hands in my pockets without the smallness of the shoulders of it making me feel like I was hanging from cheesewire by my armpits.

Of course, in an ideal world, I wouldn't have chosen January as the month I left home and headed for the woods with nowhere else to go. But I was sick of it. Sick of the madness. Sick of the threats and violence against me there and being chased down the road to be dragged back and thumped. Sick of being twelve and too young for any of it to change.

I wandered around the village afternoon, peering through early dusky, still open curtains, into the unfamiliar normality of other people's domestic lives. Boarded briefly as a few sodden footsteps in the dreamlike, intangible, crepuscular otherworldliness of every passing dwelling, oblivious to everything but the elation of being free in warm orange tungsten lightbulb bliss.

There's something unique about the combined scent of cold rain and chimney smoke in the portentous slate blue hum of winter twilight. Something inexpressibly, almost heartbreakingly comfortless when it finds you ambling in the near nothingness of your own already disconsolate company. It's an evocation of a more familiar past you erroneously think you remember, which is at odds with its palpably romantic appeal to the more somehow in-the-perfection-of-the-moment entwinement of hand in hand strollers.

I wanted to embrace someone or something with the hungry totality of my afflicted wandering. I didn't know who or what, and I didn't know if it was because I was feeling cold, wet and sorry for myself, but I felt pretty lonely, and like at least half of me was missing.

# 39

Most of the trees in the woods were deciduous, and the drench poured through them as if they weren't there. Their saturated nakedness seemed to impart an inhospitable odour, too. As though they were scent-marking their time and place, and questioning my qualifications for standing there among them. They were otherwise as familiar to me as the weeping cartouche of my own crudely carved initials; but, although my arborglyphs confirmed our once cordial acquaintance, their carriers adamantly offered me no refuge, and looked and stank ragged, like shivering strangers in the rain.

For all the running in my mind, I was still only minutes from home and, with no realistic prospect of a successful abscondment, I descended further, Orpheus-like, into the intractable despair of my inescapable defeat. I had nowhere to go and no money to go there with. I was soaking wet and my hands had become so stiff and painful from the cold that I no longer tried to scare up even an attempt to hold the front of my jacket together. It wasn't anymore an unanswered question of whether I'd ever go back home again. It was only a matter now of how many more minutes I could hold out.

When I got back, I went straight up to my room and took off my wet clothes. My anguish dripped all around me, unnoticed, and my spontaneous attempt to escape into an ill-defined freedom remained justifiably interpreted by my house-mates as nothing more meaningful than a short walk in a downpour. I hadn't even been gone long enough for the atmosphere to have changed.

Through the watery tracery of my bedroom window, the rain looked harder than it had felt when I was wandering around in it. Some things you can almost get used to.

I was numb all over. It wasn't just from the cold. I was imprisoned like a traitor to myself. Banged up in solitary and tied to the rack of my misery with thumb screws on.

Downstairs, the TV spluttered RP belches of something stupefyingly self-important and grappled with a pervasive sombre Saturday afternoon malaise for someone's unengaged eye.

# 40

I never drank designer water; considering the fashion
pretentious and absurd. The only time I felt compelled
to subscribe, I bought a bottle of bleach by mistake.

My voice broke unangelically into a smattering of sad
smithereens in plenty of time to leave me barking around my
thirteenth birthday in a cacophonous croak. It happened in a
sudden thunderclap of misfortune, just like they said it
would. My singing days were over.

I tentatively embarked upon a new career as a tuneless
teenager, but my current of desolation had swollen just about
enough to imminently threaten the already dangerously
crumbling banks of my emotional reserves. I resigned from
the church choir and began to withdraw from the social life it
had provided. Night lasted longer. I felt profoundly
incomplete.

The foreign and ancient coin collection I had begun to
accumulate with the proceeds from service duties was now
destined to remain uncrowned.

The collection had been more than a hobby to me; it had
become my pet, and I had lovingly nourished it by making
excited weekly visits to a tiny philatelist and antiquities shop
on Pulteney Bridge and bringing back home for it expensive

little trinkets of mysterious treasures, long buried and unearthed after aeons of sleep.

I was fascinated by the timeworn relics that still carried the faded heads of mythical figures from my well-thumbed history books, and beguiled by thoughts of all the magical tales each piece could recount. My regular, affectionate stroking of every philosopher's stone conveyed me through golden periods of Byzantine, Roman and Greek history. Turned the base metal of my boredom into a treasury of mysterious times and places.

My modest hoard also lent me a sense of self. I was enthralled by the certainty that I, too, now counted in the multi-faceted narratives of their secret histories, and that my fingerprints had inextricably mingled with so many other anonymous or renowned characters who had written their own happy, sad or monumental chapters on their exchange.

But the unprotected trove, which typically perched like a miniature pirate chest on the top of my bedside cabinet, had already suffered serious attacks from my marauding mother, who had regularly plundered it of some of my favourites to feed the vending machines and parking meters she discovered she could cheat with surrogates of the appropriate size from my little silver-coloured casket. Sometimes the stolen artefact was the correct coin but an anomalous issue, or from a year when relatively few were minted.

I felt bereft by the abduction of my friends. Useless, too, to know they had been taken from me and lost for ever, and that I could do nothing to prevent their theft, or my trust from being so cynically abused. To repeatedly encounter the pain of my mother's pilfering, which of course, she denied. In the same way she invariably denied involvement in anything that suggested the possibility of human failure lurking furtively in the shadowy corridors of her character.

But it was more difficult for me to deny that the reality of having caught her in the act of maliciously fingering my collection had, in some irrevocable way, defiled it.

Her dismissive rebuttals also absolved her from the responsibility of offering to provide any manner of redress for her delinquent deeds, and no offers were made. She remained, as ever, staunchly unaffected by her incomprehensible meanness. The bastion of her conscience endured defiantly intact; unbreached by any acknowledgement of her swindling mendacity.

This was the same attitude she was planning to con the Lord and inveigle her way into Heaven with. The Almighty was a commoner, after all; He had fashioned us too perfectly in His own image, and she had begun to develop the same contempt for Him that she held in excess for everyone else. She had long since bullied Jesus into a humiliating submission with her blossoming assault on his thorny crown. Now it was God's turn.

Certainty is the seed of unknown fathers. Its bastard offspring too numberless to name.

As with all religions, my mother offered her disciples truth. Like all the other truths, it was different from all the other truths, which were at best untrue, and invariably insidious falsehoods. She marketed her truth in the same way all the other truths were marketed, and invited purchases of it in affordable instalments. She spoke about it enigmatically, as if it presented itself with an unambiguously recognisable face and would not deign to sully its integrity with vulgar definition. And having so far side-stepped the odd and usually no more than half-hearted attempt to ascertain the shape or nature of it when deflecting the mumbling inquiries of the curious by indignantly announcing that God would not subject Himself to the interrogation of fools, she likewise dismissively declared that His truth and other eschatological mysteries would be fully revealed to the proven worthy, prepared and paid up only on the last evening of all days.

However, a number of less negotiable commercial complications had arisen consequent to her reluctance to elaborate upon her secret to any significant extent, and it had become uncomfortably clear to her that as a matter of some urgency, she would need to provide at least a perfunctory general conversance of what her truth actually consisted of, and devise an imaginative and uniquely CHRISTian dogma to package and sell along with it.

For many weeks, my mother studiously pawed the incendiary pages of her clandestine library, vacillating between recipes for militant anarchism and social revolution, and Essenic, pre-Christian propensities for seductive hidden mysteries and secret knowledge. Meticulously combining the seductively aromatic flavours of each with an alphabet soup of Old and New Testament passages, and adding no more than a sprinkling of the secret instructions of Moses with a liberal pinch of both the Revelations of Enoch and the Gospel of Thomas to a subtly modified Masonic maceration, before eventually straining the entire concoction through a lesser satanic god-of-the-dead sieve and euphorically exclaiming to herself that the Lord had spoken and had instructed her to stop reading.

An almost unbroken period of zealous meandering through a panoply of paragraphs culminated with the much re-worked but finally completed ultimate draft of her inaugural edition of scripture, The Unclosable Eye, which bore the playfully ambiguous subtitle, Into the Arms of God.

The initial consignment of factory fresh boxes arrived directly from the printer's press several months later to an excited reception from my mother, who hastily sliced the top of the first open with the penknife she had cut my thigh with some months earlier when I used it without asking, to reveal a brilliant scarlet, laminated jacket, emblazoned with gold lettering, and a large, ovoid, lustrous black shield, framed on either side by a single, embossed, suggestively bloodied, upright scimitar with an angel wing hilt. Although it wasn't immediately obvious, the arrangement inventively formed the image of a stylised eyeball.

Our Heavenly Sister slid her hand inside the cardboard and coaxed the first tenderly out of the box, running her fingers over the full length of it as though it were the most venerated of holy relics.

She devoured its bloody body with a long, lecherous leer, before noticing me standing there, propped against the frame of the open door watching her, and proudly turning a few degrees to tilt the front cover towards me as if she were showing off a welcome newborn.

I improvised a not entirely generous, slightly awkward, off-centre smile and nodded with begrudging approval. It didn't feel quite right, but I wasn't sure what else to do.

She made no attempt to hand me the book for a closer inspection. Neither did I expect her to. It was hers, after all, and my touching it would have been anathema to her.

From where I stood, it looked appropriately impressive. Not particularly thick, but visually imposing and substantial, nevertheless. I masked my disappointment in a raised eyebrow and diplomatically resisted the temptation to snort dismissively.

'It looks OK,' I said, trying to flesh out my nod with a bit more approval. Even toying for an irrational moment with the idea of offering a cursory compliment.

An immediate reunion with my momentarily misplaced common sense prevented a calamity. I couldn't afford to be so generous and encourage her to attack me in some way via my inevitably perceived vulnerability. My opinion of her handiwork would have been irrelevant to her, anyway. And my reticence spared me the certain indignity of at least a contemptuous lecture.

She posed in front of the bay window, statuesque, throwing a rigid figure of shadow onto the carpet. Inspecting the back and front covers of the book over and over again. Caressing them both with uncharacteristic affection. Smoothing them with the edge of her hand, as though they were finest cashmere and she was brushing an invisible blanket of gold dust off them. The edges of her mouth softly rising like a tide.

As if rudely chilled by a sudden breeze, her back stiffened. She threw out her shoulders and raised her head to stare something that wasn't there in the eye; tightening her grip on the book and squeezing the body of it hard enough for the pressure of her clasp to whiten her knuckles. Then, peeling apart the semi-rigid cardboard covers, she flicked rapidly through the pages, front to back, two or three times; the familiar, evocative, sweet peppery scent of new paper rising like ceremonial incense to permeate the flaring aisles of her nostrils. As she drew in her breath, deeply enough to stamp the flickering Gothic typeface on her lungs, she gurned one of her peculiarly earnest faces. Grotesque, of course, but not one I had seen before. Constructed, no doubt from errant elements of pride, and inflated to the brim of all out hideousness by the irrefutable proof that she had single-handedly devised an audacious challenge to the Orthodox King James. But there was something else there, too, nestling amid the myriad rubbery contours of her moue; it wasn't an expression of the same obscene consummate smugness I was so accustomed to turning nauseously away from. It was icier. Stonier than that. The sort of face a petulant young Edward the Sixth might have met the Prayer Book Rebellion with. And although it wasn't easy to ascertain exactly which fantasy lay concealed beneath the curious countenance, it seemed, from where I was standing, as though she were holding an imaginary weapon over the wounded body of an unarmed adversary, and it wasn't mercy that was running through her mind.

## 42

The seven or eight second Sunday regulars seeped like a watery ingress into the oak-beamed belly of the house through the open back door as usual, to be unexpectedly greeted by a debuting display of The Unclosable Eye, spread out like a rosy picnic on the refectory table before them.

An animated babble hastily ensued, led by recurrent interjections from my doctrine-laden mother, who had been careful to strike a meticulous balance between sober, leaderly composure and infectious vivacity, as she handed her volume of scripture to each of the assembled.

The Moorcroft Leaf and Berry collection dish, deliberately selected for its shallow shape which my mother correctly calculated would more effectively encourage the donation of paper currency, was almost full before the service began.

And for the first time, the afternoon's formalities opened with a passage from the Sacred sayings of CHRIST.

Following a gallimaufry of motivational pleasantries, my mother parted the swirling Red Sea of her pages and announced that she would open with a short offering from the Epistle of Jude.

Pausing over the text momentarily to further reinforce the already palpable sense of momentous occasion, and adroitly contributing to the heightening dramatic tension by flashing a lingering glower of calculating scrutiny into the fixated eyes of her expectant congregation, she began to read with the modulated steeliness of a call to arms: '"Enoch also, the seventh from Adam, prophesied of these, saying, Behold, the Lord cometh with ten thousands of his saints, to execute judgement upon all, and to convince all that are ungodly among them of all their ungodly deeds which they have ungodly committed, and of all their hard speeches which ungodly sinners have spoken against Him."'

It was a groundbreaking moment, which preceded an extended hallowed hush among the assembled, as they slowly set like mortar beneath the jurisdictive weight of printed words.

Proceedings were rounded an hour or so later, in an almost party-like atmosphere of elation, with a stirring rendition of Onward Christian Soldiers, and a pledge to be prepared when the Holy Call came.

# 43

Faith is an unforgiving mentor.

It was difficult for me to feel overjoyed about my mother's recently found status as a spiritual doyenne. I had wanted her insufferable hubris and canting to be destructively challenged, not endorsed by fawning adulation.

I was disappointed, too, by the recent cessation of my father's acerbic comments, and it was beginning to bother me that he may be growing not only more tolerant of my mother's ministry, but sympathetic towards it. I had no firmer evidence to support my growing concern than an uncomfortable hunch, but it was based on a noticeable shift in his attitude towards her that I was anxious to keep my eye on with a view to confronting him about.

I kept thinking about it during the dire monotonony of my newly acquired paper-round before school, as I poked Western Dailies through a hundred brass letter boxes in the pre-dawn drizzle.

What the hell would happen if my father *did* get roped into this? I really would feel orphaned. Somehow, it seemed the potential for such a scenario had grown since my withdrawal from the church choir and my growing alienation from the effervescent, pocket sized circle of ready made distractions it had provided me with.

I had stopped calling in at the vicarage altogether by now and barely saw any of the old friends I had made there. Unable to part ways with the feeling that I'd relinquished the right to continue my association with either the place or its enviably able affiliates, my social life, consequently, with one or two occasional exceptions, pretty much consisted of putting up with my own dour and uncooperative company. It was driving me mad.

I had dressed to impress in a fake-fur-collared jumble sale car-coat, and taken myself on a late January mid-evening out to the unremarkable, free-to-enter side-street attractions in the village surrounding the house, for an imaginative sightseeing amble through the otherwise deserted neighbourhood. The purring, cuculated, flickering starry darkness a familiar backdrop. The night was bitter-as-a-mouthful-of-wormwood cold and cadaverously still in the bone-gnawing chill, as though almost everything under the sky was too frozen to shiver. I felt that even my languorous locomotion was incongruously intruding upon it, like an impervious drunk cackling at his old joke through a funeral; its overweight silence amplifying even the most uninsistent of sounds. In the eerie calm, I could hear my thoughts rustle around like leaves in the lanes.

The gut-searing loneliness of shuffling homeward accompanied me so closely that I felt like the last person alive when I arrived at our black painted wrought iron gate, suspended nebulous in a light gauze of mist. I approached the scaffold of our reunion with intensifying trepidation.

The toffee-apple moon howled over the garden like a black dog's eye. An emerging noose of back porch nodded ominously towards me. And in an arctic gust of biting irrationality, right out of nowhere, I imagined letting myself into the house to discover that both my parents had morphed into vampires and were poised to puncture my jugular the moment I set foot through the door. Halfway up the garden path, the maturating fixation slowed my faltering steps to a crawl. Even then, I still just about held on to the fading belief that the scenario was unlikely to unfold. But the closer I shuffled to the house, the more anxious I became. And by the time I folded my bluing fingers around the freezing black iron butterfly door-handle, I had become so engrossed in and affected by my lamian reverie that I couldn't bring myself to turn it. I hung around outside for a few moments, trying to work out how I would beat them off or get away. Then, for the next moment or two, weighing up what I'd really lose if I couldn't.

I hadn't seen the gush of this sudden phobia coming, having rarely been troubled by Hammer Horror style scenes of supernatural fantasies. The mortifying prospect of encountering familial members of the marauding undead had never really featured among my previous concerns, and this notion had played out in my head without any obvious provocation. I was still several years away from having read Freud.

Only days before, I'd badgered most of the newsagents within the general locality for a job, and managed to land the much wished-for paper round to compensate for the loss of my regular income from choir singing. The timing of my quest motivated by the desire to buy something memorable for my mother's forty-third birthday, which was now less than a month away.

I had recently come up with the hair-brained idea of presenting her with something special; a keepsake which conveyed a sentiment that words would not. A small but meaningful token of pronouncement.

It was a deeply quixotic sentiment; childishly rash and infinitely less than well conceived. A mire of crass poetic quicksand I somehow happened to get sucked into by entertaining the improbable notion of impressing her with my maturity, extending an olive branch and establishing a new, productive chapter in our impossibly antipathetic relationship.

Despite the derisive chorus of incredulous caveats baying like bloodhounds in my brain, I went ahead and did it, anyway. Determined that one of us should make the first move to establish a new era of cooperation and respect.

Less than a week before the big day, I enthusiastically launched myself into the formidable assignment of tracking down something appropriate, and decided, after hours of fruitlessly wandering around town, to spend almost the whole of my first three week's wages on an Italian blown glass ornament I had found at the last moment in one of the smarter department stores there.

The store had been moments from closing when, just as I was leaving, and resigned to failure, I fortuitously glanced back at a display I had somehow missed on my way in and spied the shapely object sitting like a phoenix rising from a blaze of electric light through a microscopic rain of afternoon ash on the far end of a translucent shelf by the door. It caught my attention immediately. Glowing ethereal in the spotlight, I thought it beautiful. The colourful array and Amarna Fish-like arrangement of its reds, yellows, deep inky and midnight blues appealed to me immediately. The classical form, too; reminiscent of an ancient Greek amphora with twin handles, like avian wings, but with a broad, deep, globular base, seemed just right. An impatient assistant reluctantly lifted it off the shelf and onto the counter, where the sales girl there offered me a free smile.

She packed it into the smart blue box alongside it, with the manufacturer's name indented in glittering antique gold lettering on the front, which I decided straight away didn't look nearly presentational enough for the purpose. The following Monday, I dressed the whole thing up in more appropriate, specially selected hand made and printed bright red wrapping paper with sweeping, bold flower shapes on it which just about convincingly resembled my mother's own garden grown favourite dahlias.

A few days later, in the dawn of the celebratory morning, I cycled home from my paper round in time to catch my mother disappearing half dressed under an open gown into the bathroom.

It was unusual to see her stomping around the house so early, and immediately obvious that my plan for her to be sensitively roused by my well-wishes and thoroughly delighted by my unexpected presentation was already in dire straits. Nevertheless, exhibiting the maturity I was keen to impress her with, I buried my disappointment beneath an improvised decision to be almost as happy to take things as they came, and promptly collected the package from my bedside cabinet before going back downstairs to make some toast and wait for her to re-emerge.

'Happy birthday, Mum', I chirruped, with clinically uncontaminated goodwill, beaming and proud, as I ran up the stairs with the vibrant cube of her present extended in front of me like a relay baton.

Approaching the summit of the flight, I motioned to her to accept the wrapped and ribboned box, as she inexplicably stood rooted to the same few feet of landing, expressionless, and without speaking or making any attempt to move either of her arms towards me. Then, all at once, in exactly the moment I caught my breath as I came to a rest at the top of the stairs, with the determined alacrity of a second slip aiming a run-out, she abruptly snatched the parcel from my hand and without pause, threw it forcibly past me down the stairs and onto the alabaster tiled hall floor, missing the only improbable cushion of the low-piled antique Caucasian runner by several feet.

'I don't want anything from you,' she announced, icily, as she abruptly about-turned and strode dispassionately away into the soft tangerine lamplight of her bedroom, without a second glance.

She could have stabbed me in the face. I knew the little glass ornament had broken.

# 44

It was some time before I felt able to pick up the unopened package and give it a confirmatory shake. I had, of course, anticipated hearing the inevitable rattle of fragmented glass, but was still unreasonably hoping for a less predictable outcome.

I hurt like I had been attacked from behind; the pain of the assault more grievous for its unforeseen delivery.

Feeling the full weight of my lumbering footsteps, I carried the overdressed parcel, that had now wilted into a floral wreath of incongruous uselessness, to the kitchen at the end of the hall, and dropped it like a dead baby into the bin. Impotently attempting to make an iota of sense from the gratuitous butchery of my emotions.

The incident continued to swim around in my head for hours, like an Olympic crawler, while I waited for the euthanising intervention of passing time to drown it.

I can't remember if I lost my whole day in tenebrific reflection or in unfathomable confusion over my mother's cheerful indifference to her own brutality but, within hours, she denied having behaved badly and accused me of heartless abuse when I sought clarification.

She brushed the light dust of the subject off her conscience easily, in the same nonchalant way she typically did anything that exposed her to the risk of criticism. And although I had haplessly played opposite the same actress a thousand times, it was almost impossible for me to understand how she could so effortlessly detach herself from the consequences of her actions and be so completely unaffected by them.

On this occasion, she assured me that everything had been forgotten and forgiven, flippantly dismissing my bleeding sorrow as a grudge I chose to carry in order to happily remain miserable. But *I* can't forget so easily. And although the ink has faded now, I still feel the sting of the bugpin she pierced me with on that day.

Maybe she's right. It probably *is* healthier not to dwell for an entire childhood on the vagaries of such imponderables. But it's more difficult to be unaware that the pain of them has produced a hissing puncture in your soul, and whether you think about it or not, you know damn well that you won't stop looking for something to plug it with.

And I do think of it. Even now. It still circles like a rotor blade at the spearhead of its ravening pack, sizing up the slicing of another meal of me when I sneak up for air. I don't want to see it there, but I do. I'm as constantly exposed to the predation of it as I am to the bared teeth of the untold times I've lain awake in the punishing dark knowing that I should have been asleep ages ago. Flagging down my endlessly lapping, overactive brain on the greasy track of racing through the day's events and replaying them over and over again. Rewriting the script to the advantage of every possible eventuality and juxtaposing the groan of the real with the howl of the wished for. Until I restlessly roll away the millstone of my agonising hours, grinding from side to side on the impossible bed of it all, wishing the day had never arrived in the first place to leave me feeling so incurably bereft; cursing the ghost of morning because the dead of night just won't lie down.

Decades later, one of the Rolling Stones advised me, when we thought we had migrated from poetry and into the realm of keeping each other amused with a melody of more prosaic complaints about our respective plagues of insomnia, to 'always take your own pillow with you wherever you go, mate, it's one of the few things in this life that won't let you down.' At the time, for someone who generally travelled with an overnight bag on a train, I thought it possibly useful, if ultimately impracticably difficult advice to implement unless, like he probably did, you have someone else to carry your bedding around for you. I realise now, the full good sense and value of it. But it took me years to find a metaphor of my own that I could plump up enough to sleep on.

## 45

Suffering, too, is born from song; our prophets have intoxicated us with words.

My refuge from discomposure was, as usual, in music. Playing the guitar my father had bought me for my ninth Christmas, after a several month long programme of sustained imploring finally paid off, or listening to it on the radio.

Whenever I was able to, I'd air my modest, left-field record collection, salvaged mostly from racks of inexpensive miscellany outside downbeat second hand shops in un-fashionable parts of town, on the radiogram in the sitting room. I'd play them as loud as the thing would let me before distorting into a shrieking complaint, which generally corresponded to about the same time that both my parents would howl an agitated, improvised, antiphonal, synco-pated, free time chorus of *'turn it down!'* in impressively antipathetic two part disharmony.

The few good friends I kept were a year or two older than me, and entertained musical aspirations of their own. I learned from introductions to some of the more obscure albums in their collections. Wonderful things, that imbued me with life and excitement. The discovery of each novel, unpredicted chord sequence or phrase resolution felt like opening an unviolated tomb in the Valley of the Kings.

Piggy and Earwig were my schoolmate drum and bass rhythm section of a more hopeful than accomplished three-piece blues combo I fortuitously formed informally when my boogie woogie piano playing partner took to using a simultaneous combination of Fuzz Face and Wah Wah pedals on a pre-modulated electric organ and invented some Sly Stone on even more acid kind of psychedelic ballpark funk.

At the time, it was a departure too far from playing my beloved acoustic blues, so, dear, sweet, Blower, who I had met quite auspiciously and liked immediately when both of us struck up a twelve-bar while auditioning different instruments in a local music shop, with much sadness, was obliged to depart by mutual consent.

It was a huge regret that I wasn't able to persuade him out of his impassioned sojourn into the avant garde for long enough to continue with the few hours of jamming in the Octagon Gallery on a Saturday morning that I had enjoyed so much for the previous few months. But his mind had been made up, and his long blonde hair-covered back remained resolutely turned on our short-lived dalliance with the immortal Cow Cow Davenport, Leroy Carr, Little Brother Montgomery, et al, and he never relented.

We stayed on good terms for a few more years; time enough for me to develop my own love of the off the wall, too. But we gradually saw less and less of each other and drifted apart in a strangely opaque ocean, over which we could still occasionally notice each other bobbing and diving about, but in which we also somehow seemed to progressively forget how to speak. As though we had become inextricably trapped in the pull of divergent currents, and could only then communicate over an undertow of deviating time signatures with a nod or a wave; each of us conscious of being inexorably swept into different keys while still clutching one or two well spun cassette tapes as souvenirs of our collaborative musical endeavours.

It's true, the joke about the difference between a drum machine and a drummer being that you only need to punch the information into the drum machine once. It's also probably not far off the beat to say that Piggy was pretty comprehensively hopeless, and seemed to resent creating anything percussive at all; opting instead to spend most of his time behind the kit meticulously fiddling about with the wing nut on his hi-hat. Not only that, but there's a natural limit to how many times you can meaningfully explain basic patterns and fills to a dumbbell. Anyway, the whole thing fell apart completely when Earwig crashed his new motor bike around a year later and lost his arm. I heard it was bad, so I was pretty apprehensive when I called on him as soon as visitors were allowed to see him in intensive care, a couple of days after it happened. I wasn't prepared. I didn't recognise him.

Stepping into the bleached intensity of the shrine to Earwig's lost normality, the obliviously ambling ripple of people outside the window in the blossoming April air seemed incongruous.

Sitting there for half an hour, holding Earwig's only hand, trying not to inhale the wounded, nauseating smell of hospital, and gazing with morbidly fascinated incredulity at the pinned, plaster-cast, stitched and bloodily punctuated enormity of his physical destruction, I was saddened in a way I hadn't expected. And after the initial horror of the spectacle had slipped into a kind of acceptance, I became acutely aware of and moved by my feelings of affection for the boy on the bed, whose deconstructed face had looked so fresh a few days before.

In those readjustive moments, I found a new facet of friendship. But sitting next to him, unable to do anything to help alleviate his barely conscious state of indefectible helplessness, I felt my own enfeeblement compounded by the certainty of knowing that even if I could have foreseen the consequences and warned him of them, I never would have succeeded in talking him out of taking that ride.

# 46

The constancy of every world is stolen by a moment of fortune.

Maybe the simple truth of it all is that we don't choose the air we breathe. But that we involuntarily remain forever indissolubly wedded to the umbilicus of our fate and there's not a thing we can do about it. It's an encouragingly less catastrophically hopeful alternative to the reality of grafting for everything we have, only to be left at the end of it all with the unappeasable need to explain to ourselves why everyone else seems to have got their hands on so much more than us without ever having worked half as hard for it as we did.

So what do we do? We fatalistically philosophise like suggestible simpletons to soften the crippling impact of our failure.

Maybe, if we can ever manage to summon the required degree of conviction and shrug hard enough when we're putting it all down to fate, we might just break our necks with the effort and end it all there in a moment of mercy. More likely, we'll end up throwing our arms in the air and pathetically accepting that it's all been inalterably ordained. Even I could probably suck enough of my atonement from the seductive poison of that spring if I could stop chasing the tail of my accountability for long enough to be convinced by it.

Trouble is, who the hell really writes everything down to fate *honestly*? I mean, you optimistically yank the one-size-fits-all fate excuse from off the top of your list of options and try to wrap it around you like a shroud, but you can't quite pull the fragile body of it all the way over your corpulent guilt. So you still wind up with a significant part of your distended conscience perpetually exposed to the needling conviction that you could have done that bit more to avoid drowning in all the vomit of bitterness you're up to your teeth in.

However much you run around on the tracks of your vicious circles, you can't escape the inevitability of frantically philosophising away the swaying gallows of your all-too-conspicuous inadequacies, anyway.

I'm so sick of the smug bullshit of philosophy. It's as pointlessly insidious and malignant as religion. They're practically incestuous bedfellows, anyway. All you can really know for certain is that one of them is going to get you in the end. There are no extenuating circumstances. If God doesn't finish you off, you can be sure as hell the cancer of philosophy will.

My mother was working diligently on the former, as she announced that services would now be held on every Sunday afternoon since the paying congregation of CHRIST had risen to around twenty regulars. It had also become impossible for her to ignore the steadily balding reality that her Church was practically outgrowing its current facilities and badly needed to relocate to larger premises.

Following the collapse of a number of inappropriate and

186

inevitably doomed to fail negotiations with improbable proprietors and their agents, satisfaction was eventually delivered in the form of a tired if not appreciably run down building on the western fringes of the city, which offered meagre but adequate facilities including a large room, small kitchen and single lavatory, above a disused bakery, for a peppercorn rent.

It was a pivotal move. The maturing Church of CHRIST had now not only fledged but, for the unprincely sum of ten pounds a week, visibly stamped its dubious credentials on the indifferent green flesh of the local landscape.

The acquisition of its impressive new profile necessitated the addition of a dedicated telephone line for the Church at home. And CHRIST, for the first time, boldly announced itself formally on authoritative, pale yellow, regional telephone directory paper as a viable institution of worship alongside a familiar host of its unsuspecting rivals. And a credible alternative to the complacently peace-loving and over-watery mainstream.

# 47

We continually pledge our undying fidelity to words. They in turn remain constant to us in their untameable faithlessness.

There invariably seems to be something distinctly unpalatable about the indiscreet over-excitement of other people in public. An unpalatability which runs rapidly to offence when the uncontained elation extends beyond the excited party's initial obliviousness to their effect upon outsiders, and into a territory where the effect becomes not only noticeable to the offender but, from there on, is consciously employed increasingly as a weapon of assault.

My indomitable mother's smirk, which had become indelibly stained with the same insufferably effusive and unchecked self-infatuated excitement, had been quite inexplicably mistaken for a smile by a well-built, conservatively dressed, red-headed chap in his early thirties, who had been perched against a wall by the Roman Baths, licking an ice-cream.

My mother abruptly recalibrated the communicable shade of her dour demeanour in the manner of a second hand car dealing chameleon and replied to his genial beam by spontaneously announcing, somewhat confessionally, that she wouldn't mind a lick herself. A short but sparkling fountain of banter frivolously extended the topical subject of frozen confectionery before a brief, significantly wordless demarcating though still genially smiling thaw was politely signalled to conclude the initial dairy based portion of their discourse, and the aptly emolliating introductory theme was expeditiously exhausted in favour of directing the conference more profitably into other areas of outstanding natural interest.

A captivating account of the chap's working life as a relatively locally stationed army captain, whose key professional duties included the tactical responsibility for operations on the ground and the maintenance of an appreciable inventory of combat equipment, ensued. Without missing a beat of rapidly pulsating opportunity, my immediately attentive mother chirped cheerfully in with a honey-pot of enthusiastic remarks concerning the hefty bolt action of the P14 and its unusually long travel. She also said something complimentary about its Model 98 Mauser type claw extractor and forward lugs, but didn't dwell overly on the rifle's ergonomics in order to allow the soldier an early opportunity to seize the bait. Which he obligingly did by grinningly dismissing the firearm as a practically fossilised relic of the great war that, in his opinion, even then had been ultimately let down by its weight and lack of wind drift correction.

'It saw us through two wars reliably enough,' my mother volleyed back at him, defending the weapon with a ballistic glare, which softened almost immediately to a playful pout that successfully inspired the captain to promptly moderate his criticisms by admitting it had been a generally useful and pretty well designed rapid firer, nevertheless.

'Accurate, too,' my mother added, throwing most of her emphasis into a less discernibly flirty nod, 'it was a far better sniper's weapon than the Mark Three.'

The soldier cautiously weighed the curious invitation to embrace something he was unsure of behind a protrusively admiring, slowly head-nodding, slightly taken aback, lower-lip-jutting mien of approval.

'I wouldn't have thought you'd know much about guns,' he said, pulling a handkerchief from his trouser pocket and wiping the creamed corner of his broad smile with the fold of it. 'What makes you the expert?'

'Oh, I'm not an expert at all; my father left me the Enfield when he passed on,' she lied, glibly, with a supporting shrug, 'he used one in the Home Guard and bought a decom after the war as a souvenir. He had a great fondness for it.'

'Ah, well, that's quite understandable,' the soldier conceded, in a more sympathetic tone, 'the P14 was your dad's friend, then?'

'Yes, I suppose it was. I think he must have wanted it to be mine, too.'

'Well, let's hope you never have the same need for it,' said the soldier, softly, as he replaced the handkerchief into the pocket of his linen trousers and rustled a nest of loose change, as if signalling an imminent intention to wander off and buy something.

'We're living in the last days,' my mother declared, in a kind of wistfully matter of fact way, half shrugging again to convey an iron cast confidence in her assertion, and her resigned attitude to the approaching spectre of Armageddon. The bait remained unseized this time, but fingered lightly with a quizzical glance.

'I mean, look at the Cuban missile crisis eleven years ago,' she continued, besotted with the plainchant of her complaint, 'it nearly finished us all off. It's only a question of time, isn't it? They say we won't see out the century. The whole civilised world's living under the shadow of the bomb. Well, *you* must know that.'

The soldier raised his rubicund head in a moment of quiet reflection and squinted, as though diligently counting a constellation of invisible stars in the summer afternoon sunshine. 'I'm not sure I agree with you. About the world being civilised,' he smiled, 'two tours of duty in the last three years is enough to make me wonder about that.'

'Then you know first hand how iniquitous the divisions of religion can be,' she coaxed, tightening the screw and widening her interrogative eyes in anticipation of an emboldening reply.

'The oppression of dissent's always going to stimulate conflict in the end,' the soldier non-committally retorted, brushing the short cropped side of his head with his open fingers, as if to casually sweep the subject away.

'Yes, but isn't that how it ought to be if the voices of the disaffected continue to be ignored?' my mother insisted. 'Shouldn't the self-serving social and political elite be at least forced to pay a price for their undeserved privileges?'

'Are you a revolutionary?' the captain joked, hoping to diffuse a sudden tension arising from the directional change in my mother's meanderings.

'I don't think it's necessary to be a revolutionary in order to wish for a little more justice and fairness in the world, do you? Have compassion and equality become such subversive concepts?'

The soldier drew an exaggerated breath through his closed teeth to occupy the few vital seconds between deciding

191

whether to reply to my mother's inquisition or make his excuses and end the conversation with an expedient word of farewell.

'I don't know,' he confessed, quietly, offering an apologetic shrug of his own, 'all I can say is that human nature doesn't seem to change very much. The history of mankind is riddled with greed and conflicts between oppressors and oppressed, who merely change positions at the end of them. I'm not saying there's anything wrong with being idealistic; ideals are OK, they just always manage to stay a bit beyond our reach, don't they?'

'It doesn't have to be that way; it *is* possible to change things, you know, if you want to.'

My mother's eyes slithered around him like a slowly rising cobra sizing up an unsuspecting lizard, licking the appetising scent in the air around his fleshy words for a beckoning taste of vulnerability. 'Wouldn't you prefer that all people were equal to each other, and that the poor were not just used as an expendable commodity to further line the pockets of the rich?'

The captain shuffled his feet slightly to place his weight onto one leg, whilst scratching a reply from his throat with a fingernail.

'Then where would the chain of command be,' he mused, 'when you discover that equality hasn't been enough for some people, and you now need to act decisively to contain their unneighbourly ambitions? What then? Anarchy? Mayhem? I suspect we only really aspire to ideals of equality when we envy somebody else's advantages. I suppose a cynic might call that jealousy, mightn't they? And there's very little virtue in jealousy. It's the cause of far too much trouble.'

My mother shuffled both feet inadvertently, and although

192

momentarily tempted to reply, remained silent, and satisfied her need to respond by briefly opening and closing her mouth.

'So, I suppose we need to be careful not to expose our grudges too much, and try to dress all our envy up in something that looks a bit less disparaging and a lot more virtuous. Like a social conscience, for example,' the soldier continued, confidently, 'you can hide almost anything behind an appropriate concern. It's all a matter of presenting weakness as an illusion of strength, isn't it?' he smiled, standing slightly taller to announce his arrival at the conclusion of his discourse, and subtly communicate the satisfaction of his tactical advantage. 'We might call it a kind of smoke screening', he added, efficaciously.

The limbering swagger of my mother's anticipated attack slithered feebly away into a bungling submission. Then, fixing her stare on an imaginary semi-distant distraction, she prepared herself for a sobering retreat and the consolation of an easier assault on less resilient prey.

'Well, God will have the final word on the matter,' she declared, defiantly, with one of her firing squad smiles, fishing desperately for a corroborative canonical quotation while enduring the excruciating additional ignominy of drawing a deafeningly frustrating blank.

She was accustomed to being casually rejected, but not so subtly outsmarted. And in the enforced dumbness of a reflexive chewing of her cheek, as though it would somehow provide the face-saving relief of a conveniently situated cyanide pill, she sullenly denounced her cringing artlessness as preposterously unchecked excitement, and her puerile fluster as being unworthy of occupying a place in the emotional repertoire of any sensible woman, let alone one of such an exalted position.

Overflowing with the bile of self-contempt, she silently rebuked herself as she might an aberrant schoolgirl for having been so easily seduced by the proximity of a potential armoury of support for her as yet unannounced programme of spiritual reckoning.

A moment later, blaming the effect of the unseasonably warm sun for a temporary lapse of judgement, she attempted to expel the taste of her abashment in the breezy, cavernous near silence of a softly billowing sigh. It didn't work. She inhaled sharply. Seething with the impulse to upset somebody. To regain the familiar, comforting, full-bodied form of her self-satisfied sneer. If it had been possible to vomit the nauseating broth of her unbearable blunder away over every pointless passer by in the vicinity of the Abbey Churchyard, the flagstones would have been awash.

'It's a difficult word to understand, equality,' continued the victor, embarking upon his lap of honour, 'I've never really been sure of what it means when it's applied to things that can never be equal. It's funny, isn't it, how we use words with no contextual definition to describe ideas so abstract that they defy description.'

'It's the nature of language,' my mother capitulated, vaguely, re-emerging from the void of her disheartened suspiration with a marginally more convivial smile, 'I suppose we have to admire it's willingness to lead the parade without necessarily being able to see where it's going.'

The soldier politely indulged my mother with half a moment of sympathetic hush, then expeditiously threw his head back and laughed an unreserved, open, good-natured laugh, and my mother forgot herself for a moment and laughed along with him. It was an instant of harmonic confluence in which the previously gaping space between two facing armies narrowed to the tender edge of an unguarded eye.

An instant which had indeed exposed a vulnerability. Not in the captain, but in my mother, who, for a few seconds of unexpected ecdysis, stepped deftly out of her skin and became a woman.

The thunderstorm of laughter had cleared the air so precipitously that my mother no longer wished to vomit or spit, and instead sought to continue a conversation with the man indisputably her junior by a decade or more, but for whom she had reluctantly allowed herself to develop an unfamiliar flickering of attraction.

Within the sudden artless nervousness of the moment, and without knowing exactly what to say, she attempted a jumbled rush of words but articulated nothing more meaningful than another half-coughed sigh through the hangover of her smile.

'Would you like to join me for a coffee?' she eventually chirped, buoyantly, with both eyes appealing in a fanfare at full volume.

'I'd love to,' the soldier replied, glancing at the blued steel sword hands of his oversized wristwatch, 'but I'm afraid I'm expected at the Empire for an engagement in around ten minutes. It was very nice to meet you, though. Try not to do too much damage with that P14,' he smiled.

My mother made no such assurances, but wistfully returned both the compliment and the smile, and motionlessly followed his determined strut past the well populated lace windowed tea rooms on the corner of Abbey Green, before watching him, along with the rapidly fading embers of her fleetingly anticipated adventure disappear into

195

the little black hole of street traffic milling down to the river.

The unexpected breeze of the experience had ruffled her, and effected an obvious partial collapse in her usually unassailable stately house of cards that she was anxious to repair and forget about as quickly as possible. And before anyone else could notice.

As a small plume of prematurely migrating swallows billowed through her exposed rafters, the quieting flutter of unspoken words taking flight into suddenly darkening skies left her now feeling simultaneously exhilarated and peculiarly empty. She stood rooted in her disorientation, vacillating for a moment, like a stump-footed pigeon contemplating a wounded hobble to a more propitious location. Then she peered studiously around the square for an invitingly different, disengaged soul offering tit-bits to the birds.

# 48

I invariably reflect at extraordinary lengths to make absolutely certain that I don't overthink things.

My mother's interpretation of the concept of romance seldom deviated from the fictional poverty she had lovingly written into the narrative of her domestic circumstances. Who knows how many other unlikely encounters she may have harboured the memory of in the occasional defrosting of her otherwise bullet-proof pack ice?

She had, of course, at some point encountered my father, but I had never actually seen her offer him even the smallest, stalest crumb of somatic tenderness. Nor, must it be said in fairness to her, did I ever once notice my father as much as kiss my mother's cheek or attempt to take her hand. It was as though both my eminently distant but somehow still attached parents preferred the abstruse badinage of insult sparring to the explicit language of a more physical affection. At their rarely seen best and most personable, they invariably presented themselves as newly-mets, unsure of their inherent suitability and grappling with the circumstantial logistics of how to clinch that awkward first kiss.

Questions on the subject of whether the same frosty detachment persisted between the flyless walls of their bedroom remained. Although a clandestine intimacy that belied the institution of their apparent aversion to each other seemed unlikely.

Television programmes containing nudity, or even innocuous references to typically concealed areas of the human body were, as far as my mother was publicly concerned, anathema in any context. Lascivious and depraved. Her official line on such debased entertainment was that it was prurient filth, sacrilegiously broadcast from the bowels of Hell by messengers of the Devil.

The same near-hysterical reaction invariably sprang like an uncovered asp from her exposure to the most banal conversational references to pregnancy or any other loosely related reproductive subject matter of concern to any member of the animal kingdom large or small.

The mere mention of the word *sex* would invariably draw an animated reaction akin to that which a naked young glamour model cat-fighting off the lecherous advances of a longboat crew of Saturnalian Vikings might offer.

Fortunately for her, however, such hysterical states of nervous collapse depended entirely upon the presence of other people for sustenance, and therefore lacked any real power to prevent her from savouring the forbidden fruits of salacious late night programmes or dramas in the comfort of her own less critical company when my father had retired from the sitting room to bed, and when I had followed soon after on her morally superior instructions.

There, in a heightened state of furtive curiosity, she would sit engrossed, having reduced the television volume to a level that ensured her secret indulgence would remain undetected from the bedrooms.

The inaccessible world of romantic fiction intrigued her. A

fascination that would often lead her to lift erotically covered novels surreptitiously from the shelves of shops and flick through the pages with a disinterested expression, as though she were studying the typeface or something, in the possible event of being caught in the act when she thought nobody was looking.

Romance, however, was not the most notable feature of the programme purring out of the TV when I sneaked down one night to catch her red-handed in the act of blowing her fingertips through a shockumentary that left obscenity trailing like a discarded negligee in the dust.

I perched uncomfortably on the unusually bony arm of the sofa and watched his victims tearfully reminisce about the Angel of Death's butcherous indulgences on young women, pregnant and otherwise, in the horrific secrecy of an infamous Nazi death camp.

Initially presuming my mother to be as appalled as I was, I soon realised that little in her demeanour supported my assumption.

She didn't appear to have noticed me at all until a belated microscopic turn of her head confirmed the clocking of my presence. But she made no attempt to switch the programme over or off and seemed content to allow me to share it with her. Instead of bemoaning the intrusion, she casually glanced occasionally up at the screen over a picket fence of vertically extended fingers, between frequent periods of meticulously inspecting her nails.

She could as easily have been watching Disney cartoons. She didn't cry, or sigh, or gasp, or groan, but carried on filing and buffing, while a half-eaten crustless ham and cucumber sandwich occupied a floral plate on the arm of her chair.

Her insouciance distracted me. I sat through a few more

minutes of of it while being gradually distracted from the screen, before realising that I could stomach no more of either feature. I stood up to leave the room, dropping an inadvertent obscenity like a contemptuous fart on my way and trailing my less than impressed opinion of her behind me.

She parried my outrage with indifference. Then, abruptly disguising a flinch as a shiver, pulled an affronted attitude around her like a comfort blanket; tutting and clicking her tongue flippantly in a supercilious manner, as she had throughout the few minutes of programme I had watched, and declared defiantly that if the assaulted women had placed more faith in the Lord, none of it would ever have happened. I was then indignantly ordered to bed in a sudden change of attitude, and impatiently advised that the documentary was of little more significance than any other form of entertainment. Adding, like a rap on the back of the legs from a bamboo cane, that I, a child of such tender and unworldly years, couldn't possibly have understood any of it, anyway.

Infuriated by the audacity of her dismissive rebuke, I made it to the door without realising she may have had a point. That the sickening footage may have resonated with her in a way I hadn't appreciated. That it may in some way have addressed her need to understand or rationalise the apparently ubiquitous presence of evil. That she may simply have been contemplating the reality of how acceptably such inhuman acts of brutality can irrigate an entire landscape of cultural normality when collective popular perceptions are distorted by a politically fabricated hatred and intolerance of differences.

As unhappy as the incident had left me, I would have

been glad to apologise to her for my misapprehension, had I been mistaken. But my experience of her indifference to the pain of others suggested otherwise.

She made no further comment as I left the room, but planted one of her imbecilic smiles on her face, then stuffed another mouthful of sandwich into it.

I couldn't sleep. Unable to rest comfortably on such springs of disgust.

Eventually, in an attempt to devise some form of usable soporific, I considered the possibility that my presumption had been unfair, and that beneath the carapace of her contrived detachment, a heart human enough to empathise, to feel some kindred need to surrogately experience such untellable depravity, bled profusely for such suffering.


The Abbey Churchyard frequently attracted the pilgrimages of lonely and offbeat characters who occupied the neat perimeter lines of well varnished, wooden, drunk-bearing benches to scatter handfuls of grain for the avian parasites lunching others would unappreciatively shoo away with a tentative kick and the spasmodic fling of a sandwich-shielding handbag or elbow.

Among the many habitually revisited proselytising patches, the Churchyard had earned its distinction of favourite by typically responding particularly well to Our Heavenly Sister's predatory stalks and rattles, and had continued to obligingly provide upon its copious oak benching the visibly exposed but crucially affluent emotional remains of some vulnerable resident from an expensive nearby property, whom she could effortlessly espy from some considerable distance and salivatingly swoop with primed talons unsparingly down upon like a vulture. Having dragooned two of her Church members from the biddable ranks of this irregular pest catering corps to date, she was keen to expand their burgeoning number.

# 49

Wishes are the footprints of grief.

In the case of Edward Charles, my mother had no need to swoop. He was looking for her just as eagerly as she was looking for another impeccably dressed misfit to bamboozle into submission and recruit as an act of mercy. His gangling stature had, for several years, been a familiar embellishment of the Abbey grounds, and he would stoop to speak to anyone.

That's how Earwig and I met him, before Earwig's accident, when Cha, as he claimed everyone called him, asked Earwig what he was carrying in his guitar case. Then he almost immediately proceeded to tell us how he had managed a number of moderately successful bands and provisionally offered to do the same for our devoutly amateur bush-league trio. Possibly even kit us out with some professional gear.

He sounded pretty convincing at first. So much so, that we decided to accept his invitation and turned up at his house around a week later with a home-made cassette recording of ourselves to allow him to lend a critical ear and decide if he'd be interested in taking us on.

He lived alone in a small but smart Regency house on the

elevated periphery of a park at the top of a precipitous century of steps known locally as Jacob's Ladder, which overlooked the city beyond the railway. He was a fantasist. He was homosexual, too. But more obviously than anything else, he was lonely.

Although probably less than ten years older than us, he seemed remote and decades beyond our years. The careful composition of his appearance a stubborn vestige of some distant age that spilt exclusion into the air of him like a heavy scent. His anachronistic whalebone way, rendered odder by the lingering keening of his hesitant voice, communicated an entrenched world-weariness and presented him as being more seasoned than his less formal peers.

A distracting holistic awkwardness afflicted him like a muscular disease, which twisted in the manner of a clinging manzanita around his tall, thin, willowy-drooping frame. He swayed around in a constantly leg-crossing, head tossing way in his chair as he spoke, as though he were acting out his dialogue in a series of stages. The effort he invested in it all seemed laborious to me. But I sensed he was attempting to conceal something beneath calculated clouds of minor distractions. Still, there it seemed to be, poking out between them. Sprouting up from his feet like weeds through a field of plastic flowers.

I didn't dislike him. His gentleness was genuine, and his peculiar, winning, fragile charm difficult not to warm to.

Half listening to a couple of songs from our cassette, he discussed music in a way that suggested he knew little about it; returning the dialogue, as usual, to improbable anecdotes of his own experiences. It wasn't at any point a riveting conversation. Even so, I couldn't quite take my eyes off the way he wouldn't look at anyone directly when he spoke, but into a semi-distant space at one side of them instead. The result of this unnatural lack of visual engagement was to quickly communicate the impression that he didn't care about what you, or even particularly about what he was saying. Which didn't help. It was disconcerting. Maybe he had felt it necessary to fashion his sideways-on style of conversation from a fear of noticing how destructively a more unguarded look may be thrown back to judge him. Nevertheless, he liked to talk and appeared to appreciate our company. While all the time soliciting some manner of reassurance about the acceptability of whatever he said, and the confirmation that he had let nothing slip to provoke our displeasure.

I had been slightly apprehensive when the idea of visiting Cha at home was first mooted in the Churchyard, suspecting he was not all he claimed to be, unsure of the motive for his invitation or quite what we might be letting ourselves in for there. But my initial reluctance for a conversational audition with a dubious stranger almost immediately on meeting him again, turned to an empathy which extended beyond my appreciation of the lengths he went to to make us feel comfortable, and conceal from us his still evident sorrow.

The visit to his house lasted less than an hour, but we had realised much earlier that we were wasting our time, and that all he really wanted was someone to talk to.

Although it patently wasn't us, I hoped, by the time we left him on his Welcome coir doormat waving, receding visibly from the threshold of flight, that he would find whatever it was he was looking for. But it seemed from the inescapable dissonance of our mismatched meeting that the closest company he kept was with a constant coterie of implausible stories and dreams.

A few months later, I was surprised to see his familiar head of blonde hair sitting right there on our sofa, drinking tea and talking God and politics with my mother when I came home early from Piggy's house one evening. By which time she had probably realised that he was homosexual, and would have been anything but sympathetic; viewing him in her pseudo-pietistically puritanical, narrow minded way as nothing more than a practitioner of deviant sex and perversion. Even a casual reference to heterosexual sex would have been malignantly anathematic to her. Christ knows how she ever managed to have enough of it to produce a kid when it was so difficult for her to conceive.

There were still a few prattling minutes of tea swilling around in the bottom of his second cup from the pot and she was already keeping him at an arm's length, saying little with any warmth to encourage an extension of his dialogue. Her interest in his impromptu visit clearly by this time reduced to little more than allowing her impression of someone who had just swallowed something inedibly rancid to indicate her displeasure at his company. I said hello, but he seemed distracted, uncomfortable, his diffident overtures at continued conversation with my mother faltering and awkward, like a repetitively backfiring car exhaust. He left soon after I came in and stood around outside the house for a few minutes, as if he had nowhere else to go.

A fortnight later, his body was fished out of the Avon at Locksbrook.

My mother judged no-one. Except for those who did not measure up to her impossible expectations. In the scathing loneliness of her perfection, she loved herself with the unsparing devotion of a pampering mother. She loved herself as the lover of her unfailing lover. She loved herself so selflessly that few onlookers were able to remain entirely unmoved by the passion of the romance.

When aimed at others, the declaration of her affection was never more than the polished surface of sound. She wielded the promise of her love as an incentive to invest her with something of greater value. Pricing such words highly and never selling them for less.

The truth of her elusive love was that my mother ruthlessly detested anybody who did not manifestly mirror her every thought and deed. Such moral underlings were to be pitied with the lash of correction. Even dressed in the devious gauze of magnanimity, the naked glare of her natural loathing undermined her pretence and threatened to radiate through the weave of its thin cloth with the force of a thousand suns.

She assiduously presented herself in a way scrupulously devised to convince the yearning ingenuous that she believed utterly in the redemptive potential of love, but the love she believed in was earned by unquestioning obedience to her impossible demands. The vastness of its embrace according no place to affection.

She insistently proclaimed her belief in the sanctity of the family but obsessively renounced the unnatural evil of sex. She vociferously spouted the necessity for truth but contemptuously rejected honesty. She demanded tolerance but would not countenance contention. She believed in freedom of speech but not in a difference of opinion. She demanded belief in the existence of God but railed against any other interpretation of God but hers. She encouraged respect for language but used language to disrespect others. She respected her unfailing sagacity without reservation, however. More than was required to venerate the infallibility of her judgement. She believed mankind had lost its way in its unrelenting pursuit of summary self-gratification; and that it had been spared the redemptive pain of the rod for long enough.

# 50

In the freshly risen and sanctified tabernacle of the CHRIST Church room above the disused bakery, golden dust particles glistened polished in early afternoon midsummer sun, which streamed in onto the inconspicuously steaming congregation like a scriptural revelation through a wall length row of long picture windows.

Whatever the weather, my mother had for the last six months scrupulously taken to officiating in an impostrous virginal white arrangement of extravagant drapery, consisting of a long, full frock, gathered at the waist by a sash that had been subtly but industriously self-embroidered with a veritable galaxy of off-white stars and planets. The anaemic outfit being thematically completed by a similarly designed white velvet hairband, featuring rockets, comets and otherworldly spacecraft in tribute to the mysterious astral flights of Enoch, and simple, white, plain leather ankle boots which may equally easily have passed muster at a Western Evening line dancing extravaganza.

The final apologetically cacophonic strains of Fight the Good Fight limped into the post-hymn silence that fell with sufficient dramatic weight to effectively emphasise the gravity of my mother's parting declaration, taken verbatim from chapter fifty-four of the Book of Enoch, on the still closed opening pages of The Unclosable Eye, that "The chiefs of the East, among the Parthians and Medes, shall remove kings, in whom a spirit of perturbation shall enter. They shall hurl them from their thrones, springing as lions from their dens, and like famished wolves into the midst of the flock." 'My Blessed Soldiers,' she concluded, raising the undisturbed scripture in her right hand, then affixing her left to it and thrusting both into the air, as though somewhat gracelessly pitching an oversized grenade in an ostentatiously galvanising though nevertheless unprepossessingly ham-dram manner, convincingly reminiscent of Olivier's risible Saint Crispin's Day endeavour, 'we shall tear the spoils of their decadence from the hands of the unscrupulous, and refashion it into broadswords for our battle with the detractors of the Lord. We shall silence the footsoldiers of the Devil with the word of God and deliver them to their judgement before Him. In the beloved name of the Father, we, His most trusted of saints, shall cut down the enemies of light with the invincible blade of His love. In peace and Christ, Amen.'

A small but enthusiastic choir of syncopated amens filtered through the embered sighs of my mother's militating mettle and rested in an almost immediate shuffling of feet. A few polite and complimentary comments were exchanged for reassuring handshakes in a still semi-hallowed hush.

My mother mooched around in the vein of an alabaster hostess at a surreal society cocktail party, sticking her wet, hay-fevered nose in front of the departing assembled like an habitually spoilt pet Labrador anticipating an enthusiastic petting, as she traded pleasantries and promises with her fawning familiars and flattering acolytes. One or two issued a waving 'bless you, Sister,' as they scrambled for air, disappearing down the hessian carpeted stairs and out into the street.

My mother, of course, artfully contrived, as usual, to be the last to leave, after customarily scooping the valuable contents of the newly acquired brass, seventeenth century Nuremberg alms dish into a patent leather Gucci handbag and locking up some considerable time after the final stragglers had ambled breezily away, bolstered, inflated with gladdening conversation and an accentuated sense of a less undefined purpose.

# 51

There has always existed a certain uncertainty surrounding the certainty of Heisenberg's uncertainty principle, but I nevertheless found myself completely unable to ascertain my exact place in the world while simultaneously attempting to measure the precise speed at which I was hurtling toward my destruction. Consequently, my own purpose, I felt, continued to slip inexorably into the morosity of ineluctable obscurity. And considering patience, as I always had, to be no more virtuous than an unacceptable acceptance of irrefutable failure, I waited impatiently in vain for things to change.

My literary profile on the local stage, however, was gradually gathering pace on a current of encouraging whispers. Although my progressively sinking condition prevented me from viewing the negligible improvement in my fortunes as anything concrete enough as flotsam to cling to. In fact, the whole thing floated quietly past me, almost unnoticed.

I had initially been unaware of the microscopic rise in my reputation as a juvenile wordsmith among the aesthetes of the local community, and that any accolades my verse may have received had been due to the promotional efforts of the city rag.

Completely unknown to me, the Evening Chronicle had, a

few months previously, embarked upon a programme of regularly publishing my poems in midweek issues. A collection of the works having been meticulously copied and submitted to the newspaper on my behalf, though without my knowledge or consent, by a trainee teacher at my school who, through a mutual passion for music and literature had become a friend.

My unofficial literary agent enthusiastically assured me the verses had attracted a respectable degree of appreciative attention, a claim borne out some time after the publication of each by someone or other who would compliment me with the mention that they had enjoyed them.

My belated reaction to this information was to eventually purchase a back copy of every appropriate daily edition.

I didn't buy them because I was proud, because I wasn't, particularly. Or because I wanted to crow or blow my own horn about it, because I didn't. In fact, I've never been particularly precious about that sort of thing at all. I collected them because I thought it was the apposite thing to do. I wasn't exactly sure why, but it may have had something to do with the same posterity I collected everything else for. Which is probably why it didn't bother me very much when I discovered that my pile of bedside newspapers had disappeared. Thrown away by my mother a few weeks after I'd added the final issue to my collection. She had taken customarily little if any interest in them anyway, beyond appearing to resent them occupying the small area of floor beside my bed.

The incident had not been without precedent. The same fate had befallen other newspapers that had carried photos of me performing in the various school plays my mother never once atended. Copies of each were available for years at the

Chronicle offices in Westgate Street, but I never replaced any of them. Neither, of course, did she.

# 52

Our ways remain when our way has become lost to us.

I knew things needed to change.

The deferment of my increasingly tormented amble into a conscious decision about the general shape and direction of my future coincided with a spiritually edifying introduction to the esoteric world of live rock gigs at the Edwardian aircraft hangar-like dance-hall of The Pavilion.

On my inaugural visit I jostled amiably with impressively hirsute, alcohol bearing people, who filled the unabundant air with the alluring scent of tobacco and patchouli oil, and who, like me, had immersed themselves in the electrifying anticipation of discovering treasure in the sudden darkness when a multi-gelled collage flickered piecemeal into being, and an assortment of denim-clad life-forms from the planet Hawkwind wandered like chemically articulated magi onto the stage in an ocean of liquid light.

A howling chorus of approval briefly accompanied them to a short parade of silver microphone stands spanning the foreground like miniature cranes, until two thousand watts of Dave Brock's Dick Knight Les Paul copy instantly destroyed the roar, along with the likelihood that I would ever hear anything else at normal volume again. And in less time than it took for the Lord Lemmy Christ to counter the chord on the howitzer of his Rickenbacker, the entire universe of my being knew consummately that this was what I had been so convulsively in search of since the day I was carted home songless in the snow.

I saw, in a sublime moment of stroboscopic slow-mo clarity, the technicolour glory of God, while drooling transfigured, spiritually prostrate before the unfolding miracle of psychedelic space-rock.

I found religion at precisely the same time as being bedazzled by the burning bush of Stacia flinging her naked breasts about downstage while the band belted out *Brainstorm* at a volume and with a low frequency resonance that threatened to unsurgically disembowel me from two rows back.

My epiphany was as profound as the assurance of a life-long devotion. My desolation transformed in moments of sensory rapture.

The experience confirmed a suspicion I had always been vaguely aware but not entirely conscious of. That a road to Damascus-type revelation would flood me with a light bright enough to penetrate the clinging monochrome of familiarity and illuminate it with colour of such piercing intensity that it would blind me to everything I had previously known.

Days later, the Elysian landscape of my newly discovered nirvana remained true. Colour-drenched and luminous.

Saturated with the certainty that my life had changed, I impatiently paced the lacklustre corridors of my school days with restless feet itching to carry me back to the next gig at the Pav.

# 53

I had discovered the missing matter of myself. And could barely contain the elation of finally knowing that I fitted in somewhere after all.

I now flaunted my school fatigues proudly, with a new sense of belonging. Though not, of course, to the school.

For almost the entirety of the previous two and a half years, I had annunciated my existential disassociation with the allegedly educational boot camp by substantially disregarding the rigorously enforced grey flannel uniform with its quasi regimental tie and optional cycling boy cap in favour of an original canvas of illegal colour and flair, which I now substituted with a freshly painted portrait of myself disputatiously decked out in a superabundance of scintillating bohemian psychedelia.

In a good-natured and broadly concessionary spirit of more obvious irony, however, I had taken the time and trouble to specially dye both sides of my well below shoulder length hair a suitably fluorescent acid apple green, and the front to back centre portion a most invigorating and resplendent pillar box red. Both colours more or less corresponding to the narrow stripe of ribbon on the otherwise hideously plain, deathly ashen headdress of the official uniform.

My Modigliani-esque frame modelled a delightful, cream piped, brown velvet smoking jacket over a complementary floral burgundy T-shirt, faded blue denim Levi's and white daps, with different dayglo-coloured socks for my left and right feet.

I had sourced my creation for pennies from a variety of jumble sales around the city, but the bold palette and inspiration for the patchwork picture was my own. My spectrum of contraband colours constituted a uniform of sorts, but was a more honest representation of myself, which I saw no reason to compromise or modify for the purposes of learning.

Naturally, I complemented my ebullient appearance with a courteous and affable demeanour whenever I felt obliged to respond to a near constant barrage of miscellaneous quips and eye rolling witticisms from psychotically outraged staff and nonplussed, envious inmates alike.

Even when in the face of expulsion I was ordered home to change, as was the case on an almost daily basis, I invariably completed the fulsome ritual by returning to school some time later and presenting myself in exactly the same way. This ceremony continued intact throughout an inevitable, tedious and lamentably extended period of having to endure a tiresome chorus of gang-mentality opposition from masters, almost to a man, and culminated with the necessity of my explaining to the Head that my position on uniform, dress and personal expression was entirely inflexible, and that the only sartorial concession I was prepared to offer to any self important, meretricious, all show and no blow establishment, under any circumstances, was the addition of a scarlet cable-knit jersey instead of the short sleeved T-shirt in winter months.

Being reasonable, I was, however, also open to the possibility of replacing my white daps with a pair of electric blue patent leather brothel creepers in wet weather.

The ongoing threat of expulsion transpired to be nothing more than toothless intimidation, and began to gradually fizzle out after the first couple of terms. During which time I continued to write, with the begrudging approval of some, and even the respect of some more of the traditionally cane-happiest sadists there, for the school literary magazine. To which I was typically the most represented contributor by quite some margin. However, as an unfortunate consequence of the disappointingly rancorous ongoing skiving-related battle with school representatives in the final year of my incarceration, I completely withdrew my services to the publication, ignoring repeated appeals by various members of the teaching fraternity to reconsider.

The beleaguered local authority truant officer remained a regular visitor to my parents' house, despite my mother's brazenly repeated attempts to convert her.

# 54

Sorrow burns holes into the colours of our memories.

My father and I collected three members of my cousin Will's large family from naval barracks in Portsmouth, when they relocated to Bath. The family being unfamiliar to me, I had been initially reluctant to make the trip, preferring instead to watch Humperdinck's Hansel und Gretel from La Scala on TV. But on the strength of my mother's refusal to travel, as she habitually loathed all members of my father's family ancient or modern without exception, and somewhat unaccommodatingly resented spending any time with any of them ever, it appeared to have been determined without my participation that I would be offered up as company for his journey to the south coast, and was surprisingly persuaded of the arrangement's relative appeal by my father's reiterated assertion that the production of the opera was rubbish and that I would find very little reward in it on any level.

As it happened, the oddly cobbled occasion was to prove unexpectedly rewarding.

A few months younger than me, Will was a sweet, kind, personable and softly spoken kid, who unfailingly seemed to be dressed in a light scent of the lingeringly elegiac. He was talkative right away, with a collection of promptly identified mutual interests being avidly dissected as we began the journey back to Bath. Our contempt for pointless displays of authority by petty pedagogues pretty much laying the foundations of an enduring friendship by the time we skirted the airfield at Middle Wallop.

A friendship that endured unbroken until he died in a freak accident thirty years later. After he had married a Royal Ballet dancer, had children, and been honourably discharged from the army. And three days after his pococurante GP had twice diagnosed his post fall brain haemorrhage as a harmless headache.

At the beginning of the winter term, his application to grievously suffer at the hands of my boot camp was accepted, so, on his first day, we bunked off into the fields and got drunk on some cheap wine together to celebrate.

We both revelled in the natural beauty of the endlessly undulating countryside surrounding the school, and on just about any given day, and at just about any given time, we could be found by anyone but the truant officer wandering around in it, taking unforgettable notes in lessons of far longer lasting reward.

At the end of a day of studying kingfishers and goshawks from the ass-moistening mossy banks of sticklebacked brooks, after discovering the burnished silver of slow worms and antique gold of grass snakes hidden in a trove beneath rotting hunks of fallen tree, Will would often sneak back into school to use the high board and swimming pool, well into the warm, soft, glowwormed summer evening, where he'd dive and swim for ages.

Sometimes, mostly just after his father died, I'd go back there with him; but he'd become quiet and distant. When he arrived at the pool, he withdrew altogether. I even lost sight of his convivial smile. By the time he disappeared into the water, he had become blind to me. He didn't speak at all. He just dived and swam.

We were caught trespassing in the almost roofless remains of some disused barn once, when we were taking shelter in it because it was pouring with rain. The owner had called the police, and they came storming in like a trio of scrum-halfs. Next thing I knew, they had us pancaked against a wall like we were the IRA or something. We told them calmly and honestly when they frisked us for artillery, that we weren't doing any harm and didn't mean to endanger anyone else's life with our wet clothes, but that we had only wandered off the footpath and into the barn to keep dry.

They gave us the third degree with a free presentation of their reaction to our threat to national security, then radioed our false names and all the sordid details of our crime of the century back to the station to determine whether their superiors felt it appropriate for them to shoot us on the spot or take some other action to safeguard the country's vulnerable population from a society-destroying duo of ardent public enemies who had audaciously demonstrated such unsparing contempt for the law.

At first, the police were unaccountably belligerent. So much so that I wondered if they were planing to take advantage of our being alone in the sticks to rough us up a bit while they waited for word on the short wave. They'd already assaulted my integrity. I felt violated. Besmirched.

The strange fiction I had been written into was real and could significantly count against me if ever I was presented with the need to prove myself respectable. I was concerned. It hadn't even sensibly occurred to me that the dilapidated hovel merited an owner when we ducked into it out of the downpour. Now my collar had been felt and I was spreadeagled against a crumbling stone wall that stank of being lost, where I was pinned like an exhibition butterfly to an erroneous accusation of flagrant moral iniquity. Our futures hung in the balance. It was a long few minutes wait for our fate to be decided.

A crackling voice eventually came through on the walkie-talkie, which we couldn't decipher. Wherever the dice would fall, they were loaded against Will for sure, and whatever was about to happen, we both knew that his was a dead ass walking. He didn't stand a hope in hell of acquittal one way or another.

The long awaited upshot was that they let us off with a finger-wagging warning not to shelter from the rain again and ferried Will like a resigned lamb to the slaughter back to school, as he was clearly strutting his unmistakable penal institution skiving regalia. I felt bad for him. There was no way he could avoid the inevitability of a painful reunion with the headmaster.

Although, it would have been difficult for him to escape his fate even had he not been sporting those give-away regulation greys and the school crest emblazoned on the breast pocket of his jacket for the world to see who owned him.

Will's fatal truanting handicap was that he was a fresh faced kid. On the short side, too, and he looked his age. Fortunately for myself, not only had none of the officers previously encountered me at home, but I couldn't have looked much less like I ought to have been banged up with a circus of morons in a school classroom all day. I was tall, had plenty of facial hair and looked quite a bit older than I was. Particularly as I was decked out in my smoking jacket and

Levis as usual.

I cadged a lift into town from Starsky and his couple of Hutches in the back of their Jam Sandwich after impressing upon them my need to get back to work, and bumped into Will there an hour or two later. His hands were still red from the cane.

# 55

We are divided by love. Its blind exactitude inspiring us to the most passionate of hatreds.

My father readied himself to venture out late on Sunday morning, as he regularly did, but this time he seemed to shower and dress a little earlier than usual. He didn't typically invest quite so much effort into preparing for his once a week afternoon rendezvous at the Belvoir with his Royal Antediluvian Order of Buffaloes friends, either. There was something unnerving about my mother's attitude, too. She carried the demeanour of a swollen-headed fisherman holding up a sixty-three pound pike for the camera. I frantically angled for a less harrowing interpretation.

'Are you going with her?' I demanded to know, struggling to balance contempt and consternation in as few words as I could comfortably muster before losing my voice entirely in a paralytic state of neuron-crunching incredulity.

'You'd better hurry up if you want to come,' he antagonistically replied, straightening his paisley tie in the mockingly expansive, ancient, gilt, hall mirror.

'I don't!' I spat, apoplectically, silently adding 'you must be out of your fucking mind, you lunatic,' in the cyclonic fever of my own.

I'll be damned if he didn't have close to the same intolerably smug expression I'd seen a thousand times before on *her* megalomaniacal mug.

He knew full well that I had been mown down by a train of insults on the tracks of his surrender and it didn't seem to bother him a bit. He couldn't care less how I felt. And I felt sick. I couldn't have felt more like puking over his suddenly strangely unrecognisable face if he had casually turned me over to the child abusing ravages of the orphanage single-handedly. All his mocking and 'she'll never rope me into it' resistance had culminated in this cringing and spineless capitulation.

Patently, something pretty substantially conspiratorial had transpired between them. Things had obviously been going on in their unnatural little world that I hadn't even been aware of. I just stared, stupefied. I couldn't think of anything sensible to say.

As I watched him for the few seconds I was able to before inhaling my own vomit, he seemed to shrink in front of my eyes to the size of a Pygmy.

My mother occupied her self-sanctified section of the CHRIST room with a notably inflated presence that day, and launched like Enoch's wolves into the First Book of Peter, chapter four, verse seventeen, quoting again with redoubtable dramatic acumen from The Unclosable Eye, which she clutched in her left hand like a trench bomb, "For the time *is come* that judgement must begin at the house of God: and if *it* first *begin* with us, what shall the end *be* of them that obey not the gospel of God?"

'My beloved Brothers and Sisters,' she continued, flicking emphatically through her thumb-tortured gilt-edged pages to the next ribbon-draped section, and then laying the open

226

book like a suckling newborn across the heaving hummock of her chest, 'God has bestowed upon His adored Sacred Soldiers the unprecedented honour of returning His fallen flock to the rod of His reproach. It is our sacred calling to root out the pestilence of evil from this world, lest we ourselves, so trusted by the Almighty with its cleansing, fall like whimpering babes into the outstretched arms of its welcome. The Lord has provided us with the guide of His beloved prophet Ezekiel, who instructs us in chapter nine, verse six to "Utterly slay old men, young men, maidens, little children, and women, but do not touch any man on whom is the mark; and you shall start from My sanctuary."

Our Father loves us so, yet His heart is broken. And in His sorrow, He has revealed to me that the heretics who aggrieve Him are no less than the progeny of Amelek. Enemies of the chosen pure of heart and true, who have united with disciples of the Devil to stalk the Earth and lust insatiably after power and flesh; condemning the enslaved poor to forever suffer the pains of their greed. The Lord, our God, clearly commands us in Book One of Samuel, chapter fifteen, verse three, to "Now go and strike Amelek and devote to destruction all that they have. Do not spare them, but kill man and woman, child and infant, ox and sheep, camel and donkey." We, my Sacred Soldiers, must not and shall not shun the honour of our sacred duty. Neither shall we allow ourselves to succumb to the will or governance of the unjust, but to the unassailable order of our Heavenly Father alone. And we shall not rest from the rigours of our labours until He has spoken and bid us rest and rejoice together at His side, in peace, and in the eternal light of His love.'

Seated rows of Sacred Soldiers nodded affirmatively, like a neurotic pack of the interminably neck-swaying little plastic, pseudo-suede-covered dogs that faddishly occupied the back window shelves of family saloons. One or two felt moved to offer a devotional amen and another leapt to her feet into a visually unimpeded area significantly above the pates of the others and ecstatically shouted 'kill the bastards!' My father was formally introduced to the congregation as a coveted convert at the end of proceedings, and ingratiatingly declared that he believed the Church of CHRIST to be true.

# 56

At the next gig at the Pav, I drank vodka all night on an empty stomach with a friend and passed out. I was hungover for three days and grounded for a week.

The whole thing came about as an ill-considered knee-jerk reaction to an enforced period of sobriety I had been compelled to endure as a result of a complete lack of funds, and one which had left me feeling somewhat materially dispossessed. I had taken every advantage of my generous older friend's unexpectedly tip-enhanced weekend waiting wage to embark upon an immediate rehabilitative prog ramme of particularly heavy drinking, which culminated in the accolade of my being carried senseless out of the Pav by an internationally esteemed guitarist.

On the morning after the night of my paralytic return home, I took as much pleasure as my incapacitating nausea permitted in repeatedly referring to my mossback father as *man*. Enthusiastically announcing throughout my entire pre-resurrection period that the gig had been cool, and that the music was far out, (man). As I had expected, being a pedant in the affairs of address, he took particular exception to my referring to him in this way. And being so anally unbending in his attitude to the use of the correct form of it for practically everything under the sun, was incapable of not reminding me on every occasion I attempted to so engage him, that he was not, in fact, *man*, but my father.

'I'm your father,' he repeatedly insisted, not aggressively at all, but in a quite unexpectedly compassionate tone of conspicuous pique. This assertion, of course, was growing ever more difficult for me to accept.

The following gig, a week or so later, was an entirely different affair altogether. I could never have foreseen or envisaged the ineradicably life-changing effect that going to it would have.

Manfred Mann's Earth Band strolled off stage, with the pre-recorded otherworldly soprano choir bursting out of the p.a. on both sides at full volume. It was a sublime conclusion to their set, which they didn't spoil with an encore. And as the music eventually subsided, with the house lights beginning to rise, I realised the event was over and that there was little else to do but get up spellbound and disappointed from my front row seat and go home. Turning around as I did to glance briefly up at the steady stream of shuffling leavers spilling out into the aisles, I was magnetically drawn to the beautiful face of an exquisitely presented girl in a bright red coat who had remained seated in the row behind me and who, in the same moment, casually returned my immediately smitten gaze with a smile.

The completion of my total reinvention was closer than a Planck length away.

I could barely contain the new-universe-parturating explosion inside my head, and instantly fell into a semi-conscious condition of completely intoxicated emotional spontaneous combustion while being sucked spellbound into the amber of her eyes like an otherwise motionless mayfly. So hopelessly arrested by her beauty, that Marcel Marceau himself would not have offered a more convincing impression of a person rendered senseless after being smacked flat by a wrecking ball.

I wasn't aware of how long I stood there for, giddily gawping at that radiating vision of unmitigated loveliness, before becoming conscious that I had been staring inanely, and breaking the besotted plaster-cast of my sudden awkwardness by incoherently mumbling something apologetic about really liking her coat. Within seconds, we were kissing and embracing, and kissing and embracing until the hall was almost empty.

I adored Yssy with every ever-hankering molecule of my undimmable devotion from the second I set my helplessly infatuated gaze upon her. Every detail of her was as perfect as if God had fashioned into flesh an illustration of everything He intended the female sex to be. My prayers had been answered without my having ever been aware that I had offered them up for consideration. Renoir's Petite Irene had matured by a couple of summers and floated off my bedroom wall to fuse seamlessly with a cavern-eyed, strawberry lipped, Roman Holidaying Audrey Hepburn, before the unprincessly haircut on her big day out in Rome incognito. I was jellified by the impact of her charisma.

Holding onto her as if my life depended on feeling her perfect, slender, floral-scented form beneath my fingertips, we surfed the temporarily overpopulated, unseen river-edged pavement weightless, enveloped by the torrent of each other's embraces, into town. Each fleeting moonspilt moment a disappearing dream.

Leaving from the city centre in less than ten minutes, the guillotine of Yssy's last bus home assured a premature severing of our short acquaintance. I staggered towards an incoming tide of despondency on the hope-sucking alluvion of disbelief, words failing me like faith at the conclusion of our surreal encounter.

I walked her like a haul of jewels the short distance from the end of North Parade to her stop on the Orange Grove, where we kissed for the last time, before she scribbled her phone number onto a piece of card and handed it to me as the bus rounded the corner.

She pulled away like a temporary dance partner from the last of my grasp and casually stepped aboard the Number Four without looking back. They waddled away into the darkness together like a long, green, illuminated lizard with an obdurate lack of ceremony or concern. A painfully extracted assortment of my vital organs went with them.

In the gaping enormity of her place, I held the holy relic of her handwriting, but had no idea if the telephone number inscribed on the sliver of card was real, or if I'd ever see her again.

I stood inhaling the garden of her lingering scent as my heart ached in limbo at the bus stop, watching a steady trickle of miniaturising poppy red tail lights vanish into the night, and counting the unshifting minutes she had been gone.

The encounter had been a dream I had awoken from too soon; and as the empty glow of bus after bus disappeared into a tapering funnel of under-lit distance, I rubbed the vestiges of it from my eyes, while blunt scalpels of disparate emotions hacked away at what was left of my insides.

My immaculately replicated inaugural postnatal cry immediately immersed me in undying echoes of agonising speculation.

In a maelstrom of sighs, now blowing like swirls of litter into the darkness, I managed to remain almost oblivious to

232

the graceless gruntings of wittering words, as they scurried around my brain like an army of illiterate ants foraging for nuances of description. Droning on, incongruously, as they almost always do, about such things as the lush, mossy, night-stained woodlands of her warm, soft, coromandel eyes; the aromatic nimbus of her shimmering oakwood tresses, each iridescent filament clinging swagged to another, reflecting scintillas of light in fountains of glittering golds, as if every strand had been sable-brushed into life by the enraptured hand of a Pre-Raphaelite master; her gentle, disarming, honest, open smile; the slow bowed nocturne of her voice and the angelic, Berniniesque magnificence of her body. They went on and on, piling cliche upon well-meaning but inadequate superlative, and I scarcely heard them at all. The vortex of mutterings pivoting away into the ether beyond my ears, painting the unframed end of day with a crude approximation of possibly never to be seen again perfection.

My burning solitude pitched me like a nugget of coal into a crucible of insufferable melancholia.

I smouldered through the night. Barely closing my eyes.

It was an impossibly long wait until five-seventeen the following evening, when I reckoned Yssy would be home from school and callable. The delicate undertaking was not, I felt, one that could be most effectively accomplished from the strained confines of the house. Besides, I needed the five-minute walk in the fresh air to the phone box to help steady my nerves.

It didn't work.

When I arrived at the kiosk, my heart was beating harder and faster than it had been before, and a tsunami of concerns was vaulting my synapses like greyhounds. I still wasn't sure exactly what I was about to say, even as I tugged the heavy, red, rusty iron door open and edged myself apprehensively inside.

A minute later, I had still managed nothing more constructive than a series of overly anxious sighs, as I stood rigid as a scaffolding pole on the claustrophobic microscope slide of the cold concrete floor, breathing the familiar stale, acrid scent of damp directories and Bakelite, while the reverberating thunder of my pulse counted down the eternity of my apprehension.

Finally, I rustled up the requisite modicum of composure, lifted the unnervingly weighty, ominously buzzing receiver to my ear, steadied my shaking hand and rested the soft pad of my finger in the satisfyingly smooth, thin chrome circular cut-out to dial the number.

For a few seconds, it lingered there, limply, resisting repeated impassioned pleas to move. Seldom, if ever, had I felt so nervous. I impatiently attempted to sedate myself enough to function, over and over again, with the temperatingly fatalistic advice that she would probably regret what had happened and give me the brush-off, anyway. I was as prepared as I could be to be gutted.

The strident ringing tone changed, and in a coronary compromising moment, every outcome became possible. I rammed the two pence piece into the audibly disengaged coin slot with a force that took me by surprise. The unintended power of my push extravagantly more than was necessary to ensure that the call engaged. As the coin clanged into the hollow of the box with a disconcerting confirmation that the all-revealing moment had arrived, the electric hum suddenly vanished loudly, and an ominously well spoken woman's voice cracked the cut glass bullwhip of a cold hello straight into the trumpet of my ear. I was thrown. Unsure of what to do next. I had no idea if the voice belonged to Yssy's mother, and if so, how she might react to a boy calling her. Would I blow my chances right away by answering? I held back for a second, wondering how to proceed.

It seemed to take me forever to get a grip on myself and decide I had no choice but to ask.

'May I speak to Yssy, please,' I mustered.

The chiselled voice said nothing. I wasn't sure what had happened.

From the ensuing aeons of silence, I was eventually able to overhear a short, faint muffle of sounds that seemed to come and go. Then, a sudden increase in the volume of the noises off heralded an unexpectedly abrupt but reassuringly less incendiary hello, and I recognised the heavenly tones at once. 'Yssy,' I started, trying to still the seismic tremor in my delivery, 'it's Chris, we met last night.' She didn't say anything. 'I wondered if you'd like to come to the pictures tomorrow evening?'

'I can't,' she replied, after a short pause, in what I considered to be a disconcertingly matter of fact manner.

'Oh,' was all I could manage, before getting stuck for words and feeling that my whole new world was already on the edge of collapse. '...um,' I continued.

'I can make Saturday evening, though,' she interjected.

I don't remember what else was spoken between us on that fateful occasion; everything abruptly faded behind an explosive anoesis, and I was instantly launched into a state of almost total deafness by my near paralysing inner outburst of unqualified delirium.

I somehow walked the several hundred yards home on the freshest air I had ever tasted.

## 57

Dawn broke, and a chorus of blackbirds fed songs on the pieces.

Three days after falling headlong for Yssy in a rapture at a glance, I held her again. Few experiences had ever felt more natural or familiar. The germinal moments of reunion were a transcendental consolidation of our Pavilion founded affection; the entire old repertoire of embraces came flooding through pristine and unscathed. Our relief articulated in a communion of eyes and hands, we kissed in radiant silence with the sun on our faces.

I had been crippled by the fear that we would have somehow regressed in each other's absence and need to establish our acquaintance all over again. Nudge it cautiously along this time with a little more awkward formality. I languished in the perma-fretting darkness of a trio of unending summer days.

Yssy's Colditz Castle-styled convent school was conveniently situated right next to the Pav. She was a day pupil there. Same year as me. The private institution was imaginatively called the Convent School, but Yssy referred to it without warmth or humour as The Gulag, and many of the religieuse who taught her there as sadistic witches. Few being particularly interested in, or sympathetic towards her anticipated career in newspaper journalism, secularism in general, or even the fundamental emotional well-being of their browbeaten captives.

I met her at the school on most evenings in term time, outside the imposing Victorian sagittate railings that circled the austere neo-Gothic edifice like a penal corral. Almost every Saturday, we spent the whole of the day together, either in town or at one of our houses. Occasionally we'd amble around the farm and cattled fields of one of Yssy's family friends; gathering smaller pastures of straw and mud upon ourselves in a recreation which, managing to combine both the vital ingredients of walking in the country and socialising with ruminants, appealed to her more than most.

Sundays, on the other hand, were a life sentence for me. In the bottomless well of the late weekend I felt utterly alone and bereft. Except for in the easy, idling reprieves of our school holidays, when we ambled around more fields and more animals and grew closer.

The unappreciated term time Sabbath sabbatical was implicitly observed for the full two years in which the day remained routinely out of bounds. Not because it fell victim to the imposition of any ecclesiastical obligation by Yssy's non-church-attending parents; in fact, they were almost as ambivalent as me in their attitude towards many matters of the divine. No, it was a secular discipline that divided us on the Lord's day. My scholastic indifference to supplemental school assignments was not indulged or endorsed by Yssy's philomathic parents, who insisted on the setting aside of the day to enable her to catch up on the previous week's homework, and to attend to a variety of other domestic occupations. Being at the beck and call of few such commitments, at home or anywhere else, I accepted their unconvincing reason for my insufferable day of exile magnanimously and counted down the infernally dragging hours before I could see her again. On Sundays, deprived of the oxygen of Yssy's inexhaustible effusion of tropical affection, I literally feverishly looked forward to Monday all day.

There are unique and wonderful moments in which illusion and reality exigently coalesce.

Loudon Wainwright once sang that the movies were a mother to him. They were to us, too. From the back stalls seats of our inaugural visit, we suckled on them like nurslings. They raised us, nourished us, enriched and encouraged us, flickering their vital transfusion of life-blood into our veins at twenty-four frames a second.

We ornamented our still-life naivety with photographic symbolism, birthed embryonic images in developing fluid.

Mesmerised by sirens of secret worlds, we were drawn instinctively like moths around magical shafts of light that flooded like torrents of angels from the pulpits of projector booths. And they bled into reels of our own inchoate scenes of discovery like cue marks.

On at least one evening a week, we threaded ourselves warp and weft through the colours of reality and illusion in the fluttering dark, transfixed, while kaleidoscopic travelogues through unexplored landscapes fuelled our wide-eyed anticipation of impending worldly adventure. We daydreamed deep focus details of dependable lives, crafted by sedulous screen recollections, in the imperceptibly oncoming headlights of everything it was possible for us to be.

By fourteen, I had almost completely outgrown the condescendingly cliched vernacular of the average Factory

Hollywood flick. Such moralistic polarity and all-looks-and-scant-talent glop appealed to me less than wandering aimlessly around outside in the cold. I had no appetite left for being cynically conned by the commercial dreams of a financially aspirational industry perpetuated by a self-worshipping coterie of charlatans and over-painted faith healers. I wanted the grainier woods of more ambiguous realities, not fairy tales.

Trusting film to honour its explosive origins and to destroy stereotypes of correctness and virtue, we generally shunned the psychotropic offerings of Rank or Pearl and Dean in favour of the one or two more intimate indie outlets around Bristol and Bath. Smaller, unashamedly unassuming places which offered a different variety of excitement and romance with their conspicuous lack of grandeur and the independent, arthouse and foreign language films few mainstream venues could afford to screen.

The worlds in movies shown in these bijou nickelodeons were exciting, interesting and new. Arcane, though oddly familiar places where something, somewhere, somehow made some kind of sense.

Tucked like a folded grey ticket in the shadowed pocket of barely even a side-street, we'd backrow ourselves in the pint sized auditorium of our mainstay, The Grand, among a lingering scent of stale cigarette smoke and the previously enlightened, hungry for additional cabbalistic helpings of intoxicating mystery and wisdom.

The staff were easygoing there, and usually let us into all the X rated films without asking our age.

Sometimes we'd sneak in without paying when the doors opened to let the previous house leave. We didn't need to, but it was fun, and the seductive additional attraction of being comfortable and alone for longer was potent enough for us to enjoy sitting through the last reel of the feature before watching the entire double bill, complete with its repeated ending again. Once a week in the summer became necessarily more often at other times of the year.

We occupied the soft plush, narrow, horse-hair, cordovan velveteen seats in a constant huddle throughout the darker months of winter, when we couldn't squeeze a full evening out of a restaurant meal, or amble for hours from shop doorway to doorway in the rain.

Discovering the immaculately flawed perfection of poetic landscapes together and wandering into them in search of comfortable, safe, warm places to live felt like laying the foundations of a future we were yet to define. Yssy spoke their idiosyncratic language naturally. Drew and sculpted metaphors from their unique colour and form.

I learned from her quiet, self-effacing perspicacity by osmosis. It was the kind of education that suited me.

I felt better nourished on a diet of Yssy's even temper for the past six months than I had been at any time before, and it now took me two or three seconds longer to fly off the handle in response to my mother's fanatical provocation. In most other situations that didn't feature my mother, I had become even more sedate and easygoing.

My prospects now looked convincingly fair in a new coat of fresh aspirations; my sanity no longer balanced quite so precariously on the knife-edge of my mother's whims. In fact, almost anywhere away from home, tightropes had become clouds.

I decorated the bare buff and khaki covers of my school exercise books with Spirographic repetitions of Yssy's name, as though the endless pattern of its perfect symmetry were a magical rune. Through the Augean tedium of maths, physics, geography, chemistry, R.E. and lunch, I couldn't wait to see her again.

In less than a brace of seasons, my mother had stopped aiming the pot shots of her threats at me, after raising me on them as though I were her personal game bird. At any time, I could have been toppled from my cloud by being yanked off to a children's home and taken away from Yssy for good. Now, incredibly, the dread of a perennial threat that had dogged me like a disease had receded.

I had humped its ball and chain around so habitually throughout my tormentor's reign of terror that practically an entire constabulary of local police officers who had encountered me over the years in the course of their duty not only recognised me, but greeted and addressed me by name as I ambled about town. A familiarity born not of delinquency; I was, after all, almost suspiciously law abiding, but the avuncular reaction to the spiteful absurdity of my mother's countless impassioned telephone pleas to the police station to despatch a child-catcher to seize and permanently remove me from her house and life for no sane or sensible reason.

Extraordinarily, my mother's recent growing pre-occupation with the physical manifestations of her ranting lunacy had resulted in a noticeably diminishing determin-ation to have me put out of her misery. In fact, the compulsion to be rid of me seemed to have subsided so dramatically that she appeared to now barely notice me at all for much of the time. She hadn't waved the red rag of her catchphrase past me once lately. Even the eggshells I walked on had grown stronger.

My father, who had always been a stranger, became even stranger, as he abandoned the Buffaloes and his many friends there to implicate himself in the practical development of my mother's madness.

In many ways he had changed, too. In some ways, beyond comprehension. Everything he did now, which he had always done, seemed to have a religious motive. Suddenly, now, it was God who was helping people, not him. He blessed my mother's swill at the dinner table and thanked the Lord for providing it. He had grown bigoted about other religions, other beliefs, and muttered snide and disparaging remarks about them in a way he never would have before. He also read much more now than he ever did, but his reading was almost entirely confined to the volumes and pamphlets that lined my mother's bookshelves. Even the way he held himself was different. He stood straighter, prouder, became still more aloof and adopted the famous smug when he spoke of CHRIST.

In other ways, he hadn't changed at all.

He gusted into the house from work like an infantry of sighs, and without preface or preamble, catapulted an order across the hall to me to get my hair cut. The command was issued without humour and with an obvious dearth of scope for discussion. I assumed it had been delivered at my mother's behest and contemptuously refused the instruction outright. He then fired off a few other relatively innocuous remarks, most of which I had been subjected to in some capacity on a number of previous occasions. Being keen to dismiss the exchange with a shrug and leave the house without further delay, I considered the familiar, encyclo-paedic roll-calling of my various character defects unworthy of a reply and made for the door as he continued.

Yssy and I were looking forward to meeting at the Uni for a gig there later in the evening, and I had already dressed and been ready to go before my father's cyclonic arrival, but soon realised that I was unlikely to get very far under my own steam. I couldn't stagger much beyond the top of the garden path.

'Yssy,' I said into the phone, with my hand still shaking, 'I won't be able to make it. My father's just punched me in the face and opened up my eye. There's blood everywhere and it won't stop. They say I have to go to hospital and get it stitched.'

# 58

You can love philosophy and you can love religion with all the bootlicking verses you can muster, but neither of them are ever going to love you back.

I often walked the five miles to Yssy's house, from where we would frequently amble on the short distance to Hampton Rocks, our own paradisiacal green Valhalla; unspoilt and magical. A bucolic, several hundred acre hideaway of special scientific interest above the affluent village of Bathampton, where Yssy lived in considerable comfort with her parents. Churchill's friend and tutor, the painter Walter Sickert, spent the last four years of his life there.

Hampton Rocks is one of those quiet, numinous places which seem to be overdressed in words.

It's surpassingly easy to forget the imagined size of yourself there, and instinctively occupy the impressionless inches of your shadow in the massive, arching timelessness of its imperishable terrain. There, compressed into almost nothing by the weight of its antiquity, you whisper your visibility so quietly as to never be noticed at all. We placed the vanishing footprints of our kisses among the grasses and the wild-flowers, and the unhurriedly beating heart of its Pleistocene rock.

It's harrowing; the way in which time and change reshape perspective so insufferably.

It's the unremitting, torturous intangibility of the past; the visceral totality of our separation from it, the impossibility of ever re-touching or amending it in *any* way, which renders the present so insurmountably tragic. All we have left to us is the butterfly wing dust of it on our fingertips, and most of the time we're too afraid to look at it, in case even that has become inextricably absorbed into the fabric of our callouses.

# 59

Actions are said to speak louder than words; but often they are heard only when words have spoken.

I wasn't proud of it. Far from it. My malformed mumblings prematurely spluttered in an ectopic extravasation. But I asked my father, one Saturday morning at the end of June, in a nauseatingly adolescent, maladroit, pseudo-intellectual moment, 'how many identities must we adopt and dismiss before we become the person we think we always were?' I had wanted to say something vaguely intelligent, like *life is a pilgrimage to ourself*, but it got lost in translation somewhere in my head and came out all wrong. It was hideous. A cringingly graceless, unsubtle attempt to encourage him to objectively reconsider the suitability of his recently acquired self, or at least, to think about it for a moment; but delivered in the stupidly naive and preposterously arrogant vernacular of a domestically disaffected teenager who was trying in the only way he could to land a punch of his own.

My woeful solicitation to discuss the issue was dismissed with stultifying ease by my mildly irritated father who, without disturbing himself enough to raise a glance at me, immediately replied with an embroidered flutter on a millpond sigh and in a disinterested monotone added, 'as many as it takes to make sense of each's memories, values and attitudes.'

'Oh,' I said, fast deflating with the whistle of a puncture, but determined to land my jab anyhow, 'maybe some of us just populate our worlds with endless imperfections.' I was going to add the apothegm 'every birth carries a mutant gene,' or something like that for good effect, but thought better of it and didn't. I swiftly concluded the exchange there, with possibly even a sniff of partially reclaimed credibility, before leaving him alone with the more satisfyingly cryptic clues of his daily newspaper crossword.

Within an hour or so, Yssy and I had sneaked off on the train to London together, and on to the Hyde Park Free Festival, where we sat blissfully lost to the world in each other and the perfect, sunny, midsummer magic of Kevin Coyne, Kevin Ayers, Nico and Gong, while playful people threw paper plates to strangers in the crowd like frisbees.

We devoured every exhilarating moment of it. Sneaking back to Bath later in the evening, still full on its spell, clutching an iconic gatefold copy of Hendrix's Rainbow Bridge, my first glimpse of a Blind Blake record and the cassette tape bootleg proof of our perfect, dream-like afternoon.

We had, for those hours in Elysium, climbed above ourselves and conquered Olympus to reach the gods in our bare feet.

It all seemed quite odd to me when my parents actually started going out together. It was as if they had reverted to being kids of my age again, stealing off mischievously and getting up to things they shouldn't. I wasn't used to it. I hadn't seen them behave in such a way before. It was unnerving.

Previously, my father would have quietly ducked out for an hour or two, probably to a Buffaloes event, with a just about discernible sense of dewy deliverance, as though he were jumping attached to a pre-opened parachute with a muted 'Geronimo' out of a mortally perforated Hurricane, and come back too soon with the resigned air of a recaptured escapee, sheepishly sporting a bottle of Babysham in his overcoat pocket for my unappreciative mother. Or else, as on the evening of my grandfather's death, until when, she had offered no noticeable solace as company for having berated my father for his unmanly tears, she would visit her sisters or outlandish friends without him. But seldom would they socialise as a couple. I could probably have counted the times they had sauntered awkwardly out on the pretext of pleasure together prior to her having netted him to feed to the Minotaur of her Church, on the outstretched middle finger of one hand.

I had no idea where they were slinking off to in the secret of each other's unlikely company on their recent, odd, illicit evening escapades during the week. Or what they did. I didn't particularly want to know, either, and neither of them volunteered the information. But I was aware that their Saturday mornings were now spent on a shooting range in the country, where they revelled in the cavalier massacre of an unarmed battalion of clay and paper targets.

Even after their first visit, the experience seemed to infuse my incorrigible mother with a prodigiously hideous free-gurning excitement that propelled her like a barrage of buck-shot into her Sunday rants with ballistic momentum.

It was agony. Like sharing the house with Billy the Kid; the tedious way she would childishly crouch and fire her outstretched index finger at you. I could have blown her fucking head off.

# 60

Desperation compels us to play our weakest hand.

I didn't think about the range too much, but the idea that it may actually belong to my parents didn't occur to me until some weeks after they had begun to use it. Not, in fact, until I had overheard part of the telephone conversation that first placed the thought in my mind. And then, a few days later, I eavesdropped on a discussion my parents were having about it, in which they mentioned their surprise at the ease with which they had been granted the necessary firearms licences. My mother insisted that God had handled the application personally, and said something about the potential benefit of opening the range up to a wider than anticipated public. They then went on about how much money they had left in the kitty after completing the purchase. It confirmed that they had bought the land with Church donations and, as I discovered soon after from official correspondence I just happened to discover lying around in one of her bedroom drawers, had registered it in the name of a religious charity they had specifically established to facilitate their application and which, they claimed, was intended to provide support and relief in the rehabilitation of both ex and serving military personnel from the emotional rigours of active service.

In two years, the Church of CHRIST had swollen to almost a hundred local members. Another one hundred and sixty-eight mail order associate members, who had been groomed and recruited from repeatedly placed adverts in the personal pages of various national magazines, also counted among the ranks, and many proved to be every bit, if not even more zealous than the eighty or ninety who typically formed the weekly congregation in the almost full to capacity tabernacle above the disused bakery.

Inevitably, some of the long-distance members were deemed to be of questionable practical value; their frailties suggested by the scrawly handwritten signatures on their exchanges which identified them as Saint Roger from the Hounds of Crewe, The Blessed Virgin of Death, Shitbrained Sue from S-heavenoaks and Bren Gun Dave the Divine, amongst an assortment of less poetic others. My mother encouraged them all, with each being sent a signed copy of The Unclosable Eye and baited further with the assurance of a dedicated place of worship in their own locality in the not too distant future. She industriously solicited and received generous donations from all parts of the country to help fund a national promotion of the CHRISTian Church, and to secure for all donors an essential panoply of personal post-life benefits and blessings.

During the same period, my mother's arsenal had matured, too, and a dozen more noticeably less vintage handguns now augmented her collection. Almost the entirety of which she continued to conceal beneath the dining room floorboards whenever they were not being made available to each of the local members, who were actively urged to make paid use of the firearms and the shooting range as an integral constituent of both their spiritual instruction and personal development.

To encourage the profitable take-up of bullets for the Lord, members were also warned that an army of flesh alone would be insufficient defence in the impending war against the machinery of evil. My mother would often reinforce the imperative by encouraging the singalong of a specially contrived ditty from Psalm Eighteen to remind her flock that "He trains my hands for battle, He strengthens my arm to draw a bronze bow." Invariably ending the musical refrain by quoting Ephesians, chapter six, verse twelve, "for we wrestle not against flesh and blood, but against principalities, against powers, against rulers of the darkness of this world, against wickedness in high places."

Within a few months, the invitation had been extended to almost all mail order members to indulge themselves in the restorative luxury of a fully inclusive, 'educational', one week package holiday break, specifically tailored to the catering of their spiritual needs and emotional restitution. Each uncharitably expensive break pledged to comprehensively fulfil all possible requirements. Including travel to and from the range on three days, personal instruction and practical supervision, scriptural guidance and support, as well as the added provision of a carefully cooked breakfast and evening meal to complete the comfort of their stay in one of the several unused rooms at my parents' large house in a 'quiet and picturesque village location a few miles from the centre of the World Heritage City of Bath'.

To augment this smorgasbord of irresistible attractions, a taxied return trip in my mother's new Jaguar Saloon to and from the Sunday Church service, and a ceremonial introduction to the assembled as a highly revered and greatly esteemed guest of honour were offered as complimentary additional incentives.

It was another reason for me to dread going home.

Before long, however, I felt the inexorable pull of curiosity and almost against my will, began to imagine how it might feel to handle a recoil and mess around with firearms on the range.

The more I thought about it, the more inextricably attracted to the idea I became. I dropped a battery of subtle hints in conversation and waited for an invitation to try a live round or two. It didn't come. I knew she was making me ask outright. I held off for as long as I could before temptation got the better of me.

With no plausible alternative, I simply had to swallow my pride and act.

It was dissolving my spleen that my mother was able to play with guns and enjoy an experience I felt was for no good reason being denied me. I absolutely had to know, as she knew, how it felt to wield a chunk of lethal power and pump a shower of slugs into the heart of a sitting target. I dreamt about it. About packing a piece and wandering around town looking for trouble.

It was now a delicate question of deciding exactly how to proceed without completely losing face.

I felt, however, that I had waited long enough already, and justified the impending suicide of my credibility by reminding myself that other people, who I didn't even know, and who had no right to hang around anywhere near my house, much less dispossess me of the one advantage of being saddled with a lunatic in it, were being treated as preferential members of my own family. It seemed to work.

'Can I have a go on the range, Mum?' I appealed, at last, with as much self-consciously deferential enthusiasm tempered by as convincing an approach to warmth as I could muster without puking.

'No, you can't,' she coldly replied, cheerfully thrusting the bayonet of her refusal into my specially pre-softened eyes, 'not unless you join the Church and earn the privilege.'

The brevity of the exchange was determined by the certainty of both parties knowing exactly which orifice I would advise her to blow the suggestion out of. And knowing equally well that she was pathologically incapable of resisting such an opportunity to be as spiteful as possible.

'Forget it,' I shrugged, nonchalantly.

I felt deflated, and it probably showed. Even if I had managed to conceal my disappointment, she would have revelled in the triumph of her checkmate. I didn't face her to confirm it, but I was sure she was smirking.

I winced imperceptibly, and silently blasted myself for losing grip and making her victory so easy. I needed to react immediately, to demonstrably redress the naked disgrace of my failure. So I casually picked up a newspaper from the kitchen table and flicked through it glibly for emphasis.

'Your father won't agree to it, either. The range is mine, so there's no point asking him.'

'I wasn't going to,' I assured her, lowering the newspaper without looking in her direction, raising my eyebrows and shaking my head slowly, like I couldn't believe she was still banging on about it. 'It's not a big enough deal.'

By the Christmas of that year, the range had proved extraordinarily popular. And my father had officially become recognised by the Church and its members as Our Blessed Brother.

# 61

Is it not preferable sometimes, in the loneliness of our memories, to know that others once remembered them, too?

Yssy and I shopped laboriously in the snow for Christmas presents, before deciding to buy each other exactly the same Japanese print and heading off to Sally Lunn's for tea.

There's something about the relative novelty of such weather at that festive time of year which seems to promote a greater sense of amity among people who, having sought shelter and warmth, are left nursing the oddly pleasurable still wet stings of their exposure to it, and the general atmospheric tone of the crowded tea room was good-humoured; upbeat and conversational.

Yssy slid her elfin frame into the Windsor Chair at a table next to the wall and sighed, smiling something far away at me as I ordered a pot of chai from a passing waitress.

She lifted my hand gently from its temporary perch near the centre of the red and white checked mercerised cotton tablecloth and squeezed it with an excited little shake.

'They've gone to Winchester for the weekend and won't be back until tomorrow night. But they've left plenty of sherry for us.'

She almost always referred to her parents as 'they'. As though it were constantly essential for her to re-establish an acceptable distance between herself and the embarrassing wealth and lifestyle they enjoyed. It was a genial, though sincere detachment.

'They', in my own estimation, were good, easy-going, liberal-minded parents who had unconditionally welcomed me as a surrogate son into their family from the start. I liked them a lot, as I had from the immediate thaw of our initial encounter.

By which time Yssy's father had already sold his hugely profitable advertising agency, that still retained him on the payroll as a consultant. He now seemed to pocket a great deal of money for not doing very much. But the amount the agency paid him paled into insignificance compared to the fortune 'they' inherited from Yssy's maternal grandfather, a well known equestrian who made serious money from the breeding and training of racehorses. 'They' took me on holiday with them and included me on frequent visits to their friends who generally lived in attractive properties around the country. I regularly found myself at the receiving end of their generosity. As did others.

We recently left the house on the evening of Yssy's sixteenth birthday but didn't get out of the door before her father slipped her twenty-five pounds and instructed us to enjoy a night on the town with it. Almost as soon as we stepped off the bus in the city centre, she stuffed it all into the hand of a homeless chap sitting under a railway bridge and we went to the pictures.

Unselfconscious displays of affection were freehandedly showered upon Yssy by parents who treated us both sensitively, with consideration and respect. Even some way short of the years to support us, we regarded ourselves as adults and they didn't contradict us. Not only were they happy for us to spend weekends alone in the house whenever they were away, but they even replaced Yssy's bed with a double, a few weeks after her birthday, as an additional incentive to house-sit, as if we needed one. We were trusted to be responsible and to not wreck the place with our own parties. A trust we didn't betray on either count.

Alone in the house or not, we now spent almost every weekend there.

The trickle of passers by outside the bay window of the tea shop became Lowryesque in the tumbling violet twilight, with feathers of snow, falling and settled, reflecting the embers of the afternoon, making it appear slightly earlier in the day than it was. Yet even in the brewing gloom, the occasion was suffused with the saturated colour of our being inalienably conjoined to it, as it so often is when we are young, and when everything we experience feels so tangible and real. We seem to act out our lives in technicolour then, which fades and pales into more pastel shades of indifference as we age.

'I'm hungry,' I said, as I stroked Yssy's hand and waited for the waitress to bring our tea, 'shall we eat something?'

'No,' she replied, softly, after a momentary glance at the celebrated buns on some of the other tables, 'let's go back and have something in front of the fire; it'll be nicer.'

Twenty minutes later, we ambled out warmer into the thickening dark, and around the corner to the Orange Grove.

As we scaled the serpentine hill hand in hand to the house, the snow fell more heavily and stilled the luminous night to a picture. Even the air passing through us seemed to acquire an ethereal quality, and the sprinkled amber muffle from barely patched black iron streetlights spilled lacy threads of entrancing mist onto our idling footsteps.

You know how sometimes you can get an overpowering sense of eternity in the magic of a moment, and could blissfully spend the rest of your life immersed in the consummate perfection of it? Maybe it's a metaphor. Maybe it's a presentiment; a terrible glimpse into another world.

# 62

Yssy sketched me by candlelight after dinner as we sat in front of the fire listening to The Eagles on the radio, half a bottle of Oloroso lighter. Through the soft half-light and open curtains, the empyrean otherworldliness of the quietly glowing night infused the supernal tide of our wordless embraces. We went to bed at midnight, after watching the snow falling in the garden around the drive lights for an hour.

'I love you more than anyone will ever love you, and more than anyone ever has,' my mother assured her congregation, with a fiery passion, 'more than the evil rich love their money, more than the shadowy Masters of Mankind love their power, more than the odious banks and multi-nationals love their greed. I love you as our Heavenly Father loves you, because He has invested in me all the power of His love to love you with. And because He has chosen you, my beloved Brothers and Sisters, to be most greatly respected and most deeply loved.

Fear nothing on this Earth, you Children of God; we *shall* prevail. We are assured in Deuteronomy, chapter twenty-eight, verse seven that "The Lord shall cause thine enemies that rise up against thee to be smitten before thy face: they shall come out against thee one way, and flee before thee seven ways." And our Father has made it known to me, my sainted children, that death shall never be visited upon us as the reward for our endeavours. He has promised me that, as He carried His beloved servant Enoch, He will raise us in victory to Paradise aboard His chariot of fire, and our flesh shall not pay for our destruction of His foes. We must nevertheless remember the Book of Genesis teaches us that the Devil will surely attempt to divide us with doubt, and seek without rest to divert us from our path of glory. But the falling of his shadow shall not darken our journey; and with the guidance of the Lord, we shall fight with the zeal of Joshua to restore His light of righteousness to the world.'

A pervasive hush filled the room like a pall of thick smoke, as my mother recessed in the composure of a few unbroken moments of reflection and knelt in the quiet, candle-lit cathedral of her admiration for the inimitable brilliance of her magmatic eruption. Calmly cradling, in the fashion of an ancient mystic, her resting right hand in the palm of her left and staring in motionless meditation into the unseen spider webbing among the decorated far cornicing above the furthest seated.

It was in the soft soil of these fertile moments that, perhaps for the first time, the entire century of palpably affected attendees, so ably moved by their Holy Sister's address, solemnly tended the visible sprouting of their salvation in undisturbed introspection, and contemplated the impending reality of their promised place in history and Heaven. The suffocating silence was at last ventilated by a whisper of sighs.

From the fathomless depths of cumbrous rumination, a delicate, hesitant, middle-aisle seated voice tremulously attempted to flutter like a broken-winged bird into the ether.

'Are we to engage in physical combat against the enemies of goodness, Sister?'

My mother lowered her unfocused gaze slowly, and fixed the aged, silver-bearded owner with the stiletto of a stare.

'We are to vanquish them utterly with the power of the Lord,' she replied, cryptically.

# 63

And that night the angel of the LORD went and struck down 185,000 in the camp of the Assyrians. And when people arose early in the morning, behold, these were all dead bodies. *2 Kings 19:35*

The Book of Enoch reveals to us that the first two hundred angels to appear on Earth were evil. They taught man to kill, to fornicate, to deceive and to be godless and corrupt in all his ways.

These errant messengers from Heaven, dispatched to watch over the world, kidnapped and raped Earthly women to spawn a hybrid race of deviant giants called Nephilim, who pillaged the Earth and ultimately devoured mankind. The God-threateningly powerful sons and daughters of these fallen angelic-fathered prediluvian biblical giants of evil, who themselves enjoyed few things more than the sexual conquest of mortal women, continued to stalk the world unbounded in the chemically polluted outpourings of my mother's nightmares. Presented themselves in front of television news cameras to justify their wholesale economic and spiritual slaughter of undefended indigenous poor on traditionally hand-farmed land, rich with exploitable natural resources.

They were the thieving, murderous, megalomaniacal heads of industries which served to further enslave and impoverish the already desperately unenviable quality of the lives of their choiceless workforce in piss-poor countries collusively run by psychotic and embezzling despots. They were the captains of propaganda and the enviably well rewarded apologists for such kleptocracies and other havens of obscene immorality. Sowers and launderers of lies. Shape-shifting political slime, who'll come over as your friend to help themselves to the contents of your pockets, then sell you for dogmeat when they've left you too poor to feed yourself. They were the young, sexually promiscuous and depraved. They were the threateningly content, ordinary people in any walk of life anywhere, who had discovered a plausible alternative to the warmongering bigotry of holy words.

'And when these evil angels feared their dreams of violent retribution from God for their own nefarious deeds, they pleaded with Enoch to beseech the Lord to be merciful. The Lord refused forgiveness and cast their souls into the eternal pit of damnation, saying "let it be known to you that the things you have done, and your wives have done, and their sons, and the wives of their sons, by your licentiousness upon the Earth, that the land is weeping and denouncing you and lamenting the deeds of your children for the harm that you have done to it. Behold, your destruction is coming." And God did let loose His vengeance upon them, flooding the globe to destroy the vile bodies of their villainous offspring. Yet, the Devil in his cunning contrived to spare them and preserve for ever their undying wickedness. And through him the Nephilim survived the wrath of the Lord; becoming disembodied demons and stalking the world as rapacious agents of their diabolical master. It is these ghouls who encourage the godless to destroy the Lord's good Earth with iniquity in the guise of progress and enlightenment.

We, our Father's True Soldiers, shall not rest until we have rooted these strangling weeds from the garden of God and restored the light of His word to the world. And I am eternally blessed to announce to you, my children, that we have already been provided with the means to embark upon the first steps of our inevitable victory. As of Wednesday last, I am humbled to reveal that our Heavenly Father has secured for us the legacy of fifty thousand pounds from the passing to his side of our dearly beloved Sister Muriel Rossie in October. This is the most wonderful proof that the Lord our God has spoken to us and promised that He will not allow us to fail in our endeavours.'

# 64

We are too easily silenced by the tyranny of words.

I don't know what, if anything, my mother said to Cha to rebuke him for his homosexuality and contribute to him landing lifeless in the drink without so much as a kiss goodbye, but I often wondered.

Given half an opportunity, she would have very likely quoted Romans 1, 27, or Timothy 1, 8-11, or Leviticus 18, 22, or mixed and matched from an arsenal of other scriptural castigations. Any one of them alone may have been enough to end the suffering of a despairing man clinging to the straws of a solitary struggle to accept something he could not.

A year earlier, she had preached Leviticus, chapter twenty, verse thirteen, to an audibly appreciative reception. For those of you who may not be familiar with the passage, it goes something like this:

"If a man has sexual relations with another man, as one does with a woman, both of them have done what is detestable. They are to be put to death; their blood being upon their own hands." She loved that one.

## 65

Wisdom flourishes in the nursery of reason.

Yssy and I often partied at weekends, mainly at her friends' or at her parents' friends' houses. They usually began as an adventure, but I almost always found myself soon becoming tired and disappointed by them, somehow. And after a while, I typically forgot my participatory obligation to socialise, and ended up staring, more sadly than anything, into the unnervingly empty spaces between unconvincingly energetic crowds of people attempting to profitably market their indefatigable self-belief as vital attractions to each other. I never felt like telling anybody who I was; being perfectly aware of how such descriptions could seldom be trusted.

We were invited by a minor film director acquaintance of Yssy's father to a 'celebrity' party at a smart Regency terrace in Cheltenham once, where, we were confidently assured, we would meet a register of famous actors and musicians, amongst others. We arrived late but didn't recognise anyone. A few disappointed minutes of avidly confused gawping later, we realised that the event was less a celebrity laced affair than a veritable Who's Who of complete unknowns. It was a disappointing introduction to the long anticipated gala, but despite none of our new acquaintances there being recognisable; we hobnobbed amicably with a succession of amiable aspirants and enjoyed a pleasant and informative evening. Yssy perhaps enjoying the occasion a little more than me, and naturally courting popularity by being typically interested in everything that everybody had to say.

Even without making any of my anticipated new musical celebrity contacts, I had occasionally been bunking off school in recent months to provide the mostly improvised acoustic blues solo support act for a modestly well known local band at their mainly one-off university gigs around the country. But each time we stayed in a distant town or city overnight it tormented me almost beyond endurance to be so far away from Yssy. I felt lost without her. And except for when I immersed myself in a song while simultaneously dredging up an idea for the following number, I felt irredeemably shipwrecked and broken. Lonely and sick. I ate hardly anything at all or slept for more than minutes at a time. The money I earned for feeling this way wouldn't have covered the cost of all the complimentary bottles of Newcastle Brown I could drink. And although it had been Yssy who'd encouraged me to travel, had it not been for the acclaim I received for playing, the sacrifice of her company would have been worth immeasurably less than the reward.

I couldn't deny that the imbibable reward was welcome, but the applause intoxicated me more than the beer. Nevertheless, the alcohol was an essential distraction, which made it easier for me to spend long dark hours in hotel rooms with daydream hangovers and half a dozen other people who didn't want to be there, either. The front-man of the band's infant daughter, who grew up to become a painter of repute, invariably bunked down in a chest of drawers or a suitcase and sang through the night at inopportune moments.

I told my parents I was staying with classmates.

I was honest about my exploits at bootcamp, though. If anybody asked me where I had been, I told them. My English teacher, who was eventually to deny a number of school inmates a crucial aspect of their extracurricular activity by forfeiting his career as a result of being unable to successfully conceal the contents of his greenhouse when the police turned up to raid it, frequently loaned me his generously supplemented guitar case for the purpose.

My ungigged new country rock cover combo went by the modestly confrontational pre-punk handle of Chris Myass and the Screwyoos, and featured a left-handed rhythm guitarist who had lost the top third of his right index finger when he absent-mindedly stuck it under a sledge blade a few years earlier. We rehearsed at his house once, a peculiar, dingy modern monstrosity, where his brass-necked father stared tactlessly across the room at Yssy for practically the entire session. He couldn't seem to resist the need to rotate his encephalitically plus-sized, over-greased Teddy Boy quiffed cranium ninety degrees every few minutes and study her as though she were an ornament, while she sat knitting on a cream cushioned beech backed dining chair in the corner of the room, trying not to notice him.

An uncomfortable conglomeration of musical fits and starts later, I felt I could no longer let the situation ride and had no choice but to address the problem directly with an unrehearsed refrain. He begged our pardon with a contrived addendum of wounded surprise but didn't stop looking; claiming that he was keeping his eye on the cheap mantle clock gracing a crude Jacobean revival credence table stuck against a revolting pin striped papered wall and next to a particularly hideous sparkling gold and glass cocktail cabinet behind Yssy, as he was waiting on a mate to go out for the evening. Yssy had by then inched her chair gradually away from his unflinching gaze in a series of conspicuous attempts to avoid it. And although she said nothing, she had seldom looked less at ease.

I withdrew my contribution to the rehearsal shortly after speaking out, and we left. Having been accompanied to the door and waved off by the person who had made it impossible for us to stay.

I had no idea that Yssy would be so exposed to the fixation of this dullard I had never before seen, but I felt guilty for taking her there and apologised to her as soon as we set foot on the crazy paved path to freedom. She casually shrugged the awkward incident off, as if she had forgotten about it already.

It was true that Yssy attracted attention. She couldn't help it. But it wasn't deliberate. She wasn't a girl who insisted on creating an impression in a crowd, and unlike some, had no desire to market herself to passers by. Comfortable with who she was, and confident, she had no need to parade romantic invitations, or encourage no-hopers to fall in love with her to inflate her self-esteem.

But the lure of her ingenerate beauty was enhanced by the mysterious feline composure that framed it. The puissant combination radiating in tandem to produce a magnetism almost impossible not to succumb to.

Even my mother skirted close to the brink of treating her with affection, and practically doted on her as a favourite child. Not a difficult choice, given the alternative. An enviable appointment, nevertheless, and one that Yssy may easily have exploited had it been customary for her to profiteer in such a manner. Instead, she addressed my mother with a quiet courtesy, occasionally extending her respectful formality to a friendliness that expected nothing in return.

Beneath Yssy's unassuming persona, the array of her bouquet featured colours more subtle and striking than the proverbial warm, soft, feminine, strong and vulnerable. I catalogued them diligently and was besotted with them all.

Although, I attempted to restrict her direct exposure to as few of my mother's characteristics as I could. Not that it was always possible for us to sidestep the frequent sudden fire-crackers of her extraordinary outbursts.

But above anything else, it was paramount to conceal any information at all that may inadvertently reveal the exact whereabouts of Yssy's parents' conspicuous abode to my mother, lest she turn up on their doorstep waving a clenched fist of The Unclosable Eye in their faces and inviting herself into the house to appal them. They had been thoroughly and frequently warned to be on their guard against such an obvious disaster. Yssy, too, had been instructed to explain that both she and her parents lived in complete destitution in a charity-run doss house on the river, if ever she was caught off guard without me to drag her away and asked to elaborate on her address. So far, we had escaped further interrogation with 'Batheaston'.

My father invariably treated Yssy with unaffected charm and consideration, but I couldn't afford to allow us to let our defences down with him, either, and to be too charitable with any potentially damning slip of the tongue. I was beset with concerns on every visit, as it was. Each ballooning anxiety threatening to burst into a full blown neurosis, particularly if I couldn't immediately step in physically to narrow any conversation with either of my parents to a short exchange of simple pleasantries and escort Yssy, before they ran the risk of developing into anything else, to the relatively motherless harbour of my private, spacious and boltable bedroom, where we subsequently spent most of our time, both on and off my bed.

Naturally, I would have preferred my mercurial nemesis to have been normal, and to have trusted her not to wreak havoc on a whim. Instead, her internecine unpredictability had driven me to the edge of my own madness. And although I frequently offered excuses for her behaviour, I never overcame my fear that Yssy would experience an episode too many and be frightened off.

Fortunately, my precautions were effective more often than not and, for most of the time, we were left alone.

My bedroom was a modestly isolated haven at the end of an appallingly decorated landing. The walls surrounding it being presented in a way that suggested they had long ago been penetrated by a particularly vigorous species of bilious Art Nouveau Knotweed.

To provide an essential modicum of redress for the sensory assault on approach to my door, I had covered almost every inch of available wall space inside my room with a panoramic gallery of more acceptable images. Some, the featured weekly centre-spread posters from Sounds magazines, which I plastered over my ceiling, too, like an instrument-bearing pantheon of musical immortals; others, Japanese prints and Impressionist block-mounts from Athena. Filling the gaps between were one or two Tibetan tantric prints and a small, glossy, soft focus, David Hamilton photographic semi-nude of two beautiful young women. Artistic and innocuous, but guaranteed, I thought, to inflame my mother's wrath on first sight and have her tearing off the wall in some kind of mouth foamingly outraged blue-pencilling trauma. It didn't happen.

I was unable to explain her apparent indifference to the obvious obscenity and assumed that she had simply become too preoccupied with her paying guests and other distractions to be fully aware of just how much such things would have affected her in the past. Nevertheless, her unexpected tolerance of the nudity she had always so vociferously railed against had wrong-footed me. I'm not sure I would have bothered to squeeze the picture into the small space at all had it not been for the near certainty that its brazen exhibition would provoke a reaction. But no, nothing. I had miscalculated. And although these strangely invisible, partially naked young women had been ineffectually gracing my own semi-private retreat for quite some time, the truth was that I'd been lately fast losing the inclination to argue with my mother, anyway. Not only because it wasn't worth it; I mean, I know perfectly well that if you argue with an idiot, no-one will know who the idiot is, but I really didn't feel like spouting off any more.

I had Yssy to thank for my new easygoingness. I never heard her raise her voice against, or utter a demeaning word about anyone. I never saw her lose her temper or her composure, either, and my propinquity to such inspirational dispassion had progressively affected my slightly less than accommodating general attitude towards my mother for the better.

Neither Yssy nor I had offered the other a single word in anger in the two years we had been together. The cataclysmic ugliness of an egocentric shouting match or falling out never claiming a momentary place in our repertoire of responses to occasional disagreements.

Yssy's quietude was born from an armature of unusual natural strength and resilience. She never felt threatened or offended by a divergence of opinion. And was never too shy to insist or too intransigent to backtrack. Either way, she invariably considered my own preference or objection and we routinely ended up syllogising our respective points in amicable conversation. A technique I effortlessly adopted for arriving at a decision in which both parties retained their dignity and the respect of the other. Besides, my default position with Yssy in such affairs was to defer to her fourteen week seniority, and her almost invariably superior common sense and judgement; so the potential for significant discord between us seldom arose.

Even in the ongoing struggle with the bane of my composure, I enjoyed the novelty of now not being so readily drawn. I had managed to soften my mother-baited tongue and was enjoying my metamorphosis into a new and, under most circumstances, much calmer person.

'I love it!' exclaimed Yssy, as we peered through the rain from beneath her umbrella into the umpteenth shop window at a powder blue, three-quarter length pea coat, buttoned up to the abbreviated neck of a headless mannequin. 'Do you think it would look nice on me? I have to try it.'

I followed her in. 'I think it would look even better in red,' I replied, hopefully.

Beautiful as she was, she never looked more perfect than when she sported the scarlet coat I first saw her enveloped in at the Pav. And whenever she had dressed in it, the image immediately transported me back to the unique magic of that auspicious moment. I would have been more than happy if she'd never dressed in any other colour. But the coat I loved so much was getting old now, and she hadn't worn it for a while.

I watched, besotted by her simmering exhibition of dissilient sensuality, as she pulled the pale blue fabric around her slender shoulders and posed in the mirror with it like a model. The splay of her long, dark hair breezing and bouncing, caressing her angora draped shoulders as a stole. Afraid of prematurely bringing the show to a close by moving, I fixed my eyes on her almost without blinking and followed her every movement like a spotlight, as the cat-walk ballet continued.

'I think you look lovely,' I said, as she glided to the rail and lifted the Venician red version from it.

She reprised the choreography of her steps in a truncated variation, as though she had already arrived at her decision and was now merely going through the motions. Then she smiled a little, flirty, satisfied smile at me.

'I'm going to have this one,' she whispered.

Two streets away, at the offices of the local newspaper, my mother had arrived at the midway point of delivering an interview to a journalist for an article about her selfless charitable exertions on behalf of the Church of CHRIST, in regard to the psychological rehabilitation of conflict trauma-tised Armed Services personnel.

274

# 66

The ground on which we construct our reason is no firmer than the atmosphere of a dream.

The brand spanking new derelict Temple of CHRIST nestled less than half a mile from the shooting range like a festered carbuncle on one of the green carpeted western slopes of the seven-hilled city. Bought at an unmissable bargain basement price in a lull at a local property auction, it passed swiftly to my mother's raised hand unappreciated by almost any other bidder.

Already, after only a few weeks of concerted professional and volunteer attention, the extensive ex-boarding school's transformation into a fully self-contained place of worship, study and accommodation was now visibly underway, and a palpable air of excitement at its growing transformation permeated the mood of members enjoying their last Sunday gatherings above the disused bakery. Even the flaming, valedictory vocalising of my mother's final sermon there, taken in part from chapter two, verse twelve of the Second Book of Thessalonians, which decreed that "they all might be damned who believed not the truth, but had pleasure in unrighteousness," could not darken the party atmosphere.

## 67

Cursed is the one who is remiss in doing the work of the LORD, and cursed is he who withholds his sword from bloodshed. *Jeremiah, 48:10*

Services were held at the transforming temple before the refurbishment of the rest of the building and its associated properties was complete. The predominance of the colour green in its deep emerald shade for the ubiquitous drapery and coverings, including the loop piled carpeting and cushioned seating, was not entirely unnoticeable. Neither could the glaring over-accommodation of the worshipful membership in the capacious area that had once held the school assemblies be easily ignored.

My mother's response to the disconcerting dwarfing of her congregation was to insist upon it that each member dutifully obey the will of God, as divinely communicated to her in another incident of supernatural revelation, and introduce more frightened, lost and angry sheep to the flock by sedulously proselytising in all the nearby centres of population. This may now, upon the same celestial instruction, include a small number of The Poor. Providing their numerical representation constitute no more than one-tenth of the overall membership, and only then, upon the specific condition that each prospective Poorsoldier be able to clearly demonstrate a genuine outrage at the golden-throned manufacturers of their poverty, and possess the conviction in their fury to catalyse others into an impassioned desire for revenge.

Previously, God had decreed that the blessed poor shall inherit the Earth, but had also expressed concern that until such time, entrenched poverty would be likely to constitute a substantial distraction from the prosecution of His will to members who would necessarily need to primarily occupy themselves with thoughts of where their next meal was coming from.

By the end of spring, the refurbishment of the study rooms and residential accommodation was almost complete, and the Church of CHRIST was thirty-one members stronger.

The decoration in all the smaller rooms throughout the complex was simple. Spartan and functional. But the areas themselves were comfortably spacious and smelled reassuringly new and clean. The only obvious concession to aesthetics on the stark white walls above the omnipresent green carpeting of each, was a twenty by twenty-four inch Lincoln green velvet framed portrait of my statuesque mother looking distinctly arboreal; wearing a slightly puff-shouldered, mossy, long dress in a grassy garden and holding some kind of wooden, green beaker with a gold rim to her chest. It was the same photograph as the large one hanging half way up the wall at the far end of the Congregational Hall, which was pretty much the first thing you saw when you went in.

The smallest of the rooms was the bygone chaplain's office at the head of the corridor that led away from the main hall on the near side. It was the only room so far accorded a function name. This had been stamped as two capital letters on an ornate brass plaque attached to the door. Inside the H.A. were two large, immovable, seventeenth century oak coffers sporting newly fitted iron lockplates with broad, steel, fastened padlock shackles running through them. Each solid, five-foot, six-plank coffer weighed a ton, even before it had been filled and bolted to the floor. The picture on the wall was different, too. It was just about noticeable that this photo, even though my mother was dressed in exactly the same way as in all the others, had been taken on the range.

# 68

My father disagreed with my mother that the poor should be so excluded from the Church's membership, arguing that they ought to be taken care of, rather than remain contemptuously overlooked. Discussions between the two descended into full scale late night arguments, during which my mother frequently shouted my father down with such dismissive phrases as 'well, you pay for them, then!'

Clearly, a compromise had been reached by the time the Bath News and Sport ran an article about how the Church was now offering a limited daily number of free meal places for under-privileged members of the community, who were encouraged to reciprocate by voluntarily engaging in menial tasks around the temple complex. A small number of eager new members were quickly recruited from the ranks of the devoutly grateful.

An unexpected but widely appreciated consequence of the provision of free CHRIST meals for the poor, was a steady flow of unsolicited private and corporate donations of both money and food to help continue the project. Before long, several shops and supermarkets in the city had demonstrated a keen interest in taking advantage of a complimentary opportunity to identify themselves favourably with worthy philanthropic enterprises, and offered generous, regular contributions of freshly out of date and consequently unsellable stock.

The number of available and accepted early afternoon luncheon places increased significantly. Members who were able to lend a hand were drafted in to provide practical help and supervision to the almost immediately popular endeavour.

The lunches produced a number of regular diners. Some being over-stressed single mothers struggling on state benefits, who often turned up with a clutch of pre-school age children in tow. One or two others were fresh but as yet jobless post-grads. The largest contingent, however, suffered from long term drug and alcohol abuse and directed sudden associated bouts of aggression at anyone at any time for no particular reason. Often drawing warnings that they were risking being asked to leave if they continued to disrespect the sanctity of the environment by using foul or abusive language. Although the majority of them gradually became familiar with and trusting of the volunteer temple staff, and began to reveal themselves as the vulnerable, sensitive but unhappy and emotionally precarious people they were.

A couple of months subsequent to the successful implementation of his idea to provide free lunches for the poor, my father felt sufficiently moved by the plight of the same people he had now come to regard as his friends to introduce a scripturally based programme of alcohol and drug reform.

My mother, who had not made a habit of being overly visible in the refectory during the luncheon period, judged the diners and their lifestyles very much less sympathetically, and despite managing to be relatively personable when called upon to make an appearance for prayers at the opening and close of the period, could not fruitfully devise a facial expression to fully conceal her still spilling contempt.

As a result, the prayer duties swiftly and more naturally fell to my father, and my mother began to restrict her personal appearances to the more formal barnstorming occasions that required no such pleasantries.

## 69

Myth is the master of truth.

The p.a. feedback from the stand-held microphone in the Congregational Hall howled like a holy storm, while a near-biblical torrent thrashed itself with a voice of sand against the golden tinted skin of the windows. My mother waited, unfazed, unhurried, her composure never less than immaculately assured.

'We, the immortal few,' she began, pausing for a moment to test the suddenly compliant silence, 'by the endless love of almighty God, have been considered uniquely deserving of the magnificent gifts He has bestowed upon us, and which we have accepted with our deepest love and the knowledge that we are now indeed indebted to our Heavenly Father to the full value of our lives. I have also received the great gift of His solemn instruction to inform each and every one of His beloved Soldiers that we must all consider ourselves now the most valued property of the Lord by unfailingly bearing the rightfully coloured stain of His pure, green Earth, and from here on in, regarding His glorious temple as our own true and natural home.'

There was more. But what my mother meant, in plain English, was that all members were now required by divine instruction to wear green shirts or dresses whenever they occupied the temple complex. The bit about regarding the temple as their own home was about to have much more disconcerting implications.

Boxes of green shirts and simple, same green dresses were dutifully pulled open by my father, and the garments handed out to the inquisitively queueing end of sermon gathering. Unity and inspiration, deference and fate now being consolidated by the absolutism of a single shade.

The Church was respectfully cited at various municipal meetings as a model of social conscience, and local political leaders intoned favourably on the subject of its growing charitable profile. Such endorsements swiftly culminated in the securing of a modest but significant contribution of initial funding towards my father's drug and alcohol rehabilitation programme by a quartet of senior civic officials who were keen to blow their own deeply caring and philanthropic horns to an impressed and admiring newspaper reading public.

# 70

Miniature victories diminish in stature when the vanquished refuses to fall.

Spring term arrived in a shower of hail as I waited at the gym to escape for the afternoon.

I had been impatiently marking off the days before I could legally leave school in the notebook I had bought around a year earlier specifically for the purpose. And although I couldn't wait to enter the final cross, I had not subjected myself to the indignity of a full five-day-a-week incarceration there for a single stretch in the previous eighteen months or more. Managing at best, two or three days in a good week. I could also be laid up in the countryside around my school, or in town around Yssy's, with regular bouts of unspecified illness for weeks on end.

Fortunately, my extreme absence had not been fully recorded by the attendance register due to my brazen audacity and a systematic implementation of the well perfected practice of securing my roll call mark in the morning after a good singalong in assembly, then, ostensibly enroute to my first period of involuntary detention, strolling nonchalantly past the headmaster's study window, as though the sound of my determined crunching over the gravel outside it were confirmation of my pursuit of legitimate business, and bunking off for the rest of the day. The fact was, I was hardly ever there.

My attendance had dropped off so precipitously that, months earlier, the master who usually caned me for truanting invited me, in school time, to come in specially for a man to man chat about why I refused to show up for classes.

It turned out that the vicious bastard who had forged a successful career in convincing the boys that he was a genuine psycho, was actually quite a nice guy. We sat in the sun on the white painted wooden steps of the school's cricket pavilion and had a really pleasant tête-à-tête in which we discussed all manner of things, and then I went home.

Years later, after he died, I felt an unshifting regret for not having thanked him properly. And for not having spoken to him again. The disaffiliation bothered me. I wished I had accepted an opportunity to let him know that by dropping his guard and proving that he wasn't, in fact, the sadistic, psychotic, cane-happy martinet he so diligently portrayed himself to be, by rendering himself vulnerable on that one genial occasion and demonstrating that he actually cared, he had invested in me a poignant lesson in expressing honesty at the expense of personal interest. An instruction which has remained a deeply valued precept to me since.

I abandoned all pretences of maintaining any kind of meaningful relationship with the inane establishment and stopped going anywhere near it altogether for the last two or three months of my lawful internment. Returning only to sit my exams, which I did as a result of an arrangement I had previously contrived with the bemused, exasperated, often avoided, but unexpectedly accommodating headmaster.

Yssy had been set to stay on at The Gulag, but we decided we would see more of each other if we studied for our A's together at the local college. Which is, despite some not entirely unreasonably held but eventually overcome educationally based concerns by Yssy's parents, exactly what we did.

I was officially resurrected and rose from the shackles of my calaboose at Easter. Legally redelivered to the world rebranded and suddenly full of previously denied potential.

I revelled in the completion of my seemingly impossible achievement, while at the same time harbouring a nagging disappointment that I hadn't actually accomplished my objective through a single physical act of punctuating anger. Like knocking a winning six out of the ground with a member of the opposing team's bat. Nevertheless, I filled my lungs with the clean, fresh air of a long-awaited liberation now rendered visible to all, and celebrated my new circumstances with the vigour of an athlete.

Festivities continued well into the following week. By the end of which I had fulfilled another ambition and secured my first full-time job. I had now arrived at the cusp of becoming a respectable, self-supporting, fully contributing member of society.

Having accepted my first written offer of gainful employment by return post, I immediately set about decking myself out in a manner appropriate to my impending professional standing and opened an account with a gentleman's tailor in town, where I ordered my prototypical bespoke three-piece creation with an interesting array of extortionately expensive self-styled additions that ensured I wouldn't be mistaken for a chartered accountant.

While awaiting the completion of my visionary ensemble,

I took up the summer post in a rigidly conventional quantity surveyors office underdressed, but nevertheless sporting a specially purchased-on-account interim, off the peg, ice-blue, lightweight crushed velvet, shawl collared jacket and cream linen Oxford bags, without having a clue about what I was doing there, or quite what my job was actually supposed to be.

The company had hired me as a result of the favourable impression I had somehow made on its daily post-lunch ukulele playing director at the interview. An interview that, as a result of an initial, speculative phone call, I had been invited to attend for a position which didn't actually exist. I stepped through the ornately engraved, semi-painted gilt-glass door of the business and into the Twilight Zone. The bizarre upshot of this surreal arrangement was that I spent most of the time I assumed I would be working in the office, not actually working, being welcome, or even properly accommodable in the office at all, but obediently strolling around town in the sun and sitting for hours on end in the park. It was a relatively undemanding introduction to the rigours of professional life.

Although, as a result of my unexpectedly leisurely schedule, I couldn't help feeling that I had been deceived. Cheated out of a bona-fide experience of fulfilling routine clerical duties and working honestly. But it didn't really matter. I had plenty of books to read in a variety of pleasant places, and the thing that really counted was that, for some inexplicable reason, the bizarre appointment paid me. And although the financial rewards were less than impressive, they were enough, after the deduction of my living expenses, to take Yssy on holiday.

I immediately set my sights on the two weeks in Egypt I

had been looking forward to for years, paddleboating up the Nile on a sight-seeing cruise to the Winter Palace at Luxor. But almost immediately, I realised that what was left of my meagre poundage fell a long way short of providing us with the quality of holiday I'd had in mind. I lowered my sights and imagined us frolicking around in some other ancient historic location, clambering over Greek or Roman ruins instead.

By almost the end of my fourth month, I was confident that I had saved enough to buy us at least a flavour of somewhere appropriately interesting and spontaneously decided to act. Moments after casually window shopping for bargains on my first official walk around town of the day, I swaggered through the open glass door of Thomas Cook after spotting an advert in the window and, already deeply immersed in an over-excited moment of imaginative youthful adventure, impulsively bought ridiculously cheap plane tickets to Tunis for two weeks, with no hotels attached. And without at any point in the previous several months of contemplating our first self powered summer vacation together, mentioning the prospective caper to either of Yssy's parents. The holiday had been my own secret and I didn't want to compromise it or feel that I was going behind Yssy's back by revealing it to anyone else. I slipped the paperwork into my jacket pocket and wandered back out into the sun, having performed my most fulfilling and spectacular act of independence so far, and feeling like the freshly converted English equivalent of a million dollars.

A few hours later, I met Yssy for lunch, waving the tickets like a banderole over my head as she sailed towards me down Milson Street in her summer frock.

'I'm taking you to Tunisia,' I announced, excitedly, like

some fully mature swashbuckling movie romantic.

'I'd expect no less,' she replied, with a kiss.

I could tell right away that my declaration had produced the desired effect, because she threw herself into one of her typical, larger than life smiles, which seemed to possess her entirely and draw into her radiating face from the depths of her soul a complete body-full of undisguised joy.

'Are you really?' she continued, taking the tickets I was by now practically forcing into her hand and casting her eye like a Xerox machine over the travel agent's logo on the envelope.

'It'll be fantastic!' I assured her, superfluously, wrapping my arm around her waist and kissing the fresh August blooms of her long, warm neck.

She took the tickets from the envelope as we walked, looked at them, turned them over, put them in her bag and told me how happy she was.

If I had informed her that we were off to the moon in a bucket and whipped out the documentation to prove it, she would have reacted in exactly the same way, and with just as much of a consummately approving yottawatt-of-energy-infused smile. I could have told her almost anything sensational and it would have produced the same ruffling effect of a humming bird feather landing on the Pillars of Hercules.

Her parents, however, later that evening, didn't receive the news in quite the way I had hoped. The phone rang around eleven-thirty, just as I was going to bed. It was Yssy. I knew something was wrong from the momentary opening silence. 'I can't come,' she said.

71

Words linger in memory like faces of the dead.

The verdant, lush-garbed temple congregation sat transfixed behind the oversized portrait of Our Heavenly Sister, like the merry men and women of Sherwood Forest shorn of the more noticeable part of their levity. Sermons had lately increased substantially in length, with the determinedly repetitious leitmotif of the violent overthrow of evil now being reinforced by two separate ten minute periods of the chanting of appropriate scriptural verses or epithets, determined, of course, by my mother.

The latest of her heated homilies had been specifically fashioned to impress upon her flock, on pain of God's lethal retribution, the critical importance of unity and of remaining tight-lipped in public in all matters of temple service instruction, discussion and activity.

'"I appeal to you, Brothers and Sisters, in the name of our Lord Jesus Christ,"' she quoted, from the First Book of Corinthians, chapter one, verse ten, '"that all of you agree with one another in what you say and that there be no divisions among you, but that you be perfectly united in mind and thought."' The sentiment being subsequently buttressed by her breezy recitation of Proverbs, chapter

290

seventeen, verse nine, which advises that "he who conceals a transgression seeks love, but he who repeats a matter separates intimate friends", before then transposing her progressively unravelling delivery down a full tone on the Celsius scale and warning the obsequiously nodding crowd that God would surely interpret any disregard for the sanctity of all words spoken on His behalf beneath the roof of His own house by His own appointee as blasphemy.

The longer she sermonised, the more febrile she became. Until eventually, she medleyed the merging repetition of herself like a tumultuous echo, breaking the ringing loop only to round her tirade by trotting out Leviticus, chapter twenty-four, verse sixteen, to well and truly hammer the blistering rivet of her pommelled polemic home: "Moreover, the one who blasphemes the name of the Lord shall surely be put to death; all the congregation shall certainly stone him. The alien as well as the native, when he blasphemes the Name, shall be put to death."

My father vacated his chair on the podium and walked the few feet to place himself alongside my mother in what appeared to be a gesture of consolation, and for the ensuing seven minutes, both of them ebulliently led the now also upstanding congregation in the continuous chanting of Psalm One Hundred and Eighteen, verse eight, "It is better to take refuge in the Lord than to trust in man."

The final additional three minutes of the first session of chanting were entirely taken up with the repeated assertion of my mother's lead that 'I am not ashamed,' which, in its rousing collective delivery, ended at practically a fever pitch by the time she raised her hands to signal the end of the incantation. Then, with barely a pause for breath, she lowered her arms to instruct her flock to sit, and launched by the consummation of the gesture into the somewhat starchy and mannered but absolutely appropriate to the gravity of the moment, King James Version of the first seven verses of the seventh chapter of Deuteronomy: '"When the Lord thy God shall bring thee into the land whither thou goest to possess it,"' she began, casting her eye briefly over the chlorophyllic crowd to ensure that she had captured its unalloyed attention, '"and hath cast out many nations before thee, the Hittites, and the Girgashites, and the Amorites, and the Canaanites, and the Perizzites, and the Hivites, and the Jebusites, seven nations greater and mightier than thou; And when the Lord thy God shall deliver them before thee; thou shalt smite them, and utterly destroy them; thou shalt make no covenant with them, nor shew mercy unto them: Neither shalt thou make marriages with them; thy daughter thou shalt not give unto his son, nor his daughter shalt thou take unto thy son. For they will turn away thy son from following me, that they may serve other gods: so will the anger of the Lord be kindled against you, and destroy thee suddenly. But thus shall ye deal with them; ye shall destroy their altars, and break down their images, and cut down their groves, and burn their graven images with fire. For thou art an holy people unto the Lord thy God: the Lord thy God hath chosen thee to be a special people unto himself, above all people that are upon the face of the earth. The Lord did not set his love upon you, nor choose you, because ye were more in number than any people; for ye were the fewest of all people"'.

My mother timed her ensuing motionless twenty-six seconds of silence to perfection, during which time more than a few rigid recipients of the still reverberating canonical commandment were almost too afraid to break her expertly crafted spell by breathing too conspicuously.

The electrifying atmosphere was, however, eventually fractured unceremoniously by an asthmatic coughing fit from someone sitting several rows back, who had held her breath for a few seconds too long.

Such an incongruous prelude to the theatrical masterpiece of what happened next seemed to inspire my mother to dizzying new heights of audacity, and without perturbation or impatience, she invited the distressed whooper, aided by my more sure-footed father, to hobble down the aisle and onto the raised platform she occupied with a yet to be used Fender Rhodes piano.

The breathlessly apologetic woman mounted the podium barking, to be immediately embraced with a distinctly measured warmth by Our Heavenly Sister, who then sat her still spluttering charge between the exclusive, green silk velvet upholstered arms of her long-empty chair and laid her hands upon the woman's head; bidding her, after a few moments of melodramatic finger trembling, in the name of my mother's all powerful love, to cough no more. The woman respectfully obliged without a second gasp and stopped hacking immediately.

A dropping pin would have caused considerable damage to the aural membranes of the rapt and astonished congregation. One or two of whom had already been reduced to such a stream of tears that they could barely participate in the ensuing spontaneous eruption of a boggled chorus of 'Praise the Lord'.

The freshly cured female returned to her place in the assembly unaided, and my mother continued in a moment of dramatic genius, as if nothing had happened, to recount the story in Luke, chapter thirteen, verses ten to seventeen, of how Jesus had, by the laying on of his hands, healed a woman who had been crippled by a spirit and had been unable to stand upright for eighteen years.

She eventually concluded the service with another nine and a half minute chant, which consisted for the entire duration of a repetition of the earlier chorus of 'I am not ashamed', and being distinguishable from the previously enthusiastically intoned effort only by the addition of the words 'of Our Heavenly Sister's love'.

# 72

After the service had finished, a peculiar new, more rarefied atmosphere pervaded both temple and members, and a small group of deliberate stragglers implored my mother to administer a healing laying on of her hands for the treatment of their own enduring afflictions. Fully aware of the potential value to her personal reputation and status, not to mention the consequential fiscal benefits of her agreement, she consented to each of their requests on the condition that they return to church the following Sunday to receive their curative blessings in the context of the temple service, and before the witness of its congregation.

My father had very recently begun to implement his rehabilitative programme for drug and alcohol abuse, which he considered himself fortunate to be able to offer twice weekly before lunch now, instead of as originally planned, one evening a week, thanks to the received funding which made it possible for him to reduce still further already diminishing commitments to his self-employing civil engineering consultancy.

He immediately found himself immersed in the mundane mechanics of arranging the registration of addicts and abusers at the surgeries of conveniently located GPs, even accompanying his unfortunate charges to their appointments to help prevent them from falling in the initial stages of their recovery. He listened tirelessly and compassionately to their many problems and encouraged them to call him brother, which they did. He liberally demonstrated his genuine affection for them simply and honestly, reminding them of their inestimable value to themselves and to the Lord. And when they cried, he cried with them.

When they careered off the wagon, as they often did, or even if they failed to clamber aboard it at all, he never rebuked or criticised them, but told them instead, with quiet lenity, how much he loved them. And how perfectly God had made them.

Gradually, when they began to realise how close they had become to my unwaveringly supportive and nonjudgemental father, when they began to see him as their own father and not only their brother, when they began to feel the sincere warmth of his concern, they began to believe him. Parts of their lost or missing selves slowly edged back into the softening centre of their bleary vision.

Encouraged by such progress, my father sought to consolidate the Church's involvement in their rehabilitation by offering to all members of his programme the security of temporary, although ostensibly open-ended accommodation in the boarding house dormitories, which had been retained as such and were already fit for immediate occupation. Residents would be expected in turn to undertake seven hours of vitally distracting therapeutic light work duties every day, with the exception of Saturdays and Sundays. But would also receive all meals and green uniforms, as well as additional objects of recreation, in exchange for the handing over of their state benefit giros to prevent their otherwise possibly all-too-easily tempted recipients from making illicit and retrograde purchases from any personal management of them. Several participants agreed to the offer and the attached conditions without hesitation.

To facilitate the general opening up of the entire temple complex for continual use, the need to ensure that the premises remained supervised and secure had become difficult to ignore. And although the boarding houses were self-contained and situated a short distance away from the main buildings, all of which had previously been kept routinely locked when not in use, it was now obvious to my father that the entire complex demanded a realistic level of staffing to facilitate duties of support and security at all hours of the day and night. My parents, he concluded, had little choice but to move in.

## 73

'The silver is mine and the gold is mine,' declares the
Lord Almighty. *Haggai 2:8*

Subsequent to the healing of the cougher, it had been
arranged for the following week's service to open with the
agreed laying on of my mother's hands in a specially
dedicated section to spotlight the miracle of her ability to
cure the many ailments of the afflicted.

The situation threatened to spiral completely out of
control shortly after the very first hallelujah! when at least
two-thirds of the assembled greenery ecstatically scrambled
out of their seats and queued before the iatrical podium in
fervent anticipation of having their own heads felt.

It was almost an hour before my mother personally
praised the Lord and recited the Second Book of Chronicles,
chapter fifteen, verse thirteen, affirming that "All who would
not seek the Lord were to be put to death, whether small or
great, man or woman," then took a well earned break and
slumped exhausted into her chair, while the rapturous
congregation chanted a full ten minutes of 'Our Heavenly
Sister loves us so'.

'My immortal family,' she resumed, as the reverberant
embers of the monophonic chorus subsided, 'God has spoken

to me of His boundless love for each of us, His most favoured children. And has pledged to protect us always in our righteous endeavours. He has assured us in the Gospel of Saint Luke, chapter ten, verse nineteen: "Behold, I have given you authority to tread on serpents and scorpions, and over all the power of the enemy, and nothing shall hurt you." We shall forge ever onward, imperishable, and the tongues of the godless shall not be heard amongst us. We will march together before God, as we march together now, and shall abide with Him together in His holy house until the end of all days. Lift up your voices now, my sacred children, and let us offer to our Almighty Father, with all the love in our hearts, the last ten wondrous words of Psalm Twenty-three, verse six, "I will dwell in the house of the Lord forever"'. And off they went again for a further six minutes. Until my mother lifted her arms like the outstretched wings of an imminently airborne swan to signal that she was once again about to launch into prose.

'My beloved Brothers and Sisters, the Lord, our Father, who we magnify and adore as giver and master of all good things here on Earth, has graced us with the exceptional gift of His own abode. Look about you inside, for everywhere in His house is the Lord. And everywhere renders manifest the many blessings the Lord has showered upon you. Let us give a moment in thought to consider the incomparable honour it is to live in love amongst Him. And to value the untellable treasure He has given us. He has provided His most loved and favoured children with all. Should we return His generous gifts with ingratitude and break the heart that has poured upon us so much love and tender caring? Who among us would permit the Devil to turn their back on the bounty of our Father's devotion?'

'Never!' came a voice from the middle row.

'Never!' another adamantly concurred.

'Not me!' still another bellowed, to be rapidly joined in multi-part harmony by a growing legion of assent.

'My sacred, precious family, the Lord has delivered to me the solemn promise that not a single Brother or Sister amongst us shall ever fall sick of mind or experience the bitter anguish of loneliness again. He has bestowed upon me the most wondrous promise that we shall reside here with Him together always, in the arms of His almighty protection and the magnificent house that He has awarded us. And we shall repay His vast and abiding love for us with nothing more than our devotion to His word, and the paltry offerings of the proceeds from the sale our own unnecessary Earthly abodes, which we shall gladly return to the occupancy of the ungodly. Together, we are and always shall be the choicest, mightiest, most loved and blessed, true, immortal family in God.'

It was a stupendous moment of consummate, almost subliminal coercion, in which a number of hopelessly overcome members broke spontaneously into openly wept tears for a variety of reasons, and others, for other reasons, rested their heads quietly in their hands.

# 74

The ancient Egyptians worshipped a pantheon of animal gods. The crocodile, the bull, the cow, the cat, the hawk, the cobra, the jackal, the lion, the hippo, the scorpion, the pig, the goose, the vulture, the frog, and exposed the tenderest parts of their lives to the unpredictable wiles of each. When their gods took a more familiar form and became human, nothing really changed. Except for the birth of philosophy, with which man attempted to understand the actions of his disorderly inventions.

I realised, even before the call, that I should have run the idea past Yssy's parents. It would have been the proper, polite and respectful thing to do. I knew it. I just prioritised the egocentric romanticism of the prospective escapade over basic courtesy, consideration and common sense. It was a sobering experience. The worst part of the entire debacle was the feeling that I'd betrayed everyone. Almost inconsolably distraught and incredulous at my own stupidity, I couldn't have felt worse.

Yssy had attempted to reason with her parents, but to no avail.

Had the antipathy been caused by a legitimate concern that we were too young or irresponsible to holiday abroad together, I was sure we could have talked them around. But I knew it had not been. It had been provoked by a far more malignant and ineradicable problem than a negotiable matter of reason. I had offended them. It was as simple as that. Inadvertently angered them into refusing their permission for Yssy to join me by not asking them if it would be OK to whisk their daughter two thousand miles away from home and land them in her place with a couple of weeks of worry. The damage was done. I had taken their goodwill for granted. It was not an oversight that could be easily amended retroactively.

Yssy blamed herself for the way she had handled breaking the fateful announcement to them, but it wasn't her fault. I refused to let her claim any part of my ineptitude.

It grieved me beyond measure to know that I had caused such unintended upset to the people I cared about most. So, the next day, I walked to Yssy's house after work to apologise.

From the moment I arrived there, I was almost speechlessly contrite. The atmosphere, too, so strained and unfamiliar, was as if I were visiting for the first time. The heavy air in the house smelt strange and unwelcoming. The leaden, unexpected, impenetrable formality unbearable.

I didn't even ask Yssy's parents to reconsider or anything. I just gave them the full, unreserved S.P. on how sorry I was, then clammed up altogether. It was agonising to sit among people who now occupied a distance which had never previously existed, almost insupportably sad; as though everyone had suddenly become strangers.

I didn't stay there long. Less than half an hour later, I was walking every uncomfortable inch of a long way home, hauling the gravity of my desolation like a cartload of rocks;

feeling remote, detached from myself and everything around me in the differently imagined, swelteringly hot, gunnysack summer evening.

When I got back, I hoped Yssy would phone to say that they had changed their minds. But she didn't.

## 75

Our fragile landscapes are framed by a symmetry of
disconsolation.

When I met Yssy for my typically extended lunch hour at
noon the following day, she turned up with a live mouse in
the pocket of her dress, which she had taken to Sainsbury's
and bought half a pound of Wensleydale for. She had picked
it up from the canal towpath on her walk into town to meet
me because it hadn't moved for ages, and after deciding that
it had probably suffered some mishap in the clutches of a cat.
It looked OK, and we couldn't tell if it was carrying an injury
or not when we set it down near a bush in the park, but it
hardly moved at all. It didn't eat any of the bits of cheese we
broke off for it, either. So we had most of the Wensleydale for
lunch ourselves, after which Yssy put the mouse back in her
pocket and decided she'd take it home. It was a small but
welcome opportunity to concentrate briefly on something
other than the fiasco of Tunisia. Even so, our mood was
sombre, and it was hard for either of us to rise very far above
it.

'They appreciated you coming around to apologise,' she
said, taking my hand, as we sat beneath the canopy of cherry
trees overlooking the sagging nets across the empty tennis

courts, 'they knew how bad you felt.'

'Does that mean they've changed their mind?' I replied, in a quiet, forlornly hopeful kind of way.

'No.' She didn't look at me when she said it. Only when she followed the anticipated negative with an apology of her own did she raise her head slightly and rest her soft eyes on me. She gave me an appropriately dolorous but reassuring half-smile, before nestling her head lightly into the cushion of my shoulder for a moment and quietly declaring 'I'm sorry, darling. I love you.' I told her not to be sorry, and that I was very lovable.

An hour and forty minutes later, we strolled the short distance from Victoria Park to the brass-plaqued front wall at Princes Buildings where I ostensibly worked, hand in hand, but without saying very much. She left me at the always open white door of the tall Georgian terrace, where I told her I loved her, too, and watched her cross the road with a wave and head down Milsom Street in the sun.

Shortly before I left the office that evening, she called to tell me that her parents were giving us a ton of money to take to Tunisia.

# 76

I caught the bus to Bathampton straight from work to thank Yssy's parents in person. By the time I arrived at the house, my place had already been laid at the dinner table.

In the evening, we talked, and joked, and watched TV and drank sherry in the garden. And I had my family back again.

I walked home at one a.m. to grab a change of clothes for work later in the morning, after fending off the repeatedly insisted offer of a taxi, or a tipsy lift from Yssy's slightly more than merry father. This time, I wanted to enjoy every step of my stroll, to drive out the painfully dragging nightmare of the evening before.

A sweet scent pervaded the warm, still air, like a breeze. I had re-established the exquisite closeness of my relationship with everything around me and was drunk on relief. The champagne stars in my personal sky had never before so enthusiastically toasted so sudden a conversion of a more passionately enamoured nyctophile. I drank the entire, full, sparkling glass of the night the whole way home.

Three weeks later, we were being shaken around in a bout of turbulence in a Dan Air DC10, somewhere over the Med. This went down less well with me than it seemed to with Yssy, who didn't flinch.

I hadn't realised quite how much I hated flying until we

arrived at the check-in lounge at the airport terminal, where a steady succession of complete strangers walked up to me and asked if I was alright. Apparently, the colour had drained from my face and, in the words of one concerned enquirer, I had become as white as a sheet.

In fact, the result of their quietly composed interest in my anaemic appearance was to make me feel better by normalising my distress, and by the time we climbed what turned out to be practically a rope ladder to get onto the tiny plane, I had actually become much more philosophical about dying.

Even though we had taken flight directly from our repeated barbecuing by the hottest summer since the last ice age at home, we realised immediately that we had arrived ill-prepared for the most unrelentingly fierce month in the North African calender. And when, having disembarked from the comfortably cool plane, we stepped blithely out onto the tarmac at Tunis in our English-summer clothes, the searing assault of midday was more vicious than being flung wrapped in a rubber, winter weight wet suit into a pre-heated oven at gas mark ten. We could barely move. Or breathe.

In the air-conditioned post-passport control lobby, we sat among people sporting TV sets and wondered what to do.

We sat and wondered for so long that a concrete hard, clean-cut, sullen looking, middle-aged policeman with a black leather-holstered revolver on his hip drifted towards us like a raincloud. I felt nervous straight away, assuming it must have been my long hair and dazed demeanour that had attracted his attention. I had been warned by a guide book before we left Gatwick that often the officials in North Africa had abbreviated affection for men with long hair who dressed flamboyantly.

He stood in front of us like a firing squad for a full menacing moment or two of steely scrutiny, before returning our tentative smiles with a genial nod and saying 'hello' to us in English. We replied instantly with an extravagance of reassuring charm. Our efforts promptly appeared to produce the desired effect. And almost without further hint of interrogation, he pouted amiably and nodded again, as if confirming our wishful assumption that we had won him over.

Our relief was short-lived. And before we were able to fully capitalise on our expeditious breaking of his ice, he demanded to know, in a tone which suggested a motive other than the furtherance of polite conversation, if we had a hotel to move on to. We told him we hadn't. Straight away we felt that this was not the answer he had been looking for. He pouted again, stiffened, gave us the twice or third time over, then sat down next to us, took off his cap and placed it in his lap.

Undoubtedly sensing our increasing nervousness, he softened his lips and eyes into half a smile and nodded again.

'You must have hotel,' he said, in a kind of affably matter of fact way.

'Yes,' we both agreed. 'We're going to find one; we've just arrived,' I added, axiomatically, in my best 'apologies for the hopelessly irresponsible booking oversight, but I'm really not looking for any trouble' tones.

He nodded his head for a fourth time, slowly, without replying, and held the crook of his index finger over his lips for a few seconds.

'This is your first time in Tunisia?' he asked, moving his finger slightly to speak.

'Yes,' I confirmed, adding, 'we're here for two weeks.'

'Do you have plenty money?'

'Yes, we have plenty,' I assured him.

'You need good hotel. Are you staying in Tunis for two weeks?'

'We're not sure,' said Yssy, hesitantly, 'we thought we might see some more of the country. Perhaps Djerba.'

'Ah yes, Djerba, it's very beautiful,' he smiled, before embarking upon another short excursion into indecipherable realms of contemplation, gently rubbing the flaking crest of his slightly pouting lip slowly with the edge of his finger, then nodding his head again after a few moments, as if he had arrived at his conclusion and that he was happy with it. 'Come with me,' he said, authoritatively, rising from his chair, 'I have friend.'

We strolled behind him through the glass doors of the airport and onto the edge of the road outside, where he directed us with the flat of a half waved hand to stop. Then he unlocked the back door of the police car and held it open as we edged ourselves into the stifling confinement of it, wiggling onto the griddle of the seat just as his expression changed. Immediately, the rest of his body language spoke in a similarly disconcerting tone. In a moment, he had disappeared into someone else.

'OK,' he asserted, uninterpretably, before slamming the door with an ominous thud and opening his own. The full volume impact repeated like a ricochet a few seconds later, after which he turned the ignition key and ran the engine like a jukebox selection for the entire time he sat there, almost imperceptibly nodding his head stiffly behind the wheel, without saying or doing anything else. The unaccountable delay in our departure presented us with the perfect opportunity to become increasingly anxious about what exactly was happening. We sweated in silence for a long couple of minutes before the car eventually pulled off.

Our self-enforced silence stiffened the air, and the quality of conversation didn't improve. The only words the police-man spoke on the road were in Arabic into the walkie talkie he left resting like a loaded weapon on top of the dashboard in front of him. His delivery earnest, impatient. It didn't feel appropriate for us to distract him, and neither of us tried.

Fortunately, the air-con kicked in pretty quickly and we cooled down in enough time to ensure that we weren't going to roast to death without ever seeing the inside of a Tunisian police station. I felt the growing tension in Yssy's fingers, as her hand hung lightly on my leg, and attempted to reassure her with a steady succession of gentle strokes and squeezes, while marvelling at the ease with which we had been manipulated into complying with our own abduction.

Sitting bolt-upright, we attempted to pick up non-existent clues about where we were being taken; tight-lipped, not exchanging a word, as if any mood-lightening dialogue between us may be regarded as an affront to the intimidating formality of the atmosphere and compromise us.

With little else to distract us, we threw ourselves into appreciating the extraordinarly picturesque passing scenery of the offbeat road movie we had become inadvertently trapped in.

Fifteen minutes later, the policeman abruptly reanimated, as though he had been plugged into something vital, and regained his amicable disposition as we entered a Western-style, smart, boutique-lined area of the capital.

'You will like it here,' he said, encouragingly.

We both directed our simultaneous sighs at the kerb we

were pulling up alongside on an imposing street in a reassuringly salubrious part of town, and from the self-satisfied smile the policeman beamed as he turned around to face us with the confirmation that we had arrived.

Taking a lead from our now infectiously ebullient driver's already disembarking gesture to follow, we all left the car upbeat and beaming like three fully fleshed rays of sunshine suddenly enroute to a tea party.

The policeman briskly walked us a short distance through a baking panoply of colourful images to Habib Bourguiba Square, talking amiably about his family and asking interested questions about us and ours. Stopping at last outside the entrance to an impressive looking hotel on the corner of a terrace of similarly arresting buildings.

'Is this good hotel for you?' he asked, before stepping inside.

'Yes, it looks perfect, thank you,' Yssy replied, still beaming with barely concealed relief that the purpose of the journey appeared to have been proved benign, after all.

'Come, come,' he said, excitedly, ushering us in through the door to the ornate reception.

Sweating profusely, we gratefully strolled into the exquisite coolness.

'Stay,' he instructed, motioning us with an outstretched index finger to take a seat beneath a large palm a few yards from the reception desk.

He strode the short distance to the desk, bellowing on the way in an abrasive manner to the blue and braided uniformed clerk behind it.

A minute or two later, he gestured to us to join him there.

'Passports,' he said.

We obediently excavated them from somewhere near the

top of our light luggage and handed them to him. He opened them like birthday cards and scrutinised their pages intently, before handing them in turn to the desk clerk.

'My friend will take good care of you,' he smiled. 'I hope you have very good holiday and come back to Tunisia.'

He extended his hand and shook hands with both of us.

'Next time you come, you will stay at my house.'

We thanked him profusely and enthusiastically agreed that we would. Although he never at any point told us his name or where his house was.

We felt, however, as we watched him leave with his broad smile intact, that we had made a friend. And that the strange, unexpected encounter had given us a perfect start to our vacation. The full magnitude of which was to become very much more apparent in the few minutes following our registration, when the porter closed our room door behind him and left Yssy and me to fall tired, relieved, excited and cooler into each other's embrace and occupy the unfolding reality of our first own home together.

After dinner, our inaugural evening in North Africa was spent wandering the magical, still sweltering streets of the capital, hand in hand in the sweetly scented night air, among a myriad of happy people who sold us jasmine flowers and told us they loved us.

# 77

Truth remains intact when ideologies fall.

Unbeknownst to my mother, my father had been sneaking off in his car to distribute blankets and food to the down and outs in Bristol and Bath.

He wasn't looking for any kind of religious return on the deal, either.

She eventually caught him loading up red-handed when she came home early, and warned him in no uncertain terms that he was misusing Church property and to stop doing it before he became seduced enough by unfortunates to offer them a roof and be landed with an army of freeloaders.

'We don't need tramps, we need a Sunday school,' she reminded him, coldly. 'You'd be a lot more help doing something about that.'

'I think we should help whoever needs it,' my father retorted, acerbically, before driving off.

My mother had been wrong about my father's misuse of Church property. He had purchased the food and blankets with his own money.

One or two of his other new friends were now beginning to display a noticeable improvement in their physical and psychological condition for having exchanged their drug and alcohol abuse for the supportive Scripture and Friendship classes my father held as part of his rehabilitation programme. Following their move into the dorms, they began to regularly attend Sunday service, too. Which didn't quite make up for the small number of others who had gradually dropped out of attendance over the weeks since my mother's invitation to her flock to donate their houses to the Church. However, several stalwart members, two of whom being elderly widows, each living alone in impracticably large dwellings, had indeed registered their homes with local estate agents and subsequently informed my mother of their wish to accept her offer of temple accommodation. Thirteen more of her mail order correspondents, most of whom had holidayed at our house, had applied to invest considerable amounts of money to secure their occupation of multi-roomed quarters in the Residential Blocks.

I was no stranger to the myriad mysteries of life, but had never been able to understand the vital dynamics of my parents' relationship. Try as I might, it had always proved impossible for me to either identify or comprehend the source of my brassbound father's attraction to my uncomp-romisingly bohemian mother. Until now. Until I saw her total baptismal immersion in the holy waters of her exacting new obsession and his growing fear that he may be losing her to it. Then it became obvious. For my father, it was the need to not be alone, married to his insistence on the kind of solitude that precluded all requirements to negotiate any serious concessions to the romantic demands of a partner. The need to be distracted, even by her madness, from the destructive gravitational force of his own pain. Even imperceptibly more comfort than could be derived from her irascible company would provide insufferable exposure to it. It was a perfect dovetail of vital exigencies. She needed someone to need her selfish, irascible company enough for her to justify her devotion to the nurturing of it, and to make almost no other demands of her at all. The recipe for the nourishment of their unusual union was simple. It was a relationship founded and fed on the bedrock of emotional deficiency. Affection never appearing to have played any significant part in their domestic aspirations.

Even during their courtship, which more or less consisted of her leaning over the garden wall that had divided them since their early childhood and declaring, as someone might who had looked up, noticed a cloud and predicted a shower as an attempt to initiate small talk with a neighbour, while keeping at least one eye on the stormy demands of social convention, that they may as well constructively apply the time they had already spent becoming acquainted with each other and get married. He agreed without hesitation, seizing a gilt-edged opportunity to spare himself the inconvenience of needing to shop around any further. The betrothal being rounded by her hanging the remainder of her basket of washing on the line while he returned to the house to empty the remains of a pot of char before work.

The apparently insoluble mystery of how their improbable union had endured, and the attempted unravelling of the riddle had occupied me for ever like a Gordian knot.

I had always erroneously assumed that it would be impossible for my father to ever extract any reward or pleasure from his unenviable place in her malignant world. I saw now the full scale of how wrong I had been, and that happiness lives in shadows, just as well as in sunshine.

I felt relieved, but I wasn't sure it was the kind of relief I had been looking for. It was enough, however, to sustain my cogitation by wondering if the genesis of my mother's mania had been a fear of love. A fear of being hoodwinked by the seductive promises of uncontrollable feelings. Of becoming lost and forgetting too many of the reasons for her intolerance of tenderness by falling helpless into the cunning of its trap. Who could she then be, if she could no longer be so unlovably unpleasant? Would she really break the habit of a lifetime and embrace an emotion that could swallow her like Jonah and leave her praying for the comfort of its company? Sacrifice her own to accommodate another's will and wishes, and be inveigled into a costly and debilitating dependence?

I knew such hypothetical meditation would be unlikely to ever disturb the imbalance of my mother's mind. And that she couldn't have allowed herself to be tempted to stray anywhere near the jaws of such a snare, or to ever be so recklessly selfless if she tried.

'If you love that riff raff so much, why don't you go and live on the streets with them?' she barked at my father, when he came in through the back door, foodless and blanketless from the rain.

# 78

Despite their recent puke-making cordiality, and the incongruous oddity of their actually going out and doing things together, their inveterate inability to demonstrate any touchy-feely affection for each other came sailing through unscathed. Still I never saw my parents hug, much less kiss. I once glimpsed them briefly touching hands without wincing, and that was all.

I thought about their strange, unyielding aversion to physical affection often.

Of the few moments of corporeal contact I had shared with my father without the exchange resulting in the drawing of any of my blood, arguably the most memorable was a short, awkward but cordial handshake he initiated when I left for Tunisia. I was thrown. Unable to decide if the unexpected gesture represented anything more than social convention. Mechanical etiquette, that had compelled him to tentatively offer me his still elongated paw immediately after having shaken hands with Yssy's father, who had been poised to drive us to the airport. The reflexive motion had, after all, continued on inseparable from the same casual, perfunctory, arm-waving flourish, and his contact with me was no more than momentary, arguably devoid of anything more significant than the desultory gesture it was. I valued it, nevertheless. And long after he had dropped his hand and walked away, I continued to feel the weight of his warm, broad fingers in my palm. I had never shaken hands with him before.

My inability to understand the experience saddened me. I didn't know if I was glad it had happened or not. I needed simple statements, declarations of absolutes, not vague suggestions; and although such ambiguity would have been essential to my father, I could never figure out such complex subtlety.

He tapped Yssy's father's shoulder amiably as he walked past us on his return to his own car, without extending the pleasantry to me. I turned to watch him retreat, hoping for some gesture of extension to our unread dialogue, but he didn't look back.

I followed his footsteps until the regularly spaced solid taps of wood and leather heels on Georgian flags faded, unable any longer to see him clearly through the fluctuating screen of others, or recognise him at all as the person who, when he quoted scriptural passages like Corinthians' "let everything be done in the name of love" or Romans' "be devoted to one another in brotherly love" to his little group of rehabilitees, embraced his friends without inhibition. Male and female alike. Real hugs. Long and warm.

## 79

Phantoms lurk furtively in the half-lit byways of reflection, but dwell audaciously in the rustling wind of passing years.

In the medina, the ancient, interwoven, shaded and semi-shaded streets forming the bustling, narrow, labyrinthine souks were amazing and seemed to go on for ever, providing an intense, almost dream-like storm of colour, shape, incense, spice and animated conversation. Carpets, trinkets, beaten copper and painted plates, clothes, fabrics, leather craftwork and food, each eye-catching stall we passed by that lined them brought the avid owner's always impassioned, sometimes earnestly arm-clutching plea to spend a little time and money inside. Yssy and I haggled amusingly over things we never seriously intended to buy, just to be part of the vibrant and impossibly compelling carnival of it all.

In fact, the only thing we came away with on our first full day was an antique silver Berber bracelet that I bought as a present for Yssy and paid the full asking price for.

Days were shorter here in Africa, not least because the heat in the middle of them made it difficult to be anywhere that wasn't artificially cooled. Even venturing out in the post-midday sun briefly from a temperate interior immediately shocked us into feeling that we had been attacked with a flame thrower.

Night fell fast and early, stealing the soft, infant twilight greedily. But it arrived with its own fragrance, and everywhere the sweet scent of it permeated the swelter of still sultry air. It was a magical balm, which rendered abounding processions of linked-armed strollers amiable; as though we had all emerged intact into the tranquil aftermath of some collective suffering, and had in its temporary wake discovered a fresh new appreciation for the joyful company of other people.

Minarets pinpricked the pearly spotted, inky black metropolitan skyline, awash with the gently hilly homes of affluent urbanites. Flamingos flew in formation over the pitchy ripples of Lake Tunis.

Yssy and I wandered among the unquietly convivial in Kasbah Square, and through lonely, glowing, yellow thirteenth century stone covered gaslit streets, enthralled.

By the time we sent postcards home on the evening of our third day, we had already seen Carthage; deciding not to rush around in the unrelenting heat, and to spend the whole day there.

Pretty much as soon as we stepped out of the taxi in the ancient town, right outside the amphitheatre, a local tourist hunter thrust a Roman terracotta oil lamp into my hand and persistently attempted to badger me into shelling out twenty-five dinars for the questionable pleasure of owning it. I didn't know what, if any, restrictions applied to the removal of antiquities and whether I'd be able to take it out of the country. I didn't want any trouble trying to, either, so I declined.

As it happened, the fenced site was locked, as usual, on

that particular day of the week and we couldn't get in. But we stared over the gate at it for about half an hour before ambling off down the hill towards the sea.

We meandered around the town for several hours, trying to shoe-horn Dido and Aeneas into a few unrevealing later Roman ruins. But all the time, Yssy's flip-flop blister-induced hobbling was worsening to the extent of rendering her almost stationary, so we bought her new sandals and dined beneath parasols in a restaurant overlooking the ocean. Before we took the taxi back to Tunis from Sidi-Bou-Said, we had already decided to head south to Djerba in the morning.

# 80

Dense objects invariably distort the spaces they occupy.

In spite of all the publicity, and my mother's attempts to lure them, not a single member of the armed forces past or present had ever expressed an interest in, much less actually used the shooting range for any purpose whatsoever. Plenty of other people had, but no services personnel at all. An inconvenience that did not prevent her from describing the therapeutic aspect of her charitable offering as an unqualified success in a local radio interview, and announcing the extension of her holistic service to include comprehensive post-traumatic counselling every Wednesday morning with a medically experienced member at the dedicated healing centre within the temple complex.

The medically experienced member's forte was chiropody. Although she had previously spent several years as a counsellor with the local branch of the Samaritans and was keen to establish a similar facility within the Church as a way of restocking all battle-scarred minds with an armoury of scriptural weaponry. My mother praised her initiative, then promptly claimed full credit for it. Going on, with typical modesty, to describe herself in the broadcast as the true saviour of all those who have suffered.

In a barrage of outraged criticism prompted by her immodest self-portrait during a post interview phone-in, my mother imperturbably addressed each assailing opinion by proclaiming that God stood Himself above the petty remarks of mortals, and that He had manifestly both chosen and trusted her and her followers to carry out His work. She denied accusations that she had drawn any direct comparison with herself to Jesus Christ, citing obvious gender and cultural anomalies.

The net result of this fortuitous controversy, which actually appeared shortly afterwards as a quarter page article in the local rag under the provincially pithy banner 'voice of the saviour' was to attract a number of new faces at the next Sunday service and unite existing members in a feeling of persecution which, as my mother was quick to point out, was something that Jesus and his followers had had to put up with, too, and a sure sign that the forces of darkness were rattled.

She had chosen the same service to publicly christen her new Van Cleef and Arpels single emerald necklace, and speak eloquently about the spiritual virtues of the poor.

# 81

It was a slow train to Gabes that inched us ponderously over rippling panoramas of parched earth, when we finally got underway in the early afternoon sun from the Gare de Tunis. Sparse as it was, it was our first glimpse of real, unabashed, simmering and sunburned African countryside and we drank it in thirstily, as we picnic'd on fresh milk and cous cous.

Occasionally, in and around more populated localities, the loitering express replenished its predominantly human cargo so generously that even the standing space between the seats was occupied for relatively short periods, during which, despite the carriage's multitude of open windows, it became hard to breathe in the stubbornly unventilated incalescent humidity produced by so many evaporating bodies. But at other times, there were few enough passengers aboard that we could relax and exchange smiles, or even a few words of English with interested and interesting travelling companions in a neighbourly and leisurely manner.

Camelled landscapes vagabonded by, decorated with flamingos and baked ochre-mud houses. And when the train slacked lazily off to an even more sluggish crawl, as it often did at various points down the line, young and old men dressed in jebbas jumped on and off with TV sets and animals, out of nowhere and into nowhere.

A few hours into the journey, and retaining the relative novelty value of being the only Westerners in the carriage, we were abruptly descended upon by a flock of avidly waving arms and other personal space-puncturing body parts. The lumbering limbs being owned by various members of the suddenly encircling huddle of excited, newspaper thrusting neighbours who had gathered in front of us to manfully stab at the same article in each, which was written in Arabic and which, however emphatically they poked and prodded, we were never going to be able to read.

Their incomprehensible chorus was soon augmented with a symphonic refrain of exasperated wails and sighs. One soloing vocalist attempted an extended passage in an unusual time signature while ingeniously accompanying himself on the improvised percussion of my shoulder joint; frantically shaking it like a maraca between contrapuntal grunts, as though he were playing out a desperate last gasp hope that the dislocation of my collar bone would increase my understanding. We nodded and tried to catch the occasional word of English, smiled and thanked them assiduously, without the least apprehension that the concern they were trying so hard to communicate was for our safety.

A national report of an outbreak of cholera had prompted an impassioned attempt by the ensemble of caterwauling well-wishers to warn us. Our sudden friends were imploring us to be vigilant. And to under no circumstances drink any unbottled water.

In our determined ignorance, we reacted appreciatively with a limited repertoire of inane nods and smiles, as though we had been thoroughly enchanted by a peculiar custom.

Eventually, the little group of well-wishers began to back off with faltering canticles of further lamentation, as if their mouth to mouth resuscitation of a long dying dream had manifestly resulted in failure.

When we arrived in Gabes, it felt small and quiet, and we had no idea where we were going. We hadn't pre-booked a hotel. It was dark, very dark and we were tired. We'd barely even stepped off the train and into the familiar warm scent of the street vendors baked sweet-meats before I doubled over with a groan, as if I had been shot in the stomach with the blunt end of a whaling harpoon.

Yssy gripped my arm tightly, concern etched into her eyes.

'What's wrong?' she asked, earnestly.

'I don't know,' I answered, suddenly short of breath and unable to straighten, 'I'm in pain. I need to get to the loo.'

I crawled back to the station, reluctant to leave Yssy alone there on the platform, but I had no choice. It was quite some time before I re-emerged from the undecorated convenience.

A minute or two further up the road, it happened again.

Yssy hauled me gently to beneath the neon sign of a several stars less than salubrious looking hotel, a stagger from the main drag, where we pushed past a group of old men smoking in the doorway and booked a room for the night. Which I spent most of creased up on the previously uncleaned lavatory, while sinisterly oversized cockroaches tap danced noisily over the broken earthenware floor tiles around me.

## 82

My mother had begun to hold Wednesday evening women's classes in one of the larger ground floor rooms at the temple, where everything from child rearing according to scriptural principles, to the violent revolutionary overthrow of imperial governments past and preferably present was discussed with typically animated fervour by around thirty participants representing a broad span of adult ages. The conference often being spearheaded by two particularly captivating and articulate ex-alcohol abusers who had grown increasingly active in recent Church activities, and another previously chemically compromised young woman with the irregularly proportioned inscription *I didn't mean to* crudely tattooed across the span of her forehead in reddy-brown Indian ink.

Ideas of aligning the Church of CHRIST in some practical way with various sympathetic European left wing extremist groups were also aired, and remained open.

It seemed that in support of almost every call to take some practicable stance against manipulative and exploitative authorities large and small, my mother was readily able to quote an appropriate biblical imperative or carte blanche for doing so; ratcheting up as a result the militant sentiments of the passionate and vociferous women still further.

Even the sudden downpour of unforecasted rain brought

an angry call from a thin-frocked voice for the meteor-ological office to be held financially accountable for their woeful incompetence.

Whatever the topic of discussion, the most immediately noticeable aspect of the weekly events was how closely-knit these members of the Church had become. How they had begun to identify themselves as real sisters within a real family, and how committed to it and defensive of it and each other they were. Growing ever more comfortable and confident in each other's company, they had discovered a mutually supportive, exciting new love, and were patently revelling in it.

Their love for my mother, however, was about to rise to stratospheric new heights.

# 83

Yssy set out unshowered and unbreakfasted to look for a chemist and more suitable accommodation when the shops opened at nine the next morning, taking a few traveller's cheques, no Arabic, and little more than a pocketful of French words with her. I was worried about her, a lot, but was too ill to move.

Quietly composed and confident as ever, she assured me that she'd be fine on her own and back before I knew it.

She was both, of course. But not before I had embarked upon a painful succession of nervous excursions to the window to try to see her and reassure myself that she was OK.

'I've got you this,' she chirped, thrusting a dark brown bottle of something medicinal into my hand. 'You have to take two now.'

I thanked her, kissed her cheek, opened the bottle and shook out a couple of the oversized tablets onto my palm.

'The man said they were the best for upset stomachs,' she continued, reassuringly, as she handed me a small bottle of water from her bag, before gently stroking my arm. I unscrewed the water bottle and gulped the pills with a swig.

She dipped into her open bag again and rattled a plastic container of improbably large salt tablets as her hand re-emerged from it, 'You have to take these as well. There's a nice looking hotel a couple of minutes away. I'm starving.'

Needless to say, I couldn't have eaten a thing, but marvelled silently at how completely unaffected Yssy was by the same food that had rendered me so wretched. It still hadn't occurred to me that only I had drunk water out of anything it had flowed from, as I finished swallowing my small garden bird-like breakfast of bitter and salty pills.

'I think I can make it,' I nodded, heroically, desperate to convince myself, while seriously questioning the good sense of my optimism. Ten minutes later, I cautiously set about putting my affirmation to the test.

My first effort terminated abruptly before I had trotted even half way down the barely still carpeted stairs, forcing me into an ignominious retreat and an invalid's equivalent of an Olympian sprint back up them again to the freshly vacated bathroom.

My second, a few minutes later, resulted in me just about enjoying the relative comfort of a much nicer loo altogether.

We both felt quite a bit better after showering, which I managed to accomplish without incident, and from the comfort of our relatively palatial new room, Yssy ordered something appropriately exotic to eat from the bedside menu, which turned out to be an omelette.

Simply watching Yssy delicately negotiate her eggy meal was therapy for me, and by the afternoon's dose, I felt well enough to throw myself into a short stroll around the town to explore its many lavatories.

## 84

I form the light, and create darkness: I make peace, and create evil: I the LORD do all these things. *Isaiah 45:7*

The rain fell hard after the sun had dropped like a bronze penny behind the sodden green hills around the temple complex, and continued as my mother and her co-inhabitant left the midweek meeting and walked the short distance to the residential quarters together.

The uneven, pitted, mud and concrete ground between the clutches of buildings had pooled quickly in the twilight torrent, making it impossible for the women to avoid stepping through the many puddles that had formed along their way. The single most voluminous and unavoidable of them prompting a sudden shriek of dismay from the friend, who had lost her sandalled feet beneath the brown pond of cold water. The immersion of her feet almost immediately preceded the immersion of her knees which, in a bracing moment of devotion, she had flung herself to like a bundle of stones, before shaking uncontrollably as a result of having noticed that my mother's own espadrilles had remained immaculately impervious to the aqueous conditions. My mother, with commendable detachment, calmly extended her hand, lifted her friend from her mud-bath and carried on walking as if nothing had happened.

Despite having inadvertently given the impression that she had walked on the water, her off-white canvas shoes were not actually dry, as her friend had supposed them to be, or indeed canvas; but a finely woven matte plastic that closely resembled cloth and which naturally threw off moisture so effectively that they appeared to remain undampened and persuasively uncoloured by the saturating ingress of dirty water. The facts were unimportant.

Within a day or two, the independently corroborated miracle had been ecstatically brought to the awestruck attention of every member of the Church. And, even sooner, my mother's plastic footwear had disappeared, to be replaced by a clean new pair of off-white canvas espadrilles.

An impressive array of fresh and keen new faces was to be seen at the next Sunday service, four days later. Almost all belonging to those introduced to the certainty of salvation in the interim by ecstatic existing members. The curious new-comers were welcomed cordially and immediately made to feel at home. The atmosphere was, from the start, electrified by a pulsating sense of restless anticipation.

During the service, my mother invited her congregation to consider the strange phenomenon of how, unlike her, Jesus had found it impossible to perform miracles in His own home town. Following an extended period of modest self aggrandisement, she proceeded to rail vociferously against the manifest shortcomings of other religions. Describing them all as dangerous purveyors of mind bending hogwash, and the major brands as assiduously ignoring the needs of their members and the demands of God in favour of more profitably cosying up to the state and acting as little more than its back-handered political sheepdog and apologist.

She articulated at length about the prodigiously nun and child abusing priests of the Catholic Church, who appeared to lack any conviction in the beliefs they were so oppressively keen to sell to others. Labouring specifically on the subject of their one-time leader and spiritual mentor, Eugenio Pacelli, or, as the world knew him, Pope Pious the Twelfth. Who, in his determined stalking of power, colluded incestuously with his ideological blood-brothers to crush all political opposition to the National Socialists and, by doing so, encouraged a drive of millions of German Catholics into the outstretched arms of the Nazi party. A cynical symbiosis that helped identify and send millions of Jewish innocents to their deaths.

Her diatribe continued to recall how Pacelli said or did very little to deflect attention away from his apparent political preferences, and how he even publicly endorsed his treasured collaboration by describing his pre-pontificate, mutually empowering Reichskonkordat signing with the Nazis, which facilitated this rapturously received influx to the Party, as "an unparalleled triumph for the Holy See".

And how, even as the interminable perpetration of historically unprecedented atrocities continued throughout the years of the war, he barely uttered a word as pope to condemn them. To oppose the slaughter of millions, the holocaust, or almost any of the suffering that could perhaps have been avoided had he acted more in accordance with the supposed protectorship of his office and unambiguously resisted rather than indulged the Fuhrer and his incomparably unchristian ambitions.

'Were it not for Pope Pious the Twelfth,' she concluded, uncharacteristically prosaically, though visibly overcome with emotion and increasingly subject to a slight wheezing breathlessness from the dogged oppugnancy of her attack, 'history may have been written very differently.'

In full flow now, and reluctant to navigate away too soon from her beloved bête noire, the institution which had provided her with the vocabulary to describe it with every dripping glisten of her venom as the purveyor of untold sorrow and the single most festering kernel of all Earthly iniquity, she drew another exaggerated breath, as if to emphatically extinguish its ecumenical flame with a final lungful of philippic rhetoric before sinking her spittle into the flesh of her quarry like a Dachshund with a mischief of rats.

'Let us not forget, either, the Catholic Church's collusion in the unspeakable butchery of more than half a million Serbs, Jews and Romani in priest-run Ustasha death camps during the nineteen forties; many of their internees being murdered by Franciscan friars while the Vatican said nothing. Or Pacelli's fawning prayer for the fascist Franco, and the message delivered "with great joy" to "all the brave men who followed Franco's stand and fought and died for Christ," whilst presiding at the same time over his own Church's theft and sale of hundreds of thousands of Spanish babies, seized from their own mothers to punish the families of those who had fought for the rights of the poor and dispossessed against Franco's Nazi-supported government. The arrogation and sale of these stolen innocents has secured for the Catholic Church such a fortune that even now after Franco has died, not only do they refuse to stop it, but they have introduced the same barbarous commerce to a welter of other nations.

Neither should we ever forget, my children, that even before Pacelli's pontificate of shame, his fascist assisting predecessor chillingly declared to Mussolini that the Church

334

shared many of his beliefs and objectives.'

Bowing briefly to the need for breath, and exchanging a short roster of dictatorial celebrities for a single suspiration, she quickly regained her familiar camera-conscious composure and continued the cannonade of her diatribe to question the Church's historic sale of Indulgences and why, as Martin Luther had asked in his 1517 Ninety-five Theses, the pope didn't liberate everyone from purgatory as an act of Christian love, instead of only those who had parted with prodigious amounts of cash to secure the privilege. Changing direction slightly only then to expose further colourful examples of corporate malfeasance.

Details and examples of the murderous activities of blue-chip financial institutions and oil companies prefaced her pithy advice that giving money to banks and investment funds was no different from giving children to paedophiles. And after concentrating her artillery on the global banking network's clandestine multi-billion dollar investment in the propagation of war, she launched an incendiary attack on the sinister activities of hidden governments and their big, multi-billion dollar business bedfellows. Vigorously restating the obscenity of any political system devised by such agents of the Devil that threatens, oppresses and hoodwinks the ignorant poor into perpetuating the circumstances of their own destitution.

She also denounced the sexually profligate youth of the nation, who threatened to convert the country into a modern-day Sodom and Gomorrah, and the BBC for their imperiously ongoing commitment to producing ever more fatuous, lewd and degenerate filth in order to inspire an already depraved generation to venture still further into the mire of their depravity with an apparently endless reservoir of extorted public investment.

'The very lives of the meek and blessed are expendable in the hateful eyes of these iniquitous seekers of worldly wealth and power,' she lamented, further citing the slaughter of innocent civilians in the Angolan Civil War, and the genocide of two hundred thousand peaceful and innocent voters for independence in East Timor.

'And don't think the killing won't happen here when the poor start standing up for truth and fighting for what is right. They're not going to want them to get away with that!

No, my children, we must root out these evildoers, these self-pronounced Masters of Mankind who darken the very door of our world,' she evangelically declared, with the rising twist of a clenched fist, as though she were yanking out a tangle of stubborn weeds from her overrun garden, 'and seize back the treasure of a future they have so savagely stolen from us all. We shall obliterate their bastions of indecency and glorify the Lord our God with our bringing of their ruin. No nation shall hold dominion over another, nor any man call any other master. Neither shall any hold the life of another cheaper than his own, save in his righteous struggle against the purveyors of evil and on the battle-ground of the Lord. And where citadels of the Devil have sprung from cradles of vice, we shall honour the Holy Word of the Lord in Samuel and deliver their destruction. And each blood-drained land that falls to the sacred sickle of our wrath we shall harvest as our own in the name of our Father. We shall fall upon the lands of the Earth as a hammering rain of justice and flush from them the embedded stains of the godless corrupt. The once dumb animals in the fields we hear speaking with the forked tongue of the Devil shall be slain.

Together, victorious in our struggle forever, we will stride unstoppable under the banner of the Lord's protection. And with the imperishable sword of our Father's love in our hearts and the pure, sweet flavour of Deuteronomy, chapter twenty, verses sixteen to eighteen, on our tongues, we shall heed our Master's call when He commands us in those verses to vanquish His enemies, and "in the cities of the nations the Lord your God is giving you as an inheritance, do not leave alive anything that breathes. Completely destroy them; the Hittites, Amorites, Canaanites, Perizzites, Hivites and Jebusites as the Lord your God has commanded you. Otherwise, they will teach you to follow all the detestable things they do in worshipping their gods, and you will sin against the Lord your God." Which, my immortal Brothers and Sisters, we, as virtuous, true and chosen holy liberators of the world from the pedlars of sickness and evil shall not. Amen.'

A collective 'amen' physically reverberated among the seated, like the devastated Earth trembling from the dropping of an H-bomb.

Three verses of an enthusiastically sung All Things Bright and Beautiful, complete with Fender Rhodes accompaniment later, the swollen congregation chanted 'We know Our Heavenly Sister loves us' at an ear-splitting volume for a full ten minutes, with more than a modicum of unexpurgated joy.

## 85

I had been wolfing down tablets like Smarties all day. So much so that, less than thirty-six hours later, I was well enough for us to go wandering in the relative cool of the oasis and get lost among the date palms. Eventually emerging from a maze of identical footpaths onto a blazing cove carpeted in irridescent silver with the upturned bodies of dead sardines.

It was an odd and unexpected sight, painted eerier still by not having seen a living soul anywhere the whole time we had been walking. There wasn't another visible life form on the beach anywhere, either. It wasn't only me who thought the atmosphere seemed ominous; Yssy found it strange, too. She said it felt like we had stepped into somewhere that wasn't really there.

The little guide book we had brought on holiday with us revealed Gabes to be the only place in the world where the mountains, the desert, the oasis and the sea could all be seen at the same time. It was true; we could see everything, and it all looked creepily deserted.

I sat on a warm rock and used Yssy's camera to take photographs of her as she girlishly skirted the pungent shoals of expired fish in the sand. But it didn't feel right.

We hung around holding our noses and our place in the

surreal scene for a while longer, looking out at the sea and calculating a variety of distances. But, before long, both the intensifying smell and the discomposing emptiness rendered our narrowing proximity to an ever encroaching discomfort unbearable and we wandered back into the town, where a well and Western dressed young man walked determinedly up to us and, in perfect English, unhesitatingly attempted to persuade us to fly to Algeria with him in his private plane for no obvious reason. We declined, even though he insisted that he would meet us in the same place at the same time the following day. By which time, we were on a rambling, crowded, dirty yellow bus to Djerba.

This felt even more like the authentic, tourist free, Tunisian experience we'd been looking for. Now we were positively roughing it.

We passed natural embroideries of ancient olive groves and date palms, which sprang out of the sandy earth like irregularly tufted pom poms. Multi-storey dwellings roughly hewn into the sides of artificially cratered natural rock in spartan, same golden-beige scenery decorated with small, plodding splashes of brightly blanketed camels. Thawbed men drove sheep to unobvious places.

Somewhere remote, on the edge of an unusually visibly unpopulated village not far from the Libyan border, the bus slowed and pulled over to the side of the road, where several police or military officers carrying automatic weapons filed aboard and strolled menacingly up and down the aisle, scrutinising the face of every passenger before grabbing, seemingly at random, a number of Arab men from their seats and marching them off at gun point.

I was mystified, but no-one said anything. The bus started up again and we drove off. The atmosphere was subdued.

We arrived on Homer's Island of the Lotus-eaters in the paling light of Houmt El Souk's early evening and found a hotel easily, just off the main square, where seated vendors and their palette of wares were still spread quietly tapestried over the street.

# 86

Behold, the day of the LORD comes, cruel with both wrath and fierce anger, to lay the land desolate; and He will destroy its sinners from it. *Isaiah 13:9*

The days and evenings of the week were filling up with various Church activities, including dedicated days for religious instruction, shooting practice, social reform studies, and evenings for women's concerns, men's concerns, and games, which all proved to be well attended by ever more enthusiastic members.

My mother's often repeated declaration that ignorance is not, in fact, bliss, but a debilitating condition which encourages others to exploit our fears, provided the inspiration for another recent lively interactive reading session that formed part of the weekly schedule; each such instalment being specifically devised to promote the dissective study and discussion of The Unclosable Eye.

This rigorous examination of Church scripture, popular with both sexes, invariably excited much energetic debate, which often required the indisputable authority of my mother's uniquely penetrating insight to definitively resolve. Such discussion would routinely stimulate the prescription of various volumes of supplementary esoteric reading material to facilitate the greater levels of elucidation eagerly sought by her insatiably curious flock. Almost all titles being available for purchase directly from my mother in her guise as the Temple Mail Order Bookshop, which retailed them at considerably inflated prices.

Another activity Our Heavenly Sister shrewdly initiated, was to personally dispense generous compliments to any member heard making suggestions of benefit to the Church. The response to these recommendations took the form of Outstanding Contribution Notes, which after compiling in a pocket note pad, she almost immediately committed to vivid green paper and pinned with a small, ribboned rosette to the temple notice board. A calculated practice which saw warm approbation lavished upon the contributor both at the time of the suggestion and again at some later juncture. My mother ensuring that on at least one of the occasions, plenty of other ears would be hovering in the vicinity to appreciate the outpouring of respect and attention. Such panegyric attracted the enthusiastic contributions of everyone. Even the traditionally retiring tongues of the most introverted members were winkle-picked into action by invitations to revel in such reward. The result of this practice was to not only potently strengthen existing feelings of attachment and belonging, but reinforce a parity of inclusion and personal value within the family unit. A monumental sense of collective well-being and familial indestructibility resulted from the liberal repetition of this simple technique.

'I love you with every drop of love in my heart,' my mother frequently reassured her flock, often continuing with her effusive eulogy for long enough to remind them that they were not only to her, but to the Lord, the most special, adored and remarkable people ever to have lived. She repeatedly described them as her super-human children and reminded them that she had given them life, and their new life meaning.

Not that anyone had forgotten her gift, or had taken their neonatal status for granted. Their dependence on her for their continued access to freedom and value acknowledged with unstinting devotion. They had each been conscious throughout the entirety of their rebirth and were still clinging tenaciously to the breast of the lacteal words that sustained them.

Such desire for rebirth is woven like prayer into the fabric of our being. Some of us wear our lives out so completely on the ruinously menial that we're too ashamed to show off the threadbare state of them in public. Some of us save our lives for never to come best occasions, as though they were an impossibly expensive set of delicate new clothes; too smart and fragile to wear in the grind and grime of workaday dirt. We hang them away untouched in our overstuffed wardrobe of dreams, where moths and beetles devour them beyond repair, while we obliviously wait for that one special, spotlit time when we can finally feel clean enough to drag them out of the darkness and wear them for an hour or two before it all gets too late.

My mother had dressed her children well, and they swaggered around in their new clothes proudly.

And in the recently created section of Sunday ministrations that was, at the end of ecclesiastical proceedings, open-endedly devoted to the public expression of their individual testimony and pride, many members spoke with moving eloquence and at considerable length, while others wept quietly with gratitude for their own spiritual rescue and psychological recovery. The section generally being concluded by my mother, even my father, too, sometimes, who flooded their congregation with their love, trust, and respect with all the haemorrhaging gush of a ruptured sewer main.

The blissfully bleating clutch couldn't soak up enough of it, and ambled away at the rounding of the service dripping with an enraptured sense of inclusion.

Substantial percentages of salaries were lately exchanged for ever-elevated tiers of unspecified benedictions. The gainful occupation of temple beds grew.

Members and volunteers laboured diligently to complete temple restorations, including in the general refurbishment the provision of a common lounge for residents. And my father pored over his plans to purchase a nursing home for the suffering elderly, so that he could provide affordable care for them physically, emotionally and spiritually in the otherwise isolated misery of their final years.

In the brooding introspection of her solitary prayers, my mother discussed pressing military plans with the Lord.

# 87

Our greatest freedom is to forget. Our greatest treasure,
to remember.

The languid adhans of the muezzins filled our room like a
soft wind of clarinets through mutes of single, laced, pre-
dawn windows and led us into sleep after dark with the
soporific mellifluousness of their music. The clopping parade
of donkey's hooves on cobbles raised us to breakfast at
sunrise.

A dozen idyllic trap-rides and half as many perfect arm in
arm moonlit evening strolls on tide-lapping sandy beaches
long, Djerba was poised to be remembered as a friend.

On the penultimate afternoon of our island odyssey, I
stoically suppressed my aviophobic reservations and agreed
with Yssy that a more expeditious method of return to Tunis
would be of greater benefit to my health than a reversal of the
languorous train journey over almost six hundred kilometres
of land. We decided to fly in air-conditioned comfort aboard
a Jumbo Jet in a fraction of the time. Even so, I still wasn't
able to sidestep the suspicion that we would inevitably miss
out on something. The hour long flight seemed almost
indecently short.

In an attempt to recoup some manner of compensation for

the loss of any land-based experiences in the last days of our holiday, we opted, or rather, I somewhat irrationally decided and Yssy indulgently agreed to walk the nine kiln-fired kilometres in shimmering haze to the airport, along a dirt track through barely anything other than occasional, scattered, single-storey houses between stretches of sandy earth, olive groves and date palms. It was, I realised after the first two or three kilometres, a suggestion of questionable merit.

Around forty-five minutes into our increasingly blistering amble, and precisely in the middle of nowhere, Yssy turned her head towards me and nervously whispered, after a conspicuously covert glance over her shoulder to make sure that she hadn't been mistaken, 'we're being followed.'

'What d'you mean?' I replied, immediately becoming aware of exactly how isolated we were and turning around abruptly to answer my own question.

She was right. We *were* being followed, and the situation was as dramatic as it was bizarre. I was surprised to see that our pursuer was a shuffling group of nine or ten kids, ranging in age from around eleven to fifteen and lurking in a sinister cluster a dozen paces behind us, watching us with every one of its eighteen or twenty eyes intently.

I wasn't sure whether to ignore the kids and carry on regardless, or to bluff it out and yell at them to piss off.

'Let's just ignore them and carry on,' I said, decisively, after a second or two of deliberation, throwing my shoulders back and trying to inflate every inch of my appearance. Yssy agreed, as if she had already decided, and edged herself closer to the marginally less baggage-laden of my arms.

They knew that we had seen them now, and it wasn't long before they gained ground on us. All of a sudden, they

346

shuffled several metres nearer and started bellowing out minaciously in unison.

Although it sounded menacing, I couldn't at first make out what they were saying. It was Yssy who, after a few mystified seconds said 'they want money and sweets'.

I could hear the carolled call more clearly now. 'Dinar, candy.'

I turned around to face them. 'We don't have any sweets,' I assured them, authoritatively, casting my eyes over each. They were unconvinced.

'Dinar, candy,' they re-intoned, in ten part harmony.

'I told you, we don't have any,' I repeated, impatiently.

'Dinar, candy, dinar, candy, dinar, candy,' they went on.

I tried once more. Even setting my array of bags in both hands down and completing my final attempt with the internationally recognised palms outstretched and turned upwards with all fingers spread apart routine. Completing the convention with an accompanying double pocket tap and a protracted shake of the head.

This triple pronged approach seemed to work like a charm on around half of them straight away, but the rest kept up their querulous quadrisyllabic demands and looked devoutly unimpressed.

I turned around a last time to face the more harassing threat of the sun and we carried on walking without paying them any further attention. Gradually, the number of voices began to fall away, and by the time the ebbing choir had reduced to a half-hearted duet, they were faint enough for us to relax in the satisfaction that they had given up.

'I thought they were going to rob us,' said Yssy, at last, with a slightly sad shade of relief.

We even quite enjoyed the leisurely hobble of the next few

kilometres, being the only objects visibly moving through the solidly still air. Until the relentless Saharan heat that we hoped we had grown accustomed to began to marinade us in the sweet sauce of our sweat, and the payoff still to be negotiated on the hoof suddenly felt painfully unrewarding.

We arrived at the airport saturated, thirsty and uncomfortable, but appreciably intact, and without having been subjected to any further incident enroute.

All the buildings here were unnaturally stark and new. They rose out of the retiring buff semi-desert like a canker. Incongruous. As though the delicate-skinned, virginal landscape had vomited a heavy meal over itself while being crudely seduced by boorishly insistent modernity.

We sat patiently awaiting the arrival of a loitering recovery, drinking bottled water from a dispenser in the liquid-like air-con among people with still more television sets until, less than a couple of hours later, we were five miles higher aboard a reassuringly capacious Seven Forty-Seven on our way back to the country's less conflagrant capital.

Although I had dumped the worst of my lavatorial home runs a comfortable distance behind me, I didn't shake off the pain of my unidentified stomach upset completely until almost a week after we returned home to England, carrying near walk-in-wardrobes full of Berber-made clothes from the Djerba souks and bags of presents for Yssy's parents.

During the many curtain-called recountings of our African adventure over the following few days, we bored our over-indulgently attentive audience stiff for hours at a time with our effusive tales of the magical country and its friendly, vibrant, colourful people we both recalled with such excitement and affection. Yssy's mother repeatedly casting tender smiles at her, as if she had rediscovered her daughter after a period of loss and was proud that she had turned out so well. Her father nodding approval at me in such a matey way that I began to wonder what I had done to deserve such an outpouring of favour.

No doubt they were relieved we hadn't disappeared into the desert never to be seen or heard from again, and that we had made it all the way back to Blighty without significant cause for concern, but the strange thing was, we all seemed closer than we had been before. As if something extraordinary had happened while we were away.

The same magnetic phenomenon, of course, did not pertain to my own aberrant authors, who were by now living exclusively at the temple and carried on with their distractions without really noticing me.

Bizarrely, I discovered in the final week of my employment there that the quantity surveying company would have kept me on had I not given up my temporary position the day before we flew away to Tunisia in order to start college with Yssy in September. The occupants of the office I was seldom allowed to work in seemed genuinely sorry to see me go.

We spent the last days of our summer break walking in the countryside and sitting beneath trees, waving away clouds of gnats on river banks, writing poems and travel articles, and weaving colourful patchworks of make believe plans for the future.

Yssy stayed at my parents' house as often as I stayed at hers now. My mother hardly ever being around to bother us. In fact, I had barely spoken to her for the several weeks since she marched initially unnoticed up to Yssy and me in the Abbey Churchyard on the particular Saturday afternoon she evidently felt a more than usually pressing need to pass comment on my new burgundy velvet, reproduction Georgian masked-ball costume coat, with royal blue ribbon epaulettes and high, florid, gilt braided, cushioned buttoned cuffs. My broad-brimmed, pheasant-feathered, floppy, sea-green wool-felt hat, which I considered an indispensable companion piece to the coat, appeared to fare little better in her estimation.

She rendered her opinion of my appearance relatively succinctly, with a terse but thunderous outburst of touching disdain. Thoughtfully augmented by precisely the correct complement of completely over the top exasperated indignation.

The brief appraisal began deceptively wordlessly, with nothing more articulated than the incredulously pained expression she might have worn on the unhappy discovery that she had squelched through a pile of fresh dog droppings in her bare feet to greet me. This continued throughout a short spell of visibly vibrating with the rupturing intensity of formulating the absolutely worst possible insult she could articulate and culminated when, close to the climactic state of uncontrollable convulsion, she fired the words 'YOU'RE ECCENTRIC!!' into me, like a volley of dum dums.

A flurry of ear-bent steps further towards the High Street, a middle-aged couple genially complimented me on my appearance.

Now, if the vampire bat paid a fleeting visit home, I cleared any evidence of Yssy's presence in less time than it took a magical children's nanny to Feng Shui an eyesore to the strains of a merry song and concealed her in my room to prevent the possibility of any encounter at all, as soon as I heard the crunching of car wheels on the gravel outside.

At any other time, with neither of my parents there to bother us, we treated the house as our own.

# 88

We are dominated by the impossible promises of learning.

College suited my temperament much more than school ever did. I had plenty more money now than I did when I was at school, too. In fact, my student grant was not very much less than I had been paid for working. I assumed my adopted identity as a student easily, and despite the prismatic arrangements of my even more costume-dramatically self-indulgent appearance, I felt that I fitted in.

I hadn't really gone to college to learn anything; only to spend more time with Yssy, but the odd thing was, that spending more time together seemed to have the peculiar effect on me of wanting to learn. Even in the subjects we didn't share, I became unexpectedly studious.

As for skiving a lesson, the thought barely occurred to me at all.

Our new domestic circumstances centred around the intimacy of the classroom, which often continued to accommodate us well into the evenings, when we'd finish our homework together and then go out somewhere to relax afterwards. To a gig, a pub, or to the theatre or cinema.

English, politics, economics, sociology and philosophy

were the weapons we would together wield to refashion the world. Although global restructuring was never really part of our primary plan. We felt the world had already changed and that were enjoying the opportunities it now afforded us.

Finding new playmates at college couldn't have been easier. Almost everybody seemed to want to be somebody's friend. People collected people like pebbles on the beach. It wasn't difficult to find someone to jam with for an hour or two, or to be invited to a party by.

In fact, it quickly became obvious to me that I would need to devote at least as much energy to recreation as to study. It was almost impossible to find the time to accommodate quite so many investigations into ubiquitous temptations and still entertain a variety of other compulsory distractions.

I urgently needed to cultivate a serious grasp of how to structure my academic life meticulously enough to be rewardingly diverted from it, and to devise a way of prioritising the most essential of my leisure pursuits. Like discussing art and politics with a self replenishing farrago of beer and short glasses around the dartboard during my extended break on a market day afternoon in the pub across the road, ahead of staggering back lunchless into lectures trying to hide my inebriation behind an incoming headful of Hegel before I keeled over and fell asleep.

There was very nearly too much fun to be had here. And it was all so dangerously accessible. You didn't need to sell your soul to the Devil to enjoy it. Even Yssy, who was always infinitely more dignified and restrained than me, seemed to find a little extra joie de vivre to decorate her typically quiet exuberance with. You could be or do almost anything. There were welcome signs everywhere.

Friends came out of the woodwork. Literally. My earliest

best mate Minky B emerged like a desert mirage and floated towards me in a pine-panelled corridor that I was somehow failing to negotiate on my alcohol-fuelled voyage to a lecture.

However incarcerated I had felt in my iron masked aeons at school, I couldn't have felt more liberated here. I drank freedom like nectar from a ubiquity of vessels. So much, that I became addicted to the narcotic of its promise. Within months, I couldn't imagine denying myself the intoxication of it. I demanded that it furnished my future with as much of Yssy's company as I had now.

It was of course, Yssy, as usual, who dragged me back into the sobering daylight of common sense. Rescued me from the impossibly romantic gourmand of myself. Compelled me to realise that my ideas of freedom were beginning to imprison me. She challenged me to reappraise my definitions, and my expectations of what freedom was really capable of providing. I would have had little patience for anybody else's liberating ideas of restraint.

Instead of attempting to run before I could crawl, I decided to tackle freedom at a walking pace.

I didn't realise it at the time, I was too busy looking elsewhere, but there were callipers on these legs, too.

In the prolonged absence of sleep, everything becomes shadowed by dreams.

In the cold autumn evening air, a slow procession of green overcoated residents ascended the hill behind the temple to marvel vociferously at the unusually vivid sunset. It was as if the sky had set the horizon's hairline of skeletal trees ablaze and the fire had spread dramatically throughout the heavens. No-one could remember seeing anything quite like it. Drips of molten sky fell like napalm onto ruddily incandescent fields and hedgerows, and purple clouds hung between the lips of flames like bruises.

'It's a sign,' said someone, in the awed undertones of a reverential murmur.

'It *is* a sign,' someone else concurred.

Everyone seemed to intone the word *sign* with various degrees of excitement and retiring trepidation.

Before long, the spellbound group had mustered a rhythm and spoken as one, and the unanimous interpretation of the unusual meteorological phenomenon was that, as my mother declared in an authoritatively stentorian bray, 'the Lord has spoken,' adding for sensational effect, the rather axiomatic commentary that 'even the birds have retired in dread.'

The verdant group of firmament-gazing bystanders watched as the intense spectrum morphed kaleidoscopically into Rorschach ink blots that tested their fiery imaginations; some seeing chariots of death, others nuclear mushrooms, before draining into the homogeneous mush of a post-apocalyptic blue-grey which spread over the sky like a fire-blanket.

Returning to the temple, the bedazzled Soldiers exchanged a few words like 'amazing', 'astonishing', 'wonderful', and 'very red,' but mostly, they lost themselves in their personal quietness of wondering what exactly the content of the Lord's speech might be.

My father said nothing of any real note, other than that the imminent firework display he had arranged for one of the local nursing homes would have a lot to live up to. And on a different occasion, confessed he wished he'd had a camera to another member, who commiserated and tactfully consoled him with a reminder of the fact that cameras never really capture sunsets very well, anyway. My mother spoke loquaciously to everyone, and promised an immediate consultation with the Almighty to ascertain precisely what His instructions were, and how His wishes were to be executed.

Later that evening, unaccompanied and unseen, my mother sneaked like a thief through the temple passages, stealthily unlocked the door of the Holy Armoury, released the shanks from the lockplates, and satisfied herself that each coffer remained full and their contents untouched.

# 90

And Jesus said 'men think, perhaps, that it is peace
which I have come to cast upon the world. They do not
know that it is dissension which I have come to cast
upon the earth; fire, sword and war.'
*The Gospel of Thomas*

The thirty-three temple residents now constituted my
mother's inner circle of friends, if not exactly confidants.
Most had bought their prestigious positions with money, but
all with love. Even the seven dorm dwellers would, if called
upon to do so, give a sizeable portion of their previously
liquored livers or non-hypodermically healed right arms for
her. She had lent them back their lives; now she stayed up
well into the small hours, long after my father had retired to
bed and dreamed of soup kitchens and community work
programmes, planning exactly how she intended to call in
the loan.

The impact of her impending performance needed to be
monumental enough to immortalise her; to unequivocally
cement her name into the upper echelons of international
folklore. To ensure that by her selfless devotion to God, she
would become even more loved and worshipped than Him.
God would be left with little choice but to marvel at her

martyrdom in rapturous admiration.

Dare she even believe it? That through a gesture of sufficient magnitude she would forever command the infatuated devotion of the Lord?

Without the legion of armed forces personnel she was hoping to recruit, her options remained disappointingly limited. She had bargained on having quite a bit more time, too.

The ball was rolling now. She had, perhaps a little impetuously, forced her own hand.

She would need to play for time, to inform her inner circle that God had instructed them to take courage and to be patient while He formulated the finer details of His apocalyptic plan.

Three weeks after the formal announcement of her undisclosed intention, the BBC revealed that in an unprecedented display of unity with the global business community and the ushering in of a possible new age of greater, ethically based industrial co-operation, the pope had taken the unique step of accepting a private invitation by a consortium of multi-national companies to meet informally in London to discuss mutual interests and symbiotic objectives, early in the New Year.

The Lord had finally spoken.

# 91

Regular hors d'oeuvres Sunday services were now dished up more decoratively, and with the pronouncement of a more conciliatory flavour, so as not to arouse any rumblings of concern or suspicion among unenlightened visitors and the less than unconditionally committed. Confrontational and militant rhetoric could easily be, and had been credibly defused and excused as typical biblical poetry and metaphor to the previously disconcerted few, but now it had become provident, essential, not to attract any unwanted or detrimental attention. Clandestine late night services for the immortal Holiest Forty were a notably different affair, however.

The prevalent mood was one of conspicuously sombre excitement.

'My beloved Brothers and Sisters, we stand on the cusp of glorious immortality. God has chosen us as the saviours of His world. The indisputably elite of His revered saints. He has promised each of us, His own Sacred Soldiers, His greatest love. And has rewarded our fearless fidelity to His word with a place of the highest honour at His side.

The brutally oppressed and impoverished masses will bow eternally to the magnitude of our miracle in prayer. And remember us always in worship with reverence and awe. We few alone, we heroic, invincible few, now upon the cusp of glory shall, through the power of our faith and love deliver the exploited masses from the shackles of a slavery the Catholic Church endorsed for more than a millennium after Saint Augustine declared it a gift from God. We shall release the suffering multitudes from fear, as our Father released us, and from their crippling curse of filling the bottomless pockets of demonic tyrants forever. By the light of our Lord we shall reveal the pied piper to be no champion of the downtrodden, but as the child and servant of the Nephilim we, the true prophets of Heaven know him to be. The Devil's own back-scratcher. Whose iniquitous purpose in our world is to magnify the wealth of his office by perpetuating the ancient tradition of papal trickery to threaten, enslave and misguide the hearts and minds of the Godly. To tighten the chains of dependence that bind the hands of the dispossessed and pick the last penny from the pockets of the poor.

Read now with me, my dear children, with all the love in your hearts, from the Book of Exodus, chapter thirty-two, verse twenty-seven, on page thirty-six.' The invitation was followed by a collective rustling of pages.

'"Thus says the Lord, the God of Israel, every man of you put his sword upon his thigh, and go back and forth from gate to gate in the camp, and kill every man his brother, and every man his friend, every man his neighbour." This is how the Lord God instructed Moses to rid His ailing world of idolatry, as He instructed Elijah to slay the four hundred and fifty prophets of Baal, as He commands us, His so fearless, noble, resolute army of just and Holy Soldiers now.'

For the Holiest Forty, a new regime of discipline had begun, too.

My mother held compulsory early morning fitness classes and initiated a timetable of motivational 'happy chanting' in twenty minute periods, five times a day; starting before breakfast and ending after dinner with 'We shall not fail the Lord'. Half an hour before lunch, and again before dinner brought similar cries of 'We are the saviours of the world' and a single, mid-afternoon reminder that 'Our Heavenly Sister loves us so' completed a trinity of essential ruminations.

An hour a day of meditation on the subject of greatness and immortality, my mother's and each member's own, and an hour of Mutual Support Activities or, more informally, the telling of spiritually affirming stories, which invariably concluded with each story-teller's promise of perfect love and unfailing devotion to my mother and their indispensable Brothers and Sisters in battle, were also now rendered compulsory, and all commanded unstinting participation.

My mother's countenance had recently darkened, however. Not nearly to black, of course; nothing would succeed in deepening her colour to such an unrescindable tone. But she had, nonetheless, become increasingly preoccupied and distracted, and it now took a second longer than usual for her to remember who she was.

She concerned herself with logistical considerations and the acquisition of tactical information regarding her target. Although, one of the most disconcertingly recurrent subjects of her reflection was the rapidly increasing visibility of the advanced age of almost three quarters of her battalion.

# 92

Yssy and I began to wear the long, black, unlined woollen capes to college for the winter, that we had brought back from Tunisia. It was an impractical fad which didn't last. They were too warm for the autumn, too cold for December. And despite our concerted attempts to blend unnoticeably into a bromidic background of hiemal grey, it was impossible to conceal the outstanding colour of our unnerving resemblance to a conspicuously comical duo of too young to be entirely credible eighteenth century highway robbers in them. I stopped wearing mine altogether after a week or so of determined effort to persevere with the inconvenience of it flapping around me like a straitjacket and preventing me from using my arms. Buying a silky, coal black, silver embroidered suede Afghan coat for myself instead, which I wore for just about long enough to enjoy before giving it, in an act of spontaneous charity a few weeks later, to a skinny kid shivering under shirtsleeves in the street.

While my mother and father continued to draw up preparations for a major festive occasion at the temple, Yssy's parents' took a short European break to secure a deal for their new luxury product design sideline, leaving Yssy to extend their invitation to me to spend the whole of the Christmas period with them at home in Bathampton. She apologised on their behalf for their inability to deliver their invitation in person, and proceeded to wander somewhere around the introduction of a loosely related subject, but I had stopped listening. Immediately rendered oblivious to almost anything else in earshot, I spontaneously arrayed her nearside cheek in a flourish of pneumatic kisses and couldn't think of anything I would rather have heard.

I was sure I understood why her parents had asked Yssy to invite me herself, and was touched by their consideration on both counts.

I was not, however, anywhere near being similarly informed about anything relating to my own parents' plans for the New Year. And had no idea whether they intended to sell their house or keep it on. I was concerned that as I had received no assurances about my tenure there, I may be faced with the reality of soon having nowhere to live. Even when I confronted them directly about it, they were non-committal; refusing to be drawn into a conversation on the subject. It was a disconcerting situation. Once again, my uncertain future was giving me cause for concern. I tried not to allow my anxiety to affect me, especially when I was with Yssy, but it did.

All I could really do for the moment was be reassured that the house had not yet been put up for sale or rent, and concentrate on the more felicitous prospect of spending the whole of the festive period with my surrogate family.

I was almost wishing my time away in anticipation of it. Besides, the commitments of college life and the necessity to habitually listen out for the car pulling up in the drive while anticipating my sanity's kiss of departure at the sound of the momentarily homecoming harpie, who probably only made the effort out of a warped desire to provoke my indignance by insistently inviting me to join the Church and live amongst them at the temple, gave me a pretty good excuse for needing a holiday. And although it was true that I hadn't suffered the assault of her fleeting visits quite so often lately, the experience lost none of its incongruity when it came blasting into my sedate evening like a gunshot out of the blue.

Other than on those mercifully brief and infrequent occasions, my mother seemed more than content to forget all about me. In fact, a week before Christmas, she confessed with unusual sincerity but with a levity I found difficult to enjoy, that she had completely forgotten I existed.

My father, on the other hand, never now mentioned the Church to me, or tried to wind me up by preying playfully on my hatred of it. In fact, his attitude towards me had grown noticeably more cordial of late.

While the CHRISTians chanted and told each other stories about love and benevolence and goodness and sacrifice on Christmas eve, Yssy and I played Monopoly and laughed and drank sherry with her parents; eating mince pies and Belgian truffles until after midnight, when we went to bed. To wake up with the pale, watery blossom of sunrise in the undilutable perfection of being together on Christmas morning.

Needless to say, it was a Christmas like no other. I had wasted the previous incarnations on collecting a Santa's sackful of scars from opening presents I never wanted.

The seasonal decorations around the house were supplemented from our earliest conversational breakfast yawns with our own unaffected high spirits and merry-making, which percolated through various rooms in a complementary stream of ornamenting colour. It was impossible not to be swept along with the tide of it all. Even so, I found it difficult to avoid reflecting for a moment on how such natural displays of affection and goodwill contrasted with sepia scenes of festive conviviality needing to be prised from the flattened tube of my parents' indifference like the last scraping of toothpaste.

With a little help from the TV guide, a time had been democratically arranged for the opening of presents by the end of our post-breakfast coffee. Another convention I had not previously encountered in a household that had traditionally set no store by such formality.

Following the exchange of gifts, we posed with champagne flutes around the drawing room in crimson cracker crowns, for photographs.

Yssy, sporting her parents' principle Swiss wristwatch present and the gold clasped, seed pearl necklace I had given her in a hollowed out paperback book to disguise it, tugged on my arm and smiled a simultaneous invitation to follow her as she moved away from the open fire and headed towards the dining room. Sailing across onion layers of discarded multi-toned wrapping paper, she disappeared through the open French doors while I abortively attempted to clutch her temporarily trailing fingertips.

When we arrived at the centre of the large Bokhara spanning the full width of garden-viewed latticed windows, she took my hand and looked at me for a moment, as though she were about to say something, then dropped it gently and instructed me to close my eyes. Almost immediately, I heard the familiar sound of paper-crinkling. A few seconds later, the command to reopen my eyes was whispered into my ear with a kiss.

On the momentarily unfocussed restoration of my

eyesight, I traced Yssy's finespun fingers with dappled, filigree laces of tree-branch shadowed sunlight playing on them, as she raised her hand towards me to extend a water pattern gift-wrapped canvas she had painted, exhibited and won an art club prize for early in the autumn. I studied the slightly smaller than LP boxset-sized parcel as she placed it in my palm, without at first guessing what it was.

When she reported to me that the picture had sold on the first day of the show, I naturally believed her. On seeing it again for myself a few days later, it carried a confirmatory red spot in the bottom corner of its frame. I was pleased but disappointed, sorry that I wouldn't see the painting again. I had mentioned many times how much I liked it. But things were not quite as they seemed, and the red spot was a well-meaning ruse. Even without my encouragement, Yssy had planned to give the picture to me all along when the exhibition closed.

I folded my fingers around it, turned it over, shook it, then quizzically began to unwrap the present, before revealing the third of one side that enabled me to recognise it, and just before beaming broadly enough to break into a laugh when I realised what had happened.

Yssy laughed along with me, but in the moments it had taken me to remove the remainder of the wrapping, her smile had fallen like a scrap of the paper, and as I reached for her hand, she glanced quickly away with a detached, plaintive expression I had never before seen.

Immediately, I was affected by her unaccountable dis-composure. Shaken. Watching her for a moment, confused, I attempted to unravel the assailing mystery of it by assuming that she had been unduly troubled by the uncharacteristic deception; and despite wanting to be convinced by my explanation, I wasn't. The weight of her demeanour seemed to suggest more than an embarrassed apology, and I felt instinctively that something of greater significance was amiss.

The troubling atmosphere persisted, and my anxiety grew. Concerned and confounded by my inexplicable exclusion, I needed information and studied Yssy's face for clues, unable to permit myself the incongruity of intruding on her reflections. Opting instead for a sudden, unassuaging sadness of my own, and the feeling that I had taken something I shouldn't.

I kissed her cheek lightly and brushed it softly with the edge of my thumb, before attempting to surmount my discomfort by contriving a comical, exaggerated inspection of the picture from all ways up. But even as I performed my hopeful routine, she continued to look down, away from my eye, silent and still. Until a few seconds later, when I forced another arbitrary laugh in a continued effort to break the gloom, and she looked up at me, as though she were relieved, and smiled.

The banquet of Christmas day ended with a television hangover, and Yssy and I spread ourselves into midnight over a Liberty print sofa in unaccompanied treelight.

The next day, of course, we strolled up the garden to Hampton Rocks.

# 93

The skin-flaying scud howls inextinguishable from the sea, imperceptibly arching the single shrub over the misty eye of the crag. Forever wrenching its departing crook deeper into the empty of its shadow.

The irrecoverable asset of youth is the riches of belief it abounds with. They purchase and confect the possibility of almost anything.

Typical of other young people, Yssy and I were keen to see our blossoming plans bear fruit, gain some financial independence and have a place of our own. But in the mainly leisurely meantime, we did just about whatever we wanted to. And most of it was pretty effortless and almost impossible not to enjoy.

Everything we did etched memories, that I chronicled like diary entries. Each decoratively friezed mortise and tenon morning radiated irridescent like an acetylene jewel.

Such joy rendered the sharing of even relative banalities rewarding. We grafted our dreams and dreads to each other like rootstock, synchronised our periods of pleasure and occasional ennui, and landscaped endless landscapes of togetherness with no contingency for concern.

Even now, from the rose-thorn splintering spectacles of

this unnavigable distance, the rippling flood of that immersive happiness remains as close as if it had never ebbed.

I feel it, among the ever-present kisses and tears; its alive. It has grown for all these years inside me. It's the one part of me that hasn't aged.

Geographical landmarks have become part of my blood-line. Lost children clinging to the umbilicus of memory.

It's all still there, radiant, aglow, right in front of my weakening eyes, even if they belong to someone else now.

On New Year's Day, after lunch in Dunster, we all drove to Devon and had ice creams on the beach.

## 94

We gaze for understanding into the dimness of words.
Straining our eyesight to the point of blindness.

I hadn't seriously considered the pile of holiday essays I
still needed to produce to secure various coursework
marks until we started back at college, where I handed in
sheepish excuses for their absence and spent hours in the
evenings trying to catch up. For Yssy, who was far more
disciplined than me, it had been easier to write them, finish
them and put the commitment behind her pretty much as
soon as term ended. And although we often tackled our
homework together, I wasn't always quite as meticulous
as her; occasionally falling victim to my unshakeable habit
of awarding almost any trivial distraction preference and
leaving everything of any importance to the last minute.

It was already over a fortnight into term and I was
still a long way behind. Anxious to make a significant impact
on the discomfiting deficit, I diligently spent most of the
daylight hours of Saturday in the college library while Yssy
stayed at home and waited for me to call her to let her know
that I had finished, so we could meet in town and bus up to
the Uni together to watch the Welsh band Man in the
evening.

Writing essays was purgatory for me at any time. A tedious occupation. And I really didn't feel like sitting at a table all day. But not wanting to let either myself or Yssy down, I was determined to complete them once and for all, and finally navigated a relatively painless way through the backlog. In fact, I had gradually gathered momentum through the morning and was on such good form by lunchtime that I even stayed at college long enough to launch a respectable assault on the first few hundred words of my next assignment.

By around mid-afternoon, I was completely up to date and felt appropriately pleased with myself. I stretched my spine over the back of my chair to articulate my satisfaction and relief, took myself down to the common room and called Yssy on the payphone.

'I'll meet you opposite the bus station in an hour,' I said, 'I've done it, but I'm starving, I need to eat something.' I put the receiver down and walked up to Kingsmead Square to get some chips.

I sat at one of the plastic tables in the back of the diner with a few scattered, overcoated others, collectively ambling wistfully through the invigorating scent of diluted dark malt vinegar on deep fried potato, while maintaining the isolating convention of pretending not to notice each other.

I finished my chips, had a cup of tea next door and made my way through town to the bus station.

The rising surf of evening had not yet broken; the light was still good, but the acute blue edge had blanched out of it. A horn of moon edged lustrous into a cerulean wash over the Churchyard like a thistle.

We'd probably spend a while in town before heading up the hill. Maybe hang around in the listening booth of a record

371

shop or two, then sip away an hour or so in the bar at Claverton Down before queueing outside the hall there for a place near the stage.

I arrived at our once traditional antiquarian bookshop meeting place opposite the bus station, ten minutes before noticing Yssy walking towards me on the other side of the road. It wasn't an ideal spot to rendezvous on a Saturday afternoon. Buses were parked and parking on both sides and it was difficult to see across to the opposite pavement between them for very long. I was immediately forced to backtrack a few paces before disappearing from view altogether behind a stopping double-decker; but it pulled off almost straight away, and by the time I had covered half the length of my original obstacle, I could see Yssy clearly; catching her eye with a wave and converting my gesture to an exaggerated pointing suggestion that she stay where she was. She waved back with a big smile, holding a long, cream envelope in her other hand, which she then proudly fluttered to and fro in an arch above her head, as though I would recognise it and be as excited by it as she was. I had no idea what it was or what was in it. It was still a week short of my seventeenth, so I guessed it wasn't a present, but I beamed back at her, and to myself at her typically uncontainable boundless enthusiasm, before repeating my signal to stay and embellishing it with another point to explain that I would cross over when there was a break in the traffic. And precisely as the next bus pulled up in front of me. I backed along the length of it to a clearing behind, from where I could dive out as soon as I had the chance.

Re-emerging onto the road between two parked buses to cross, I couldn't see Yssy at all now. I looked up and down the suddenly open opposite side of the street where she had been, perplexed. Then I stepped back onto the kerb and scanned the sparsely peopled pavement on my own side. Convinced I hadn't missed her there, I stepped out onto the tarmac and skimmed the opposite pavement again as I continued to cross.

I didn't get it at first. It took me a second to notice that the traffic had stopped, and another before I could just about decipher a shape between the gaps in the small crowd of hunched figures already gathered around a slither of Venetian red coat in the road.

The previously colourful array of everything I could see drained in a moment of dread. The road unrecognisable, the buildings, the street unknown to me, I attempted to shout Yssy's name, expecting to re-summon normality immediately with the desperation of my call. Then to run, either toward the crowd or away from it, but neither my voice nor my legs would respond. Time stopped. I had no idea how long I stood there for, not knowing where to look.

Gradually, I became conscious of a myriad of sounds losing their dynamics and morphing into an indistinct drone, then reducing in volume to a barely audible hum as the fragmented scene before me slowly began to rotate and proceeded to spin. Darkness hit me like a jackhammer. Catapulted me away from every particle of daylight. I became a lost child again.

# 95

There is no scream loud enough to break the silence of heartbreak.

When I sleep, I no longer fly.

Between restless hours, I dream of endlessly searching for Yssy in the sunless emptiness of unidentifiable landscapes, where even a single, fleeting glimpse of her evades me. Wherever I discover she has been, she has moved on from by the time I arrive there. And as interminably as I try, I am never able to catch up with her.

Occasionally, I see her for a moment in a stranger's face, but it isn't her who looks back at me, and I tear my wishful glance abashed from unsuspecting eyes, caressing her name; sealed, unvented, in the reliquary of my inability to speak it aloud.

Unfamiliarity is a familiar companion to me now, in the intimately foreign, unnavigable wilderness of where she once walked. And though I can not allow myself to imagine her wandering so unbearably alone, still I do and must believe that somehow, in the perfect, endless, overpopulated afterlife of dreams, should I once remain asleep for long enough, I *will* find her again.

Was it a blessing or a curse that I didn't see Yssy step out from the kerb? How could I ever know? However much I remain, as I do, wedded like a bloodstain to the open wound of the moment.

Wilde inked me in as a footnote to his page when he advised us that 'each man kills the thing he loves'. It's true. A paragon of consonance was shattered into eternal silence by a handful of words when I incautiously issued the details of our arrangement to meet and determined Yssy's fate as surely as if I had ferried her across the Styx on their mortal contagion myself. I am guilty beyond contention. She would never have left me to travel so light had love not stood on the wrong side of the street and compelled her to cross. You can label it destiny or providence, or any other meaningless spittle of drivel, and you can philosophise until its reassuring riddle sticks in your craw and chokes the last gasp of reason from you. But you'll never smuggle your culpability out of the picture and no warming wind of ataractic waffle will blow away the cold, blue, naked truth of any of it. The portrait of your unfolding destruction is never going to look any less shocking than it does. Period.

A few days before Yssy died, I had a premonition as we were leaving the cinema. It hit me like a lightning bolt out of nowhere. We were holding hands walking past The Bunch of Grapes pub, just yards away from The Grand, when it stopped me in my tracks. I couldn't move at all. I just stood rooted to the flagstone, feeling sick and cold; staring and staring at this picture I knew was there but couldn't decipher the details of; as though someone had thrust it in front of me in the dimness of the alley, but it was too darkly painted to see. Yssy asked me what was wrong. I couldn't tell her. 'I'm OK,' I said, without looking up, but it was a lie. I didn't know how, but I knew she had gone.

Within months, my family had gone, too. I had lost my reason for counting myself among it. Neither did I bear the pain of my subsequent rapidly diminishing visits to the remaining members of it easily.

Less than two years later, Yssy's parents separated and moved away from Bath. I never kept in touch or saw either of them again.

I never saw the little Japanese print Yssy bought me for Christmas again, either. It had disappeared from my bedroom wall when I returned home a week after her funeral.

# 96

And the four angels who had been kept ready for this very hour and day and month and year were released to kill a third of mankind. *Revelations 9:15*

It had no doubt previously been expedient for my father to exculpate himself by refusing to accept the reality of her madness, but I don't believe he ever for a moment permitted himself to rationally consider the actual flesh and blood implications of my mother's deranged ambition. I'm not able to explain his indulgence of and involvement in her nightmare world, beyond my reasonable assumption of his emotional need to physically remain with her. Neither am I able to bring myself to condone him; even though it's difficult for me not to accept that to him, my mother was and continued to be the essentially harmless fantasist she always had been.

To his credit, however, something had abruptly altered his opinion of her and had pricked either his conscience or the free-floating balloon of his prodigal common sense in the plummy dark of the late January pre-dawn morning.

The first breathy yawns of sunrise creaked haunting as a slow shiver up the spine of the hills that ran like a frame alongside the ominously purring engine of the hired coach on the temple drive, which now, in the eerily purple-lit frost, offered the accommodating gape of its door to the surreptitiously resolute ply with pre-loaded small arms and boxes of ammunition by several of the primed and ready holiest.

'No!' My father bellowed, manfully, as he marched up the path to the drive and grabbed my mother's trailing arm in a pinch, 'that's it, you've gone far enough. You're taking this beyond a game now!'

My mother shook off his grip indignantly and glared a branding iron stare into his unblinking cornflower blue eyes.

'Beyond a what?!' the blowtorch of her outraged howl returned from the snarling curl of her lip, hovering inches from his face like an incensed drill sergeant giving a lethally punishing command of execution.

'You're not going anywhere,' he insisted, 'and neither is anyone else.'

'How dare you issue orders to me,' she growled, incredulously, pushing him with both hands to teeter a step backwards, 'do you know who I am?!'

'Yes, I do,' he said, softly, earnest concern spilling through the velvet voice of his compassion, 'and it's time to go home. You need help.'

'It's you who needs help, you apostate! "That prophet or that dreamer of dreams shall be put to death, because he has spoken in order to turn you away from the Lord your God!"'

'I am not turning you away from God,' he gently replied, regaining his ground and attempting this time to take her arm with more discernible affection.

'No!' she howled, throwing off his hand, taking half a step back and drawing the attention of a number of milling and filling holiests by continuing to quote Deuteronomy, thirteen, verbatim, by heart, in a shriek, as though rapidly reciting a life-saving incantation. '"If your brother, the son of your mother, your son or your daughter, the wife of your bosom, or your friend who is as your own soul, secretly entices you, saying, 'Let us go and serve other gods,' which you have not known, neither you nor your fathers, of the gods of the people which are all around you, near to you or far off from you, from one end of the earth to the other end of the earth, you shall not consent to him or listen to him, nor shall your eye pity him, nor shall you spare him or conceal him; but you shall surely kill him; your hand shall be first against him to put him to death, and afterward the hand of all the people. And you shall stone him with stones until he dies, because he sought to entice you away from the Lord your God."'

'I'm taking you home, dear,' my father reiterated, tenderly, extending his arm for a third time, 'you aren't well'.

'Seize the apostate!' she ordered, convulsively, but no-one moved. '"Anyone who attacks their mother is to be put to death",' she carried on, barking rabidly, 'Exodus, twenty-one, fifteen!'

'I'm not going to let you do this,' my father continued, determinedly, but with an appeasingly gentle smile. 'I'm not going to let you hurt anyone. Or yourself. If you don't come with me, I'm going to call the police.'

This was a bad move. He was immediately surrounded by a group of ageing greenery and two of his ex-substance abuse friends.

'We can't let you do that, brother,' said one, with reassuringly menacing calmness.

'I'm afraid you don't have any choice, brother,' my father retorted, with similar sangfroid.

He turned and began to walk resolutely back down the

drive, toward the temple entrance. Three or four paces later, he found my flying mother limpeted on his back, followed closely by the two younger men who, between them, succeeded in dragging him to the ground.

'I'm sorry, brother,' the menacing one said, slightly more breathlessly this time, 'but we really *can't* let you do that.'

My mother, in the exaggeratedly unruffled imperiousness of her best movie villain modulation, abruptly issued the order to tie my father up and lock him in the Holy Armoury, whereupon, he was subsequently dragged by each arm unceremoniously down the drive, into the building and put away according to her command.

The lethal equipping of the coach continued apace with the return of the two assailants less than fifteen minutes later, and was satisfactorily completed before an army of overwhelmingly elderly combatants tentatively appeared, then hastened like an energetic shudder out of the chill and boarded sporting picnic hampers and lap blankets.

The atmosphere on the coach was initially subdued and reflective, and even attempts by the jovial ex-alcoholic driver to initiate a spirited sing-song met with at best, a half-hearted mumbling of distracted efforts, amounting in total to little more than an apologetic rendition of a theme. The result of which fell some way short of inspirational, but nevertheless, could still have easily passed as a discriminating composition by Stockhausen or Cage.

My mother was unusually quiet, too. Whether she was reflecting on the divine bestowal of her imminent immortal glory, or had been overly affected by the extraordinary confrontation with my father, wasn't easy to deduce. She perked up briefly around Swindon, enough to seize the driver's microphone and quote a short passage from the

Second book of Chronicles, chapter fifteen, verse thirteen, to remind her window-wiping warriors that "all who would not seek the Lord, the God of Israel, were to be put to death, whether small or great, man or woman." But even this abbreviated flurry of invective failed to inspire her to launch further, more venomous diatribes, so she sat back down again and watched the stark, grey countryside canter by outside.

## 97

Thou shalt not kill. *Matthew 5:21*

Going had been unforeseeably slow due to a multi-vehicle accident and subsequent lane closures, which had reduced traffic to a virtual standstill for almost an hour at Newbury. By the time the coach party had pulled into Heston for their final loo break and to fill their pockets with ammo, the pope had already arrived at Heathrow aboard a private plane. And the extensive retinue of official black cars parked in anticipation alongside the runway like an outstretched snake with the head of a marked police escort, was poised to slither him off to the Confederation of Associated Global Interests symposium at the World Commonwealth Building in Pall Mall. It was now essential that the CHRISTian delegation avoid any further delays and remain ahead of him.

Back on the road, my mother eventually shook herself resolutely out of the nestle of her reflection and once again rose like a chimera from the ashes of reverie to address her mostly meditating troops.

'My beloved Immortal Ones,' she began, tapping the driver's ribbed chrome, goose-necked microphone with her clear-polished fingernail for no apparent reason, 'the weight of history sits upon our steely shoulders this very day. This fateful, victorious day, we shall open a window to the world through which the light of the Lord will shine forever. Today, the glory of our mighty deeds and valour shall be celebrated on Earth as it will be in Heaven. And God will grant us, His holiest and most beloved of angels, the promised gifts of eternal love and everlasting life at His side. And though the Devil may try to instil doubt in our hearts, the solid rock of our trigger finger shall remain steady as the Word of the Lord. For we shall have no fear, my heroic children, as nothing in this world can breach the unfailing armour of our Father's protection. We shall sow a garden of seeds this day never to be crushed by the actions of man, and the fruit of our sacred duty will live in the hearts of the righteous for ever.'

The rally defied the existing solemnity of the atmosphere, and despite the almost imperceptible hesitance of a not quite yet fully confident understudy's performance, the coach shook with the force of a resultant collective 'amen' and the subsequently roused passengers spontaneously broke into several minutes of 'We love our Sister dearly,' which only stopped at Earls Court when the driver slammed on his brakes to avoid rear-ending a delivery van.

Everyone knew exactly when to liberate the revolvers that had been pre-taped to the underside of the seats before the coach had set off from the temple, and several members were already stretching their hands below the metal frames to reassure themselves of the presence of their murderous company. Other members were quietly reflecting and wringing the sweat from their welling fingers.

My mother continued to glow, ever more elated; her exultant grin and battle-ready countenance befitting a martyr who strutingly paraded the aisle of the coach administering final little noontide touches of Harry in the night.

Driving up Whitehall, it became obvious that hordes were flocking to the Mall. Every one of the pedestrian approaches to it from around Admiralty Arch were clogged with jostling bodies. Large numbers had lined the pavements since well before daybreak.

Outside the World Commonwealth Building, the excited gathered fidgeted and chattered jovially across their many rows on the pavements and verges. There were accompanying swarms of uniformed police everywhere. The scene was mirrored at the Palace end, where several roads were closed and large crowds had swollen for hours around the royal residence. Small groups of Met officers and bollards blocked access to the mall from both sides of the mansion.

For some reason, my mother hadn't reckoned on quite such a large gathering of sightseers hoping to catch sight of an inch or two of the first serving pope to set foot on English soil.

The clamour was an inconvenience, but didn't really change anything. Most of the original plan still held good. They'd anticipate the motorcade from a position on the south side of Trafalgar Square, wait for it to approach the World Commonwealth Building, follow it at speed, then draw up along side it and, immediately subsequent to my mother's initiation of the ambush by racing from the coach, cutting down the pontiff in a hail of fire and claiming her eternal prize, start picking off any available lingering industrial dignitaries from the pre-opened windows and door.

It was essential to the success of the campaign that the crucial sequence of events be meticulously observed, but it remained in essence an undeceptively simple plan, and everybody perfectly understood their own part in the procedure.

For the first time, however, my mother secretly questioned the sense of it.

Perhaps, she thought, it really would have been better to have arrived at the scene in the early hours and secured a strategic position with a clear and uninterrupted view of the target. But what if the coach had been stopped enroute, as vehicles often were on the roads at that time of night? It may well have blown the entire operation. Maybe she could have led a small group to stand in a favourable place in the frost overnight, while the rest of her task force followed up by coach in the morning? Then, even if the early bystanders had been subjected to routine searches, there would still have been an operational back up. No, she resolved, dismissing the idea she had already considered a thousand times with a snort, bystanders were *bound* to be searched. Particularly those closest to the barriers. They had been invariably frisked at other major events since paramilitary groups had stepped up their activities on these same streets in recent months. It was too risky. If anyone had been caught carrying a weapon, it would have alerted the attention of the security services to the probability of a conspiracy and the whole plan could have been scuppered, along with her possibly never to be repeated opportunity to permanently figurehead a spectacular list of spiritual immortals. The triumph of the entire undertaking hung on the crucial element of surprise.

She relaxed. The better part of plan was still best, after all. Even if it meant that there would be no chance now for anyone to disembark enroute, walk the last few hundred yards to the WCB and mingle with the crowd for a prime position beforehand.

The only remaining vital and unknowable aspect of the

entire operation was, which end of the Mall would the motorcade be coming from?

# 98

My mother saw the policeman approach before he was close enough to start rapping on the driver's window with his black leather-gloved knuckles. He took a long look into the coach as he did so.

'Move,' he said, before the driver had let in air.

'Agent of the Devil!' my mother hissed, as they pulled away to circle the square.

From what they could see, there were various marked police vehicles parked at the Arch end of the Mall, and groups of officers planted strategically around the area in front of and behind the admiralty building. They didn't appear to be armed, but there was sure to be undercover everywhere, and *they* almost certainly would be. There may be marksmen behind the windows of other properties along the Mall, too. Maybe even on the roofs.

The symposium was scheduled to convene at midday, before breaking for lunch at two and continuing open-endedly into the evening. It was ten to twelve already. The pope could only be minutes away.

Three times around the square and everyone was beginning to feel anxious about attracting suspicion. Justifiably so. They hadn't escaped the extra beady eye of extensive police surveillance already.

At the beginning of the fourth lap, parallel with the Arch, the crowd had suddenly become restless. Something was happening. Slowing down, level with the now last closing road gate beneath the structure, it was just about possible from the expanding ripple of commotion to make out what it was. The motorcade was crawling up the Mall. From the other end.

Unable to stop for the stream of traffic immediately behind it, the coach had already overshot the entrance to the Arch by at least twenty yards and wouldn't be able to back up without drawing a blue swarm of immediate attention. They had no choice; they absolutely had to go back around the square yet again and get a clear run to break through the barricade. This was a startling setback. It was not only time and security that had suddenly turned against them. The traffic was slowing. Dramatically. The coach driver tried to pull out, overtake, blast his horn and shout, but the slowdown had affected everything, and there was nothing he could do to get anywhere any faster than the crawl he had become trapped in.

My mother became almost hysterical. 'It's the Devil! It's the Devil!' she kept yelling, over and over again, pacing up and down the same few yards of aisle in a hand-wringing rage. A minute flew by and they were still inching due north, diametrically away from the Mall. In another minute, the pope would be safely out of his car and inside the building.

'Oh Lord, grant us this one miracle,' she wailed, desperately, glaring wild-eyed through the front window at the shoal of practically motionless motors ahead.

Suddenly, the traffic began to flow. Just as a policeman stepped forward, raised his arm and flagged the coach down.

'No!' My mother screamed, 'Go! Go! Go! Go! Go!'

There was a frantic scramble to rip the handguns from their under-seat holsters and a muted chorused clicking from the releases of their safety catches immediately ensued. The collective thud of sliding windows opening to their full resounded like a brief symphonic passage of rapid-firing tympani shooting off quarter notes from the pit through a muffle of silencers.

The coach rounded the corner with two swaying police motor cycles in hot pursuit, then the next corner, just as the lights were turning. It flew onto the pavement to round the final set of red lights with a screech at the last, building up enough speed to crash explosively through the ornate iron barrier and send several pieces of it flying as it fell.

The motorcade had already stopped outside the World Commonwealth Building, less than a hundred yards from the Arch, but the pope remained seated in the back of his car. The coach, with its door now gaping, screamed to a tyre-smoking halt alongside the papal limousine and my mother raced out towards the bemused pontiff, weapon in hand. But not before one of her elderly greens had fled down the stairs ahead of her in a frenzy of excitement, losing his footing on the abrupt stop and fracturing his hip in the fall. My mother had just enough time ahead of tripping over his trailing leg and ignominiously mounting him on the fly to let off a single round, which killed the tyre of the pope's Mercedes on impact, before a rugby scrum of special branch officers landed on top of her and a second, with revolvers drawn, piled onto the coach to confront another bewildered and dithering rabble trying to get off. The incident was over in seconds.

It was a shorter immortality than the one my mother had hoped for.

# 99

History is written over legends of happier days.

All my rocks have become sand now. There's nothing left of stone but grains to hold. Form has spilt away through the time-cracked stranglehold of my grip; only the immutable, adamantine density of its mass remains.

Seasons outpace my breathless steps, herd my limping days like sheep, lead me as a hastening torch-bearer in the falling night to a home I will not reach.

Over the following years, my mother stabbed a total of three cell mates with improvised implements, denouncing them all as agents of the Devil. None fatally.

I still see her occasionally, on visiting days, when she calls me by a different name and tells me she loves me, as she always has. And how I have wronged her so by not returning her love.

Each time I see her, she asks me how Yssy is. And if I still sing.